David Crackanthorpe was born at Newbiggin in the county of Westmoreland, where his family had lived for some eight hundred years. His antecedents include Richard Crackanthorpe, the 16th-century logician mentioned by Sterne in *Tristram Shandy*, William and Dorothy Wordsworth and the notorious Daniel E. Sickles, a general in the American Civil War. He studied law at Oxford University and practised as a barrister in London, where he married the Irish actress Helena Hughes, now deceased. He has written a biography of Hubert Crackanthorpe, a young writer of the 1890s associated with the *Yellow Book*. He lives in France where he has worked as a forester, gardener and cultivator of olive trees. *Stolen Marches* is his first novel.

'A relish for the colourful, telling piece of detail, some sharp characterisation . . . a refusal to prettify or simplify events and their effects and, at the same time, a respect for a good story and a well-orchestrated plot'   *The Times*

'Everywhere, the prose keeps up a continuous murmur of threat and risk. All France is here, and treachery, love, self-sacrifice, accident and ambition tighten the story's tensions'   *Mail on Sunday*

'Excellent novel which skilfully evokes a dramatic period of modern history'   *Manchester Evening News*

'A story of love and betrayal, ideals and deceptions, that brilliantly evokes the morally and politically ambiguous world of post-Liberation France. It marks the debut of a remarkable new writer' *Living France*

'If you like the books of Sebastian Faulks and Charles Frazier, then you might fancy David Crackenthorpe's French wartime novel *Stolen Marches*' *She*

David Crackanthorpe

STOLEN MARCHES

review

First published in 1999
by HEADLINE BOOK PUBLISHING

First published in paperback in 2000
by REVIEW

An imprint of Headline Book Publishing

10 9 8 7 6 5 4 3 2 1

ISBN 0 7472 6085 0

Typeset by
Letterpart Limited, Reigate, Surrey

Printed and bound in Great Britain by
Mackays of Chatham plc, Chatham, Kent

HEADLINE BOOK PUBLISHING
A division of the Hodder Headline Group
338 Euston Road
London NW1 3BH
www.reviewbooks.co.uk
www.hodderheadline.com

TO THE LATE COMPANIONS OF THE ROAD

Part One

Chapter One

Seagrave had waited late in the station buildings, to carry a message expected on the Baudot telegraph from the resistants in the Cévennes. He'd continued going through the motions of sweeping corridors and offices long after the women who did the real cleaning had gone home. The little camera, as usual, was in the pocket sewn for it into the waistband of his skirt, on the inside. You never knew when it might be called for. To photograph a schedule of trains that could be attacked as they wound into the hills was more dependable than trying to memorise the details. So it happened that he was there now behind a window in one of the many arches of the viaduct, ready to make his way down and out into the boulevard before curfew hour.

Through the window as he passed it he caught movement in the goods yard below and shifted back against the wall of the stair to watch. All information was potentially valuable. Down in the yard was a company of grey soldiers, calm under plane trees in fresh leaf, a last light reflected off the metal of their weapons. This yard with its trees and familiar buildings was more like a playground than a goods yard, just one of a million school playgrounds. But there in the middle of it now was a frightened shuffling civilian group, men and women beside the vans that had brought them in with their small hurried bags and bundles and their hats and coats in the warm evening, civilians obedient as the soldiers but with so much more to lose. It came as a shock, even if no real surprise, to see his father-in-law among them, tall and patient. Though they knew each other little and never met now that Seagrave lived apart and in hiding, he nevertheless felt an instant call made on him, some appeal to honour, probably. He put a hand under the skirt and withdrew the Minox camera. There was still just light enough in the May evening. He had no help to bring but he could record the scene as an act of piety, of a kind. It was a dangerous gesture of no practical value but these last months the captured Minox had become like a colleague to fall back on in times of isolation.

He slid open the casing of the camera within the acoustic shelter of his hands. Constant fear made you cautious by habit, when it didn't make you reckless, and even the insect buzz of the Minox advancing its film might catch attention down there in the yard where nothing stirred. There was dust on the panes of the window and he eased open one half by a crack wide as a hand. The camera was at his eye. The head of Denise's father was half turned from him, in profile. At one side a few metres off under the trees Seagrave noticed for the first time another civilian, a squat figure at liberty, compact in its field of force. A man who wore a black felt hat adjusted to an assured angle and who watched attentively from under its wide brim. This observer was surely not in personal command of a small-scale quotidian operation in the station yard of a town like Nîmes. He looked as if the net of his powers spread far wider than that. Besides, Seagrave knew the local Vichy officials well enough by sight and had never seen him before. With an involuntary motion obeying the force field he shifted his view away from the figure of his father-in-law and onto the civilian at the periphery. He could risk only a single photograph. There was the buzz for one thing and the rarity of Minox film for another. Exposures should be for the general good, and that could include being able to identify this man later on. Pressing the metal trigger he felt the familiar little percussion. The civilian onlooker had been clear in the lens and now, as Seagrave drew the camera back into his dress he saw the man look up at the arch and the window for a long moment. He seemed to take in the frozen situation at a glance, and its implications, and his look, as their eyes met, was clear and sharp, and bare of any illusion.

'Fetch me that woman down from there,' he called to an underling behind him, and pointed to the arch. But at the same moment orders were shouted in the direction of the waiting people and repeated by other voices like rifle fire echoed off a nearby wall. No doubt the train they were to travel on was signalled and it was time to board for the long journey. The underling hesitated, caught in the crossfire of orders, and Seagrave ducked back from the window and made for the wooden stair which was his escape to the world of the streets. What could he do by staying longer? Tell Denise a story of risking his life to watch her father entrained for the frontier and the black world beyond? No. Still less show her a photograph of the scene, there where she lay in the stifling ward, waiting to travel the frontier into her own darkness.

Now as he slipped out of the masonry of the viaduct like a rat into the boulevard the light was going fast, a last band of fading pink behind the hill and the Roman tower dominating the town. He could hear shouts behind him, up on the railway lines and down in the square below the arches. They were looking for him but he was well ahead. Under the trees of the great double avenue aligned on the tower he sensed the presence of shadowy figures. The precinct of the station was a dangerous place to be at any time, even if your papers were in order. The lurking figures might be friends, might be potential enemies, might be imaginary. Chronic hunger made you fanciful. Or they could be sons or fathers or brothers of men held and interrogated in the Milice headquarters near this end of the avenue, unable to stay away as if their presence under the trees could in some way succour the kinsmen in blood-smeared cellars or back rooms where the cries rang out.

Seagrave wanted to break into a run, but that would be fatal – and nearly as bad to walk too fast because a man, even not a tall one, hurries so differently from a woman hurrying. He went forward with a quick, practised gait, feminine as he could make it without inviting trouble, a walk on a razor's edge. A train was rumbling in along the stones of the viaduct, into this station twelve metres above street level so that your first and last sight of the town through arched windows was like a monumental scene viewed from a theatre balcony. The mother-of-pearl backdrop and the first stars were certainly theatrical tonight. Was this the last train from Montpellier bringing students home from the university? No, the faculty had been closed since March. It must be the arrival of the cattle trucks for the deported. Seagrave cut down a side street where tall garden walls alternated with fine houses of the old bourgeoisie and artisans' workshops in what must have seemed in peacetime a pleasant promiscuity. Separation of the classes here was no less real but a good deal less gross than it had become in England, Seagrave thought for the thousandth time, too hungry and too urgent to have any new ideas about it at this late stage of the War. He had a colleague here who would lend him a bicycle, his own left behind in the railway buildings. Bicycles were beyond price, but between colleagues of the Resistance there was a communard spirit, even if you were a foreigner. In fact especially if you were a foreigner. If you were a native socialist it was no good expecting much help from a native communist, and vice versa, but as Seagrave scrambled over his friend's wall with his skirt hauled up to his waist he wasn't thinking of these internecine rivalries. His lot, mostly by chance, was thrown in with the communist railwaymen, but the friend whose dark scented rose garden he was passing through now as an early nightingale tuned up and fountains trickled somewhere among the mosses, the jasmine and the palms – this friend didn't count him as an adversary, political or otherwise, so he believed. For him Seagrave was an anomaly he'd got used to.

'You'd run far less dangers in your own army than you do here, even if you were captured. They don't torture prisoners-of-war,' he once said.

'I have to be here. I don't belong in any army. It's here I have to fight,' Seagrave had replied in the rather histrionic vein of declaration echoing clandestine broadcasts he and others listened to in garrets and cellars and stone cabins on the garrigue outside the town.

And everyone felt and knew that the end was near. You could feel the occupiers feeling it too: their discipline was slackening, morale low, there were deserters – Armenians, Poles, Alsatians – who had begun to join the armed groups in the Cévennes, while in the towns the Milice had become even more venomous than before, lashing like sea snakes in a net. The civilian onlooker in the station yard looked clever enough to know that time was running out for the persecutors. What then was he doing there? Perhaps he had a personal account to settle, a vengeance to witness, or maybe he planned to save someone at the last moment. But he'd sent a man after Seagrave and for the present all Seagrave wanted from life was a bicycle to get back in the dusk to his particular stone cabin in the maze of stony lanes on the aromatic hillside. He knocked quietly in the prescribed code on the garden door of the house and it opened almost at once.

'Etienne,' Seagrave muttered unnecessarily.

'I see quite well who you are my dear Stephen. Between us and these walls there's no need for rigmarole. We're not among the people, here.'

'That's who I belong with. Remember I clean floors at the railway station these days.'

'You'll never belong with them. You can't.' Philippe d'Albaron was very sure about this; it was a point they'd discussed in days when they were students together, on the last train. 'We're mere survivors. Unconsciously, they see us as decapitated,' he claimed.

In the unlit stone passage behind the garden door Seagrave quickly explained his situation, omitting mention of the photograph. That seemed safer. The snarl and whine of the fast cars used by the Milice could be heard from the direction of the avenue, several of them, and one which now came along the side street beyond the wall, going slowly, then turned away parallel to the avenue.

'Who would that man be?' Seagrave asked. 'I've never seen him around the station before. I thought I knew them all.'

'By your description it's Fernand-Félix. An important man from Vichy. A coming man. He's staying here in the house. He's my father's lawyer.'

'Then this is the worst possible place for me to be.'

'On the contrary. It's the one place no one would look for you.'

'Your father won't like it.'

'Fathers are best kept in the dark. About everything.'

Seagrave followed Philippe up a back stair of this mansion built in the 1820s for an enriched member of this poor but ancient country family. 'The Restoration in France was the time for arse-licking parvenus, like the Restoration with you,' Philippe liked to say, though secretly proud, Seagrave believed, of the sagacity of his forebear who had been raised to the rank of marquis and whose fortune, made by speculation in building land in this part of the town, was still not exhausted. Philippe's father never came up to this part of the house but lived, as he had always lived, in the great gilded and tapestried rooms of the first floor. Up here Philippe did what he pleased and had who he wanted and led an existence as unlike his father's as possible, though he stopped short of refusing the services of his father's domestics who still looked after both of them as if their world must never come to an end. 'I'm not interested in making a martyr of myself,' Philippe said, but he daily ran risks for the Resistance which would ensure a grim martyrdom if he was caught, and which he carried off with the same resource and panache as his uncle Charles, head of all the resistants of the region.

'There's nothing to eat but I'll get a bottle from the cellar. I may even bump into my father there, creeping about. It's the only place we ever meet.'

'Doesn't he keep it locked?'

'No more. My father is at bay.' When he came back he carried two or three bottles cradled in his arms. 'Papa was down there as foreseen. I had to do without any Armagnac.'

'What did he say when he saw you go off with those?'

'Say? My father speaks if I speak to him.'

'And did you?'

'I enquired subtly about Fernand-Félix.'

'Well?'

'He's making a political tour in the region – here, Montpellier, Toulouse. Papa understands about that sort of thing. What's that folklore figure of yours? The Vicar of Bray. Fernand-Félix won't want to be caught on the wrong foot in the wrong camp in a few months' time. That's how Papa sees it and he should know, he's being very careful himself.'

'Is that why Fernand-Félix has come to see him?'

'I suspect Fernand knows quite a bit about my uncle Charles. Probably he hopes to be put in touch through him with some of the right people, the people who are going to count, the ones who are using Charles now as long as heroes are still the thing and getting ready to ditch him afterwards. Another headless survivor.'

'And will you be ditching him afterwards too?' Seagrave asked, because he owed a debt of gratitude to Charles d'Albaron and also because he was familiar with Philippe and his shifts of ground.

'I see you coming a long way off. You take me for a shit and an opportunist,' said Philippe without answering the question. 'Who was going on that train you were watching?'

'Denise's father. And other Jews.'

Philippe considered this for a moment without remark, but within his silence Seagrave felt much unspoken commentary, as if Philippe and his father in spontaneous communion were mulling over the accumulated solecisms of his, Seagrave's, private life.

'There could have been political deportees among them,' Philippe said. 'No doubt someone who knew too much and Fernand was there to make sure he boarded the right train to a safe

9

station. There's so little time left, he's a prudent man.'

Far above, a line of aircraft could be heard droning inland from the sea where the allied carriers stood off the coast of the Golfe du Lion. They would drop their load of arms and explosives by parachute high up in the Cévennes for the benefit of non-communist maquis groups that the Americans felt they could trust. The population was not their concern and the politically motivated groups down here in the plain had still received nothing from the sky and probably never would; so Philippe had heard from his uncle. 'But the future's for us all the same,' Charles had said in his exalted manner, 'because we know how to assume it. Destiny and the historical process are with us.' He was fairly new to the rhetoric but his followers didn't mind that. Soon the planes would swing round over the forest slopes and return safely to their base out at sea. You knew the nationality of the aircraft by their height from the ground. The Americans kept well up, but already several liaison officers were known to have been dropped from English aircraft and Seagrave knew, and foresaw without pleasure, that sooner or later when the armed maquis came down from the hills and the longed for end was at hand, he would come up against one of these officers, and be required to explain his presence here in the south of France without a uniform to identify his place in the conscripted ranks. That was a reckoning to be faced later; for the moment there were danger and starvation to occupy your thoughts.

'I haven't asked you about Denise.' The manner didn't mask Philippe's obvious certainty that it was useless to ask about her; it was a hopeless and ill-founded topic in every way and better avoided. Philippe had known Denise at the university but not well. He was, after all, not an exile from his caste. He poured the last of the bottle of Mersault into Seagrave's glass and turned away to a side table to cut a crust of bread and a couple of slices of sausage, dark, hard and shrunken from storage like a body preserved in a peat bog. 'We'll move on now to the Vougeot. Red wine sustains resistance.'

'The haemorrhage started again yesterday.'

'Internally?'

'From her mouth.'

'Can they stop it?'

Seagrave didn't answer the question, which seemed hedged with too many others, concerning past and future and his own feelings which Philippe well knew to be unavowably mixed. Sometimes he thought Philippe envied his double life even when reminding him he was far too young to afford to have one. 'You're not of an age to be so emotional about your affairs,' he would say. 'In our prime we should be ruthless. It's biologically determined. Anyone who pretends otherwise is impotent or a hypocrite.' But these comments seemed dated now. The climate these hard days was wrong.

'She's back in the hospital,' Seagrave said. 'I go there before I go to work at the railway.'

'You go how? As a woman?'

'Of course.'

'Strange. In the women's ward.'

'You get used to it. I keep my mouth shut and I don't stay long. She wouldn't want me to if I could.'

'You mean . . .?'

Philippe stopped there and Seagrave took up the line of association. It was a relief to say it. 'Because she knows Ida Karoly was pregnant when they sent her to that camp. And she knows how I got her out and away to safety.' It was a time when special trains crept across the face of Europe and special camps sprang up like deadly mushrooms from the indifferent grass.

'It wasn't elegant to let her know that in the circumstances.'

'I didn't let her know it. She made her own researches. Sometimes I wonder how it was Ida got to be denounced, we lay so low.'

Philippe's eyes, at the mention of Ida Karoly, had closed in and narrowed like the lens of a camera focusing on the objective it was desired to capture. For an instant's possession, a snapshot, not an erotic servitude like the one Seagrave suffered. That would be what

11

Philippe thought because his culture was a culture of surface, dissemination wide but not deep. Still, Seagrave believed that when Philippe first saw Ida she had done something to him that lay outside his usual expectations. Or perhaps he only thought that because what she'd done to him so far outstripped all his. For an adolescent as she'd seemed to be at first – not quite a woman, to be honest still really a child; anyway under age whatever that was for a Gitane. Perhaps there was no such thing for them, but her extreme youth and the almost measurable accretion of beauty from one moment to the next had let into Seagrave's ready mind a flood of pity – that was how he thought of it – like the first rush of light into a sealed room.

'And the little brother?' Philippe asked casually.

'Still in the camp in the Camargue. Even with your uncle Charles's help I couldn't get them both out.'

'Perhaps he's all right there.'

'Perhaps. Unless there's an epidemic or he starves to death.'

'We'll see, if anything can be done . . . as soon as it's possible. What's he called, that boy, again?'

'Luis.'

Need for sleep reached out to them before they got to the second bottle of Vougeot, exhaustion of undernourished organisms in a fight like the fight for breath, incessant, at the edge. The sky was silent now, the pilots back in their hive. From Philippe's father's quarters there was equally the silence of the grave. The old butler with whom on most evenings he kept up a conversation of mutters, nods and clicks like that of grounded birds, flightless, bypassed in the evolutionary onward sweep, had at last been sent to bed. Hungrier no doubt than his master as Monsieur d'Albaron owned farms out in the plain and certain provisions destined for his plate alone came in by the garden entrance on dark nights.

'Papa has retired. Another taxing day drawn to close. Fernand-Félix must have come in and we didn't hear him.' Philippe's voice was tailing off as he spoke. Twenty-four hours more had passed without arrest, one more day towards the end, away from the threat of interrogation, a bullet in the neck, the cable hung from a plane tree with you as pendulum, turning as the strands unwound with your weight. Seagrave poured the last drop of Burgundy into his glass but never drank it because at about the same time the nightingale in the garden fell silent, opening a void of sleep into which he and Philippe fell where they sat, in the hard chairs with the warm night air washing in from the open window.

When he woke the shutters were back and the sky beyond the trees of the garden was showing the grey early light. A sharp star like a ray passing through a keyhole appeared between leaves. Philippe was missing but from another room Seagrave heard movement and almost at once he appeared with a cup in his hand.

'Coffee,' he said.

'Where did you get it?'

'My father may be everything a regrettable anachronism can be but he has his resources. Black market. He daren't say anything when I take my cut, the time's turned against him. People like my father are going to have to shrink and submit in the days to come.' Philippe sounded pleased about this, too pleased. He held out a dusty bottle of Armagnac, just opened. 'Put some of this in it. There's no bread left.'

'What are you doing today?' Seagrave enquired as he went back into his skirt and long-sleeved peasant blouse and the scarf he wore about his head and the stockings he must wear however hot it might be because of the male character of his calves, the shoes too small, the clips disagreeably pinching his ear-lobes but suggesting, he hoped, female self-adornment without pretension. Above all with no pretension of any kind.

'Rendezvous with Charles at Montpellier. I have a message for him. And he'll have errands for me, as usual.' It was these errands that put Philippe into such daily danger but you could see as he mentioned them how they excited him by their importance.

'Is the message from Fernand-Félix? Have you seen him already this morning?'

'You're very quick and you're as my left hand to me but I can't let you know what my right hand's going to do.'

'Be careful.'

'Of what, especially?'

'Shark-infested waters.'

'A shark can be played, if you know its ways.' Philippe sounded exhilarated, as if he'd breakfasted on Armagnac. Seagrave checked the bottle. It was unbroached.

'You think of playing with the sharks?'

'The best game of all,' said Philippe, and there wasn't any time to argue about it. Risks were for everyone. You must assume that a friend saw danger as clearly as you did.

*

The entrance to the hospital was closely guarded, ever since the day in February when, with the complicity of someone on the medical staff, several captives had been rescued from care by their comrades and taken away to die untortured in the forest. Seagrave walked quickly, head down and back rounded, past the men of the Milice with the gamma insignia on their armbands. Nothing else distinguished them from anyone else in this haggard population; they wore no other outward sign of atrocity; they were men from the fields mostly, working men, ordinary people. Their eyes rested speculatively on Seagrave's figure as he passed. In the ward the beds were close together, there were few nurses, and the usual smell composed of fatigue and pain and the discharges of the incurable hung on the air. Later when it was hotter it would be worse, terminal in the built-up despair of the day. On the high ceiling the flies awaited the heat that would stir them into ceaseless back-and-forth patrol like the Milice on the streets. Seagrave sat on the hard stool by the side of his wife's bed and waited too.

Her eyes were closed and her head half turned away from him, and from the corner of her mouth extended a strip of bandage whose other end she held in one hand. Near the mouth the bandage was discoloured and as Seagrave watched it this stain advanced, gaining ground perceptibly like an index of the illness itself. Denise's face was white and the skin on her hand thin as a membrane, covering faded veins.

'It's getting better,' she said, 'flowing slower. In the night I was changing the bandage every ten minutes.'

'That's good then.'

'Good? For who? For what?' Her voice was muffled by the bandage and now she turned her head to look at him. 'Have they come for my father yet?'

'I haven't seen him. I don't think so. But it'll all be over very soon.'

'I know it will,' Denise said, not meaning the War, which had been superseded in the scale of her interests. 'I wish it was already. And anyway I know you're lying.'

There was no answer ready for this. With all that had gone wrong between them Seagrave's way of sticking as near as possible to the truth with Denise had been constant. Misguided and harmful but constant. It was his self-image that was at stake. His inconstancy in other departments was undeniable.

'What happened to the boy?' Denise asked, still looking at him from the pillow a few inches away from him where he sat at the head of the bed.

'What boy?'

'You know, Etienne. Her little brother. I know you had to take them both. Both or neither. It's like that with those people, they live in litters.'

'Another despised and rejected race,' Seagrave said, and at once regretted saying it. Perhaps Denise hadn't caught his words; she showed no reaction to them.

'So what did happen to him?'

'He stayed in the camp. The litter's broken up.' An expression of some wish satisfied passed over the features within a whisper's reach of his mouth. Seagrave wondered how she knew about Luis but supposed that the enquiries made had been professional in their way. Her father had been an influential man. Seagrave's little hovel out in the garrigue had been under observation while he and Ida and Luis lived in it with the secrecy of refugees.

'You'd better go now,' said Denise. 'Perhaps I'll be better tomorrow.' Suddenly she withdrew her other hand from under the blanket and let it advance like a small wounded animal across the sheet towards him. 'Don't forget I would have had you back even so,' she said, and he took the hand for an instant and let it go again.

'I had to come without the bicycle. I've got to walk.' She turned her head away without answering and lay as he had found her, wasted and light and still as a feather on the grass. When he stood up she spoke again.

'She's had it by now, I suppose?'

'Yes.'

'Where?'

'Out of harm's way.'

'Where?'

'In Switzerland.'

'You sent her to your sister.'

'There was a truck going into the mountains, near the frontier.'

'I don't know which one to feel sorrier for. Her or your sister. And what was it?'

'A boy. Another for the litter.'

Denise raised herself on an elbow and turned her head towards him. Her eyes were very wide, like an animal at the end of the chase. 'We have connections in Switzerland. When I'm strong enough . . .' Whatever it was she meant was in earnest but you could only guess at it. Seagrave felt glad that Ida was so securely hidden. The Sephardic families of which Denise's was one formed a potent society, loyal and vengeful. Living so long in a time of camps and a climate of denunciation made you paranoid, there was no doubt. Seagrave left Denise's bedside without saying any more. He felt his chance of surviving the coming weeks was in some way a fraud at the cost of her certainty of never seeing them out. It was a shameful relief to get away.

Outside you were held between the heat in the sky and its hard refraction off the cobblestones and pavement and the walls of closed and shuttered houses, boltholes from the universal fear. The goods yard of the railway, the marshalling yards and administrative offices were in this part of the town, separated from the hospital buildings by a wide boulevard and the parade ground of the barracks, used now by the Wehrmacht as a park for armoured cars and troop carriers. Seagrave's ostensible duties as cleaning woman started in the offices here, and later would take him on to the main station in the centre of the town. Between the resistants in the administration and those outside whose work was sabotage Seagrave was the link, carrier of messages and photographer of schedules, while the team of other women, the real ones, covered up his presence or absence, sheltering him with their ample fearless feminine identity. As he crossed the boulevard the first warning siren sounded far off, followed soon by another from the roof of the barracks, but these sirens whose functioning was rehearsed on the first Wednesday of every month had never been followed by anything more than the distant droning of Flying Fortresses heading, like yesterday's smaller fry, for the hills or the sea. Sometimes you heard the droning without remembering any sirens; they were subject to the censorship that occludes, with habit and luck, irrelevant noises. So now no one heard the sound unless, like Seagrave passing the barracks, they were close to the source, and then an uneasy but not urgent sense of the ominous, a reminder that surprise is part of war, was all you were likely to feel. He wondered briefly if it was a first Wednesday today . . . no, the date was the twenty-seventh, it couldn't be.

In the streets the cafés were crowded though they hadn't much to serve; shops had queues of women outside; people went on their way, on bicycle or on foot. Seagrave longed for a glass of beer, hesitated at the terrace of a café, remembered his dress, hurried on. No rain had fallen for weeks; there was no freshness in the air but a haze of urban dust and piles of rubbish on unswept streets. Looking across the parade ground he discerned above the roof-line of the barracks the first aircraft in formation, small bright insects in the sun advancing slowly at great height, harvest flies drawn by the sweat and swarm of human activity. They were making due north from the coast, not towards the Cévennes but in the direction of the Rhône valley, its arterial communications and vital bridges. Seagrave walked on past the barracks and into the yard where the offices were in which the most valuable information about rail movements could be gathered. He entered by a low door and the dark, dirty staircase designated for the use of women employees to show that their working lives were only an extension of destined domestic servitude. Of course the women were not Party members. They had no vote, paid no dues, made up no constituency, were not wooed for that. Each time he came in here Seagrave knew the relief of only being seconded to this under-class, not part of it. The railway official who was his contact rose and left the little cupboard-like office as Seagrave entered it with cleaning materials and the camera under his skirt. No words were exchanged but a flick of the hand indicated those papers on the desk useful to photograph. It was cool in here and quiet, the window giving onto a neglected garden away from the busy side of the yards and the local theatre of war. The buzz of the Minox in action and the shrill whistling call of swifts circling the garden and past the window sounded in a vacuum of silence and calm. The photographs were soon taken and Seagrave, for the form, ran a broom round the floor in the direction of the corridor. He was standing still for a moment watching the excited chase of swifts when a new whistling combined with theirs, overrode it in a sharp crescendo backed up by others like a mounting canon of trained voices. It was the impression of an instant, then the first bomb fell on the far side of the buildings, followed by a train of explosions across the lines, the barracks, the parade ground, the street, the houses beyond. The explosions continued in that quarter like blows to a body within hearing but mercifully out of range of your own. Picking himself up from the first shock Seagrave ran down the dark stairs and out into the open forecourt.

Fat pillows of dust hung over the parade ground, but from beyond, the inhabited quarter, there were smoke columns rising to tower over the houses, spreading out as they gained height on the current of heated air, forming a cloud which soon obscured the sky and veiled the sun and hid from view the aircraft whose noise grew as the sound of explosions died away. It seemed there were more aircraft, many more out of sight up there behind the smoke and the black and orange stain of the sun. A minute later as Seagrave was running across the parade ground the second wave of bombs began to fall in front of him in the streets. Behind, in the railway zone and over the acres of lines, the shunting yards and the rolling stock standing there, all was stillness and peace. The bombs must be falling near the hospital, around it, among the houses adjoining. It was a close cluster of explosions, accurate work from such a height. All that was wrong was the target. War effort was being squandered like a defecation of dollars over the homes and shops, the cafés, the nurses' hostel, the wards for surviving wrecks of men from the war before. The pilots of these planes were too high in God's sky to tell one complex of buildings from another; they had picked a target in their remote viewfinders and they were right on it. No fire would reach them where they were, floating in the blue; the second wave of planes was followed by a third and by the time they all returned to base the lesson left behind was exemplary, with the dying choked under fallen masonry, trapped in the furnace of the day's heat.

There were no police controls round the entrance to the hospital now, people moved about without purpose or function, overseers and overseen, sound and sick in the common ruin. Seagrave made his way among them to the wing of the hospital where he'd walked away from Denise with relief an hour ago or less. He found a shell of walls, a line of craters, a flue of smoke to the sky with dust falling back out of it where the roofs had been. Somewhere down below the beams and stone would be the bodies of the patients in what had been this ward. He climbed into the hole with no particular motive. If his father had been alive he would have told him that as a man he could do no less, or anyway as a gentleman, Seagrave reflected grimly. There was no trace of life, the bodies were as deeply buried as those in the cemetery up the road, far deeper than the torn corpses of the summarily executed about the countryside. They would be dug up, that was sure, and identified if possible and even among them there might be one still with breath, but Seagrave would be elsewhere when all that happened. He had film to deliver, his link in the network to hold; lives depended on it. He looked quickly round in case somewhere among the rubble there might against all probability be something belonging to Denise that he should take, by superstition, as a trace, not a memento. Everyone should leave some trace.

There was the sound of many voices through the dusty air, shouts and from time to time the noise of falling masonry. A roof here, a wall there. Soon he saw he was not the only scavenger: other shadowy figures were moving about the ruins, hunting, sifting. He was just one of a number, survivors more conscious of life by finding themselves so close to the newly dead. He turned away, feeling a sense of expropriation. Perhaps that was a kind of last salute.

By the time he reached the streets organisation had begun. The occupiers swarmed about in their powerful vehicles, the air of defeat they'd lately worn now replaced by a look of triumph, fingers pointing to the sky to show the people the real enemy. Trucks were already rolling up, bringing all the male population of any age who could be collected at gunpoint and set to work with bare hands on the ruins. The May sun was like the sun in July, fanatical against the unsheltered. Women weren't yet being forcibly recruited but no doubt they soon would be, those on the streets anyway, in the open like Seagrave. He hurried by back ways towards the main passenger station where the next link in the chain of Resistance waited.

Here there had been no bombs although this was where the arterial railway lines ran, from Spain and Toulouse up to the Rhône valley and the north. If this was the sector it had been intended to hit the attack had fallen wide. Mighty wide. The boulevard was deserted, men already conscripted. The building occupied by the Milice, two storeys above raised cellars where interrogations ran their audible course, stood in sunlight behind guarded ornamental gates, iron railings wrought in the form of spears in close-stacked rank as if tribal infantry bivouacked hereabouts. But the Milice didn't bivouac and never rested, especially now they knew they would soon be stamped out themselves, like scorpions unearthed. Seagrave crossed the double avenue to reach the station offices, a stooping, uninviting figure, that was the effect aimed at as he passed before the Milice headquarters on his way to the entrance each time he came here. It was an ordeal which far from increasing his courage by practice reduced it by attrition. It wasn't just the heat of the day that provoked the sweat he now felt run from his neck down the upper part of his body to the loins. This happened equally at the approach to the station in cold weather. Exactly at the moment when he seemed to be getting safely past the gateway a black Panhard of the type used by the Milice swept fast in from the Montpellier road, passing beside him and into the gates at a distance of a few feet. The man next to the driver signalled Seagrave violently away with a gloved fist and as the car went by he saw that the man held between two others on the back seat was Philippe d'Albaron. His face looked puffy and discoloured and the hair in disorder stuck to the side of his skull as if after an accident, some bloody concussion since he'd gone off to Montpellier that morning to pass on Fernand-Félix's messages. Probably he and Seagrave wouldn't meet again. These gates were seldom passed by the living on the way out unless, all intelligence extracted, they were entrained to the hinterland. The sight of Philippe so near prevented Seagrave from keeping his head down as he usually did, and in that half-moment he read in Philippe's expression an unmistakable message. Get away without delay, it said. I don't know how long I'll hold out or what I'll give away when I can't hold out any more. Get out fast, we know we aren't made for heroes, the expression of Philippe's eye plainly signalled before the iron gates closed behind the black vehicle of these investigators with so little time left to play with.

Chapter Two

FAMILIARITY WITH THE railways was a help when it came to getting away in a hurry. It was lucky too, if one let oneself think it, that the Americans had bombed the wrong locality so trains still could run. By evening Seagrave was in the hills with a sleeping bag, a change of clothes and what cash had been in the cabin, and that night he spent in the open on the fringe of a forest of evergreen oaks near where he'd jumped the train as it wound slowly uphill through the first valley of the Cévennes. He'd waded through the river under the moon and settled into cover. It was cooler up here and the night sky more brilliant. He ate the heel of a stale loaf, the last two inches of a sausage, some raisins stored up since the time when Ida had been there in the garrigue to make the most of their rations and keep him warm. He thought of her as he lay on the stony earth and leaves, and she wove in and out of his waking and sleeping consciousness as if she was the thread stitching him together like a filled sail. But these days and nights were not the season of love in the old sense. Even the well-fed occupiers had begun to desert, so it was reported, the inspected brothels reserved for them. Apprehension and anxiety were the great agents of detumescence in conqueror and conquered. Things would be different soon, when the tide turned; they probably already were different for people like Fernand-Félix who rode it whichever way it ran.

Men driven from the town by danger or to evade the pressgang of labour beyond the frontiers were often alarmed by raw nature as

23

they met it in the forests. Here the nightingales sang throughout the night from branches just above your head, and the boar came down to the river to drink, root about on the edges of the pasture, wallow in any damp patch and propagate their kind in noisy stampede through the undergrowth. But to Seagrave all this was like the accidents of some sort of homecoming. Not that the fauna here was at all the same as in his native region but the forest night-life code was recognisable. The animal world exploited, for its joys, the absence of mankind. It was like that in the woods at home when the men with guns or axes withdrew. At home – the phrase came naturally to mind but the place itself, the long line of dim hills and the red earth and cloudy sky, was held in a compartment of memory where all was distinct but the sense of any reality was missing. Too much had happened since then. Requited desires had appropriated reality's immediacy.

He had little sleep but felt refreshed at first light as if some part of mind and body had enjoyed a deep healing rest. There was a long walk ahead of him into the mountain where he hoped to identify himself as comrade with a group whose whereabouts he had been given, in one of the high, trackless valleys. If he fell on the wrong one he might quite likely be shot at once or otherwise disposed of since there was not only mistrust of informers but enmity between maquis operating independently, savage in isolation, ruthless about the coming political struggle. There was competition for arms parachuted in for the elect but taken by whoever got there first, and each group was as jealous of its integrity as if married to it. And Seagrave's friends on the railways with their detachment here in the hills were the most purist of all due to belief that the historical dialectic was approaching its moment of synthesis. He himself held no strong views about this, kept his mouth shut, played his small part in the class struggle because a competent photographer had been needed in the railway offices and because he was known to François Paradis, the admired chieftain of the group at Nîmes. François had disappeared some months ago and no one knew what had become of him. The worst was feared. The others mentioned him now without the usual mixture of awe and derision, but with sorrow as for a monument engulfed. As for Seagrave, his thoughts of François were always coloured by his feelings about Ida because François had been their ally from the start, when they needed a roof and a refuge in some out of the way place.

'She's not much more than a child; if she's not taken off the street she'll be destroyed,' François had said. 'No one here will do it. They'd say she should be in a brothel where she'd be safer. Perhaps it isn't the same for you. When I was a student I read some works of Monsieur Lawrence. The English practise more the eroticism of the heart, that's clear from the books.' And he had found them the stone cabin and provided backup in different forms to make existence possible without correct papers, outside even the fringes of what was left of proper social order.

Seagrave wondered if the group, when he found them, would have food for him. It was said that in the mountains there was more to eat because the peasants were helpful and if they weren't they could be encouraged to be. Some of the groups, so his friends said, had swollen their numbers by recruitment more among the hungry than the committed, and peasants in outlying farms had been made to feel the difference. The morning started cool under the trees but by midday the heat of the ground and that of the sky seemed to meet in the dense canopy of branches and the air as you breathed it entered the lungs like warm lead. He was high up by now and there was no water here, the stream in the valley bottom, visible from time to time through a break in the trees, was followed by a path, but paths were to be avoided. Now thirst drove him down there, towards a pool seen from far above where the stream ran under rocks while the path seemed to skirt them some way off on the farther side. He went down through the undergrowth, trying to follow a rough track perhaps used by boar but which had a trick of leading you into the heart of the thicket and there dying out. The descent was slow and hard but at last he found himself on a shelf of rock overlooking the water. He must wait long enough to be reasonably sure the place was as deserted as it seemed. He lay down among the myrtle and thyme and let the sweat run down his neck, under his arms, between his legs. It was a trial of strength. The only sound now was the trickle of water over the stones a few metres below him. No. It was not quite the only sound. He could hear another, the faint noise of some insect, irregular but monotonous. It was too soon in the year for cicadas: this must be a small relation, some unimportant locust scratching itself in the heat to make the music of courtship. But there was something else about this sound, something in its peculiar, familiar pitch, recalling some other aspect of adolescence. Then Seagrave understood with a jolt like the surprise of sudden gunfire that what he was hearing, from somewhere quite close, was the sound of radio transmission.

This was most unlikely, on reflection, to be the enemy. The enemy would not be up here communicating in code and hidden among the trees and rocks. The sound of the enemy's radio messages, peremptory and public and guttural, was familiar to everyone, heard on the streets, issuing from armoured vehicles, from offices, from inside the helmets of motor cyclists. This was clandestine in nature, and therefore friendly. Seagrave went cautiously down to the pool. There was no one in sight but the radio was near, at work somewhere behind the rocks. As he reached the water it stopped. He had been seen. He raised both arms with palms spread open and looked about him, moving slowly and not changing his ground, but the scene appeared deserted, just unedited nature and himself. It seemed that if he stayed where he was the other or others would sooner or later show themselves, whereas if he went on his way he could be taken for a potential informer and attacked from behind his back. He removed his shoes and entered the shallow water, drank and splashed his face and neck and shirt. Then he knelt on the stones and immersed his head. The water was cold and clean and seemed flavoured by the mountain herbs it had run through since leaving its source not far above. When at last he straightened up he found a figure in camouflaged uniform in front of him on the other bank of the pool, covering him with a revolver to which the fist holding it imparted a slight tremor.

'Stand up with both hands behind your head.' The order was spoken in French with evident ease but a slight accent not at once placeable, maybe Belgian or Swiss. But Seagrave had already seen what identified the speaker's origins, the little woven crowns embroidered on the shoulders of his jacket. He was face to face for the first time in four years with a compatriot.

Seagrave calculated that his own French, in constant use all that time, would sound native to this officer who would be expecting nothing else up here. 'Welcome to the Cévennes. And *vive* Churchill,' he said, and smiled encouragingly because he saw a certain nervousness in the protuberant eyes fixed on him with resolution.

'*Vive la France*,' the officer returned politely but without lowering the revolver. They stood looking at each other in a manner Seagrave thought of as two Englishmen each weighing up the pros and cons of being forced by circumstances into relation with the other. Of course the officer couldn't know this, nor could he know that his distrust of Seagrave was nothing to Seagrave's of him, a distrust with deeper roots and a much wider range of reference. Still, there might yet be something to be made of the situation.

'We're probably looking for the same group,' Seagrave said, throwing this out like a fly cast on the water.

'What's your identification?'

'It was *baiser sans moustache*, but it may have changed since I started on the run. I've seen no one since then.'

'That isn't what I've got.' A sort of brief stealthy smile under the officer's own moustache caused an easing of his stern expression. 'But it is rather a good one.'

'What have you got?'

'It's me asking the questions,' said the officer, making a small thrusting motion with his revolver, but there was already a shift in the balance of moral if not of physical authority. Seagrave was the native here, and as such, in this man's estimation, entitled to recognition of this priority. 'But in any case if they've changed the codeword without letting us know, then it doesn't much matter any more.' He looked carefully from Seagrave to his bundle of belongings and back again. 'Are you armed? Please open that pack.' When he saw the contents of this spread out on the stones he put his revolver away and called over his shoulder in English, 'Soames. You can come out here.' Then he added in French to Seagrave, 'A soldier. For the radio and other tasks.' Soames appeared from among the beetling rocks, tall and thin and heavily burdened with packs like a wayfarer in a narrative painting – *The Road to Compostela* perhaps – sojourning in a strange mountainous land.

'Permission to drink, sir.' It was more a statement than a request and he squatted promptly by the edge of the stream and drank out of cupped hands, his long legs bent under him like hairpins.

'This chap seems to be pretty harmless,' the officer said in English, 'but keep a close eye on him.'

'I will that,' said Soames, who also had a gun, Seagrave saw – some kind of light repeating rifle consisting only of a metal frame, barrel and chamber, held firmly under one arm. He looked hard at Seagrave from head to toe as if noting particulars that could be vital later on. A look of surprise slowly crossed his face. 'He's a Froggy I suppose?'

'Of course he is,' muttered the officer. 'Try and remember to say Frenchman.'

Seagrave thought of Philippe and how immensely this situation would amuse him. 'All the groups have names as well as codewords,' he said. 'Do you know the name of the one you're looking for?'

The officer weighed the question up. It was obvious enough that he and Soames, despite their radio and maps and select equipment and training were simply lost in this endless wilderness of forest, deep identical valleys, featureless receding ridges fading into the horizon. Perhaps they had been dropped by night in the wrong place and hadn't got their bearings. But already Seagrave could see how they could be valuable. Drops of arms by parachute were controlled by radio contact from the ground, and the radio contact was in the hands of liaison officers. Resistants with the wrong political sympathies got no *parachutages*, it was as simple as that, neither the Allies nor the French Provincial Government wishing to see these hordes descend heavily armed into the cities of the plain and take control of them as soon as the enemy was out of sight. Seagrave waited patiently for an answer. The officer after all was a trained man, and training inhibits spontaneous action. Appreciation must follow assessment, which has its own procedures.

'The Aigoual-Cévennes,' the officer said at last, seeming to have ticked off mentally all the criteria of decision. 'They have one liaison officer already but he needs an assistant. It seems they're a very big and well organised contingent. And we've brought certain special new radio equipment. That's what Soames is mainly for,' he repeated, and Seagrave noticed this rather evasive insistence on Soames's multiple function. It looked as if Soames was a source of support his officer couldn't well do without, a psychologically indispensable follower.

'Those are the people I'm going to,' Seagrave lied, 'and I know the way to find them from here.'

'You're joining them?'

'Yes.'

'Where have you come from?'

'Nîmes.'

'I thought the Aigoual-Cévennes maquis only recruited in the mountains.'

'I was a link in their chain of information down there. But things got too hot. My first contact has just been arrested. I can be more useful here now.'

The officer didn't look as if he thought Seagrave would be much use anywhere, but that was the lack of uniform, badges of training, marks of rank. To him, Seagrave was a spare civilian who should be under arms, but he had to take him as he found him, especially as he claimed to know where they were and how to get away from it. 'If you're sure of getting there we'll join you. Save our time. I've been trying to get new instructions over the air. We'll steal a march on those chaps. They think I'm lost.' He laughed, showing under his moustache a set of prominent teeth. 'Stupid buggers sitting out there on boats. My name's Roper by the way, Hughie Roper.' He held out a hand and shook Seagrave's with a firmness that didn't quite convey the affability you can count on. Perhaps it was still too soon for that.

'Etienne, Paul,' said Seagrave citing his two forenames, and then shook hands also with Soames who seemed to take this with some suspicion and said nothing. Seagrave considered Soames's various packs with interest. 'You wouldn't have anything you could spare to eat before we start? I've had nothing since yesterday and very little then.'

'Soames. You can fish out the chocolate, if it isn't all melted. Best thing on a march. Source of quick energy,' explained Roper whose flesh under stretched skin seemed to break out with all the fuel that had been stoked into it. 'And I'll have a nip of this,' he added, taking a flask from one of the many pockets of his combat dress. 'Do you . . .?' He held the flask out hesitantly, clearly unsure whether it was wise to offer alcohol to a man who if under discipline would surely have been in the ranks.

'Thank you,' Seagrave said. He drank well from the flask and handed it back. 'I haven't had whisky for a long time. You can't get it here.'

'That doesn't surprise me,' said Roper. 'You can't get much of it in England. And this has to last.' His expression showed he thought this had been a one-sided transaction unlikely to be offset in the future. 'If you're ready now we'll get on. Don't forget we're very close behind you.'

'Don't worry,' Seagrave said.

'War's a worrying time,' said Roper and sounded as if he meant it. Soames now straightened himself up by stages and humped his burdens ready to move on, like a complex piece of articulated apparatus in an explorer's encampment, laboriously reassembled after each halt.

'Let's just hope he knows the right fucking way out of here,' he said, looking at Seagrave as though to try him out.

'That'll do, Soames,' said Roper, and they started off in single file along the path, and then uphill away from the stream and through undergrowth of holm oak and juniper until near the crest this gave place to chestnut groves, long grass, and finally to beech with clear ground and mast underfoot. Between the trees was an immense view over rounded hills locked bafflingly into each other and down dark valleys running out at a great distance into the plain. On the eastern horizon could just be made out, in the clear heat of the afternoon above the haze, forms of snow-carrying peaks pushing up patiently as loaded elephants into the sky.

'Brings bonny Scotland to my mind,' said Soames.

From what part exactly of the north of England did he come? Out of the many shades of accent sounding to a profane ear more or less one, to Seagrave's the particular voice of Soames, a melodic rise and fall, soft under a harsh surface of tone, had brought back his own part of that distant land. It was a far cry, disturbing and intriguing. 'That's the sea over there,' he said, indicating a sheet of white between sky and earth on the flat southern extremity.

'There's the sea,' Roper translated for Soames.

'Aye, I can see it's there,' Soames said, seeming to watch from his great height for sail on the waters – Norse, Scots, Spanish, French, maybe even the gross hulk of carriers, like a bleak sentinel on a Cumbrian tower.

'They bring the sheep this way to pasture in the summer. Thousands of them. We're standing on the sheep trail. They'll come any day now. It's the transhumance.'

'Where's this maquis of yours?' Roper asked impatiently. He looked too hot under this sun to think comfortably about sheep. 'This is an exposed ridge, whatever the sheep may use it for. We're plainly visible from the air.' He turned to Soames. 'Don't stand there in the open like a crane. You're visible from the air.'

'You wouldn't know there was a war anywhere,' said Soames, who seemed, for a soldier, to have unexpected licence to say what was in his mind.

'That's not the point. The point is we'd look frightful bloody fools if a fighter came low over this way.' Roper went off behind a tree to urinate, taking longer over this than seemed usual so Seagrave wondered if he'd seen some movement somewhere among the trees and looked in his direction. Roper was just doing up the flap of the pocket where he kept his flask. 'Wake up there, Soames. Let's get going,' he said.

'We cut down the next valley,' Seagrave said. 'We'll find them there in a ruined farm. It's hidden and there's no road.'

'No road? Why? Why's it ruined? Has it been bombed?'

'Depopulation. It was subsistence farming here and the people couldn't subsist on it any more. They migrated to the coal mines.'

'You seem to know all about it. Did your people come from up here and go down . . . to the mines . . . or somewhere?'

'That's about it,' Seagrave said.

Roper turned round to Soames walking behind them. 'There you are, Soames, should make you feel at home. Coal mines here. This chap's family worked in them. You told me yours did too, under the sea off the Cumbrian coast.' Soames looked at Seagrave with no change of expression, then he laughed.

'A small world all right,' he said.

From near the head of the valley no buildings could be seen, no sign of old clearings, no field, nothing but trees, a uniform cover enveloping the slopes and anything there might be on them. Seagrave stopped at a point where the gully widened to become the dry bed of a torrent, smooth stones reflecting the sun's glare.

'I think it would be best if you wait here with Soames and I go on to make the contact. They're very sensitive about strangers. We don't want to surprise a guard who asks the questions when it's too late.'

'I'm not sure about that. It means trusting you,' Roper said.

'And you don't?'

'Trust isn't what this war is about. I thought you would have known that in an occupied country.'

'Sometimes you rely on it to survive. We've learned a lot about survival and trust these last years. And from experience you wouldn't get in a little island.'

'I grant you that,' Roper said reasonably. 'No need to get heated. As a man, I trust you, of course. Man to man. Personally I mean.' He seemed to grapple for a moment with distinctions finer than he was used to. 'But as *unknown human potentiality* . . .' His face had lightened. The strain was past. He had found the category where Seagrave belonged. Seagrave felt relief too. He saw himself through Roper's eyes, placed and slotted. 'As such, I judge you'd better carry on. But while you're gone I will orientate myself by map and fix co-ordinates and communicate with them by radio. If there's any trouble – from any source – I can call up air support from right here. Better be clear about that.'

'It's the best news my friends will have ever had,' Seagrave said before clambering down over the rocks below them. He knew now where he was and thought he saw the moves ahead. He wasn't turning up empty-handed, a mere additional unit for the maquis to feed and arm, but it was vital when he found them to get to the top quickly, not leaving Roper too long alone with his radio. How long would it take him to tactically reassess his position with the help of the men out at sea? Because once he'd done that he would stop being the asset he now seemed, brilliant, unique, negotiable.

Identifying himself was easier than Seagrave had feared. It was at once evident that wine flowed up here freer than water. From the breath of the resistants it spread on the warm air of afternoon like aroma of jasmine, inescapable. Seagrave was lucky enough to arrive before amiability had degenerated.

'Tartas was a friend of mine,' he said straight off to the first man in hearing, using François Paradis's codename. 'Like a father to me,' he added, judging a little sentimentality might go a long way.

'How do you mean, he was?' The aim of the antique rifle wandered about in the air.

'We haven't had news of him for a long time.'

'You haven't had news of Tartas? No news for a long time? Hey lads, here's one looking for news of Tartas.' From the shelter of the surrounding trees laughter sounded forth. 'Without news of Tartas, think of that.' The laughter increased, until a strong voice called up from the buildings.

'What's that noise? One of you come down here.'

'You'd better come with me,' said the man with the rifle. 'If you want to know what became of Tartas just follow me.' He led the way down to the ruins and through an archway into a closed court, his rifle balanced in his fist and swinging as he walked. It might even not be loaded, such was the shortage of ammunition. But this group had done good work derailing trains, blowing up bridges if they got their hands on any explosive, felling trees across roads by night where convoys were expected to pass.

These buildings had no roofs but the vaulted cellars were intact, dark when you entered from the sunlight, and cool. 'François,' said the escort into the darkness, 'here's a *type* who says he knows you. A foreigner. Unarmed.'

'But it's Etienne,' said the strong voice from the depth of the cellar, and François Paradis came forward, embraced Seagrave three times holding on hard to his upper arms with powerful hands as if to infuse some of his own vital force. When he let go he dismissed the escort with a wave of one hand, friendly but final.

Wasting no time Seagrave explained about Roper and the radio and the urgency of using him while the going was good. 'He must believe we're the Aigoual-Cévennes. Long enough to get at least one good *parachutage*. I think he can do that quickly if he isn't made suspicious. His French is good, and like a lot of Englishmen he isn't as stupid as he looks.' Seagrave knew from experience that this disparity between appearance and capacity was something that tended to elude the French and had to be rubbed in.

'Well, for a little Englishman you've been very clever,' said François laughing and banging Seagrave on the shoulder. There was a triumphant gleam in his eyes. 'A very cunning young Englishman. But your Major Roper doesn't know about that. I understand you. I'm not as stupid as I look either. You don't want to answer any English questions. You'll have to one day, but not yet. He might arrest you.' He laughed again. 'But don't worry, we wouldn't let him. I would shoot any man who tried to arrest *mon cher petit* Etienne. Now go and get your Roper and his assistant. I will come and meet you halfway to receive these gentlemen with the right ceremony.'

When Seagrave got back to them he detected tension between Roper and Soames. Soames was occupied with the radio equipment, bent over it with his face close to the works like a watchmaker.

'Soames has problems with the transmitter. Can't get through, he says. You were a long time.' The whisky flask was now lying on a rock within easy reach. 'I know where we are and it's not where the Aigoual-Cévennes maquis is supposed to be.'

'They were attacked. Had to move off in a hurry.'

Roper weighed this up in his usual way. 'But you knew to come here.'

'I only left Nîmes last night. They'd sent a telegram.'

Roper looked incredulous. 'A telegram?'

'We've a coded telegraphic network on the railway. It's called the Baudot. Used all the time. They sent a man down into the valley to do it.'

'Well, have you made the necessary contact?'

'They're expecting you now.'

'Is my fellow-officer with them? Did you see him?'

'The group split into two. He's with the other half, so I was told. They say that's why you were needed, to work with this half.' There was a shift in Roper's expression like a passing change of light. Seagrave believed he was privately pleased at the prospect of this autonomy and for that reason asked no more awkward questions. Probably the other officer was senior and capable of marring Roper's enjoyment of his brief authority. He might be difficult about the whisky flask too. 'It's a great moment for my friends and a great honour. They count on you,' Seagrave said, watching him. 'Apparently the other liaison officer has been very effective.'

'Has he, by Christ?' said Roper in English.

François Paradis certainly bore out the forecast that Roper was counting on. He welcomed him near the entry to the farm with his men grouped in rough formation behind him as if on parade for an exceptional circumstance, a general at least. They may be a bit of a rabble, thought Seagrave, but they look dangerous, which is what Roper should be expecting. And hungry. For food, for arms, for action, for women in this all-male hideout. That was a contrast with the feeling in the towns where there were plenty of women but too much fear. Here, it seemed different, action and its perspectives were the allies of the libido stirring under the surface like heated oil. Soames towered over the resistants and as soon as Roper had withdrawn with François into the cellar he established with them the soldier's implicit pact that the common lot called for improvement. Within minutes he had a bottle of wine in his hand and his cigarettes had been passed round and non-verbal signals of solidarity given and received. The radio and the rest of Soames's burdens were neatly stacked in a corner of the court like a trophy of arms while the legionary rested. Seagrave wondered if the transmitter had been put to rights. If not, Soames was taking advantage of his officer's absence to catch up with him on drink when his duty clearly was to get his material into working order without delay. Seagrave went over to where he sat on the ground with his back against the wall, tapped him lightly on the shoulder and when he turned indicated the stacked equipment, raised his eyebrows, and tried to mitigate this interference with a laugh which he hoped was encouraging. Soames stared at him, then raised the wine bottle and took several hearty swallows.

'Fine stuff, goes straight home like a horse,' he said, and got to his feet, standing with his back to the resistants and facing Seagrave. He leaned down and spoke in a low voice, almost as if muttering to himself. 'You don't know me but I recognised you straight off. Don't worry, I wouldn't give the game away even if I knew what it was. Keep it from old Roper as long as you like.'

Seagrave felt more relief than surprise. 'I thought you might be from up there.'

'Knew t'auld voice, very like,' said Soames laying it on.

'From whereabouts, exactly?'

Soames named a village on the coast a few miles from Seagrave's birthplace. It was a mining district, the seams of coal exploited since the seventeenth century in workings which ran out some way under the sea. A couple of the pitheads leading to these lay on land belonging to Seagrave's family which had been steadily, not excessively, enriched over the centuries as a result, much less than others owning ranks of pitheads that marched over the violated land like monuments to armies slaughtered in useless wars. Another consequence often was an enmity in the bone, ancient, indelible, towards families that had profited, on the part of those that had burrowed and sometimes died in their interest under ground or water. 'I left a long time ago, at least it seems a long time,' Seagrave said, as if that made any difference.

'People wondered, in the villages,' Soames said.

Seagrave could imagine it. Wondering was the word up there for the darkest suspicion. But war after all was a house with many mansions; he had passed it in one of them, and not the safest. He looked quickly at Soames to see his reaction, if any. The eyes which seemed buried as deeply in his head as coal under the sea showed no sign of hostility but a sort of patience as if Soames had worked out that that was what was going to be needed with this fellow-countryman.

'How about the transmitter?' Seagrave asked.

'Working a treat.'

'You mean . . .?'

'I reckoned there were no urgency to send anything out before you got back.'

'Quite right. These people here are my friends.'

'Good enough for me.'

'Well, it could be you've done me a very good turn there.'

'I wouldn't wonder,' said Soames, using the word this time to show that he would never expect a man from the same part of the world as himself to act on pure altruism.

'Thanks a lot anyway.'

'It's nothing,' said Soames, but this was not the case. Seagrave weighed up his own motives in this piece of trickery. What was there in it for him? The minus side was that Roper could certainly make trouble for him later on when he found out about it, stirring up a lot more questions for the day of reckoning. Looked at like that his motive seemed to have a lot to do with securing a base with people who had befriended him, a foreigner in their occupied country. Also with serving them, he could honestly say. Chance had put a bit of power his way; he was using it without too much scruple in the general as well as his own interest. There wasn't much merit in it but not much harm either. He was genuinely winning the esteem of people whose esteem would one day be very valuable to have. The ethic in which he had been born and raised seemed to fade in the bright light of this common realism.

Soames drank the last of the litre of red wine he had been given and then set up the radio so that when Roper emerged, staggering slightly, from the cellar he could report the technical hitch resolved.

'Good show, Soames,' said Roper, over whose blue eyes a thin film seemed to have spread like a lens. 'Start sending this out at once. We'll see how soon we can get those chaps off their arses and into the air.' He passed Soames a sheet of lined paper covered with closely written detail, and they settled down together in the corner of the court with the maps and the writing pad and the stridulations of the radio, transmitting, receiving, retransmitting; summoning from the ships in the Golfe du Lion the flight that would deliver to this remote spot in the mountain the wherewithal – the Stens, the ammunition, the Amonal – to transform these weaponless men into effective guerrillas for liberating their land and reaping the warrior's rewards.

Chapter Three

FRANÇOIS PARADIS HAD imposed an ascendancy, by perseverance and nature, among his colleagues down in the tightly structured world of the railway at Nîmes. Here in the mountains with a private army his dominance was Napoleonic. He had the wind in his sails and the advent of Roper with the radio added the tide to his authority. The first *parachutage* came in the night following Roper's arrival, two or three long thin canisters dropped into the trees near the crest. It wasn't much but it was a beginning. The alchemy by which any success glorifies the leader was set off by this novelty. Seagrave could see the process at work because he was immune to it. His own allegiance to François dated from further back and was individual rather than collective. He felt himself a stray running with the pack but not in it. Roper however had attached himself to Paradis like a devotee and thrown in his lot with the maquis and his commitment was as collective as possible. 'I'll get you all the arms your chaps can carry and more,' he said like a lover with gifts. 'Recruit. Build up your numbers. I'll do the rest.'

Naturally, Roper had orders to observe and briefings to respect. He was there to direct the supply of arms but the decision that arms be supplied was antecedent to him in the strategic chain. Any zeal of Roper's to equip this maquis was a reflection of higher will in superior places. Liberation was coming and the maquis, especially the correct maquis, were to play their part in it. Any day now the landings were expected somewhere along the vast flat mosquito-ridden shores of the Languedoc coast. The Camargue had been flooded to make it impassable to an invader and the occupying forces were concentrating defence on the shores of the gulf to the west of it. Intensive resistant activity in the hills inland was encouraged by every radio message. Harass the rear, those were the orders, when the armies land they will sweep through the plain, roll up the enemy like a fouled carpet and restore the republic to itself and you. Drops of arms were more ostentatious, carried out by day where they would be seen and reported and foster belief in massive mobilisation in the hinterland.

It seemed sometimes to Seagrave that Paradis was restless with this scenario. He resisted calls, relayed through Roper, to deploy his men more energetically in sabotage operations, split them up, openly invest points of vantage on roads in the foothills. He appeared to be waiting for something, the pivot of history perhaps, the ripe moment to galvanise the masses. He brooded over the days and weeks while Roper continued to mediate supply and instruction. More *parachutages* followed the first but in what seemed a parsimonious trickle, a canister at a time, while there was a steady flow of men arriving from the towns, young and untrained and with backgrounds impossible to check. Who knew if some of these were collaborators climbing on at the last minute, to show themselves with clean hands? To Seagrave's surprise François didn't seem to worry about this.

'For me what counts is the future, and in the future it's numbers that will count. Any cleaning up can be done internally, later when there's time. Time for everything.'

'And if there's an informer among them?'

'I'll sniff him out. If I smell something rotten I know what to do.' Justice, or judgement, was certainly expeditive in the maquis. François had a personal guard, a few followers sticking close to him, saying little, moving swiftly, and from time to time a new recruit would disappear as if the mountain had swallowed him up. 'We're children of the Revolution. Not all the farrow die old,' François said, leaving Seagrave unsure if he was citing some folk adage of his peasant forebears, or an aphorism of Lenin, or if he was just continuing with the elaboration of his own personality, sententious as a leader's must be.

All the same in such uncontrolled affluence of personnel there was danger. By the end of June the maquis numbered more than a thousand men, camping in the forest, fed with increasing difficulty, their only discipline suspense. By then it was obvious that Roper was getting worried. As a professional he looked on this growing rabble with alarm and it was noticeable that the flow of canisters from the sky had almost dried up.

'The Major's got the wind up,' said Soames. 'He says this lot are bandits. He gets orders on the air and he passes them on and they don't get followed. These people have their own ideas. He says you can't have any of those in the Army.'

'It's their country. They're bound to have ideas about getting it back.'

'I reckon there's a lot of politics behind it.'

'And what would you say if there is?'

'I wouldn't have to say owt about it at all.' Soames spoke disdainfully as if politics concerned a class of humanity apart. 'But I won't forget what you told me.'

'What was that?'

'The Major's bandits are your mates.'

'I said that when there were fewer of them.'

'Aye, you don't know where half the buggers come from.'

'Is Roper letting them know by radio that he's worried?'

'Not every word the Major writes on his little pad gets sent out. Like he thinks it does,' Soames said, and Seagrave thought he should leave it at that.

Things became critical halfway through July while everyone waited tensely for the landings. Roper as part of his training for liaison work had received first aid instruction and among Soames's burdens was a basic medical equipment. It was known that the maquis worked in isolation and much military thought had gone into choosing the ingredients. They included an item no British officer in foreign parts should be without, a snake-bite kit, and this was just as well because on this July day one of the late recruits was bitten by an adder while alone at some distance from the others, in a quiet place among deep vegetation.

'What was he up to by himself?' Roper asked suspiciously when Soames came running to report the incident.

'He was shitting, sir.'

'There's a field latrine. Why wasn't he using that?'

'He's a loner. Like they say here he prefers to go in the nature,' said Soames who was picking up French fast as the weeks went by.

'Copped a bit more nature than he bargained for,' said Roper, and presently went out with the serum and hypodermic syringe. The victim may have been a loner in some respects but he was a talkative one. Probably he was grateful to Roper and his tongue was loosened by reprieve. Among the core of first resistants the fact of Seagrave's nationality was as secure as with Soames, orders having been given by Paradis to that effect. But this newcomer may never have heard the order; no one may have thought to pass it down as far as him on the periphery. When Roper came back he found Seagrave and marched him into one of the cellars.

'That man I've been jabbing knows you. Seen you in Nîmes,' he said furiously in English. 'What's your game? Who are you? Where have you been all the war? What are you doing here?' He didn't wait for answers to these questions but went to the doorway and roared into the open air. 'Soames. Here. At the double.'

'I've been working four years with the Resistance. Ever since it started,' Seagrave said.

'You should have been in the UK. Consider yourself under arrest. Until I've received orders about you you won't leave this cellar. Soames, get through and report we may have a young deserter on our hands. Request orders for consequential action.

What's your real name? Where are your papers? Passport?'

'They're not here. I left in a great hurry. My name's Seagrave.'

'Full names.'

'Stephen Lowther Seagrave.'

A peculiar expression passed across Roper's face and the surface of his eyes, as if the speaking of these names had scored a hit somewhere in a sensitive area of social taxonomy. 'You sound more or less . . .' He failed to complete the sentence but turned again to Soames. 'Did you know this man was an Englishman, Soames?'

'Had it quite plain from you he was a Froggy, sir.'

'Well, go and report we're holding a civilian calling himself Lowther Seagrave. Well-spoken. Claims four years' working with the Resistance. We'll see if anyone knows anything about him in Intelligence. Get on with it, Soames. And you, you've got some explaining to do to me personally. I've had doubts about this maquis of yours for some time. You've played a double game with me. I don't believe these are the people I was sent to liaise with. Seemed all right at first, not now. You may have put me well and truly in the brown stuff. Up to here.'

'You seemed to hit if off very well with Paradis. Haven't you checked up by radio?'

'Half the messages don't get answered. They're doing a war on the other end of that radio; they've got more urgent things to worry about than one Liaison Officer's doubts, that's all Soames seems to be able to get by way of an answer. But later on they'll change their tune. If I've been directing arms supplies to the wrong lot I could get court-martialled.'

'Well, no one can argue that the arms aren't going into the hands of genuine resistants.'

'It isn't for you to decide what gets argued higher up. They make their own law. What I can decide here and now is to suspend direction for any further drops. But first I want to know just who these people are, and what your connection with them is. And where I am.' He shouted again for Soames, and began rapidly writing a message of some length on his pad. 'Get this off urgently. Don't go to sleep on it,' he said when Soames appeared. 'Report back as soon as it's done. Get acknowledgement of priority request for orders.'

'Sir,' said Soames, taking the paper but giving the word a negative, sceptical ring. He strode away like a stork, making you wonder how in the Army anyone could ever have marched in step with him.

Roper sat down on the edge of a table which had been supplied to mark this cellar as his headquarters. He stared up at Seagrave and from time to time patted his revolver for reassurance in these difficult circumstances. 'What have you got to say for yourself?' The question was delivered in a bark but there was doubt undermining the military form. The whole environment of the maquis was unamenable to the disciplines Roper knew and on top of that he was faced with Seagrave, possibly – it was shameful but necessary in this world to admit it – a person with connections. Seagrave sat on another corner of the table. It seemed to him that Roper was a man with a problem about making up his mind. Not for the first time he wondered if it wasn't Roper's French that had mainly qualified him for this mission.

'I wouldn't be in too great a hurry to stop the arms drops if I were you,' he said.

'Why wouldn't you?'

'François Paradis won't like it.'

'So much the worse for him. I can handle François Paradis. What is he? A guerrilla captain. Has to face reality in the end and take orders. Anyway I have stopped them.'

'Is that what Soames is doing now?'

'Correct.'

Seagrave experienced a conflict of interests, or loyalties. Paradis was a friend and benefactor, Roper a compatriot. Roper was the agent of the liberating forces but he was also a personal threat. The Resistance, and this branch of it, were Seagrave's arm and unit with claims on him. He decided to go for compromise. 'If you stop them definitely, it would be wise not to let François know at once that you've done that,' he said.

'On the contrary, I intend to inform him straight away.' Roper had apparently made his mind up at least about that, and with all the more rashness that he probably thought it didn't matter. 'You may think it's all right for you, Lowther Seagrave, to play both ends against the middle but it won't do for Roper.' He stood up, straightened his revolver and marched towards the doorway. 'You're under orders to stay here until my return,' he said, turning on the threshold. 'If you give me any trouble I'm empowered to treat you as a deserter in the field and shoot you where you stand.'

'Good God,' Seagrave said. 'Better not do that.'

'I won't hesitate a moment. And as I suspect no one knows of your existence you wouldn't be missed.'

Roper looked as if he meant this, something about Seagrave having got under his skin. He spoke histrionically; this was because they were playing parts in the theatre of war. Seagrave himself had been pushed into a small part by circumstances, that of laconic amateur, but it wasn't how he felt himself. After a time he went out to see how Soames was getting on with the transmissions. He could count on Soames, he thought, to get away from role-playing and the imagination. Soames wasn't there. The radio blinked and twittered, stuck on the sandy earth in the sheltered corner of wall, alone like a virgin betrayed on a beach. Further off under the trees some of the maquis waited, grubby, unshaven, lean and drastic. Seagrave approached.

'Has anyone seen the English soldier?'

'The *flamand rose*? He followed his commandant. At a safe distance.' They nicknamed Soames, who was popular, the flamingo on account of his legs like jointed sticks.

'Which way?'

'Down the valley.'

'Where's François?'

'He's down the valley too.'

'And how's the *type* who met the adder?'

'His testicles and all the system swelled up horribly but he's on the mend. They're subsiding. He's been relieved.'

'I wish I could say as much,' said another man. Far away in the forest a few shots sounded, a rapid succession and then silence but for the sawing of the cicadas, echoing round the inside of your head like the sound of firing in the sphere of hills. All heads turned but no one spoke. For a moment it seemed as if the giant stage prop of action had been wheeled forward to the footlights, then wheeled away in the long silence that met it.

'Shooting a *sanglier*,' someone said. 'But what can one pig do for so many?'

'I counted three shots.'

'A *sanglier* is tough. You have to be sure of him.'

'Perhaps we should dig a pit and light the fires.'

'A *sanglier* isn't a sheep, you fool. He has to hang.'

'After you're castrated him,' offered another voice, dipping into folklore stock.

'Everyone knows that.'

The July heat was intense, and the higher up you were on the mountain the closer you felt to the sun, trained on you. Across this furnace presently appeared the figure of Soames, solitary and loping at the double through the trees, and without stopping back into the enclosure where the radio rasped on alone. Seagrave had never before seen Soames run, his greatest concession to any order of Roper's to do so being a lengthening of his stride. He followed him into the yard.

'Have they decided what to do with me?' he asked, putting himself before the war effort. Soames removed the headphones and looked Seagrave squarely in the eye as if challenging him to work things out for himself.

'Situation's changed,' he said.

'Meaning?'

'For a start, you can relax. There won't be any decision taken.'

'Roper said . . .'

'In the Army, lad, there's a space between a thing said and a thing done. That's a recognised fact.'

'But he'll be back any minute.'

'Like I said, things are different. You'll see.' Soames put the headphones back on and returned to the transmitter, where as soon as there was a break in its febrile broadcast he proceeded to tap out a lengthy message. Seagrave waited for this and the reply to it to be apparently complete, feeling rather as if he'd eavesdropped behind a hedge and held his cover till the spasms subsided.

'In that case what was all that about?'

'Directions for arms drops.'

'I thought they were suspended.'

'In the Army . . .' Soames began patiently, but just at that moment François Paradis appeared in the yard, spreading energy and action, his henchmen close at his heels. He beckoned Seagrave to follow him into the cellar.

'That Major has been making problems,' he said. 'He came to find me where I was specially to make them, nothing else.' François sounded aggrieved, but also as if a certain unwelcome load was off his mind.

'Roper takes his responsibility seriously. He's had a lot of special training for his duties. That's why he sees problems. He has a structure for every situation.'

'I don't know which structure will fit him in the situation where he is now,' François said and his hearty laughter was echoed by the henchmen.

'And what is it?' Seagrave asked though the answer was advancing towards him out of the dark on its own. François took his arm to lead him into the back part of the cellar where he had his sleeping quarters behind a low wall. There was a photograph of Madame Paradis and two or three children on a wooden box beside the remnants of an old bed.

'The English soldier, he's a very sensible man,' François said. 'He understands quickly. His French is primitive but just enough . . . for coming to terms.'

'How much does he know?'

'All he needs to know.'

'But without . . . participating?'

'It seems he followed his commandant at a distance. He stayed at a distance.'

'But you've spoken with him. Was that at a distance too, from what happened?'

'The boys saw him among the trees and brought him down. The firing surprised him perhaps, and he let himself be seen. Or perhaps it was on purpose, you can't know with the English. They're cunning.' Seagrave took remarks like that as recognition of how well he had learned to merge.

'So you sent him back to the radio after the negotiations.'

'No negotiations were necessary. That's what I mean, he understands quickly. He's a natural resistant, in the bone.'

'Signalling now for more *parachutages* . . . as if from Roper?'

'When the time comes to make ourselves heard, I must have arms.'

'The people who send them think they're for harassing the enemy in the rear, not political adventures.'

'If we see the enemy's rear we'll harass it. I promise you that. But you see, Etienne, I'm not a soldier like the Major. I think further ahead. With over a thousand men behind me in a country without a government, think of that! Just free. Empty cities! Think what it means! Every minute will count.'

'And every gun,' said Seagrave in whose mind's eye a picture was taking shape like the rapid coalescence of patterns on a liquid surface. 'It'll be what's called a power vacuum, that's what you think, isn't it?' He felt a certain excitement himself, the alluring promises of anarchy. 'But the Provisional Government will come in with the allied armies, straight off the beaches and into the towns. The world won't be empty. There'll be the tanks and the men and aircraft and the new government all together. Your thousand untrained resistants won't add up to very much. Maybe not even enough to justify executing an ally in a remote forest.'

'Listen,' said François, and sat on the end of the bed with his fists clenched together between his thighs. 'That's how you're supposed to think. How we've been made to think. But our chief Charles d'Albaron doesn't believe in the Languedoc landings. He says that's a bluff. He knows the English, he was at the Quai d'Orsay. They did the same in 1704 when the Huguenots in the Languedoc were waiting and the English promised an army to save them. Their ships were seen standing out in the Golfe du Lion, and then they sailed away again. They never came to the Languedoc beaches, no invader ever has come to them. They're too wide open. History has reasons for repeating itself.'

'That was 1704. Besides there are Americans out there, they dropped bombs on Nîmes. I don't think they know anything about history.'

'They don't need to. You don't know anything about the tide by seeing the surface of the water. We believe these landings will be further east, the other side of Marseille, to cut off all the enemy west of the Rhône. They're ordering us to make disturbances here as a blind. But no one's told us. We're not in their confidence. The advantage if we know how to use it is that our cities will be left on their own.'

'Why should they be?'

'Because the enemy will be a trapped animal rushing to get away while the jaws close in front of him. And when he clears out, all the armies will be busy somewhere else. Here, there will be a hiatus.'

'Leaving us . . . d'Albaron and you, and any others with the same ideas, with a clear field.'

'For a few weeks, for a few days even . . . who knows now? But that will be the moment for hammering in the political nail.'

'And what about Roper? Afterwards, when questions are asked?'

'That's not my problem. Not a problem for me. It could be a problem for the soldier Soames signalling in Roper's name. It could possibly be a problem for you, but not if you're as intelligent as I think. In the work we'll do between here and Nîmes, in the next few days there'll be plenty of occasions when the Major could disappear doing his duty in action. You too could disappear, Etienne, but I think like Soames you can see that need not be necessary at all. Silence solves a lot of difficulties.' François rose from the bed and put an affectionate arm about Seagrave's shoulders. 'I don't want to lose you, Etienne. You will always have a place of honour with us. Not just because I'm fond of you either. You brought Roper to us and we'll never forget it. If I had a medal I'd pin it on you.' He embraced Seagrave formally on both sides and added in a low voice as if it was a citation for the award, 'remember silence is a treaty too. It can't be broken.'

*

Charles d'Albaron proved right about the landings. The enemy reached the same conclusion as his and began movement of fighting troops eastward on August 13th. Next day the 11th Panzer Division attempted to cross the Rhône and lost twenty-four hours crawling over the few bridges still intact. The landings took place along the coast of Provence on the 15th while the Panzer Division reformed and rumbled through the heat towards it, then by the 17th the Division was ordered to retire northwards to the principal battlefields. Through all the country to the west of the Rhône the remnants of the occupying forces, scum on a retreating tide, flooded back the way they had come in, across the wine-producing plain, the olive groves, the historic sites, the gardens and villages of the garrigue. They knew they were abandoned to their fate, they stole trucks and cars and horses and bicycles, they formed a murderous urgent rabble savaging anything in its way and leaving behind, so it was thought, stocks of equipment and arms too cumbersome to take away in the stampede. These alleged stocks, as soon as rumoured, became the object of cupidity and focus of concern. Would anything be left by the time the men came down from the hills to grab them? Or would the townsmen on the spot, whatever their political persuasion, get there first and clean up? Power and its posse of shadows rode at the far ends of all avenues. François Paradis and his men, now numbering over fourteen hundred, moved down through the forests in the second week of August and by the 20th were in place, with many other maquis units, near the meeting line of plain and hill, ready to fall on the *Marschgruppen* in their panic retreat through the countryside. Paradis, as a railwayman grasping the potentiality of the main line down to Nîmes, took his position within quick striking distance of it, near a little country station built improbably of brick in the style of Henri IV and equipped with the Baudot railway telegraph.

After his talk with François, Seagrave had thought of another detail, obvious but not covered by their elliptical exchanges. Soames, by François's account, had been at a distance in the trees when Roper was last seen alive, having followed him into the forest although under orders to man the radio. Why had he followed him? And why would François have gone on to dispose of Roper unless he was already sure of Soames and his subsequent co-operation? There was more between François and Soames than François had thought fit to tell him. He was left to find out for himself, construe the facts offered and reach his own conclusion, or regard them as covered by the law of silence, interred, prescribed, passed into the eternal night. But it didn't seem possible to say nothing at all about it to Soames. At the very least, he and Soames must be prepared to tell the same story; that was the minimum precaution for later when the present and its small accidents would become part of the larger, recorded fiction. He borrowed a bottle of red wine from one of the maquisards and took it to Soames's corner, the radio post, where Soames sat with his legs stretched in front of him on the ground. Both radio and camp were quiet, a large party having gone out to ring the area of forest where a *parachutage* was expected.

'Care to share this bottle with me?'

'Thanks for the idea. This I've got here is the last drop the Major was saving for when the balloon went up.' It was clear that Soames meant to parley from a position of strength. He, after all, was now in no danger from the resistants, while Seagrave's situation with them was subject to trial. The weight in the alliance had shifted and in a sense his life was in Soames's hands.

'Then I'll join you.'

'Very welcome to it.'

Seagrave sat down in a similar position to Soames beside him against the wall, emphasising rather than reducing the effect of contrast in their height since Soames's feet seemed so much farther off. Seagrave took the whisky flask offered.

'There must have been quite a bit of this.'

'The Major had no other personal effects.'

'Nothing to go back . . . I mean for the family?'

'Orders were to carry nothing. That's what I've got myself, nowt but a Sten gun. We'd to think of ourselves as nameless units in a grand calculation.'

'From which Roper has been subtracted.'

'There'll be a lot of those by the finish. Cancelled units.'

'When will you report him missing?'

Soames turned a degree or two towards him as if following a moving target. 'That's the number one question. It depends on Mr Paradise.'

'You mean when he doesn't want any more arms dropped.'

'You've got it.'

'When you do report it . . . what if they order you to leave this maquis and join up with one of the other liaison missions?'

'Aye, well there the answer depends on you.'

Seagrave wondered how this could be. Was Soames, like François, making a covert threat? Or offering closer collusion? The first seemed likely because Soames had evidently thrown in his lot with the Paradis maquis far beyond the need of duty. He had either been bought or he shared François's political zeal and would stop at nothing in aid of the party. There were a lot of communists in coalfields everywhere, not surprisingly. 'Why on me?'

Soames passed him the flask again. 'See it this way. The order comes over the radio just when everyone's on the move. Thousands of blokes swarming all over the country and never in one place long enough to answer questions. I can obey the order and look for another mission, tramping through the forest with my pack. Dying of thirst in the heat. Or I can fail to receive the order. Or I can receive it and fail to carry it out due to the insuperable fucking difficulties.' After this long speech Soames breathed deeply, drank some more whisky and relapsed into his more usual tranquillity, still as a stone.

'And where do I come into it?'

'If you're sticking with this gang and going to town with them to fight it out then so will I. A sight more interesting than reporting back to the Army before I have to. But I wouldn't do it on my own. They could decide to dump me if I wasn't indispensable any more. Frankly I'll tell you the Major was right about one thing. They're a bunch of bandits.'

'Paradis's a friend. They won't dump you as long as I'm around. If I keep in line.'

'That's just about what I've been saying,' said Soames using his patient voice.

'So what's going to be the verdict on poor old Roper?'

'Missing on reconnaissance. Searches drawn blank. Reports say enemy not taking prisoners. So presumed dead.'

'I'll have another go of the whisky.'

'So will I,' said Soames and when he had the flask back he extended his right hand, took Seagrave's, and shook it vertically once with a motion of accord like a mason slotting the locking piece into a stone wall.

*

About ten days before the maquis moved downhill Soames negotiated the biggest arms drop so far, at least thirty canisters, and was ready to press for more but now the first and fatal dissension appeared in the relation of Soames and his radio correspondents. The big *parachutage* was agreed on the understanding that the maquis would prepare an ostensible landing ground on an area of pasture and trees at the high limit of the forest, remote but exposed, by felling the trees and flattening walls and other obstacles to access or descent from the sky.

'What do they want that for?' Paradis asked, using Seagrave as his interpreter with Soames.

'They must be planning to drop troops in support of the landings.'

'Have they said so?'

Seagrave consulted Soames and his logbook where messages were recorded in whatever terms, Seagrave suspected, that struck Soames as the most opportune at the time. 'They say they want a landing ground clearly visible from the air and large enough for an assembly point. They suggest at least fifteen thousand square metres.'

'Fifteen thousand square metres? It's a *parc à l'anglaise*. This is some dirty trick,' Paradis said. 'They're hooking us like bait. As soon as we start we'll be attacked. It may make the enemy believe in the landings but it'll certainly be the end of most of us.' He thought very briefly before he spoke again. 'Tell them we'll start tonight after dark. We'll clear a space big enough for the *parachutage*. They must drop that at first light so we can defend ourselves. Then we'll finish the job in the nights after.'

'Right away, sir,' said Soames when this was passed to him. 'I like a man who makes up his mind. That was the Major's trouble,' he added to Seagrave. 'You'll see there'll be no more trees felled nor clearing done after tomorrow morning.' This forecast proved correct, and twenty-four hours after the successful *parachutage* the peremptory questions began to come over the air with growing urgency and insistence.

'Time's come to give the sad news about the Major,' Soames said. 'Suppose they tell you to stay on and take over?'

'How can I do that if I don't understand enough of the lingo and can't make myself understood?' And after Soames had made his report and finally received instructions to work his way to the nearest superior officer and put himself under orders, he closed down the radio and packed up the gear in the regulation manner as if for a last march. Seagrave saw him laugh privately and for the first time as he landed a powerful kick with his distant boot on the assembled packs in the corner where he'd toiled over them through the heat of these weeks, a prisoner of his own technical skills while others were at large in the forest like the boar and other marauding fauna.

Chapter Four

As RISING YEAST THE numbers of the resistant forces swelled and the maquis edged forward into the fringes of the plain, thousands of men armed or unarmed, hanging like a myriad of bats in the shade of any tree before swarming into the open when the last night-time came round for the occupiers. Orders went out on August 8th from the Provisional Government for the gendarmerie to desert barracks and join the maquis, and these trained men brought their arms with them. But none of them stayed with Paradis's unit where they were considered corrupted agents of the established order, slaves and potential informers to the bourgeoisie. Any who offered themselves were sent on their way to other, less ideologically correct formations. François during this tense overture was everywhere and nowhere, omnipresent in authority but personally removed, wrapped in his plans and dreams, uttering orders but by his abstraction communicating a vague, potent vision of coming conquests.

The heat of the garrigue was even fiercer than up in the forest as there was less air, less shade, and no water. If you found a scrub oak high enough to cast a shadow over you the ground under it was brutal, stony, barbed with spike and thorn, infested with insects that entered the shelter of your clothing and made for the moist zones of foot, armpit or groin. Even the aroma of crushed thyme under your weight was too rich with heat. Soames relished all this.

'Jesus, it's about as far as you could get from a wet summer in

Ravenglass. Coming down here was the best thing you ever did yet in your short life.'

But Seagrave was in a phase of nostalgia, a delusive and occasional cycle that he suffered. 'Ravenglass,' he murmured. 'A cool veil of rain off the sea. Here we'll be roasted alive in an hour or two.'

'Come on, lad,' said Soames. 'You come through a battle or you don't. Don't let it get you bothered.'

'It doesn't,' said Seagrave remembering the stealthy danger of the streets, the denunciations, the patrols, the Milice.

'Sometimes it's bad going back where you were afraid before,' said Soames, and took his shirt off to get more of the sun on him. When his chest and back turned a strong cinnamon red he seemed to enjoy it all even more. 'This is what it was like in the desert. Never see it round Morecambe Bay.'

*

The retreating *Marschgruppen* were split between those travelling the highway from Spain under constant air attack, and the smaller units routed on lesser roads near the foothills. To delay the progress of these was the task assigned to the maquis. It was a relief to escape the infernal open garrigue from time to time, to go and blow up a bridge, collapse a tunnel or block a road with rocks. Certain of the maquis sent men farther afield in commando bands to raid and forage and mine approach roads with Amonal, but Paradis shook his head silently if anyone proposed such errands to him. In council with his fellow commanders he concentrated on defending the railway line against schemes by non-railwaymen to cut the permanent way, as had been done, on the urging of the Allies, wherever saboteurs had been able to get at it long enough.

'That line's the key to the cities,' he said, and let none of his own men stray far from it. He himself occupied the Henri IV station, spending a good part of his time near the Baudot, and so he was the first to hear that the tail-end of the occupying forces had abandoned

Montpellier on August 20th and part of the army from Toulouse was due through this sector on the 22nd or 23rd. When he reported this to the council, presided over now by Charles d'Albaron, a reception was planned for this force with ambush, air attack by radio liaison, mines, snipers. The manpower of the assembled maquis was now enough for a pitched fight and d'Albaron chose for this an area between Nîmes and the hills where major roads crossed and joined, with a fast river to one side, the railway to another, and a wooded escarpment on the third. The main attack would fall like a thunderbolt from the woods, Paradis being instructed to take a position beyond the river at a point where in dry weather the submerged wall of an ancient weir appeared above the water.

'Hide among the boulders. You can cross with your fourteen hundred men in ten minutes. You will provide the second wave of attack, when the enemy is fully engaged facing the first.'

Paradis resisted this scheme, pointing out that the railway line ran closer than the river to the chosen ground, and that from his present position near the station he could bring his men up along the line much faster. 'A thousand running along a slippery wall,' he said, 'you'd just need one man with a machine gun to mow them down in enfilade.'

D'Albaron watched him thoughtfully before replying. Unlike the other men who wore the soiled remnants of the working clothes they had left home in, or unassorted items of uniform taken from corpses of the Wehrmacht, Charles always had a supply of well-made grey flannel suits and silk shirts. His long graceful form, not unlike Philippe's, with a wing of fair hair over the brow, was seen everywhere in the region where resistants held the ground. He never seemed to sleep, never missed a rendezvous, travelled on foot or bicycle through the mountains where constant search and rewards were out for him and remained polite, elegant, remote. Though not loved he was, in the manner of the people here, honoured.

'I want you by the river. Split your force in two,' he said. 'Agree a signal to give the men on the line when you advance over the weir yourself so the attack's co-ordinated. Work out the timing by rehearsal. This is a concession I'm making. I don't make a habit of it. I have to count on you.' He could have added that this concession owed much to the fact that the maquis of Paradis was now the best armed if not the largest, no one knew how, and that this circumstance put him at an advantage if he chose to dig his heels in.

'I appreciate your tactical flexibility,' said François, showing by this ambiguous tribute that he perfectly understood.

After the meeting, while the others dispersed among the trees with the quick silent movements of forest animals, Charles d'Albaron beckoned Seagrave aside to where the decrepit crate of a Citroën car in which he had come was sheltered from view by a clump of reeds. 'I was told you'd been arrested,' he said. 'Glad to see you free. But as a British subject you'd have been treated as a prisoner-of-war not a criminal. They're very correct about these things. You'd have been lucky.'

'I got away when I saw Philippe taken in. That's why I'm here. To ask you . . .'

'We have no news of Philippe. He's been removed from Nîmes and not reported by any of our people anywhere else. He's probably dead by now.' Charles spoke of this with detachment and the tone of regret he would have used for any other resistant in his organisation. There was nothing more to be said and Seagrave turned to go. 'Wasn't there a liaison officer up there in the forest with Paradis? Where did he go?'

'Missing,' Seagrave said, keeping it to a minimum.

'Nothing else? Just missing? Gone on holiday perhaps?'

'That's all I know.'

'I see. Well, he was your compatriot not mine. And I wasn't responsible for him but I'd advise you either to know something more, or know nothing at all.' Charles took Seagrave's arm and walked a few paces with him, leaning down so their heads were close together as if for a confidence. 'That girl you had, the one we helped you get out of the camp in the Camargue. I never knew her name. She's safe somewhere?'

'Ida. She's in Switzerland with my sister. She had the baby there.'

Charles wasn't interested in the baby but at the mention of Switzerland he sighed deeply. 'In Switzerland. What memories. But she must be one of the very few *gitans* there. They're not very Bohemian, our Swiss friends. And with your sister. I suppose it's only just . . . a representative of the *Untermensch* . . . I don't know the *gitans* as a people but I respect them as an idea. They have no embassies but the desires they arouse are their ambassador. Philippe said the girl's beautiful.'

'Yes, she is,' said Seagrave, though events and privation had more or less robbed him of any clear memory of how she was in the flesh, leaving him, like Charles, just keen about the idea. 'She's very beautiful if she's your type. Evidently she was Philippe's.'

'Poor boy. I don't know his tastes but I expect he found plenty of that in the short time he had.'

'Not as much as he wanted I think.'

'Who does, who does?' D'Albaron withdrew his arm. 'I hope to be sent to the embassy in London when it's all over, we'll meet there. Don't forget to look me up.' He spoke the last phrase in English.

'I will. If destiny takes me there again.'

'Don't be so absurd, my dear, it must. That's where your life is, your future's there,' said Charles showing all his small sharp regular teeth at the prospect of all that the future promised him personally. 'The future's all in the capitals – Paris, London, Rome. You'll see, when the shouting dies down, these provinces, they're quite simply a graveyard for you and me.'

*

Detachments of auxiliaries, exhausted and demoralised, passed along the roads on August 21st and d'Albaron let them go, harassed only by snipers and an ambush here and there. A much more powerful and combative *Marschgruppe* was reported to be behind them, advancing fast and vengefully across the foothills with armoured cars, burning, executing hostages, raping when there was time. It was onto this force the assembled maquis were to fall, wildcats from the forest fringe. By the morning of the 24th the trap was set, an allied mission had appeared and air support was promised, the road was mined. François Paradis had split his contingent, keeping six hundred men with him on the railway line and the rest by the river, in the charge of a man familiar with the terrain.

'Don't let him put us with the lot by the river. Summat's brewing this end,' said Soames as if he'd received a signal from the ether. He needn't have worried. François had no intention of separating himself from the radio any more than from the Baudot. When the traverse of the weir had been rehearsed at dusk he took his leave of the men by the river, crossed the weir himself with Seagrave and Soames and set out back to the station. His last words to his deputy were, 'Put a man up a tree who can signal you in when the time's ripe, just in case you don't get the sign from me.'

'Up a tree he would see you advancing along the line.'

'Go by the fighting on the ground. Don't wait for me and I won't wait for you. Good luck. See you later on.'

This didn't sound to Seagrave much like the close co-ordination demanded by Charles d'Albaron at the council, but François was seasoned; he was moreover his own master, to the extent that his force was his independent creation, armed by his own devices. In the heat of a situation like this the only thing for subordinates to do was hang on to the authority immediately above as if it was the last noose in a lifeline. To reach the station they followed the bank of the river by a path winding among poplars, then cut across some vineyards and through the yard of a deserted farm. By the moonlight two emaciated horses could be seen standing under a lean-to, their heads hanging down.

'Those horses,' said Soames. 'They're lashed to the timbers of the roof. They've straps under the belly. God knows how long they've been there like that.' He sounded angry.

'Tell him it's because if they lie down they'll never get up to work again. Too weak. There's nothing to feed them on. Animals in war have to go on like us till they drop,' François explained when Soames's point of view was translated.

'We could water them. It's not their war,' Soames said.

'François won't like that. Hold us up.'

'Fuck François,' said Soames in a voice that needed no translation.

'Any man's peculiarities are to be respected. Especially if he's the man who works the radio,' François said, and waited uncomplainingly while Soames found a bucket and went for water from a ditch under the poplars, and Seagrave foraged in the ruined barn. When he came out with some handfuls of hay François asked, 'Is that all you saw in there?'

'A couple of old bicycles.'

'Is that so? Patience is usually rewarded,' said François, and soon after they reached the station he had another reward, as Soames intercepted a message from a fighter pilot reporting heavy convoys of troops and vehicles departing in the moonlight from Nîmes, streaming along the road towards the Rhône and the bridges.

'The pilot says there's so many they must be the garrison,' Soames added. Seagrave saw the light in François's eye as he addressed himself to the Baudot.

'They've gone,' he announced at last after a long exchange, a long wait and a last exchange, rapid and exultant. 'The town's as quiet as a tomb. With the curfew no one knows the swine aren't around any more. We've got a little time, a matter of hours. We can't lose any.'

'Here's what was brewing,' Soames muttered, while François attempted to make contact with the next station up the line, ten kilometres away in an industrial town with goods yards and engine sheds.

'A train . . . a train,' François repeated to himself again and again while the Baudot remained silent, unresponsive. The moon had cleared the trees and now shone full into the little office where the radio and the Baudot stood on a desk by the window, a light strong enough to read by, and the sleepless frogs under the poplars and along the river hammered through the airless night. 'It's no good. The curfew. If I go on I'll give the alarm. We must go ourselves.' As usual his time for reflection was very brief. He turned to Seagrave. 'Go and fetch those bicycles. You'll have to wheel them through the vineyard. I can't spare your colleague.'

'If the peasant sees me?'

'Take a gun. Always have a gun. We're the angels of peace, terrible but just.' François laughed as Seagrave ran out into the brilliance and deep shadows of the moonlight. When he got back with the bicycles all six hundred men had been roused and were waiting, a dense silent crowd, on the platform and around the station. This wait in the moonlight became, in memory, part of the stress and delay and hope these months seemed made up of, but the current of excitement ran through this, the last wait of all. No one had been told what was happening and no one asked but Soames was undoubtedly not the only one to have his ideas about it.

'They call this stealing a march,' he said. 'By crack of dawn we'll own the town and the others will still be watching the crossroads.'

The moon had floated low towards the profile of hills on the horizon by the time the train was heard, approaching slowly and easily like a patient death along the line under the trees. When it reached the station it drew up almost without a sound of brakes, and stood there, engine heaving and harness of chains on the truck doors rattling gently to the accompaniment of the frogs' nocturne. The trucks were closed as coffins, with no slit for air, and each had the word *Wehrmacht* branded in red on either side.

'Mount quickly,' François called out in a low voice clear in the comparative silence. 'It'll be tough but it's only thirty kilometres. About an hour.' Before the train started he went along the line of trucks fixing the chains outside while the men stood crushed against each other in the dark and the night heat, the fit so tight that if you dropped you couldn't fall, if you stifled you would die wedged upright.

In the first truck, Seagrave was locked into a corner by taller and heavier contiguous bodies, his head below most of theirs so he was deprived of the small space of air under the roof. He tried to concentrate his mind on an image from childhood, a still, dark pool under trees, surface opaque and depth unplumbed, a pool to the centre of the earth. The slight vibration and the sound of the wheels over couplings were other things you could concentrate on. If the train was attacked, they wouldn't know anything until bullets tore through the woodwork; they would have no way of getting out until the truck fell apart around them like a matchbox. Near to Seagrave's eye a joint in the side allowed him a thin crack of vision onto the sleeping world outside, of trees, a quarry, a wood, the moon illuminating a country of vines and orchards as the blind train passed through with its imprisoned army. Perhaps it felt like this in the wooden horse traversing the Scamander. Soames was beside him straddling the radio pack and with his head grazing the roof, but no one used up air by speech while the journey lasted. At last the first shuttered streets at the edge of the town passed by the crack in the woodwork as the train slowed down to crawl to its destination in the marshalling yard.

When the six hundred climbed down onto the gravel and stones of the yard Seagrave looked round at a familiar scene. The walls of the bombed hospital were on one side, the plane trees and goods sheds and offices on another, and to the open eastern side the sky above distant streets already pointed the index of another white-hot day. The town slept, stupefied by defeat, occupation, atrocity. One man appeared at the door of the offices in his underpants, startled as a flushed rabbit, and was summoned by Paradis with a wave of his revolver before he had time to bolt back into the warren and telephone.

'You're coming with us,' Paradis said, and sent someone else into the building for the trousers of this late conscript. Then, standing on the step of the locomotive he had driven here, with the men waiting like a herd to be directed to rich pastures, he addressed them, in a louder voice now charged with the explosive of success while the dawn filled the world, so it might seem, with fresh utopian promise.

'Brothers and comrades,' he said, 'we're here by our own efforts to free our own town. We're the first here and we will be remembered for ever as the men who liberated our fellow-citizens from the foreign enemy and the enemy at home. I mean as you know the dead wood, the dead weight, the bourgeois millstone. The Banks, the Army, the Church, the bosses. It's for us now to make our own new order with hard heads and fists. Because there's a lot of cleaning up to do. Traitors and torturers and all those who collaborated – whether upright or horizontally–' here there was a long murmur of assent – 'all must pay the price of their crimes. Count on me for severity but not for savagery. A court will be constituted this morning. I want no excesses among you. Any man who disobeys an officer will be tried and shot, that's a promise. For a few hours I'm leaving you for an important mission. You will be commanded by the officers you know. Obey them. You will go at once to the Montcalm barracks, kill any enemy still found there, and seize every arm, every vehicle, every bullet in the place. Take no prisoners. I want every man to have a uniform and at least two weapons. There may be some rabid rats taking refuge in the Arènes. We know the solidity of that building of our Roman forefathers. A strong detachment will enter it by the underground access, discover the vermin and exterminate them. I will join you at Montcalm before making my headquarters at the Hôtel Impérator. My doors there will never be closed to any man who needs me. *Vive la France. Vive la République*,' he ended, citing this last institution with what seemed to Seagrave only moderate fervour. Probably the name to be given to the new structure of state had yet to be decided, but the Hôtel Impérator as a first address had good resonances. Besides it was where important people always put up if they could afford it. Seagrave's father-in-law had persisted in the habit of taking his apéritif and dining there every night at his own table among the tables of Generals and Colonels of the *Hohenstaufen* Panzer Division. Probably it was at the Impérator he had been arrested on that last evening.

'You and Soames will come with me,' François said as he came down off the step of the locomotive. 'I must have that radio near to know how long we've got.'

'Will we install it in a suite at the Impérator?'

'*Mon petit*, the moment of destiny isn't the right time for mockery. I've chosen the Impérator because it's central and has big rooms and everyone knows where it is.' In spite of such good arguments he sounded defensive. 'I'm a railwayman but I know the inside of the Impérator,' he added, and Seagrave regretted teasing him. François was carrying all the weight and risks of a daring action, perhaps that was why he had teased him, so pre-eminently the man of the moment.

'You know I think it's a privilege to go wherever you go,' he said, feeling at the same time that he and Soames were being taken on this special mission for reasons having nothing to do with the radio. This impression was reinforced when the only other man with them proved to be a resistant of no rank in the maquis, a young subordinate tractable to the point of simple-mindedness and noted only for his height and breadth and silence, like a barn door. The lately co-opted railway employee, a Polish or Latvian worker lucky not to have been in a concentration camp, was overjoyed to find himself part of an armed insurrection, and in exchange for a Sten gun led François into a locked garage where there was an old rusty van.

'She functions, she functions very surely,' he said with a heavy accent, and proved his claim by starting up the engine which turned over at once with a tired but regular wheezing. 'Petrol full to here,' he added usefully, placing his free hand under his chin, and François gave him a bang of congratulation on the back.

'Not many cases of petrol full around these days. There are times when everything goes right, on oiled wheels,' he said, and climbed into the driving seat.

The men were moving off quickly in the direction of the barracks on one of the seven hills of Nîmes as the van turned in towards the town centre. The streets were deserted – no patrols, no closed cars carrying captives, no shops taking down shutters as there was nothing to sell. François drove as if pursued, to the total exertion of the forces the van still possessed. They drew up before an imposing porte-cochère in the centre of the old town, in a small square dominated by a clock tower.

'Keep your eyes open all round. Only fire in self-defence or to give the alarm.' François posted the young resistant at the gateway where he stationed himself heavy and still with the Sten held out before him like a farm implement. The clock on the tower struck six as François applied the great steel knocker on the double doors to the courtyard.

'Shut these doors behind us when we're in.'

'What is this place?' asked Soames in an undertone.

'Banque de France,' said Seagrave who knew the building from passing often by it to the market nearby. He pointed up at the eroded lettering carved into the stone arch above the gateway.

'Ah,' said Soames. 'Then I don't doubt we'll be here to cash a cheque. And a big 'un.'

When one of the doors crept open by a few centimetres François inserted the barrel of the Sten which he carried as well as his revolver. 'Lift off the chain or we'll blast you to pieces through the walnut,' he said convincingly, and after a moment's delay the door swung half open and an unarmed custodian in shirt and trousers and slippers stood in the gap. François took hold of this man's upper arm. 'Nîmes is liberated,' he said. 'You're a free man again but unless you do exactly as I say you will be executed in this courtyard as an enemy of the revolution.'

'Revolutions, revolutions,' the man muttered, 'the Banque de France has seen a few of those. What do you want?'

'Take us at once to the Director of the Bank. And don't make any noise.'

'*Monsieur le Directeur* is not up at this hour.'

'Get him up.'

'Doing that could cost me my job.'

'Not doing it will cost you your life.'

The custodian led them across the courtyard and through a small doorway to one side of the formal entrance. The monumental and elegant sobriety of the interior reminded Seagrave of the d'Albaron mansion without the many portraits of opportunist ancestors in their factitious insignia of chivalry.

'Please wait here. *Monsieur le Directeur* is easily upset at this time of morning. I will inform his secretary.'

'And we will come and help you inform him. Also the Director. He will be the best informed Director in the pay of the Vichy administration. He'll know what's coming to him and those like him before anyone else,' said François, jubilation breaking through his calm.

They mounted a stair with a wrought-iron balustrade and stopped before carved doors on which the custodian humbly tapped.

'These are the private apartments,' he said, barely above a whisper, and when nothing happened François thumped on the wood with the butt of his revolver.

'You wait here and guard the corridor,' he said to Soames as a muffled sound was heard on the other side of the doors. 'Have you understood?'

'Miss all the fun,' Soames grumbled, and stood, an intimidating figure in his uniform, planted in the centre of the corridor with the door behind him.

'What does he say?' François asked. And then, 'Tell him there'll be plenty of recreation for soldiers later. You'll see.'

The door was opened by a very young man wearing a silk dressing gown. 'Yes?' he had time to say before François pushed past, then turned to examine him.

'Why aren't you with the Resistance? What's your age?'

'I'm employed by the Banque de France to stay here and be at the disposal of the Director,' answered the youth who had certainly grasped the situation with commendable realism. 'I'm nineteen and there's more than one way of serving the *patrie*.' He pulled his dressing gown closer about him.

'I'll remember your face,' François said. 'Fetch the Director and no little games on the way.'

The secretary retired into the back part of the premises where his voice could be indistinctly but urgently heard, probably speaking through the panel of a door.

'So your Director's a pederast,' François said to the custodian, who shrugged his shoulders and put on a deprecating expression.

'Monsieur is a widower who likes the company of young . . .' The sentence was left unfinished because François didn't wait for the end but charged forward, followed closely by Seagrave, in the direction of the voices.

'Open that door and come out with your hands in the air,' he shouted, 'or your friend here gets a bullet . . . in the place you know.' He turned and winked at Seagrave and by the time he turned back the door had eased apart and a bearded figure wrapped in bath towels appeared in the opening.

'You are importunate. The law protects every citizen's domicile from irruption between certain hours. Be assured . . .' But before the terms of this assurance could be stated François had taken a step towards the Director and stuck the muzzle of the Sten in his belly.

'To the safes,' he said without preamble and the Director, as

realist as his assistant, fetched the keys and led the way in his towels
down the ceremonial stair to the basement, Soames bringing up the
rear, his boots striking martially on the marble paving of the hall.

'Fun's only just beginning,' Seagrave said.

'I worked that out while you were in there with yon fairies,' said
Soames.

François, who carried a buckled canvas bag slung on his shoulder, entered the safe alone with the Director and began to close the
door after him.

'There's no light or ventilation in there,' the secretary warned
in a voice sharp with the novelty of fear, and François left a gap
for the light he needed. The operation took no more than a
minute or two and when he reappeared the expression of his
features seemed subtly changed, as if aged by a few years. He
looked replete as after a good period of appetites humoured and
met. The Director was still inside the safe behind him when he
took hold of the secretary by the arm and pushed him forcefully
in to join his *patron*, then slammed the door on the two of them.
Then he turned to the custodian who stood at the foot of the
stair, guarded by Soames.

'They can amuse each other for an hour or two without
coming to much harm,' he said. 'We may shoot them later
anyway. Report for the keys at my hotel, the Impérator, at nine
o'clock, not sooner and not later, and meanwhile do nothing if
you don't want trouble.'

'No trouble at all. No problems and no trouble. I only aspire to
be of service, *mon Général*,' the man said, his terrified eyes shuttling
back and forth between François in front of him and the safe door
beyond, in the recesses of the basement.

'Good.'

'*Vive la République*,' said the custodian tentatively.

'*Vive la France*,' François corrected him. 'The republic's for later.
We'll see about the republic.'

'As you say, *mon général*.'

'As I say. But I'm not a general. I'm an ordinary man like you except I'm not a passenger in the train. I stoke the furnace. And believe me, in the new order we won't need generals or priests, or directors or catamites de luxe or the profit motive.' François stopped this speech when he saw the custodian's eyes travel, surely against the man's own will and better judgement, toward the swollen canvas bag. 'I'm wasting time here. The train waits for no one,' he said impatiently, and headed up the stairs as faint cries could be heard behind the steel doors of the safe. Not even the custodian, more anxious about the immediate than the long-term future, remained in the basement to answer them.

The campaign exchequer amassed by this raid stayed under François's close control and he told no one what was the total of the booty. Up at the barracks which they had rapidly occupied all the men who had come with him to Nîmes received within a couple of hours a sum on account of pay, and it was made known that the rest who arrived later from the battle in the country would have the same. The canvas bag still bulged. Soames at first refused to accept anything, saying he was in the pay of the king, then softened and agreed to a small amount to cover essential recreation in case not offered gratis.

'I'll go sick if I don't have it off pretty soon,' he said.

François found a moment to take Seagrave aside, onto the balcony of his rooms at the Impérator, overlooking the garden and its cool fountains. 'This is just for now, on account,' he said, pushing a roll of banknotes into the pocket of Seagrave's shirt. 'We owe you a lot. I don't mean of this. You can have as much of this as you want. I mean you've a lot of friends among us who won't forget. One day when there's more time we'll talk about it more. I've given orders that no one goes home before the town is . . . cleaned up. That may be some time. But you're a foreigner. You needn't stay with us. It might be better if you didn't. The scores we have to settle aren't your scores. There'll be things you won't like.'

'And you'd rather do them without witnesses?'

'Don't be so sharp with me, Etienne. There'll be plenty of witnesses, but they won't be asking questions or answering any. You're going to be examined sooner or later by your own people.'

'They won't torture me, you know, if I don't tell them much.'

'The intelligence services have many ways of getting to know what they want to know from someone.'

'Why would they want to know anything about your way here in Nîmes of settling scores?'

'Because the Americans don't like people who they think are subversive.'

'What does it matter what the Americans like? In the new order I mean.'

'A lot of money will be needed. It has to come from somewhere,' said François simply.

Seagrave watched the swallows circling as he had done on the day of the bombing. 'I've got affairs here to see to.'

'What you should see to is finding that girl who had your child. Most of our women have homes, but who knows where she is now?'

'She went to my sister.'

'Your sister?' A look of incredulity passed over François's face. 'In England? How?'

'In Switzerland. Charles d'Albaron had someone going up into the Jura with a truck.'

'And you think she's still there, with your sister?'

'I think so.'

François considered this for a moment. 'I have sisters too. Sisters don't like that sort of girl, usually.'

'I know that,' said Seagrave, although the truth was that this fact now materialised in his head for the first time. So far it had only hung in the background like the intimation of a cloud out at sea, a vague form remote from actuality. François put an arm round his shoulder as he always did when Seagrave's too sanguine expectations of life looked like giving insufficient defence against reality.

'It isn't far to Switzerland. You've got a passport. Go to ground now and when the armies go north, follow them. We'll give you a van. And all the money you need as I said.' He stepped back into the salon and rang for a waiter who appeared at once, as if posted outside the doors of the suite of rooms. 'Get a bottle of champagne. Whatever you served to the generals who've gone home.' He turned back to Seagrave who stood in the doorway to the balcony, the veil of the curtains shifting in a slight current of air created in the heat by the shade and spray of the gardens below. 'I may not be here for long,' François said as a kind of apology though none was needed, and when the champagne appeared he toasted with the first glass Madame Paradis in the village where they lived outside the town, and Ida, safe in Switzerland.

In spite of his personal attachment to Paradis and the habit of hierarchy learned in the life of the maquis, Seagrave had no intention of letting himself be forced back into clandestinity for political reasons. He no longer wanted to lie low. When the Allies showed up he would decide how to proceed and what story to tell. It wouldn't help then to have been in hiding, what would help would be the manifest membership of a band of heroes, bloodstained and victorious. 'Unless you order me out I'll stay with the maquis and so will Soames. As long as there's something to do.'

'I think I know what you really mean, Etienne. You mean while it feels new. For that long. I sympathise. I drink to the new. And you mean while it's interesting to be a hero among heroes. I drink to heroes.'

'In a way, yes, I mean all that. And I drink to them too.'

'Don't be ashamed. Everyone feels that. I feel it. So, that's how it is. You want to be with us while the . . . inaesthetic things happen. You know I can never refuse you. You belong to the movement. I drink to the movement.'

'What happened about the Director of the Bank?'

'I gave orders to let him out. I'm a soft man. Madame Paradis tells me that. "François, you're soft as a woman," she says. I drink to women. Here, we must send for another bottle of this. Get Soames to join us. I drink to Soames. I drink to novelty.'

'And I drink to you. And the train. And the railways.'

Chapter Five

THERE WAS NOVELTY FOR all tastes, in the swift action of the next hours and days, though less blithe than the raid on the Banque de France. The Milice, naturally, came first. Among the maquis and in the population there arose a violent storm behind the usual Protestant reserve. The cellars of the Milice headquarters near the station were found empty, the last prisoners liquidated and only mementoes left of their experience, names smeared or scratched on walls and in stone corners where they had lain or died. Seagrave, among the first to go in, found no trace here of Philippe d'Albaron. He could have been transferred elsewhere as his uncle said, or if not had perhaps thought it degrading to inscribe himself in these chambers of horror. The men of the Milice had disappeared too, but thanks to the guardian of the lodge at the préfecture it was quickly known that those who had not taken sanctuary with the Church had done so with the representative of the Vichy state. The convents and seminaries were for later, they could wait, hiding their guests in chapels and cells; but the offices of the administration were high up on the list for early invasion and the presence there of wanted criminals, enemies of the people, was enough. As he went into the cabinet of the *préfet*, with that official standing nervously the other side of the vast flat bulwark of his Second Empire writing table, François Paradis said, 'I was never in this building before. Workers don't get invited here. But liberators need no invitation.' He put his revolver on the desk as a gesture of politeness while the dozen men who accompanied him kept their arms trained on the *préfet* and his assistants in the shadows.

'What are these weapons?' asked the *préfet* rhetorically. 'It's I who represent the republican authority here.' His voice trembled slightly but otherwise the delivery of this remark was in the tradition of public diction, stately, orotund.

'There's a vacuum of authority since your colleagues started back to their own frontiers, and we're filling it,' François said. 'I require the surrender of the human vermin under your official roof. You have three minutes and then without compliance your safety is not guaranteed. There are hundreds of citizens howling for you in the courtyard. If you comply you will be protected for as long as we need to try and judge you and put you before a firing squad. That will be a quicker end than the one waiting for you outside now. I'm offering you a week or two of life which is a lot when you have a mob at your door.'

These tactics produced quick results, like the castor oil treatment used by the fascists. The ten men numbered by the guardian at the lodge were produced with the urgency of matter no sphincter could retain. They looked almost pitiful in their ignorance and terror, a few peasants, a couple of renegade railwaymen, a failed law student known to Seagrave. Citizens, fellow-men, *semblables* in some way. They were hurried away like the last faecal excretion of the late body politic.

Afterwards it was said by some that there had been no trial. A few of the more important figures including the *préfet* passed to execution months later by more formal procedures; many escaped to spend secure, devout years inside the convents, in orange-scented cloisters along the Côte d'Azur, under the aegis of bishops who in their own way and in their proper orbs and cities had only carried out instructions from above, like these *protégés*. But the court-martial of the men taken from the préfecture was summary, without appeal. It was held in the vestibule of the building where shouts from outside penetrated the glass and stone of the fabric to echo in the vast spaces of hall and stair, the lobbies and corridors and offices. The crowd had been shut out in the avenue beyond the high spiked gates of the préfecture on François's order. Through the windows, Seagrave could see three or four men who had somehow got into the courtyard and were climbing the branches of a great tree growing there to shade the carriage sweep. One of them had a rope looped over his arm.

'If they catch them they won't just hang them,' François said. 'Those people out there haven't had the pleasures of action. While we listened to the nightingales in the forest they heard the victims behind the walls. If we don't want to see these *ordures* torn to pieces under our noses the only way is to announce their immediate execution after trial. The mob respects procedures. That's one of the keys to power.' This argument may not have had juridical validity but there was a grain of mercy in it, and what François recommended was what was done. The ten men were marched with arms above their heads from the préfecture, among the crowds and protected from them as far as they could be by their executioners, up to the Arènes where they were lined up against the arches and shot without delay. The whole operation had taken half an hour and many others like it came later, but there were also more popular remedies applied in the following days, when the first rage had become more systematic. In some of these, where cornered prey might defend themselves, the armed maquis did the work. Otherwise, and particularly when it was a question of making the punishment fit the crimes of certain women, the populace managed on their own. It wasn't the whores who suffered, they had given away nothing that wasn't offered on the open market. It was on women who were thought to have had pleasure from the deal that vengeance fell. Seagrave and Soames, on guard outside the office of the newspaper which Paradis had commandeered as one of his first actions, saw a large crowd approaching the Arènes with a woman in their midst, belaboured as she was dragged along.

'Who is it?' Seagrave asked an elderly citizen who was watching the scene like himself, leaning on his walking stick.

'Madame Polge. She fucked with all the high officers and lived on champagne and oysters from Brittany, and her car was always full of petrol and her linen laundered white as snow.'

'Some people did worse things.'

'She did worse things. She had orgasms while Frenchmen were tortured to procure them.'

'Do you really believe that?'

'It's common knowledge,' said the citizen. 'Look at her, how well-fed she is.'

It was true that Madame Polge, with the last of her clothes torn off her, seemed very comfortably fleshed out for the times. Her long dyed-blonde hair was undone and fell about her face and shoulders and down her back where the first angry marks of disgrace already showed.

'You see how she's covered? That's not decent upholstery you're staring at, young man. That's the stuffing of vice. But they'll knock some of it out of her, look at them now. Go on, lads, give her a good taste,' this pensioner shouted in a hoarse voice, leaning forward supported on his stick and stamping with his free foot on the pavement.

'Looks to me like an old man who could use a leak,' said Soames who watched these proceedings with disapproval.

The woman was dragged forward, like the terrified animal she was, to the terrace of a café standing on the corner of the boulevard, thrown face down over a table and held there by many hands. From her house someone had brought a riding crop of the sort carried by senior officers of the *Wehrmacht*, possibly left behind at the last hurried leave-taking, and with this the woman was now flagellated, though not as soundly as the pensioner in his frenzy seemed to demand. Her cries were muffled by hands about her head, shearing the corn-fair tresses down to the darker stubble at the roots. Seagrave, although this scene was partly hidden from him by the crowd, saw and constructed enough in his imagination to feel in the thick of it, and a revulsion against his own excitement heaved up from the pit of his stomach as he watched and heard. Mercifully the action was brief. Madame Polge in her ruined state was put up against one of the arches and shot as the men of the Milice had been, but by worse marksmen so the stigmata of entry appeared about her figure like the scores on a badly hit target before she fell to her knees. Some in the audience were not satisfied. A broom was brought from the café and its handle used to defile the orifices of the dead or dying woman buckled on the cobblestones. As Soames strode forward the feeling in the crowd seemed to turn from approval to doubt so the effect of his uniform and height and red beret probably only coincided with a fall in temperature already underway. By the time he reached the body the crowd had begun to disperse, movement turning to a flood of people in another direction, running down other prey. As he stood there a waiter came out of the café and with his apron shrouded the remains of Madame Polge – queen of the black market, impresario and star of the enemy's orgies, as next day's newspaper described her.

The senior citizen, left behind by the popular rush, looked dejected now, stranded on the pavement under the trees, life after this highlight unlikely to offer anything but a slow decline.

'Why are you still here?' he asked Seagrave. 'Go on after the others. There'll be more sport. You've got young legs, you can keep up.'

'I'm on duty,' Seagrave said stiffly. 'I'm standing guard.'

'What is there to guard here on the street corner? At least your colleague, the foreign soldier over there, he's guarding the corpse.'

'The newspaper office.'

'That's the collaborators' paper in there. Is that why you're guarding it? Are you going to bring them all out and shoot them too?' The old man became more cheerful with this prospect of things looking up just when it seemed they had gone definitively flat. 'I could give you the names of a few people to take care of the same way. And their addresses.'

'There are no collaborators in there now. They've been turned out. We're producing our own edition.'

'Are you, are you. Well I know what that means. Politics. Just don't forget I know all that's been going on. And I can tell you something else, because I know. And that is that you haven't got long, whatever your politics are. When the peace comes the same people will climb back, they'll have changed their hats, that's all. The only solution is to put as many as possible under the ground. Quick.' He raised his walking stick to his shoulder with a parody of regimental precision. 'Bang bang. That's the way in the time you've got. Listen, I'll give you my card.'

It was while he was fiddling in his wallet with stiff, slow fingers that the doors of the newspaper office opened and François came out carrying in his arms like a new-born infant the first pile of the first day's edition, the voice of the people and their party. Seagrave read the headline.

THIS MORNING!
THE PEOPLE'S FORCES
ALONE
HAVE LIBERATED NIMES!

His own photograph of François on the steps of the préfecture with his bodyguard and Soames in the background was printed large but fuzzy lower down the page. The text described the daring invasion by train in the night, the taking of the barracks and the arrest, trial and condemnation of criminals but made no mention of the call at the Banque de France, though there was allusion to the need of financial succour for the families of heroes who had left them to offer lives in the cause.

On the second page appeared a detailed account of street fighting in unnamed quarters of the town against the rearguard of the enemy, and their ignominious defeat. This item puzzled Seagrave, who had heard nothing of these encounters. In fact the train journey had been launched the moment it was learned that the enemy had already struck camp and stolen away. The explanation was lower down the page in a paragraph of less prominence describing the action out in the country which had been in its own way heroic too, ending in the suicide of the defeated commander and the taking of large numbers of prisoners-of-war. The forces that had taken part in this fight were expected at any time in the cities of the region. It was on these men and their commanders that François had so flagrantly stolen a march, and there would be accounts to square. The fiction about street fighting was no doubt an item for the coming audit.

'Take these,' said François, his voice breaking into the current of this guesswork, 'and run down to the station with them. They're for everyone. Free. Hand them out. Broadcast them like banknotes. When these are finished come back for more. Everyone in the town must have a copy of this day's paper to keep and remember.' There was a manic element in his energy now, like a man who has overestimated his own resources. 'What was that firing?'

'A woman who had sinned. There she is, under that apron.'

François looked over at the body, a poor bare animal crushed at the roadside. 'I don't like to see that. It has to be allowed but I don't like it. Not like that. Who is she?'

'The monsieur here can tell you all about her, and a lot else besides.'

François led the pensioner away into the offices, supporting him under the arm. 'Come this way, granddad, we'll put you in tomorrow's paper. It may be the last. Make the most of it and tell me all you know,' he said, as if he foresaw his own downfall since registering the fate of Madame Polge.

There were familiar faces around the station, and many of the people concealed behind them or just beginning to emerge looked hard at Seagrave, trying to place him in the pack of cards, the shuffled identities and roles, the dangerous, the safe, the denouncers, the heroes, the active and the passive. The pack had been stacked and marked so confusingly in the last months. He began to give out the day's paper, at first tentatively, then insistently. The public was mistrustful. Even a newspaper offered for nothing was a form of commitment. One man, middle-aged in a dark suit like a doctor, held Seagrave's arm for a moment and peered into his face.

'Excuse me,' he said. 'It seems to me . . . you make me think of someone I've noticed sometimes, here in the station. But . . .'

'I used to go dressed as a woman,' said Seagrave who had almost forgotten it.

'That explains it then,' said the man. 'Or partly. You're a transvestite? I belong with some of my friends to a club . . . congenial even in these days . . . if it interests . . .?'

'Thank you. It doesn't. But I appreciate the invitation. Here's a free copy of today's paper. Please take several of them. Distribute them at the club. It's a historic issue.' He hurried along the hall towards a crowd of travellers just off the train from Montpellier. In a crippled way things still ran, residues got through, customary services were roughly maintained on the railway or at the congenial club for inverts. Similarly, the brothels had more or less held their turnover, even if the pleasure was more and more fraught with anxiety or shadowed by griefs.

The stock of newspapers was soon finished. Printed confirmation of the news already circulating by word of mouth created a ferment of excitement, heavy, angry, urgent, among these citizens worn by privation. They would soon find scapegoats of their own like Madame Polge. Seagrave hesitated as to whether to obey orders and return for more copies, or go the opposite way, up into the garrigue to see if the cabin that had been his home was still there. As he stood undecided he heard his name called somewhere behind him, from the street, among the stalled trams lined up between the avenue and the station. The voice was small and hoarse, not a child's but the voice of someone still touching childhood at arm's length.

'Etienne. Over here.'

He could see no one looking his way among the moving figures and everyone was on the move, leaning into the immediate minute, pressed along by the onrush of arousal like a stand of wheat in the wind.

'Under the tram.'

'Who?' Seagrave asked in a low voice from habit of secrecy.

'Luis. Here. Under the tram.'

He ran across to the trams. Under the first and second in line there was nothing, but huddled like a hiding hare between the wheels was a human form under the platform of the third, showing only as a blackened bundle, of rags, limbs, head. Seagrave squatted and put an arm in under the footboard. 'Luis. Come out. It's safe. There's nothing to be afraid of now. Come out.' He felt a hand take his.

'Where are the soldiers?'

'Gone. Everyone's free.' Suddenly and without warning he felt the key turn of the first emotional release, the relief. There must be tears on his face. No matter if there were. Only Luis was there to see them and they rose like a spring for Luis and his kindred, for Ida and the child, the others in the camps, for those like himself who had been afraid of death and afraid of fear. He pulled Luis out from under the tram as if delivering a birth. 'How long have you been there? What were you doing?'

'Waiting for you. I knew you worked sometimes at the station. I heard someone say the trams don't run because there's no electricity.'

Holding him Seagrave felt the thinness of unnourished arms and shoulders, breathing the odour of a delayed adolescence long unwashed for lack of soap in the place where he'd been.

'Where's Ida?' Luis asked at once.

'In the mountains. When we can we'll go and find her. Your Ida's safe there.' Luis looked as if this news of his sister being far away might be enough to finish off what was left of him. 'We'll try and telephone. I've got friends with the telephone. You can speak to her soon.' Luis had certainly never used a telephone and probably scarcely believed in its reality. 'How did you get out of the camp? Tell me while we go along. I've got some money. We'll find some food and wine to buy and take it home.'

'To the cabin?'

'Of course to the cabin.'

'Where did you get the money?'

'Naturally it came from the Banque de France.'

Luis laughed with the laughter of the camps, unpractised, lips too thin drawn back over teeth too sharp so you could see how little they'd had to work and grow on. 'Naturally,' he agreed. 'Ida always said to remember you're a *caballero*. That's where a *caballero* would go to steal his money.'

'It was a joke.'

'I think it was the truth.'

This was a reminder of the way these people had – this family, Ida and Luis – their genius for reaching across subterfuges you were hardly conscious of yourself, in any account you gave of what concerned them through you. 'It doesn't matter now,' Seagrave said.

'Can you go back there when you need some more?'

'Luis, I've told you before, I suppose you've forgotten. We don't need to steal money.'

Luis laughed again, his starved laugh. 'That's good. It means you've stolen enough,' he said.

Seagrave remembered that in Luis's vocabulary words like steal had no particular ethical or social status. They antedated, as terms for what you took and held in your hand because you needed it, the intervention in life of law or morality. Transfer of possession could be effected by giving, or by stealing. No special merit attached to the first and no reproach to the last. And in the camp there had surely been no other way to keep alive. 'How did you get away?' he asked again.

'The commandant opened the gate and told us to *foutre le camp*. He said the English were coming to drop bombs and shoot everyone. We could hear the aeroplanes flying all the time, looking for people to shoot.'

'They weren't looking for people like you.'

'How could I know that? And how would they know what I was? Anyway when I got to the river they did start shooting at the camp. It must have been the camp, there isn't anything else there since the Camargue was flooded, just the camp and the water.'

'And how did you get over?'

'I pulled down a big branch from a tree and hung onto it and the current took me to the other side at the next bend. It was a long way and the current was very strong. How did Ida get across? She doesn't know how to swim either.'

'She hung onto me and we did the same as you.'

'And then?'

'I had bicycles hidden in the trees.'

'Didn't she struggle and push your head under the water? That's what most women would do.'

'No. I told her to close her eyes and think it was a horse carrying her over the Rhône.'

'Other women would have struggled.'

'You don't know what other women would do, Luis.'

'I had a woman in the camp. I had her twice. She was one of the nurses. They were only whores really, and drunk most of the time. They were angry because no one could pay them. She said I was too young but I showed her. Then she called me her monkey. But Ida's different. She isn't like other women.'

Not for the first time Seagrave felt envy of this closeness. Ida and Luis grew so tightly together from the one root that the image of each of them seemed to have that of the other superimposed, neither of them ever to be seen altogether on its own. That was why it had felt so terrible taking Ida away. It had meant cutting them apart.

'You were wrong to leave me in that camp. Bad things happened there,' said Luis reading his thought as easily as if it showed like a strip cartoon run across the screen of his brow. 'There were pederasts too,' he added, throwing them in for good measure.

'I didn't want to leave you, Luis. My friends arranged so I could go and get Ida because of the baby. All the babies died in there, you know that. But I think they had to pay a lot. They couldn't pay for you as well.'

Even now, Luis didn't ask about this expected unknown child which had separated him from his sister. Admission to his world was according to a code of his own, arbitrary but natural. Possibly the baby would never be admitted and there was no point in advancing it as a candidate for his notice. If it came to that, the baby had no place yet in Seagrave's own inner world. He thought of it impersonally, as if it had presented itself at the door of his life on its own initiative like a friend of an acquaintance presuming on a welcome. To Ida it must feel quite different, for her there was no escaping the baby's claim.

'I'm terribly hungry,' Luis said.

Looking at him Seagrave wondered how in that state of malnutrition he could have had any successful congress with the nurse. Luis's limbs, blackened by the Camargue sun, were like sticks, his chest a cage too narrow for a bird to stretch its wings, his pelvis a dry fleshless scaffold. It must have been the sort of spontaneous overflow no material privation can staunch. Like emission in a dream, in other words. A bad one too, from what Luis had said. 'We'll look out for someone working the black market. It's the only way to get a solid meal and you need a few of those before Ida sees you again.'

'She won't mind what I look like.'

'I mind.'

'Yes, she would be angry if she thought you'd starved me.'

'She wouldn't think that.'

'Perhaps. But she might feel it.'

Luis seemed a long way now from the child Seagrave had seen driven off in a sheep truck to the camp of the Bohemians two years ago. His experience there had given him what he must consider a firm grounding in the ways of women, the theoretical gap between what they thought, and what they felt. He was becoming almost a man, counting on a little knowledge of the field to see him safely through it. But when they reached the cabin in the garrigue he looked about him, put up his hand to the stone surround of the door and the cracked wood, and was suddenly a child again. A storm of tears blew up so that eyes and nose and mouth ran with the torrent of relief, from fear, exclusion, loneliness.

'When we lived here I didn't know I was a dirty little *gitan* to be shut in a camp,' he said, his face crushed in the humiliation of it. 'I didn't know we were different and dirty and made diseases like rats. Now I know. Rats must live in ditches, like in the Camargue. Not in houses.'

He spoke between gasps of distress which seemed to be gaining on him, the storm so violent Seagrave feared something might snap, in his head or heart or wherever is the centre of balance between sanity and shame. 'It's all right now, Luis. It's over and you're home. It's all right.' The words sounded feeble and the message thin but it was a sort of first aid.

'It can never be over.'

'We'll have a real house later. When Ida comes back.'

'Rats live in ditches,' Luis repeated but the storm was passing, perhaps from exhaustion.

'Eat first. We'll decide about the ditches afterwards.' Seagrave poured the red wine into tumblers and cut the bread, and gave most of the ham to Luis.

'You're laughing at me. You laugh at everything.'

'Most things seem absurd,' Seagrave said, thinking of his own problems coming up with the British authorities.

'Not the camp of the Bohemians.'

'No, not the camp of the Bohemians. But the nurses a bit, all the same.'

'Oh yes,' Luis said, brightening up. 'As nurses they were absurd.

In a way. Depending what you had.'

'They gave the right treatment for some complaints.'

'Good treatment, yes.'

'As long as you didn't catch anything else.'

'She showed me a certificate. I asked, after.'

'Was it up to date?'

'Well perhaps not very,' Luis allowed. 'But she . . .' He seemed to check himself on the threshold of what he had to say.

'She what?'

'She looked clean enough. Down there.'

'So you didn't jump in with your eyes shut?'

'No.'

Seagrave laughed and poured Luis a lot more wine. 'I'm not laughing at you. I don't think you were at all absurd but a very serious boy. Of course appearances can be . . . but with the certificate and a bit of luck . . .'

'You have to take a chance sometimes,' Luis said with wisdom and overview perhaps supplied in genes and hormones through an infinite line of travelling forefathers.

'Often.'

'But not you, Etienne. You don't have to take them.'

'Why not? You think I'm too old?'

'You've got your own woman. You can't have any others. She isn't an ordinary woman.'

'Only she's not here.'

'We'll go and find her,' said Luis knocking over the bottle as he leapt to his feet. 'We'll bring her back to the garrigue. You said it's all over. No one needs to hide any more.'

'No, but we must wait until the armies go north. Then my friends will give us a van and we'll go behind them.'

'Is it far, where Ida is?'

'Not so far, but across the frontiers. And you haven't got a passport. We'll have to think about that.'

'Your friends will find me one.'

Seagrave doubted very much if they could but he didn't say so. His relationship with Luis was always delicately balanced between trust and disillusion. 'We'll ask them,' he said, to bring it down to earth.

'Don't go away without me.' Luis had good reason to look afraid. Seagrave was his only hold on the world of safety. And love.

'I won't unless there's no other way. Then you'd stay with my friends.'

'If you weren't there they wouldn't want a dirty little *gitan*.'

There was probably some truth in that and Seagrave reacted accordingly. 'I never want to hear you say that any more. The people who had those ideas have been driven away. They won't come back and other people don't think like that.'

'You don't know what I know about what people think. I learned things . . . not just from the nurses. Nothing belongs to the *gitans*, that's why they live on the road or the ditch. But I want to have something's that's mine. A place that's mine.'

It was a programme that would have to wait and take its chance in the new world. For the present that world was lurching forward like a blinded tank. From the direction of the town, downhill and across the quarries, came the sound of firing, individual volleys, sharp, co-ordinated and surrounded by intervals of silence. Firing squads, Seagrave thought. Cleansing, not ethnic like the one that had driven Ida and Luis into the camp of the Bohemians, the designated enclosure of their kind, but simply hygienic, the work of wiping up. Soames would be wondering what had happened to him. More important, François would be wondering. He might be needed. History was being written while he and Luis ate and drank their black market victuals. From still farther off, somewhere on the low hills beyond Nîmes and towards the sea, there came through the silences a rumbling of powerful motors, advancing it seemed through the vineyards of that region which the invader had found so rich and left so famished. There were no aeroplanes in the sky now, they were pursuing the enemy far away. This sound could only be the liberating armies coming from the sea and with the spider of administration hard on their heels, the self-appointed Provisional Government and the personnel of justice. Time was running out for summary cleansing. François must have known this all along. His ambitions had been passionate but local in scope. He'd leaped into the opening time had offered but the jaws were closing and the utopian visions clouding. What was left from the adventure was a heap of the executed, a place in the long history of the ancient town, and in François's canvas bag a still undistributed sum from the bank as to which a reckoning would soon be required.

That reckoning began before the armies and administrators reached the town. Charles d'Albaron came down from the hills with the men who had stayed to fight there after Paradis had taken the moonlight train. They were together, the two of them, in the newspaper offices when Seagrave got back there and both, in different ways, seemed relieved to see him come.

'My dear Stephen. Since I saw you you've been living very close to historic incidents. Closer to some of them than the rest of us. But I've been explaining to our friend François that history slows down after these accelerando passages. It always comes to that in the end. Better if it comes in good time before too much harm's done and brave men get into trouble. If the Revolution had slowed sooner a lot of valuable lives might have been spared.'

'No valuable lives wasted here. Not a handle to the name of a single one of them. Just a bunch of *ordures*,' said François with irony. He was watching d'Albaron cautiously, studying his polished exterior like the reverse side of a hand of cards.

'Quite so, my dear, quite so.' The grey flannel suit was dirty and crumpled from the battle but the silk shirt was clean and the tie, discreetly striped, looked as if it might be the device of some kind of club. 'But the republican habit breeds procedure. Believe me, in a few days all the cities of the region will be alive with functionaries with texts at their fingertips. We may think the state's been swept away by our victory and left us free. The functionaries know the regulation of the state never dies. They're like the olive grove without the beauty. You burn it down and it sends up stronger growth from roots underground. That's what the administrators have been at while we were fighting for them – spreading out stealthy roots.' There was a note of bitterness in his voice that had nothing to do with the maquis taking lawless initiatives without reference to him, their commander in chief. This bitterness was innate, it was against a triumphant middle class. Seagrave knew the signs, the reaction was like a tune he'd heard played too often before. D'Albaron uncrossed his legs and shifted in his seat. A look of discomfort, almost alarm, crossed his face. 'There wouldn't be a bottle of cognac somewhere? Sovereign remedy. Where there are journalists there usually is one. It's about the only thing you can count on them for.'

'I'll send someone to find it out,' said François, and passed through into the windowless rooms at the back.

D'Albaron stood up and began to pace the small office with his long stride, the even surface of his manner broken up by whatever was going on underneath. 'It must be the water out of that well. We all drank from it, in that heat. Some of the others have gone down already. I thought I was going to be luckier.'

'The thing with abandoned wells is the dead animals . . .'

D'Albaron interrupted this statement of the obvious. 'Anyone and anything can fall in a well. The Huguenots threw nuns into them here in Nîmes. Jews were burned for poisoning them. Never mind the details. While there's time I've got to tell you I've learned that Philippe is alive. No one knows why. But he's been seen with a Vichy politician, an acquaintance of my brother's.'

'Fernand-Félix?'

'You know him? How surprising you are.'

'No. But I know he was at the Hôtel d'Albaron some time ago.'

'How did you know that?'

'Philippe told me, naturally.'

'Yes, I see. So they met there.' He thought for a moment as

shadows of pain seemed to drive across his features like a rapid flight of clouds. 'Where's Paradis with that cognac? Listen, Philippe's in danger now, another sort of danger. I'm setting up courts martial in all the cities under my authority but a lot of people are going to slip through. That's why men like Paradis are in such a hurry to catch them. Anyone who's talked too much but maybe committed no other crimes that we know of. If Philippe's one of those I can't protect him. Perhaps Fernand-Félix . . . but if you can find him, warn him to stay right out of the way.'

'I don't understand it. I last saw him driven into the Milice building. Anyone might talk there. They mightn't even know they had.'

'The real question is, who got him out and in exchange for what? The new danger's at home. It may be time to . . . close ranks.'

Seagrave saw that his mind was on the class war again – like Paradis's – while he was also suffering more every moment from whatever had poisoned the well. Just then François came back with the cognac and d'Albaron drank three or four successive doses of it from the neck of the bottle.

'With luck that may kill the worm. But I must leave you for the *chiottes*. At once.'

'Just one other thing,' said Seagrave quickly as d'Albaron made for the door. 'The last day . . . Philippe was going to meet you. He had a message for you from your brother's guest, he told me so.'

'He never showed up.'

'Then the guest must have turned him over.'

'And pulled him out again. It's an old trick, to buy a man.'

D'Albaron couldn't wait any longer and as soon as he was out of the way François took Seagrave by the arm and led him into the dark premises behind the office.

'What was that?' he asked as they went.

'About Philippe d'Albaron. A good friend of mine.'

'What did he mean about buying?'

'No idea. He's poisoned himself with water from a well.'

'Is Philippe d'Albaron all right?'

'It seems he is. In a way.'

'If he's your friend . . . though with them, can you be sure, that's the question. Now, Etienne, you must do something more for us. I haven't long to explain. Only as long as it takes the commander in chief to evacuate himself and return. Poor man, I know how it can be. The cognac won't make any difference.' François seemed to be putting off taking the plunge.

'Well? What have I got to do?'

'You must put us even more in your debt. By the way, did I see that child, the little *gitan* waiting down there? So he made his way back. Decidedly you have a family round your neck. Or are you going to throw them back in the ditch?'

'Of course not.'

'I never even thought it. Now here's what you have to do. D'Albaron has had complaints from the *préfet* and the Director of the Banque de France. We should have shot those parasites but we didn't, we were patient. And Charles d'Albaron is only luke-warm about the dialectic and the people. What else can you expect him to be? The leopard's spots. I won't say any more, but that makes a problem.'

'A problem about . . . the cash?'

'You're right. I have to return it. D'Albaron's a hero, a real one, no one can ever deny that. And if it isn't restored he'll be in trouble for the rest of his life with the new powers. With the General.'

'Won't you be any part of the new powers after all? Even here?'

'Higher up in the party they say I've been in too great a hurry. That isn't how the dialectic works, that's the word sent down. I've seen before what happens to people who make mistakes about the dialectic. But I can look after myself. Not so easy to eliminate.'

Seagrave felt the chill unsweet breath of reality after the weeks in the mountains and the violent adventure of the last days. The long arm of the party was as fearsome in peace as the enemy or the Milice in war, it seemed. He wondered where, if anywhere, he himself stood with those higher up who might opt for François's elimination. At this moment, plumbing sounds from lower down in the building came up through the walls.

'Look here,' said François. The canvas bag which never left him was on a chair by his side. He opened it and took out a quantity of wads of notes held tight together by bands of brown paper. 'Get these inside your clothes, quickly. No one will suspect you because much as we love you you're still only a foreigner. The French suspect the French. It leaves plenty to hand over to d'Albaron in a minute. Here, take a few more. Go up to the garrigue and bury it. Look after it for us.' François laughed. 'We'd better be sure and use it before they devalue. Don't let anyone see you, anyone at all, not even the boy. Those people . . .'

'Are thieves like everyone says?'

'You can't say I said it. But he's only a boy. Like this there's just you and me in the know, and just you to know where to dig it up when you . . . the day it's needed again.'

Seagrave put the notes inside his shirt between the skin and the waistband of his trousers, letting his belt out by a notch or two and pulling it in tight.

'And now get out as fast as you can go,' said Paradis, and went ahead of him back into the office, arriving there just before the return of d'Albaron, pale and aged by years from his ordeal in the *chiottes*. He was too done in to take much notice of Seagrave as he left, beyond a wave of a hand.

'Let me know, won't you . . . when I see you next . . .' he called out in a voice from which the élan of victory seemed to have drained away.

*

The armies rumbled into town later that afternoon to find it liberated without them though they were received as heroes, especially by the bourgeois part of the population relieved to see on the streets a force more orthodox than the maquis. Seagrave by then was up in the garrigue, aware that his own moment of reckoning was near at hand. The first troops were French but Anglo-Saxons would not be far behind. Soames would have to report himself to someone, the actions of the maquis would begin to go on the record, sooner or later Seagrave's anomalous presence among them would have to be explained. Or justified. Luis, fuller of food and wine than ever before in his life, had fallen asleep in the shade of an olive tree, so fast asleep he looked like a casualty of war, a child of the streets blasted into another world. Seagrave had buried the bullion in a hole as deep as he could dig it in the stony ground without making such noise that even Luis might wake. Then he arranged over the spot a pile of stones loosely heaped as if scraped in from the soil prior to cultivation. A row of beans, he was thinking, two of tomatoes, when he heard a footstep and a long shadow fell across the ground in front of him.

'Worst problem for a gardener up here would be water,' said Soames, 'but then you're maybe not thinking of gardening.'

'How did you find me here?'

'Mr Paradise told me the way. It's a hot march. I've come to say goodbye for now. There's a British unit turned up. If I don't report for duty . . .' He laughed, as if he knew pretty well how to deal with that situation if he had to.

How long had he been there, silent among the trees, the sound of his footsteps masked by the cicadas? If François had directed him here it was because he thought Soames was no sort of risk, being about to vanish on the military tide. Or could it be that François had thought again and wanted a witness to the exact spot where the loot was planted? Had he sent Soames to keep an eye on him? Seagrave saw how possession of large sums in cash engendered suspicion even among friends and now Soames seemed to him to be studying the ground and the pile of stones with more than ordinary curiosity.

'I hear that cash got sent back to the Bank. Seems a terrible pity,' Soames said. 'Still, everyone got a handout first. Very open-handed,

Mr Paradise. That sort of luck comes once in a lifetime if it comes at all. But some men would have kept the whole swag for themselves. Not thought of debts.'

There was no doubt about it, Soames had wind of something. But of what? Had he made his way up here on his own account for his own curiosity? Or to stake an accomplice's claim? This buried money could hardly be thought of as really belonging to anyone in particular at the close of a war in which the state had been on the wrong side; nevertheless François might some day become answerable for it. On the other hand, if it was François himself who had sent Soames as an observer then Seagrave felt annoyed but he wasn't going to make any unnecessary secrets. 'Do you want to know what I've been doing?' he asked.

'I can see you've been digging a bloody great hole,' said Soames, nodding towards the pick on the ground. He sounded entirely innocent and his eyes had their normal patient expression.

'I've buried what's left over of the takings from the Bank. All that wasn't handed back.'

'Glad to hear it. No one will ever drag a word out of me,' said Soames. 'Not even the Gestapo couldn't. Mind you, with any luck they'll be on the receiving end before you dig it up and head off to Monte Carlo.'

'I won't do that. It isn't mine.'

'It isn't any bugger's,' said Soames putting it in a nutshell.

'I'm looking after it till François wants it again. What he does then is his problem. I don't even know how much there is.'

'You mean you didn't count it?'

'I preferred not to.'

Soames laughed at this loud and long. 'When you get back they'll put you in a museum. Last gentleman of the old sort. Species died out in the Great War. Lonely survivor found and offered by explorer John Soames in 1944. Or '45, depending.' His laughter had woken Luis under the olive and he now appeared, half asleep and staggering over the rough ground as if drunk. 'So this is the lad you told me about.' Soames held out a bony hand to Luis who took it hesitantly.

'He got out and made his own way back. Hadn't eaten anything much recently as you can see.'

'What are you going to do with him?'

'We'll stick together if we can.'

'You mean he'll stick to you. As long as he needs you.'

'That could be.'

'Then one day he'll disappear. Does he understand any English?'

'No.'

'It's not my business but I'd just like to know. Did he see you bury the cash?'

'He was asleep. He doesn't know anything about it. He doesn't need to.'

'Ah. Well as you know I'm not in the way of being a gentleman. Not even the new sort and they're two a penny. But if I was you I wouldn't ever tell him.'

How to explain to Soames that Luis was his brother in all respects except the genealogical? It wasn't possible. Soames's notions of caste cut both ways. 'He doesn't need to know anything but if he ever does I'll tell him,' Seagrave said, watching as Soames demonstrated to Luis the functioning of poor Roper's revolver. Neither of them was listening to him. Soames spun the drum with a flick of the finger and gave the gun to Luis to hold which he did, weighing it, feeling the precision of its parts, looking down at it with eyes of astonishment and disbelief.

'I hope that's unloaded,' Seagrave said.

'Don't mother the lad. Only get kicked in the teeth.'

'How is it you know so much, Soames?'

'I'm above ten years older than you, that must be how. Same difference just about as between you and him.'

Seagrave's bicycles had been stolen so they walked back into the town. The crowds were gathering again or had never dispersed, and in the distance was heard the energetic cacophony of the municipal band playing the same few marching bars over and over as it approached from the direction of the station, up the avenue. There was to be a parade to celebrate the arrival of the troops, the men in decent uniforms with stripes on their arms and medals on their chests, marching in step to drum and trombone. There might be some minor general at their head, it was rumoured. The hour of the maquis was drawing to a close. Nevertheless the maquis would be in the march, somewhere, sloping along at the end of the parade perhaps, sweaty, thin, tobacco-starved, sex-starved, starved but alive. Seagrave and Soames broke into a run to find them in time and take the place they'd earned in the ranks.

In fact the maquis came first, immediately after the band so communication was drowned. But as they went by young women ran out of the crowd to kiss them and old ones to push cigarettes into their pockets on the march. Charles d'Albaron, bowed with dysentery and grey as his flannel suit, was at their head, François Paradis and the other chiefs behind him. Luis ran alongside the column where Soames's towering form marked the place at which Seagrave had been engulfed among the six hundred. Soames was especially acclaimed as he loped along, the red beret riding clear of the sea of heads like a Phyrgian bonnet, symbol of enfranchisement.

'Did you find a woman all right?' Seagrave shouted, having lost sight of Soames the night before and thinking of his imminent return to Army life.

'Whole herds,' bellowed Soames boastfully. At least one was following with Luis and signalling to Soames over the mass of men between while he waved back at her like an actor singling out one fan from among many. 'She was the best of the bunch. Best I ever had, actually,' he shouted. The girl was dark, wiry and eager, and looked as if Soames for the moment was all she hoped of life. But when next Seagrave looked that way she had disappeared. Perhaps she had overstepped the bounds allowed to an amateur in this Protestant stronghold and been reclaimed for correction.

The parade circled the boulevards, passed in triumph between the theatre and the Maison Carrée and entered the final stretch down to the Arènes. There were people on the roofs, families hanging from windows, children in trees, all shouting though their voices were so drowned by the band that mouths and teeth and tongues seemed to exercise in a silent mime of passionate enthusiasm. In the gardens of the Esplanade beside the central fountain a platform had been erected and here there was to be a mass assembly and speeches, probably many speeches, long and windy in the rites of republican rhetoric. The maquis on reaching this point began to split up and mix with the crowd while the regular troops marched in. There were many fewer of these but their cohesion epitomised the change which would end in the ousting of the maquis cohorts. As the troops stood fast the maquisards washed about them like broken swell at the foot of rocks. From time to time a maquisard fired off his rifle or Sten into the air but the effect of indiscipline was too contrasted, even the girls looking doubtful about this solecism. The band formed up at the foot of the platform and continued pitilessly with its repertoire while the *notables* were awaited.

'What's going to happen next?' Luis asked. 'Will they shoot some bad people?'

'It's too late for that. You've missed that part,' Seagrave said. 'The bad people if they catch them will be tried by judges and juries. And the ones they don't catch will fade into the background. In the crowd.' He looked round at it, this crowd. It was rejoicing in a way an English crowd couldn't rejoice. The secret was lost. Rejoicing here was something dangerous, hot and hungry for sacrificial offering like the exemplary end of Madame Polge. With flashing eyes and mobile sinewy mouths drawn back in laughter not humorous but fertile and ecstatic. And of course among these ecstatic faces were many of what Luis had called the bad people, impossible to tell from the rest, particles in the sea.

'I like the way they go mad here,' Soames said. 'It always ends up horizontal. With us they just put you in a straitjacket. Can't even get your hands round the front.'

At last someone was hoisting himself up onto the platform, raising his arms for silence and attention. It was a long time before he had them because the mood of the moment was, for once, against verbalisation. But everyone knew it had to come, that was the rule of culture. The speeches would mark the passage back from anarchy and its cathartic joys into lenten reality. The mayor spoke first, distributing eulogies among the Army, the Free Forces of the Interior and their brave leaders, then the people themselves. The future was evoked in the most upbeat terms like a product to which there was an alternative. Punishment was promised to those who merited it but with emphasis on the Penal Code and its right practice. A reference to the presumption of innocence called up angry shouts and the mayor, with elections not far away, hurried on from this faux pas but never fully recovered. His stride was compromised and he looked relieved when it was time to hand over to the general. The crowd was pleased too. There would be no nonsense about innocence from him. The general spoke briefly and to the point. He assumed command of the maquis and ordered them back to barracks where officers of his own would see into their discipline and organisation. When he heard this Seagrave looked into the group on the platform to see how Charles d'Albaron would take it, but d'Albaron appeared to be paying no attention to the general. He was staring with intensity at a figure making its way through the crowd, then mounting the platform as if by right, a dense, compact, controlled figure of a man with supreme confidence in his own value, greater even than that of the general himself. It was Fernand-Félix, and immediately after him came Philippe d'Albaron looking as if he felt himself already on the first step of the staircase to the temple of influence and power. Obviously this must be a private joke. Philippe had somehow got on the right side of Fernand-Félix and onto the platform with him and was making the most of the comic possibilities. Seagrave began to push forward closer to the scene. The Minox was in his pocket and there were a couple of exposures left. It was an ensemble too rich in ironies not to put on the record.

Fernand-Félix had taken the place of the general and was by now addressing the populace: '. . . values and virtues of the Republic, my dear friends. Our traditions of hospitality to the asylum-seeker too long compromised. Our judicial culture, one of our gifts to all nations . . . degraded. Momentarily. And our unique Latin human-ism checked, diverted from its course . . . by *force majeure*.' The delivery was weighted, balanced, like a forensic text. No oratorical fireworks but imparted like a secret confidence flattering to each individual listener, with a kind of intimate complicity in the shad-ows of implied historic error shared by all. That way, he seemed to hint, lay the general shriving. Perhaps because no one knew who he was or where he came from he was heard with respect, and in the long, calculated pauses the audience joined in the tension of hanging on with him for the ripened fruit of his thought to fall into his hand. So much so that Seagrave's progress seemed to annoy no one and even Luis, following him, was let past without complaint.

'What are we going to do?' Luis asked.

'Get near enough for the camera to catch the expressions on their faces.'

'Their faces have no expressions,' said Luis shrewdly.

'That's just what I want to record. The numbness of the historic moment.'

They had pushed their way as near to the platform as they could get, the bandsmen around it offering a fine background for the picture. Fernand-Félix looked as if he was coming to the end of any advantage there might be in the occasion. There was a change in his voice, a slight lift of pitch, as much concession as so Cartesian a speaker could make to the vulgarity of peroration.

'Women and men of Nîmes! We will meet again. Soon. And in better times, a better climate. We will recognise ourselves better then. Purged of the late misunderstandings . . . certain errors . . .

There will be elections – to the *mairie*, the Assembly, the Senate. On that day I will come before you again. On that day our destiny together . . .' Seagrave depressed the trigger of the Minox, slid it shut and open to charge the last exposure, focused again and found, as he took the photograph, that Fernand-Félix was looking straight down at him, into the lens, from the distance of four or five metres separating them. Seagrave was conscious that he had done something irrevocable, his own destiny had lurched and turned like a ship striking an iceberg. If Fernand-Félix hadn't recognised him out of his woman's disguise, he had recognised the occasion and the camera. That was demonstrated now in his face and would be read beyond any mistake in the photograph. Seagrave turned away and pushing Luis before him tried to lose himself as quick as he could in the popular mass but the way out for some reason was slower than the way in had been or seemed so. It was like working against the grain in the throat of a carnivorous plant. Egress was not favoured by the organic environment. Without looking round he was aware that someone was following him through the crowd which was by now becoming irritated as the 'Marseillaise' was being sung. The pursuer's apologies were spoken in urgent tones as if his errand was an official one. Perhaps he was catching someone who deserved to be caught, and they made way for him so that he came up with Seagrave near the perimeter of the gardens, under the trees near the law courts and out of sight of the platform. It was, as he had expected, Philippe d'Albaron, and Seagrave read on the plan of his features the outlines of unwelcome surprise. Cordiality was conspicuously missing. Their friendship was entering a new phase.

'*Mon vieux*. What indiscretion. What a mistake. Just when Fernand was inscribing himself in history's brightest page. He's upset.'

'You might think he'd be pleased to be photographed. Did he send you after me?'

'Naturally he wants to know who you are. He thinks he may have seen you on another occasion.'

'What are you going to tell him?'

'If you help me by disappearing fast I'll say I couldn't find you. But go at once. In fact it's the only safe thing for you to do. Fernand . . . has followers. They'll trace you.'

'As a matter of fact your uncle told me to warn you to keep out of the way of *his* followers, in case you've done anything they wouldn't like. But I expect you're safe enough now.' Seagrave felt angry without being sure of an objective justification, but Philippe waved his remarks away with an impatient hand.

'We're all at a turning point, including Charles,' was all he said. He was looking hard at Luis as if the sight of him gave the key to some inner dilemma. 'Is this . . .?'

'Ida's brother Luis.'

'Yes, it's a remarkable resemblance.' Philippe said no more about that and started to turn away, at the same time drawing something from his pocket. At that moment Soames appeared out of the crowd behind him.

'Well, I'm off. Back to the colours. The Army waits for no man. See you again some day or other. It's been an interesting time. Pity we lost old Roper, he'd have enjoyed this.' Soames spoke in a deliberately neutral tone as if he was reading the back of a postcard.

Philippe turned back and held out one hand to Seagrave while with the other he passed something to Luis as if giving him a casual tip of no account. 'Don't waste time,' he told Seagrave. 'If you go now with your friend here you'll be all right, Fernand won't find you in the ranks of the British Army.'

When he had gone Luis showed Seagrave what he had been given. It was a small visiting card on which Philippe had crossed out in pencil his father's name and title and written his own. The crowd was breaking up and several excited groups were beginning to converge on the law courts where judges who had functioned during the occupation were believed to be sheltering. It looked as if it was their turn for trouble. Soames was gone, marching through the breach which seemed to open up at the approach of his uniform and the sound of his steel-tipped heels.

'I like that Englishman,' Luis said.

'And the other?'

'I remember him from before,' was Luis's answer, and he dropped the card on the ground with the rest of the unswept papers and other rubbish of these days of popular abandon.

Whatever was behind his change of front or shift of ground, Philippe's advice seemed good and it lifted Seagrave's doubts about what to do next. He and Luis must disappear. The conviction was reinforced by the sound of armoured cars along the boulevard beyond the Arènes, possibly the British unit Soames was going back to. If he stayed, Seagrave might have to do the same. He had heard too, from Soames, about the Military Police. Meanwhile there was Ida and the child, there was Luis . . . Personal claims should be put aside in war, he knew, and the War wasn't over, but he felt that he had fought his, his contribution was made and the personal claims were lifelines holding him like a net. He sent Luis home and set off himself to find François Paradis. Transport was what was needed. Of money there was plenty. Luis would have to be left near the frontier while he crossed into Switzerland. Two refugees without papers would be hard enough to get back but money could take care of most things. What they needed was something capable of crawling along behind the armies, across the improvised bridges and into the empty Alpine forests. François had offered a van. It seemed to Seagrave a very long time since he had been out of the region, felt the freedom of the road and the changing scene and the privileges of ready cash. His war was over and the peace about to begin and he experienced a vast flow of relief. Luis too had a heritage of the road. They would find Ida and bring her back to the garrigue and face any other problems, even Fernand-Félix, which after what they'd been through would seem, he felt sure, as trifling as a feather.

Part Two

Chapter Six

THE ARMIES SWARMED FURIOUS as ants over the wounded countryside, as if under orders to strip the mortified flesh back to bare bone. Then came the agents of the Provisional Government. Seagrave and Luis in the commandeered van crawled behind them all at a distance, moving on small roads, retiring into trees at the sound of a convoy, crossing rivers after dark by wooden bridges thrown up alongside those that had been bombarded, sleeping in forests. Sometimes they would wait a whole day near the crossing of an arterial road crowded with armoured vehicles, but the official fighting down here was past, the aeroplanes migrated, the valley of the Rhône once more a corridor, a military isthmus. Civilian vehicles were very rare but as long as you got in no one's way there was no one to stop you for questioning. In spite of the omnipresence of armed force there was a hiatus in control and surveillance. This added to the sense of freedom of the road for Seagrave but for Luis that was already innate: the road was an international language open to any user.

'There was one in the camp, his name was Karoly too, maybe he was our cousin, I don't know – he'd been everywhere on the roads. He'd been in Russia. He'd even been in England.' Luis sounded as if he could hardly credit this last exploit. 'At a horse fair. He said all of England's flat except where the horse fair is and there are lakes and mountains. Everything's very wet everywhere, he said.'

'I know the fair. It's near where I was born.'

'Can we go there to the horse fair, when we've found Ida?'

'It's not like the Camargue. It's not just wet, it's cold too.'

'It was very wet and cold in the Camargue when they let the sea in and flooded it. And in England there are no camps to shut up the *gitans*.'

No, but plenty of internment of one sort or another all the same, Seagrave thought. But perhaps his view was jaundiced by certain early resentments. Born into a patriarchal world he had felt undervalued and short-changed. His father, having so much, had given so little to this youngest child, the probably accidental offshoot of a second marriage in his old age. Seagrave believed his father had remarried to be looked after, not to rear new dependants he would never have time to get to know. At his death Seagrave had received a legacy of two thousand pounds from an estate valued at a quarter million. It wasn't the meagreness of the sum that rankled, it was the parsimony of consideration. He had taken the money with him to Montpellier when he enrolled in the university and by the outbreak of war it had gone the way of other adolescent incidents, burned up like a cigarette end. He was glad to see it go as if it had been the small change lifted from a corner of his father's dressing-table.

All the same he'd loved his birthplace, now his brother's property, with romantic passion, riding on the breast of bare fells or lunging in mystical ecstasy down the wooded cleft of river valleys, knowing that these moments of secret empire were numbered.

'What are you thinking about, Etienne?' Luis asked.

'The horse fair.'

'It's easy to know when someone's thinking about a woman,' said Luis laughing, his hand in his pocket. 'So was I.'

'Easier to think about than find, in that part of the world, believe me.'

'You mean a beautiful one. You've only had beautiful women. If you'd had to go to one of the nurses in the camp you wouldn't be so particular. You'd see how easy it is anywhere.'

'I expect you're right, Luis. You're like Ida, usually right about most things.'

Luis didn't deny this. 'You'll be happy again when we find her,' was all he said.

'And you?'

'So will I.'

'That isn't what I meant.'

'Oh me, I don't need a woman to be beautiful. Or special. A travelling woman is good enough for me.'

'But not as a sister.'

'Not as a sister.'

His first sight of them had been just out of range of the full light of the street lamp, on the pavement opposite to where Madame Polge would one day be immolated. Two children, they seemed – a big one and a little – so patently and pathetically for sale in the night shadow of the Arènes. Legitimate whores were in *maisons closes* by that time of a summer night, regular children safely under supervision at home. Seagrave too was lonely that evening, a sexual stray. Ida never asked, later on, why this had been so. She didn't want to know about it.

'Not every woman likes it. Some aren't made for that and if they're not doing it for money . . .' was all she had to say.

When he came near and looked down into her face under the lamp he felt as if some secret knowledge had been confided to him, like a key to time and the distant absurdity of death. She looked back at him with no change in her expression but the level expectancy of someone who already knew a lot about looking out for herself.

'It isn't dear,' she said, taking account of his student status. Probably, being not so far from her own age, he was a more welcome prospect than most clients to be found as the night wore on. She had a space under one of the arches of the railway viaduct behind a wooden partition, some sort of disused workshop where no one came to disturb her occupation. There was no sign of any family, no connections with the world of her own people, no protector. Perhaps she hadn't been at it for very long. The two of them were thin but not starved and they and the few clothes they wore were clean.

'Where can the boy go?' Seagrave asked.

'He stays. There isn't anywhere else for him to go. He isn't any trouble.'

At first this felt restrictive but Seagrave quickly got used to it as neither Ida nor the boy seemed to feel the least unease. If he'd been made to wait the other side of the partition his exclusion would have seemed even cruder, Seagrave could see that. Luis's presence at all times added to the feeling which sprang up almost at once in Seagrave that he was somehow responsible for the welfare of these two, even if predominant was desire to keep Ida for himself and off the street where others could get a share in her. In spite of her experiences she seemed undefaced, quite unscathed as if she'd washed the memory and impression away each time with the seminal residue.

'I'll find somewhere for you to live and you won't do this any more,' Seagrave said.

'Just with you,' said Luis, his expression opaque.

'Just him,' Ida agreed, smiling with the wide, unreserved smile she had for rare moments of acknowledged happiness.

'Not for money,' Seagrave said.

'I don't think you have much of that anyway,' said Ida.

'I've got enough for a bottle of wine. What does Luis like to drink?'

'Wine,' Luis said. 'Ida drinks half as much as a man and I drink half as much as her.'

'That simplifies everything,' said Seagrave, and left them there under the arch while he went to the station buffet and bought a litre of *vin des sables* – elixir of the seashore.

In those early days things were still easy, relatively easy, in the Free Zone. François Paradis provided the cabin in the garrigue, property of a cousin of his in Marseilles, and later on obtained papers for Ida and the boy. Ida couldn't say, or refused to commit herself as to when exactly they crossed from Spain or by what route. Luis spoke only French so it must have been years earlier, probably during the Civil War. How old was she? She didn't know. She could read but she was innumerate, except for the counting of change, an operation with no abstract element.

'If I had years in pieces in my hand I could tell you how old I was but the past is like water.'

'Haven't you got any family?'

'No.'

'Where's your father?'

'Father? On the road anyone can be your father and no one. People on the road aren't like peasants. They don't have any land or any place. So they don't have to have any fathers. You must come from peasants or you wouldn't ask the question.'

All that seemed pretty evasive, but what really could there be to hide? 'You're right, in a way I do,' Seagrave said. 'What's more it's what I'd like to be.'

'But you're a student.'

'I don't have to go on. I'll change. We'll buy some land and have horses.'

'How much land does your peasant father have? Enough for a big family?'

'He had enough for a lot of families.'

Ida looked suspicious as if he'd told her his first lie, the one that opens the way to all the others. Where would the process end? Soon he might abandon her and go back to his wife. 'Then why aren't you rich like the sons of the rich men in the Camargue?'

'My father didn't give me anything. He died. My brother has it all.'

She looked relieved. 'Better be like me and have no fathers at all. Or like Luis.'

'You mean, and like Luis.'

'It doesn't matter,' Ida said, sweeping this quibble aside.

'And your mother?'

'They shot her, in the mountains. In Spain.'

'How old were you?'

'I've told you,' Ida said, exasperated to tears, 'I don't know how old I am ever.'

'How big was Luis then?'

A protective or evasive expression seemed to come into her eyes and to cause a change of colour there. What colour were they at any time, if you tried to pin it down? Like the forest leaf it depended on mood and light – bronze, hazel, green earth colour, or the shade of black soil which yields a second harvest in the one season?

'Luis doesn't know anything about that,' she said.

Neither she nor Luis was supposed to know anything about his work in the Resistance, either. That was safer for them. Seagrave's absences became more frequent after the occupation of the Free Zone in November but the cabin in the garrigue where life was difficult but happy was his bolt-hole. During periods of hiding he taught Luis to read and add up. At this time his wife Denise moved out of their flat and back into her father's house in the grand street where the occupying colonels installed their headquarters, only his status as professor giving him protective cover. Less and less of it as the months passed. Money and supplies were not the problem for him and his daughter as they were for Seagrave and Ida and Luis. The yellow star and the systematic menace were the problem and there was nothing Seagrave could do to help or even share it, so he reminded himself. He was an alien and a resistant, he was occupied ground, he was impassioned, all he heard of the voice of duty was an echo far behind. He had become a renegade, in everything.

*

In the region of the Swiss frontier the forests are deep, endless, empty, clement in the month of September, watered by pure streams and crossed only by huntsmen. Seagrave bought a supply of ham and sausage and wine and hard bread for Luis on the black market in villages lower down, and left him with the van for shelter and cash for eventualities.

'Can I have a gun?' Luis asked.

'What for?'

'Pederasts.'

'You're inventing them,' Seagrave said, though he knew about the ones in the camp and believed in those, and even had doubts now about Philippe since the episode of the visiting card. He put Luis with a gun and the van not too far away from a village in case of emergency, not close enough, he hoped, to foster suspicion, and then he made his way on foot to the border. His passport had been renewed at the end of '39 and still had three months' validity without questions. The photograph showed a student with half a smile, half a hint of unspent concupiscence like a list to starboard, and a look of full credulity in its own candour. He hoped it wasn't how he looked now. At the frontier post they asked if he was an officer and he told them he was a student proselyte of the reformed church of France.

'A Huguenot?'

'Exactly.'

There was a delay, not for deliberation, just for cogs to mesh.

'*C'est la tradition. Passez.*'

Apparently he was at the favoured end of the exclusion/inclusion spectrum: that was something gained even if the gain was brief. It was unlikely to extend to Ida and the baby on the return journey. His sister Jean would have to look into her connections or her husband's and find out where the frontier could be filtered through. They'd probably helped refugees before. Surely they would. Jean was fifteen years older than him and from a different mother and she and their elder brother had always kept their distance from the infant Seagrave and increased it when he began to grow up, as though the link if stretched far enough would become slighter, weaker, and finally snap altogether, relieving them of any further concern. When he came to think of it it wasn't a very brilliant prospect for expecting help now. Still, there'd been a war. He found a post office and eventually got through to his sister on the telephone.

'Hello Jean, it's me, Stephen.'

'Stephen!' The tone was guarded. 'Where are you?'

'Near the frontier. I'm waiting for a bus.'

'Where are you going?'

'I'm on my way to you.'

'Are you in uniform?'

'I'm in the uniform of the Resistance. That's anything that covers you.'

'I don't know what you mean. I'm talking about the King's uniform. Aren't you in that? The War isn't over yet.'

'Listen, Jean. I'll be at your house in Berne by tonight. I'm told everything in this country still runs like clockwork. The War's elsewhere. I'm sure your house runs like clockwork too. I've come to fetch Ida and the baby, that's all.'

'I see.' There was a long pause during which Seagrave wondered what formula of welcome it would grudgingly give birth to. 'Well. They're not actually here in the house, you know. But I'll be glad to see you, naturally. I'll warn Hans.'

'Warn him about what?'

'That you're coming for the night, of course.'

A night didn't sound like a very long stay after five years but perhaps it would be quite enough for Hans. 'Where is Ida?' Seagrave asked.

'We sent her to the Murtensee where we keep a boat. It was safer.'

'You sent her? You didn't take her?'

'Stephen, you do sound rather quarrelsome. Perhaps it's just the telephone. We'll talk about it all when you get here. Take a taxi from the station so Hans won't have to . . . you've got some money with you I hope?'

'Enough for a taxi from the station.'

'And to get back again? To wherever it is you've come from?'

'I'll see you tonight, Jean.' He rang off. The conversation had been discouraging. He saw how absurd of him it was to expect to find Ida still in his sister's house. François had warned him. Sisters don't like that sort of girl, he'd said, and he meant sisters who were human. Never mind. Ida would have hated Jean too, for the conscious rectitude built into her and holding her up. Ida was certainly better off down by the Murtensee where no doubt there was a comfortable boathouse, a car and probably a caretaker. He would ring Ida tonight. She would have been all right there on the shores of the lake, safe and well supplied, Jean and Hans would have seen to it as the minimum demand on decency. Probably they would want any outlay they'd made reimbursed, that wasn't unreasonable and he was prepared for it. Already by an unconscious progression or decline he found himself falling back on the thought of the loot buried in the garrigue, as onto a bedrock. This was hardly the moment in Europe's tormented history for the finer scruples.

In the train from Geneva to Berne he thought about Ida. She had never been long out of his mind during the last two years but almost never, admittedly, in the forefront of it. He supposed there must be some mechanism for screening off painful mental presences, as in bereavement, after a certain time. The separation from Ida had been unbearable when she was in the camp but part and parcel of a personal victory when he got her out of it and on the way to safety and comfort in a neutral land of plenty.

The cleanliness of this train was extraordinary. Under the occupation nothing had seemed clean. These wheels ran sweetly, rapidly over the permanent way as if that too was kept scoured bright. Well-tended vineyards for the production of fresh white wine ran down to the shore of the lake where boats adorned the waters just as if the whole panorama had been assembled inside a bottle. What would Ida have made of this static world, with her genetic itinerary? He could picture her face, the features a little full by natural abundance, the eyes, viewing this scene, perhaps turning to the greener end of hazel, and an expression hinting that absurdity had been located in the beauty spread out, crisp as a cloth for a *déjeuner sur l'herbe* in this tragic world. Hans was waiting to receive him on the platform at Berne.

'Stephen! My dear old chap! How have you weathered all the unpleasantnesses of these last years? You look thin. You must put down many of our steaks and cheeses while you're here.' Hans's English was nearly perfect, if a little heavy. Jean had never learnt more German than necessary for ordering the servants about, and she and Hans and their children used English and only English in the family circle. Moreover Hans had attended an English university – London, Seagrave thought it was. Outside the station a car driven by a chauffeur was waiting. 'Jean said you would take a taxi but I felt the least I should do . . .' Hans sounded abstracted, the politeness was as the boats on the lake had seemed, more decorative than convincing. You wouldn't trust yourself to it for a venture out onto the deep. They sat silently side by side on the deep-buttoned upholstery looking at the back of the chauffeur's head through the plate-glass screen. What was this car? A Daimler? A Mercedes? No, it had a neutral, transatlantic feel, probably it was a Packard. Hans's Bank would have plenty of associations over there, sister organisms. 'So you stayed all the time in the south of France?' said Hans in a tone between interrogation and indictment.

'And Jean safe here with you.'

'It's my country, here. Of course my wife should be sound and safe. But you . . . it seems you had different concerns. And reasons.'

'Reasons that are my concern,' Seagrave said firmly. He wasn't going to take any admonishment from this balding neutral profiteer. Hans grunted something in German to himself and fell silent again. 'Have you heard from pompous old William?' Seagrave asked. It was a question, put like that, which might get a rise.

'Your brother works very hard in his Ministry. He has no time for personal correspondence. He is a colonel now, a *full* colonel. He wears some red on his uniform.' Hans sounded as if this distinction was enough to make him breathless just thinking about it. Or perhaps that was a front, a conjugal habit of deference for keeping on the safe side of Jean and her temper.

'So he's more of a civil servant than a soldier actually.'

'It's a very honourable work,' said Hans piously.

Communication in the family wasn't going to be any easier than it used to be, that was clear. Hans, as far as the family was concerned, was like a relief curate, he took the service on his own in the absence of the others, often exceeding them in zeal.

'You have generations of public men and . . . and position behind you,' he said. 'Your grandfather was . . .'

'I didn't know him; he died long before I was born; it doesn't matter to me what he was,' Seagrave interrupted. Hans shrugged his shoulders to show impatience.

'You've been too long a time away from home,' was all he said, but much more was implied – chiefly that Seagrave, with all the chances that had been his with such antecedents, forefathers in one public role or another more or less since records began, was on the contrary sinking as steadily as ever out of the civilised view, the home prospect. The word home evoked always the same image like another scene in a bottle, a bottled specimen, a foetus in formaldehyde. The building of red stone growing from red earth, extended and rooted like the prelapsarian oaks standing about it. The great lapse had been, historically, whatever it was that could make people from one locality like Soames and himself feel that they came out of different worlds when in fact the sphere of their enjoyments and hopes was the same, formed in the same words. Perhaps in a lifetime it wasn't too late to salvage something from that, put it back into joint in some way. 'I don't suppose I'll go back there,' he said.

'You might have to,' said Hans.

'Why?'

'When you need support one fine day, young man, that's why.' Hans spoke with the complacent irritation of one who in his present state of opinion would certainly vote against support if it had anything to do with him.

Hans and Jean lived in a big house behind high walls and ringed by fir trees in the suburbs of Berne. The sunset, by the time the car turned in through the gates, was happening on the other side of the range of mountains which cast a purple shadow, bathed in light the colour of mother-of-pearl. Jean stood on top of the double flight of steps to their front door, dressed in this light and shadow as if about to render her part in a big operatic crisis. She opened her arms wide as Seagrave stepped out of the Packard onto the broad raked gravel surface of the forecourt.

'Darling!' she cried, using this word for the first time ever, as far as Seagrave could recall, in their sibling intercourse. She'd put on weight over the lean years of war. Great blue eyes shone out placidly with a quite misleading air of placidity from a face whose coachwork, like that of the Packard, had been inflated by the sweets of capitalism. 'But you're so thin!' She had wrapped her arms briefly round him and then put him from her like a black sheep for the dip.

'Well, Jean, I must say *you* look wonderfully fit. And smell delicious. What is it? *Joy* of Patou? Something or other of Balenciaga?' His ideas of scents were indistinct but these names had the right ring of peace and plenty.

'Don't be so silly, Stephen. It's just a thing they make here out of their crocuses or something. Alpine primavera. Now the War's soon going to be over I'll never buy another bottle of it.' Compliments, he remembered, were no good with her. She probably felt them as a trespass in the pleasure garden of her narcissism, anyway they were repelled with ignominy, always. To get her favour you had to toe the line in other ways. 'Do get Stephen a glass of sherry to take up to the bath he must be longing for,' she said to Hans as they entered the salon, a high room with a porcelain stove and a bronze chandelier like the antlers of a moose.

'Are those a few of Hans's ancestors there?' Seagrave asked, looking round at the walls lined with portraits of wooden, cheerless worthies hung each one in the dead centre of an oval frame as if born to execution there.

Jean giggled, and Seagrave received the impression that though there was no glass to be seen there would be a good deal less sherry in the bottle than when Hans went off to the Bank that morning. 'Poor Hans. Aren't they ghastly. He got them at a sale. The whole lot as a lot.'

'One wouldn't know.'

'Rubbish. You knew perfectly well. It's why you asked.'

'Fine frames anyway. An investment in themselves, I expect.'

'There's nothing to despise in a man spending his life making money. It's a very good thing to make,' Jean said, her thought performing a sharp lateral movement. At that moment Hans reappeared with the sherry for Seagrave, a tall glass with a mist of icy condensation. 'What about me?' said Jean peremptorily.

'So you would like a little . . . sherry too?' asked Hans in a tone of synthetic courtesy.

'I didn't say anything about little,' Jean said and he went away again without protest as if knowing only too well what that could lead to by this time of the evening.

*

In the bath Seagrave thought of Ida being wretched in these surroundings. How long had she been kept here? She would have experienced it as a prison, the organisation and deployment of wealth like the panoply of control and correction. He hoped it hadn't been for long. By the lake she would be free to sit on the ground, sleep in a corner, cook her meal under the trees if she felt like it, live as she did in the garrigue. He had been going to telephone her before anything else, and now he realised that without deciding to do so he had put it off. Anxiety was undermining fervour. They'd been apart for so long and so much had happened – to him anyway. Her existence, presumably, had been more or less uneventful while his had been one of constant hazard.

And excitement, it had to be admitted. Had she been faithful for two whole years? That might depend on accident. A defensive smokescreen arose spontaneously in his mind as soon as these questions were half-formed. He hadn't himself, but that was different. Or was it? The smokescreen blew over and fully obscured the terms of the human enigma and made any conclusion unnecessary. You don't have to formulate a stance in a fog of unknowing. He went downstairs in his clean shirt and the tweed jacket he never wore in Nîmes but had brought specially for the occasion.

'Haven't you got a tie with you?' asked Jean. 'Hans will have to lend you one for dinner.'

'I want to telephone Ida where she is before anything else.'

'Telephone? You don't imagine there's a telephone there on the lake, do you? Telephones cost money.'

'How do you keep in touch with whoever you've got there?'

'What do you mean, whoever we've got there?'

'Ida's not alone, surely?'

'Did you think we'd supply her with a domestic staff? You seem a bit vague about the realities.' Jean emptied her glass and held it out to him. 'If you just go through there into the butler's pantry you'll see the sherry bottle where Hans left it. No, on second thoughts, just bring the bottle.' Humming to herself she gazed down into the coloured patterns in a glass paperweight she held in her other hand, as into a crystal ball. Then she laughed, not at herself but at the absurdity of life whereby the comfort and sustenance she derived from the sherry bottle had to be paid for and fetched, poured and renewed instead of flowing directly into her system as of right from an indebted universe. That anyway was Seagrave's interpretation of her laugh, and it added to the anger he felt building up inside his chest.

'I'll get you the bottle when you've answered my question.'

'Which question?'

'Is Ida alone down there on the lake? How far's the nearest house?'

'They're not exactly houses, any of them, and when I last saw her she had the baby with her so she was hardly alone.'

'When was that?'

Jean stood up and moved off towards the pantry in her long dress, wandering slightly from side to side in her course like a barge between wind and water.

'When was that, when you last saw her?'

'Ask Hans. Do ask him. He keeps things like dates in his head so much better than me.'

Without reflection, Seagrave sprang forward and took her by the wrist of the arm holding the sherry glass. Four years in the Resistance and the cathartic violence of the Liberation habituated you to rough and ready action.

'I'm asking you. I sent her to you. You knew I loved her.' He tightened his grip on the wrist angrily. 'Where is she?'

Jean didn't need historic events to unleash her own capacity for rough action. Or perhaps it was just an accident flowing from an impulse to free herself. Swinging round her other hand with the paperweight in a wide arc as if to hurl it against the wall, she landed on the side of Seagrave's head a blow which sent him lurching back in surprise and caused her to drop the paperweight onto the parquet floor where it smashed into fragments. She then collapsed onto the nearest chair and with eyes wide open burst into operatic tears. At the same moment Hans appeared in the salon, changed into a velvet smoking jacket and black bow tie.

'Oh dear, oh dear what a pity,' he said. 'That was a valuable item of several hundred Swiss francs' worth from my collections.'

'Balls to your collections and your paperweight,' sobbed Jean. 'And your ridiculous pictures while we're at it,' she added, addressing herself to them where they hung, a stolid captive audience. 'Balls to them, every single one.'

'I think there's been some quarrelling here,' said Hans, looking resentfully at Seagrave. 'You should remember how easily upset our dear Jean is. If this went on she would fall into depressions.'

Jean didn't look depressed at all, nor as if depression was just around the corner. She had an air of triumph as of rectitude successfully defended. Seagrave wondered if she'd become a shade paranoid. Living through the War in a neutral land and in the unadulterated society of Hans might have tipped the scales. 'I'm sorry,' he said, fingering the tender place at the side of his head where a bump was already coming up.

'And what possibly could it be about?'

'All I wanted was some more sherry,' Jean said. 'And I still do.'

'That's nothing to do with it at all,' said Seagrave in a voice which sounded hollow in his own head. 'I want to know just what arrangements you made for Ida and where she is now. And when you last saw her. And who . . . sees to her needs.' Hans was on his way to the pantry. 'Go on please, I'm waiting,' Seagrave said when he got back with the sherry bottle.

'Down on the Murtensee we have a little chalet . . . for the children, in summer . . . near the water. And a boat on the shore there too. For the summer.' Hans was prevaricating.

'And that's where you sent Ida, I know. When did you go there last yourselves?'

'Not very recently. Business has kept me here. Work goes on, you know, even when the whole world is . . .'

'When?'

There was a long silence in which Hans looked at Jean and Jean, still sniffing from time to time, looked down into the pale cold surface of the wine, a sherry so dry it seemed like arctic air liquefied.

'Then you haven't been to find out how she is and there's no telephone there. What about the winter? Has she been in touch with you? What's she been living on?' There were so many questions spinning in his head it was impossible to know where to begin, the questions spun about like starlings going to roost.

'Money was provided at the beginning, after the birth of the baby,' said Hans.

'Where was the baby born?'

'It was born here, the night she arrived from the frontier.'

'But it wasn't due . . . for two months at least.'

'What's that to us? There was no warning. Fear and hunger, and I suppose . . .'

'But everything was all right?' The question seemed inadequate as it was spoken.

'Nothing about it was all right,' Hans said vehemently. 'It was a great burden to us and an imposition. And an *expense* at the time. The doctor, the nurse . . .'

'I'll repay whatever you spent, I expect to. But since then? What have you done about her since? How do you know if she's safe there on the lake? It isn't so far away, if neither of you went didn't you send someone to find out?'

Hans was sitting in an armchair with high wings, obviously his special chair for when he got home from the Bank. In his hand he had a big cut-glass tumbler with what looked like whisky, and in the other a black cigarette which he was forgetting to smoke so the ash fell from time to time onto the parquet. He looked apprehensive and also, in his heavy way, defiant, like a slow youth caught between customary self-satisfaction and some rare reprehensible private practice. While he was apparently considering what to say next Jean brought her refreshed attention back to Seagrave and his plight, or what had led to it.

'How about your young wife? How is she?' she asked loudly. 'I remember hearing you'd married a Jewish girl at the university. Did those wretched people have difficulties down there in the south?' She spoke in an easy, social voice as if the answers to these questions were in themselves immaterial, anyway to her. What mattered was putting the present problem into perspective. 'Now we'd have understood if you'd sent *her* . . .'

'She was killed when the Americans bombed the hospital where she was.'

'When was that?'

'On May the 27th.'

'What was she doing in hospital? What was the matter with her?'

'Does it matter what the matter was? You could say the bomb turned out to be it.'

'Was she pregnant too?'

'We hadn't even lived together since 1942.'

Jean gave a loud barking laugh. 'I've never heard of that stopping a girl from getting pregnant.' Seagrave felt defeated by the distorted emotional character of her reactions. She disapproved of the Jewish wife dead or alive, that was obvious, but still more obvious was her total rejection of the very idea of Ida and any claim she might have had. He strongly suspected that Ida was no longer on the Murtensee, they knew it and were only waiting for him to work it out for himself.

'So she's gone,' he said, still hoping to hear this denied. Hans and Jean volunteered nothing. 'How long ago?'

'She stayed there more than a year, we know that,' Hans said.

'But you don't know where she went?'

'Of course not.'

'Didn't you try to find out?'

Hans made a movement of great impatience, a passing but general upheaval like the leap of an inanimate device responding to electric current. 'What can you possibly be thinking of? The girl came into this country illegally, I protected her illegally, I housed and hid her illegally. She had no papers and no money and she gave birth to an illegal child when she'd been here two hours in our house. Do you suppose I would go and ask the police to help me trace her?' He stumped furiously off to the pantry with his whisky glass.

'You don't mean the baby was illegal,' Jean corrected him. 'Illegitimate is what it was. Wrong word.'

'*Ein bastard*,' Hans could be heard muttering through the clinking of glass and ice cubes in the pantry.

'But mine. A Seagrave bastard.'

'As long as you're sure of that,' Jean said. 'If you are I suppose I'm glad for your sake. Though how . . . not that it'll do you any good now they've disappeared.' She sounded so final about this there seemed no point in hoping for any more information from either of them. Their certainty was all the intelligence they had to give. It remained only to go to the Murtensee and search the place for any message or sign Ida might have left.

'Are there Romanies in this country?' he asked.

'Those without residence papers have all been . . .' Here Hans was forcefully interrupted by Jean.

'You had no business sending that girl here to us,' she said in a loud voice of defence. 'You put Hans in danger, and what was she anyway? Where did you find her? On the street. And it seems you even lived together! A sort of animal . . . a beautiful animal I know.' Then Jean seemed to want to reclaim this tribute that had slipped out. 'Well at least I suppose seductive . . .'

'Rather a beautiful animal like that than a rotten human being.'

'A creature you buy. And you send that to your family . . .'

At this moment a maid in cap and apron came into the room. '*Madame est servie*,' she said with a strong accent.

'We've had to do without a butler for an eternity,' Jean said. 'I make them announce in French. I can't bear to hear a word in German more than I can help.'

'I suppose it is a sort of contribution to the war effort,' said Seagrave but she wasn't listening. She rose and swayed forward in the direction of the double doors on one side of the salon which Seagrave supposed led to the dining room. In spite of everything he was very hungry. Perhaps if you were young these emotions of hope and rage just made you the more hungry. He certainly felt young enough beside this ageing pair with their excess weight, their surplus in the Bank, their petrified sexuality.

'You should return to England as soon as you can. Take the advice of someone who has seen a lot of failed lives from the vantage point of a Bank. The Bank of life, I like to say. Go back and try to start again. Perhaps William can help you, forget about all this. It was all an unhappy mistake and a terrible blunder.'

*

In the morning before Jean was up Seagrave found Hans outside on the gravel, ready for the Bank. The chauffeur was holding the door of the car open to receive him like a massive deposit.

'I won't be here when you get back. You can send me a note of what you say I owe you.' He passed Hans an envelope with the address of the cabin in the garrigue, and another which was blank. 'Please just write down the directions to find your chalet by the lake. I'll go and see if there's any trace.'

'Believe me you won't find anything.'

'How are you so sure of that?'

'Because naturally when I knew the place was empty all traces were removed. I told you last night, it was a situation for me full of dangers.'

'I want to go there all the same.'

'If you insist, wait here for the car. I'll send Rudi back in an hour. But be very discreet please. If you meet anyone, don't answer questions. Speak only English. I'm trying to be helpful so you just do what I say. Stay there as short a time as possible and return with Rudi.'

'Do you have informers in this country too?'

'We have laws. And everyone shares the duty of enforcing them.'

'Then you do.'

Hans stepped into the Packard and closed the door sharply behind him, and with a subdued but potent churning of gravel the car passed away out of the courtyard. Seagrave went in and put his things together, then wrote a note to Jean. On reading it over he found that it added up to nothing but impotent recrimination and he tore it up. Anyway the woman was sick, that was easy to see. Ethical reproof wouldn't pierce the armour. How had she got to be like that? Or was she always? Here his thought process entered one of its zones of obscurity like a fast-moving vehicle hitting a bank of fog. Perhaps in his own way he was as selfish and pig-headed as her? No, impossible. Absurd. But what was sure was that they were too close for comfort, let alone safety. Perhaps. When Rudi and the Packard turned in through the gate he felt a deep relief. In a few moments he would escape once and for all from here and the puzzle of sibling identity. As he crossed the court he heard Jean's voice behind him, calling him from inside the house. He turned to see her emerge onto the top step where she came forward and leaned over the stone balustrade, her elbows propped on it, looking down at him, breasts resting on her forearms, her face puffy with sleep and the undispersed humours of the night before.

'Where are you off to?'

'I'm leaving, Jean. First I'm going to the Murtensee.'

'And then?'

'It depends. Perhaps the police. Or the French Consulate if there is one. Ida had French identity papers with her even if she had no passport. Or the British Consulate, I may go there. The baby could be counted a British subject in a way.'

Jean came hurrying down the steps with an expression of alarm. 'Don't do any of those things you're talking about, Stephen.' She took his arm and led him out of earshot of the car, under the fir trees where a gravelled path ran in an unyielding line between trimmed laurel bushes.

'Who looks after the garden?' he asked out of simple curiosity.

'It's Hans's pride and joy.' Neither of them saw any need to add to this statement and they walked on a few paces in shared silence. 'Don't stay on in Switzerland any longer being a nuisance,' Jean said. 'You've no idea how difficult and unpleasant they can make themselves when they try. It wouldn't do any good. This is a country for settled people, solid people, not strays. She's gone for good. You'll get over it. You just think you loved her. Go home. Your life's a mess. Go home and forget all this.' They had reached a circular open space among the trees with a round rose-bed in the middle of it, edged with brick tiles upended in the earth. There were a few roses still in flower, the blooms blood red as well and thrusting a heavy scent onto the still air of this enclosure. Jean gave his arm a quick squeeze and let it go. 'I know she isn't anywhere here any more. Give it up. You have to forget her,' she said.

'How do you know?'

'I needn't say any more and I won't.' Her face had closed and fastened itself up as if bolted like an armoured screen round the information she was keeping to herself.

'Then I'll say goodbye,' he said, turning to walk back between the laurels.

'I'll look around for a nice girl for you, rich and suitable,' she called after him as a bribe, he supposed.

*

There were vineyards about the Murtensee, and in the villages near the shore were gardens with vines and oleanders standing in big earthenware pots. The microclimate must be gentle here. The glass screen between Seagrave and Rudi was as tight shut as the face of Jean so there was no question of any conversation. The Packard turned off the road down a sandy track under poplars. It had rained in the night and the track was under water in places where the ditches had run over. Now the sun came in laterally but still strong among leaves just beginning to turn and threw broad blades of light across drying sand, grass, sheets of fawn-coloured water. The track came to an end where the cultivated grove of poplars gave way to pines flourishing free of discipline, not in ranks, leaning as the wind took them, various in age as an animal population. The Packard drew up and Rudi turned round and stared hard for a moment at Seagrave embedded in the whipcord upholstery of the back seat. Then his mouth opened back in a smile showing large white teeth which met with the keen precision of a machine tool. The smile vanished as suddenly as it had come, leaving an impression behind it of having seeded and spread in fields of experience which Rudi wished to hint at without specifying. Clearly he knew something, but what could he know? More than was right for his station, Seagrave found himself thinking atavistically before he checked the thought. He got out and approached to speak through the half-open window.

'Where's the chalet?'

Rudi answered in German, a language of which Seagrave knew no more than the words of shouted command to be heard on the streets of Nîmes these last years, then Rudi pointed forward into the pine wood and closed the window before lighting a match for his cigarette. Obviously neither he nor the Packard was going any further, and Seagrave set off through the resin-scented air without looking back to see if, as he suspected, Rudi was watching him go with that intolerable smile on his face. He wished Soames had been here, with his Cumbrio-celtic flair for whatever lay on the other side of any surface. He'd have known what to make of Rudi. He stopped in his tracks. But of course. Rudi had been sent here before on missions. Not with the Packard, naturally, he probably had a motor-bicycle, or else Hans owned another car, less showy. He would have been sent to spy out the land, possibly even – who knows – to bring money so that Ida and the baby wouldn't actually starve to death or draw attention to themselves by begging for help elsewhere. The smile certainly indicated something more but Seagrave refused to think what it might be.

He went some way on level ground under the pines and reached a high sand bank with a slope beyond dropping to the dark edges of the lake drawn in green shadow. Farther out a breeze stirred the surface and sunlight caught the broken facets of the water moving in answer to the wind. A small island stood in the offing, wooded and rocky, otherwise the shores in all directions except here under the pines were dressed in vineyards, and the nearest village, appearing as a huddle of pinkish roofs and yellow stone, swam up the gentle slope of hillside from the water's edge. It was an extremely peaceful scene. Positively soporific. Far away a blue sail seemed gratuitous as a touch of paint put in as an afterthought on a canvas too bland. Scattered in the pinewood a number of small wooden huts could be made out, distant from each other and discreet as wildfowlers' hides. Which of them was the one belonging to Hans? Rudi might have told him but the message was in German. Surely the man must have some French? One could go back and insist but it was half a mile each way. Ida had lived in this wood for more than a year, there must be an indication somewhere. What was he looking for? What did he expect?

If she'd chosen to leave here she would have left a mark, travelling people always did that, on a threshold, on a wall, on a tree. Soames, he felt sure, would have found his way straight there. He tried to put himself in a Soames-like frame of mind – patient, blind to obstacles, open to the collective unconscious. Anything on a threshold would have been cleared away by whoever Hans sent, probably Rudi. That left the trees, and there were certainly plenty of those. It would be a tree by a track or path, a way used by other wayfarers, that was the key of the system and its aim. A sign, to signify, must have a chance of being read. Lovers' hearts on the bole of a beech with passers-by are sure of a responsive readership for generations to come. But here there were no visible paths. There could nevertheless be habitual passages, lines of transit. He looked about more carefully and saw at a distance among the trees a structure like a sentry box. 'The toilets, lad, everyone makes for those,' Soames's voice seemed to point out. He went over to the sentry box which leaned slightly one way as if built on sand, as indeed it was, but seemed otherwise solid. He opened the door and found when inside that this amenity was constructed over a deep pit. The odour was ancient, disused, not disagreeable, perhaps what you would inhale in a tomb opened after decades, say half a century. Sand probably is an excellent filter, he thought, and then washed regularly by the rain . . . the effluent would seep off and find its way into the bed of the lake.

He walked slowly from the sentry box back to the chalet,

examining each tree, and when he got there he walked round it and inspected the wooden sides within reach. It was built on piers near the water's edge where there was a small boathouse, no more than a shaky roof over a dock with sides shored by pine trunks and a water-logged sailing dingy with lowered mast under it. It didn't look as if Hans or the family made much use of this place, probably it all dated from the more modest days of Hans's own childhood. There was nothing to be found here. It was a strange thought that Ida had been here so long, walked about so often among these trees, bathed in that water, used that sentry box. That is if this was the right chalet. And then she'd abruptly disappeared. His belief was that nomads had passed this way and she'd joined them, from atavism or despair. In that case there would certainly be a message somewhere. He repeated the search going the other way, with no result. He would take a last look at the sentry box before going round the other huts. He patiently examined the inside woodwork, the fixed seat with a circular hole, the back of the door. The lifting wooden latch. And there, behind the latch and visible only when it was lifted were some letters, more scratched than carved, done in a hurry. *Ik*, he read, Ida's initials, his heart lurched as if kicked while it ran. Then, *DELA*, the last letter unfinished, broken off. De la? De la what? Where? What could this mean? If the letter was unfinished so too perhaps was the word, if it was a word. Seagrave let vocabulary flick through his mind unchecked and random as consciousness, like a crossword zealot. It came to a brutal halt at a word very familiar these last years – *délation*. Denunciation. It was the word used every day during the occupation for what happened any time, on any street corner, usually after the curfew. *Délation*. Ida had been taken away but permitted time to come here, perhaps for the baby, before embarkation in the truck or car to the frontier. There could be no doubt about it, she had been reported to the police. The only question was, which frontier? Seagrave ran back through the pinewood to the poplars and the Packard.

'Take me to Berne,' he said to Rudi in French and speaking in a loud voice that left no room for pretence of misunderstanding. 'And open that glass. I want to talk to you.' As soon as he was in he rapped on the screen and it began to drop slowly like a furled sail.

'You knew the girl who was here?'

'Oh yes.'

'Where did she go?'

'Disappeared. Like smoke.'

'Where to? I know she was taken away. What do you know about it?'

'I know nothing. I'm paid to be a chauffeur, not an information bureau.'

This denial was obviously the signal for a bribe. 'Stop the car, I have to piss,' Seagrave said. As the Packard came to a halt in the depth of the poplar grove he stepped out, drew the pistol inherited from Roper up in the Cévennes and stuck the cold end of the barrel through the window and into Rudi's ear. The head recoiled but he was ready for that and followed the movement, pushing a little harder. 'I'm absolutely serious. I need the information and I'm not paying anything for it. The police would take her to the frontier?'

Rudi rolled eyes full of fear and deceit towards him. 'That's what they do.'

'Which frontier?'

'All frontiers were the same. Switzerland had only the *Reich* after the frontiers.'

'Which country then? Austria? Germany? France?'

'She came in from France, didn't she? That's the way they'd send her back. But what difference? They all ended up going the same way, so people say. All the refugees, the Jews, whores, gypsies, all the same way in the end. A big clean-up.'

'Who denounced her to the police?'

'I know nothing about it,' Rudi repeated, and when Seagrave jabbed the barrel a bit further into the side of his head he said it again. '*Nichts. Rien.* Nothing.'

'Did you come here often, while she was here?'

'Every time I was sent. And then–' Rudi twisted his head a little towards Seagrave and gave out his smile once again, though not quite so cocksure – 'one or two other times as well.' He hesitated, and as the pistol was withdrawn he added, 'She could have made good money, that one. With the right help.'

'Get out with your hands behind your head.' It would have been nice but imprudent to do Rudi some serious harm. 'Face the trees.' He looked over his shoulder to make sure the engine of the car was still running, then raised one foot and planted it in the small of Rudi's back, projecting him forcibly into the wide ditch half filled with water. As he scrambled out on the far side Seagrave got into the chauffeur's seat and drove forward along the track at a good speed and out onto the main road. It was a car with a big engine and Rudi was several kilometres from the nearest telephone at midday in a countryside whose population would be at the trough. Seagrave would be in Lausanne by the time Hans knew anything about it, in Geneva before he had decided what to do. Hans's position would be a difficult one. He might rather wait and see if Seagrave turned up on his own in Berne. Recrimination would be safer than involvement with the police, and Rudi could always be compensated. When he reached Geneva Seagrave parked the Packard between the Jardin Anglais and the Hôtel Métropole, had a whisky in the hotel bar and posted the ignition keys to Hans at home with a word thanking him for his hospitality. Then he went out and found a taxi to take him to the frontier. He had saved himself a lot of time and the driving had absorbed anxiety into enjoyment of speed and the power of the engine.

He must go back at once to England. William in his important post at the Ministry of Defence was his only hope left. Ida and the baby, pushed back across the frontier, would have been arrested at once on the French side. It was known that some of the racially nomadic people in the north had been rounded up and sent over the Rhine, no one knew where, to camps along with the Jews and captured resistants, or what was left of them after questioning. He must face William and the more traditional forms of questioning in London. His record with the Resistance could be attested by Charles d'Albaron whose name from the Quai d'Orsay rank and file might be known to the Foreign Office. He would leave Luis near the coast with enough cash to . . . to what? To survive. Everyone had to take his chance. The armies were reported advancing on the Rhine and prisoners of every sort would by now be streaming on the roads back to their own lands, starving and sick. With luck, a lot of luck, Ida would be among them. But a woman with a two-year-old child – supposing the child survived too – would not have much chance in the chaos, weakened, frightened, penniless. The Ministry of Defence, so he believed, would find her. Ministries were powerful things. He didn't know, it wasn't yet known, what millions had entered the camps, people without names or addresses, unrecorded, unnumbered hosts out of reach of ministry of any kind.

Chapter Seven

From a ruined orchard outside Dieppe on a slope abandoned now by the tanks Luis looked at the grey sea in the distance and shuddered.

'Is England a long way out over there? I can't see it,' he said.

Seagrave felt bad leaving him here, even with plenty of money. 'If I don't come back before the weather turns cold, try and get back to Nîmes. Find Monsieur Paradis and tell him what's happened. He'll look after you.'

'He'll give me to the gendarmes and say I stole the van.'

'No. I'll write him a note. Give him this. It'll be all right.'

'I'd like to go to England too.'

'You can't, Luis. Shelter in the van and be very careful with the money. Practise your reading and writing, you'll need that.'

*

There were plenty of boats out of Dieppe and at Newhaven Seagrave had no difficulty in boarding a train without a ticket. The Resistance had taught him methods he hadn't known about before, and a foreign kind of cheerful non-compliance. However, the cheerfulness received a shock at the sight of the streets of London. Wreckage was far greater over here than in France in spite of the strip of silver-grey sea in between. Here, the rape had come from the sky and people still looked up at it in fear. The violation of France seemed, compared with this, more moral than corporal. And here there was much less feeling of deliverance and joy, as if the springs of exultation lay trapped under the bombed masonry.

William Seagrave's first reception of his young half-brother was not warm. 'So it's you again after all this time. Jean told me you'd been to her. How did you get my number at the Ministry?'

'Hans gave it to me.'

'He shouldn't have. Poor security. Of course Hans is only a neuter.'

'A neutral.'

'That's what I said. I'm extremely busy. Come here at six thirty this evening. No. I'd better have a look at you first. Where are you staying?'

'Nowhere. I thought you might put me up for a night or two. I have to talk to you.'

'I've no doubt you do. You'd better go to a club.' William named one of his own, very far from the most exclusive, and to that sombre Pall Mall palazzo of blackened stucco Seagrave made his way from the Embankment after passing a couple of hours hung over Westminster Bridge, following the tide like other men adrift, the sick, the wounded, the unposted.

'For God's sake go out first thing in the morning and buy a suit before you show yourself again in any of the public rooms here,' William said as soon as he saw him. 'The darker the better, then if it's cheap and nasty it won't show so much.'

'Isn't clothing rationed?'

'Go to that second-hand place in Covent Garden.'

'Would you?'

For an answer William merely pointed to the red tabs on his uniform and a couple of medal ribbons he wore. It was important to humour him and above all not argue with him if he was to be any use. Like everyone William looked tired and grey and unready to put up with any aberration from the norms for which he and they had sweated and fought it out. That was understandable and Seagrave was determined to be extremely careful. Toe the line.

Knuckle under. Unlike Jean, William had got thinner. This paring away of some of the glowing, polished lacquer of superior flesh that had been on him when last they met was, aesthetically, an improvement. He listened in silence to Seagrave's abbreviated and ironical account of his activities in the Resistance as to a subordinate's report.

'You seem to have enjoyed yourself a good deal.'

'I was trying not to make too boring a recital out of it. I mean the band of heroes kind of thing,' Seagrave said.

'Most people serving here and doing their duty have had to put up with a good deal more than boredom. And heroics.'

'Well it's not really my fault if there's that difference, William. Where I've been perhaps the action was just a lot more exciting.'

'Special duties under orders are one thing. Seconding yourself without any authority to our friends over the channel is quite another. I think you've made yourself liable under the Defence of the Realm Acts. Your fault was staying away when you could have come back, my boy. We've got to face that and I don't know how you're going to get off the hook. The penalties under the act are very heavy. I probably shouldn't be dealing with you privately at all. If your name wasn't Seagrave I wouldn't be. But it is.' After this speech William pondered for a minute, plainly turning over in his mind some far more important interest of his own that might be put in jeopardy. Something, Seagrave guessed, that he was full of but felt rather reluctantly was better kept to himself. It seemed worth probing a bit further.

'What's in a name? But thanks all the same for the kindly family feeling if that's what it is.'

'Feeling be ... I don't think family feeling was what interested you when you got yourself tied up with a Romany waif and stray, according to Jean. Don't you know there are hundreds of thousands of them along the roads? No. The fact is I'm up for Parliament at the next election. Which may not be far away. This is just about the worst moment imaginable for a public family disgrace.'

The value of this new information was at once apparent. 'Where are you standing?'

'Where d'you think? Where we've always stood.'

'Then you'll get in whatever happens. Unless of course . . .'

'Unless you get put inside or shot and the local papers decide to make a field day of it.' The room they were sitting in was empty save for the armchairs lined up like leather coffins open to receive the late members whose portraits filled the wall-space. William's voice seemed to boom out and echo off the glass of these pictures, flooding the room with its plummy sound. 'Near a mining district there's always a substratum of votes ready to swing the wrong way,' he said more quietly. 'What you must do is lie low.' He went over to the door and looked about in the hall and appeared relieved when he got back so presumably he'd seen no one alive there either. 'You stay here for the time being and don't talk to anyone, in your own best interest. If asked you've been on special duties. Those chaps keep their mouths shut so you do the same. We'll see what can be worked out. As soon as possible you'd better go abroad again . . . somewhere or other. Have you got any money?'

'Nothing to speak of.'

'So something will have to be done about that too,' William said bitterly, then added after a pause, 'Have you ever thought of Canada?'

'Not much recently. In the south it was more the Americans in the sky dropping bombs who we . . .'

'I meant have you ever thought of emigrating there? They say Canada's full of possibilities for young men who've got nothing to keep them here.'

'Isn't that what they used to say about Australia, more or less, in the days of transportation?'

'Take my advice, Stephen. Don't try to be funny. Your situation's no joke. This war hasn't been amusing and the jokers people appreciate are the ones who went through the bombing with them.'

For the moment William was too necessary to be argued with.

'I'll do whatever you say. I won't show myself until the election's good and over. When is it by the way?'

'I'm expecting it in the spring, and you can't stay here all that time. I must have you out of the way before then. Wait here a couple of days. I'll telephone and come and see you.' William got up to go, straightening his uniform and lightly stamping his feet to send his trouser legs into line with the shoes and each other. His slightly bulging eyes, not unlike Roper's in their assertive righteous blue, were just on a level with the crown of Seagrave's head.

'I've got an important thing to ask you. It's what I came back for. The fact is I need help.'

'Oh Christ,' said William, and slowly lowered himself back into the leather armchair, legs spread like a man in armour being hoisted onto a horse. 'Not a hanging matter I hope? I heard from Jean you'd stolen Hans's car and assaulted the chauffeur but very decently they're letting it pass. So what is it?'

'Can your Ministry try and find someone, a refugee sent over the Rhine to one of the civilian prison camps? She has a small child with her.'

'I see. Does this mean you're still chasing after that girl you sent to Jean?'

'Yes it does. The child's your nephew.'

'Jean says the girl was hidden but then she vanished without as much as a word.'

'Not quite. She had time to scratch part of a message and I found it. She'd been denounced to the police.'

'How do you know? I don't believe it. She was protected,' said William, banging the table in front of him. 'Persecution mania, that's what comes of mixing up your categories. If I'd picked up a girl for the afternoon at Brough Hill or Appleby Fair I wouldn't go and actually *live* with her afterwards. Besides those people always think someone's reporting them to the police. They always have. And quite often they're right. Why should they be above the laws just because they think the conventions are beneath them? Same goes for this girl of yours. If she had no right to be in Switzerland and no papers they were quite in order, in my view, to chuck her out.'

Seagrave found himself too angry to hold back in spite of his good resolutions. He leaned forward so that his face, when he spoke, was close to William's and he could see the assertiveness of the blue eyes turn to surprise. 'I sent her to them to look after because she was mine. She'd been put in a prison camp in France for people of her race. I don't know who denounced her and I'm accusing no one but I do say she wasn't protected as she ought to have been. All Europe's been crawling with denouncers and betrayers and the trains were crammed with victims who've never been seen again. On my way at Dieppe I met a French Jew who'd escaped. You talk about the bombing here. You've seen nothing in your Defence Ministry shelter. The continent's a chamber of horrors.' The anger was wearing off but the damage was probably done. William looked more disapproving than ever. 'I'm sorry, William. The fact is I've been terribly anxious about them. They may both be dead by now but there might still be time . . .'

'And how many hundreds of thousands of these refugees d'you suppose there are? And where?'

'No one knows.'

'But it's the Defence Ministry in its shelter you expect to help you?'

'You, really. I don't know anyone else.'

'No of course you don't. You haven't been here. You didn't even go to Oxford. Never made yourself part of the life of your . . . not supposed to use the word but you know what I mean. And you haven't come back to join it. You've come back on the scrounge, morally speaking. I don't mind saying you needn't expect help from me except to get you out again before there's any trouble.' William spoke partly for himself, partly for his caste as a whole.

'In that case it could be a mistake counting on me to keep my head down until after the election.'

'You wouldn't do yourself or the girl any good behind bars.'

'Without help she'll never be found. She'll die in a camp or at the side of the road in a ditch. If you won't help me I'll give myself up and apply officially. The child's a British subject by birth. I'll start with the newspapers and see what they say. My stories of the Resistance could interest one of them.' William appeared to hesitate but not for long. As he didn't seem at all surprised by these remarks it looked as if advancing by menace must be quite current practice in the worlds where he operated. 'There isn't half a day to be lost. I'll get on the telephone and say I'm staying in this club.'

'You won't do anything of the kind,' said William. 'You'll wait discreetly here while I take soundings. Which needs time.'

'There isn't any time. Aren't you something or other in the Cabinet Offices?'

'I am indeed.'

'Doesn't that give you enough pull?' William didn't answer this but nodded his head thoughtfully a few times instead. 'I'd have thought you'd have more pull from there than you'll ever get as a county MP. Why don't you stay in the Cabinet Offices?'

'Wars don't last for ever. Time to bale out. Get on the scene with the early birds.'

'Well I hope the pickings don't disappoint you,' said Seagrave, who on the contrary sincerely hoped they would prove a dreadful come-down.

'There's no reason to think they will. They were pretty good last time.'

Seagrave had no large illusion about the efforts William would go and make. He wouldn't move heaven and earth, which was what was needed – that wouldn't be in his interest. It would point to personal involvement. No, he would make impersonal enquiries from the safe side of a security screen and using someone else, some subordinate, as stalking-horse. Meanwhile Seagrave could only wait. With what hope? Ida was a needle in the haystack of displaced people beyond the Rhine, which the allied armies had yet to cross.

The fighting was proceeding in France, in the Jura and the Ardennes, the region into which she had been expelled, and at the same time the bombing of the cities over the frontier grew daily heavier. She could be held in one of those cities, like Denise in the hospital at Nîmes. The Rhine was the sharp edge of the world and beyond it was the land of the black sun and the unknown horrors the Jew in Dieppe had spoken about.

Would Ida be better off now if he'd left her to her fate under the railway arches four years ago? William would have done that. As soon as this question surfaced in his mind Seagrave knew it had been waiting for him, inevitable, in hiding. If you adopt an animal that was making its own hard way before you came along you take it out of the free category of the stray and shut it up with your benevolence. The animal may be reduced, it may die of it in loving captivity. But you as a human being, or as a man if the animal happens to be a woman, you've obeyed natural promptings, used your powers and shown your colours. Your obedience to your nature is supposed to be the reward for all concerned.

These reflections came over him like low cloud in the late September sky, so heavy it was impossible to believe in light anywhere in the world. Yet in the Languedoc even in this end-of-war season the grapes would be picked, the mushrooms gathered, the boar hunted through hot afternoons. No doubt François had made his wine in the vineyard he had near the edge of the Camargue. Politics wouldn't be allowed to get in the way of that any more than of William shooting at grouse in the downpours of the northern August. But Ida hadn't wanted to be left under the arches like an animal you've stroked, fed and walked away from. Looking into her eyes he'd read a narrative of fearful solitude. Why was she so alone, apart from Luis? Her answers gave you nothing you could take hold of but you could sense some untold forfeit behind them. When you stopped seeing her as a woman you could see she was a castaway child. On that first occasion Seagrave had even wondered if he'd committed a crime under some term of the

Penal Code. Later he dropped this particular worry. Whatever her age Ida was as adult as if she'd lived already for centuries along the dusty highway.

'Do you want to stay with me?' he'd asked, though an hour had been enough to know he couldn't let her go. To begin with, he'd taken two rooms in an old, quiet, fairly respectable hotel near the station.

'I'm a student at the university and this lady and her brother are . . .'

'I can see what they are,' said the patronne. 'If you pay the week in advance and as long as you're their only visitor it'll be all right. Not otherwise. And no cooking in the rooms.'

When Seagrave emphasised the importance of this rule Ida said that she and Luis always ate in the open air, cooking and eating in closed rooms was an unclean practice, and they would continue taking their meals under the railway arches though sleeping here with him.

'Where are you going?' she asked when he showed signs of leaving them for the first time.

'To where I live. I'll come back very early in the morning. I have to take the train to get to the university.'

'To where you live? Don't you live with me now?'

'Yes, I do, but . . .'

'But you've got a wife. Have you got children?'

'No.'

Ida stood up from the bed – an old-fashioned, walnut affair large enough for a family, with a deep feather mattress on the edge of which she'd sat doubtfully, holding Luis by the hand – and made a move towards the door.

'I like you and you're honest and kind for a man, I can see, but I don't like you so much I can share you with another woman, and have only the pieces she leaves. You must leave her. And come to me or when you get back from your university I won't be here. And you won't find me. I know how to earn my own living anywhere.'

Seagrave couldn't know it yet but Ida never wept, her eyes were deep and dry as desert wells. What happened when she was distressed was that these wells became fathomless and their green turned dark at a depth where no sunlight reached. Seeing this phenomenon for the first time he surrendered at once.

'Give me till tomorrow night. Stay here till then. I'll fix everything, it'll be all right,' he promised.

'I'm not jealous, it isn't that. But it's unclean to share a man you love from the first day,' Ida said in elucidation. Evidently it was very important to plot correctly the borderlines of cleanliness in her world. They were something he would have to learn since it looked as if they were not exactly coincident with those in the world he'd known till now. 'And unlucky. It's the same. Anything unclean is unlucky. Uncleanness is against *baxt*.'

'What's *baxt*?'

'Fate. Good fate is *baxt*.'

'But fate's just fate, good or bad,' Seagrave objected. 'It just is.'

'Then *baxt* is much stronger,' Ida replied. It certainly sounded more interesting than mere destiny.

If cleanliness was one of the keys to *baxt* then as far as the conventional variety went Ida gave herself and Luis and Seagrave himself every chance. She seemed to him fanatically clean. When they were installed in the garrigue she started heating water on the wood fire before dawn and passed the better part of the morning scrubbing, wringing, drubbing their rags of garments on the white stone, his and Luis's in one lot of water, her own in another. Clearly that rule had to do with *baxt* too. But she mended nothing. The laws of cleanliness ignored textile breaches and rents. *De minimis non curat lex*. Ida didn't need to know the maxim taught to law students everywhere. From another angle it seemed to Seagrave that *baxt* had a lot to do with intuition but of course he knew that this was what men tend to think when faced with any item too elusive for analysis. Intuition couldn't be broken down. Looking back on this from the sombre premises in Pall Mall he decided that when he saw Luis again he would examine him on the subject of *baxt*-lore. Luis was old enough now to consider philosophical questions while still young enough to throw fresh light on them.

Against an IOU and a bundle of French notes of indeterminate value William had advanced a hundred pounds. It was done without spoken remark but under a thunderhead of resentment. This allowed Seagrave to spend the minimum of necessary waiting time in William's gloomy club where the food, what there was of it, was filthy, and the furniture like the inside of a punitive headmaster's study. He explored parts of London he'd never really known at all: Southwark, the City, the docks. Every now and then a deep, heavy explosion somewhere in the town shook the grey skies and echoed down from the cloud-cover. Beer, he decided, was more drunk-making and far less healthy than wine. But it helped him discover how in the vicinity of the great railway stations and their clustering pubs he felt most at home, this vast town reduced here to a turntable, every archway and line leading to somewhere less terrible. Or else bringing you back to these streets the haunt of whores, commerce of easy humanity in all shapes and forms. This was a part of the ruined world's capital where you could lose your chains of class and emotion for a few minutes as you dropped your trousers, and all that just at the price of a ten shilling note. Then when he thought about it Seagrave saw this was probably the standing charge for someone like himself. Lower down the perceived social scale the tariff might be lighter.

*

After weeks spent in William's club with no news of results from his enquiries, a letter came for Seagrave. The hall porter handed it to him with a knowing smile.

'A missive forwarded from your ancestral regions, sir,' he announced in his old, trained voice, not without a note of contempt in it since anyone could see that Seagrave was not a good representative of his order.

The envelope showed that the letter had been sent on here but originally addressed from the main mining town on the northwest coast. The letter weighed in his hand like a grenade. There was no one about in the club by now except ancient members dying in corners like abandoned beasts of draught, patient, evil-smelling, slow to go. All the active population was elsewhere and in action. Seagrave took his letter into the morning-room and sat himself in one of the great windows looking out onto Pall Mall. It was in fact an autumn day of great splendour; after early rain a golden light relieved of dust fell between the neo-classical façades and onto the faces, tired but eager, victorious, ironic, of the people passing below in the street. He opened his letter.

'Dear Etienne,' he read, and turned the page over to see the signature. It was from Soames. His spirits rose.

I hope that's right to call you Etienne here, I'm putting Stephen on the envelope so I hope they forward this letter quick to the right place because I think you'll want to hear what I've got to tell you. My news first. I'm out of the Army, I left a foot behind in a tank. Not much of the tank left either, there wasn't. So I'm invalided out and waiting for a replacement foot to rightly fit the knob where my ankle used to be. I won't moan but . . . not much I won't.

I was over Brough way yesterday looking over the horses. You'll know if you remember the fair on Brough Hill is the end of the month. Went on all through the war. The Romanies are there already with their caravans. It was a dry morning, plenty of blue sky and the horses playing and running along the moor edge. Puts heart into you to watch it. And what do I see when I look round me but that boy of yours, young Luis coming over and rattling at me in French. *In Brough-under-Stainmore* – can you think of that? I don't suppose a French word's been spoken there since 1066. And it's a long way from Nîmes where I saw him last that day we marched past. My marching's certainly past, I'm past marching all right. But there I go again, the old soldier in the pub. So what are you doing here, I ask him coolly, as if this was no real surprise these unsettled times. Very excited, Luis was. Looking for you, he says he is. That's how I knew you were somewhere abouts. How did you manage to get over, I ask, and up here to a place like Brough? A stupid question actually, you only had to look around at all the others to see they must have brought him along in the caravans. He crossed the Channel with a bunch of them who'd been living for years on nuts in the forests. They crossed in a fishing boat and landed up some creek on the East coast. It seems these people don't go in for recognising other folks' wars nor things like frontiers. They run under them like water under a door, he says and this lot he met in France always make for the northern horse fairs, like I do myself. With them it's something religious.

Well there you are, old Etienne. The boy's over at Brough with no passport and no identity card or ration book, I'm at Whitehaven after I promised him I'd try and reach you, and for all I know you're in custody telling what you've been up to these last years of total war. But if you can get here it's just as well if you do. You were right and I were wrong about the lad, he's as faithful as a dog. Sooner or later when he sees the other Romanies heading back south from up here where he reckoned to find you he'll start running like a dog on the roads. And then he'll get picked up and put inside.

So I went over your way by bus this morning. Whole place looked closed up for ever. Only inhabitants the crows sitting in the trees for hundreds of years without seeing a living soul. I'd have drunk your health and mine in a couple of pints at the Seagrave Arms but that was shut like a coffin. So if you want somewhere to go you're very welcome here. I get a woman in for the cooking. I hop down the road to another for the other thing. Any time you like.

Yours faithfully,

John Soames

You can leave a message at my local. It's called the Wordsworth – here's the number . . .

Contrary to strict instructions Seagrave rang his brother.

'I'm going up to Whitehaven,' he said.

'God Almighty, what for?'

'Private business that can't wait.'

'We agreed you'd stay here. I suppose it's a skirt.'

'It isn't. How are the enquiries going?'

'Nothing's come up yet.'

'Better put some pressure on. It's a small world up there.'

'I know, and the least you can do is keep out of the light. Take the night train. Don't draw attention to yourself. The local papers know I'm standing.'

'It's up to you, William. Hurry things on. If you want to contact me there's a pub where you can leave a message in the name of Soames. The pub's called the Wordsworth.'

'It would be,' William said savagely, 'and that would be where you're to be found. Hoping for an hour of splendour in the grass I dare say.' Plainly he hadn't believed that it wasn't a skirt at the bottom of this new outrage. All the same, pleased perhaps with the allusion, he emitted a rare laugh, barking and hollow like Jean's before ringing off.

Seagrave expected to catch Soames at the Wordsworth at opening time and he was right. 'John, ye're wanted,' he heard called out. 'A nob.' Some mirth and muttering followed this, then a voice said, 'Aye?'

'It's Etienne.'

'You're still a free man then.'

'So far.'

'Well to get to Whitehaven in case you've forgotten you can change at Lancaster and take the down slow. Or you can change at Carlisle and board the up slow. They both get here at the same time.'

'So if I oversleep at Lancaster I get a second chance.'

'Aye that's it, and I'll be at the station. It's foolproof.'

'How's the foot?'

'Fucking horrible,' said Soames sounding quite cheerful.

'See you tomorrow morning.'

'That's right.'

*

He knew the line from Lancaster. It followed the coast and ran within sight of his birthplace crouched in towers like beasts coupling on the wooded hill, not far above where the river ran out to sea. He chose the up slow from Carlisle through whose windows no primal scene would be thrust at him. Soames was on the platform, in uniform and on crutches.

'I'll keep on wearing it till they notice I'm not a hero any more,' he explained about the uniform. That stage hadn't yet by any means been reached, as was evident from the loving looks thrown at him in the street by young girls on their way to work in the offices of the mines. 'We'll drop in the Wordsworth by the back door and have a bacon and egg and a pint or two.'

The early sun was coming over the line of fells to the east but there was a cold wind off the Solway Firth. Looking over the roofs of the streets of miners' houses Seagrave saw the flat shingle stretching away to a line of harmless sea in the far distance. But the tide here could trap the unwary like an informer, relentless, secret and grey.

'How do we get over to Brough?' Seagrave asked with his mouth full of bacon.

'Ah, well there now, that's a thing,' Soames said slowly. 'It's a fair old way. A stiff logistical problem.'

'But you've cracked it already, I know.'

'You're someone always in a hurry,' Soames said reprovingly. 'Well yes, I have, like this. I've an old Standard car belonged to my poor dad. And – think on this – I've got a special petrol allowance for wounded heroes. Worth more than gold. But as I can't drive without a foot it's not much use to me, but you can. And we can bring the boy back here with luck before he comes to harm.'

'They should have made you a general, Soames.'

'They may do yet. And a Knight of the Bath. I'll keep it for storing coals in.'

They were too close to their geographical origins for these jokes to feel comfortable. In France they had an equality tempered by the advantage of Soames's greater experience and age. Here, there was a drop ready to catch them.

'How about another before we go?'

'I'm for that,' Soames said, and called for it through the open door of the parlour of the Wordsworth where they sat illicitly drinking at nine in the morning. 'Back in Nîmes we'd be having this out on the pavement.'

'But there's no Wordsworth there.'

'You can't have it all.'

They chugged through the mountains and along lakesides at the foot of oak woods in the Standard left by Soames senior, a car that had been very carefully looked after as far as its bodywork went but had developed more or less complete failure of synchromesh on any forward gear.

'My dad must be turning over in his grave to hear you,' said Soames with relish, early on before Seagrave had got the hang of it. 'You need to double de-clutch on the way up as well as down. The old lady don't like things rushed.'

Seagrave drove very carefully and as smoothly as possible, not just on account of the gearbox but because he could see Soames wince with pain at the slightest jolt. His foot, or rather the end of his leg, was wrapped in what looked like an oilskin container held in place by buckled straps. 'They only change the dressing twice a week now, but Jesus it's often enough,' he said. 'You have to drain the stump of noxious substances. I don't mind telling tha, lad, it's enough to make any strong man impowtent for a full twelve hour after.' There was no doubt he liked sharing out the gruesome details. Maybe it was some compensation for what he had to go through.

They crossed the Eamont and Eden rivers near their junction and followed the Eden southwards through the villages of that broad harmonious valley. Almost the only other traffic on the road was convoys of military who shouted and whistled at the sight of Soames's red beret and polished brass. 'Lucky fucker,' they roared, 'roll on Christmas.'

'They think I've fiddled a bit of compassionate,' said Soames, and returned each time a solemn salute as if his thought was too much on winning the War to have much to spare for pleasantries. As they approached Brough other cars began to join the main road from lanes and side turnings, all going the same way. Just outside the town they came on the first horses, tethered on the grass verge or running on open ground where heather-covered peat hags rolled down from the fell above to break like Atlantic waves against the barrier of the King's highway. As soon as he saw horses Soames's attention was released from his foot, from the object of their journey, from the countryside he'd been surveying with a soldier's trained eye and fixed itself on the animals with a passionate intensity. Seagrave remembered before the great train ride into Nîmes when they'd found two horses strapped to the beam above to prevent them falling in the night, and Soames's fury. Now it seemed the attraction was even more intense on account of his wound. Watching him, it appeared to Seagrave that Soames joined in the free motion of the horses by a process of imaginative transmigration. He became the flowing of their movement, the flexion of muscle, the strike of hoof.

'When you get your new foot you'll be able to ride again with it,' Seagrave said. 'I knew a man who rode paralysed from the waist down.'

Soames whistled. 'Now there's a thing you'd never really want to happen,' he said. 'Paralysed from the waist up including the brain I could just live with.'

The caravans lined each side of a narrow road running for a mile or more along the flank of the hill above the town.

'Whereabouts did you see Luis?'

'Just about where we are now.' They had left the car and come up the road among the crowd, Soames advancing unevenly with his crutches like an animated tripod. It was the first full day of the open fair and there were hundreds of caravans and thousands of people.

'We could ask one of them where's the boy who only speaks in French.'

'You can't ask Romanies questions about other Romanies,' Soames stated. 'They think you're from the police or the sanitary inspector. Or worse still the Army. If they answer at all it'll be a pack of lies.'

'I can try.' He went over to a caravan where he'd caught sight behind the curtains of a woman about the right age to feel motherly towards Luis if she'd seen him. 'I'm looking for a travelling boy who doesn't speak English. Only French. And I think he'll be looking for me. We're both of us spending our life trying to find his sister.' The narrative seemed to be getting complex and the face of the woman in the caravan as secretive and shut in as the fruit of an unknown tree. 'All three of us, we lived together in France.' Seagrave advanced cautiously as if seeking a foothold in a marsh. 'But the *baxt* was against us. If I can find the boy now maybe that'll show the *baxt* has turned. And then we'll save the girl too wherever she is.'

'You've no *baxt* if you're unclean,' the woman said. 'What had she done, this girl?'

'I don't know. Unless it was unclean going with me. To go and live with a *gadjo*.'

'No, it was before you,' the woman said, her eyes rolled up as if reading the past in blue spaces between the clouds. The gesture made Seagrave feel both suspicious and afraid of what she might add. She came closer and crouched on the step of her caravan to peer into his face. 'You're not like a *gadjo*. You could be one of our men, almost.' She straightened up and withdrew sharply, retreating into the shelter of the caravan and blinking as if too strong a light had suddenly broken on her. 'But there's no *baxt* there. None for you, none for her, none for her sons.'

'It's her brother I'm looking for. I asked you about him.'

'The brother's dead, long ago. You're not looking for any brother. They judged the brother and punished him and turned her away. That's why she's unclean and always will be unclean.' Seagrave backed off and turned, feeling as if he'd been assaulted by a crowd. His last glimpse of the woman as he swung away was of a sign she was making in the air in front of her. 'No *baxt* for her or anyone near her,' she called out as if paid to propagate far and wide the condemnation learned on the occult wavelength.

'I think you upset that lady. She probably expected money,' said Soames who had watched from a discreet distance.

'God damn her for a witch only fit for burning,' said Seagrave, intemperately for him.

'Or she upset you, I can see that.' Soames put a hand on Seagrave's shoulder. 'Take a bit of weight off, me lad, I've cramp in both armpits.' He leaned down heavily with a reassuring pressure. The autumn sun gilded the polychrome of the caravans, bathed the piebald horses, the green and tan of the fells around, the dun-coloured stone. There was no wind here and the Eden valley stretched far northward below this high ground in the full ripeness of the season as before the Fall. You could follow the rivers weaving and winding a serpentine course for miles between tree-lined banks. But Seagrave felt his spirits darkened like a black frost falling on this oasis. Soames tapped him on the chest with his field-glasses to reclaim his attention. 'I think I've spotted young Luis. Down by the river.'

'What's he doing there?'

'They're soaping the horses. It's good sport. They soap the horse first and then one of the lads rides it into the deep water to rinse off. You have to look slippy, riding a soapy horse with no saddle. And that's what he's been at.'

'Did you do that too when you were a boy?'

'I did, aye, every day of the fair, every year.'

Seagrave searched the throng down on the sands by the river through Soames's glasses but he couldn't see any sign of Luis. 'If that bloody witch was even half right he'll have fallen off and drowned himself in the river,' he said.

'We'll go on down then and fish the little bugger out,' said Soames, and led the way into a field where horses were grazing. 'There's a short cut at the bottom here you can't see . . . nor be seen . . . now I remember a young lass . . . well maybe not so very young . . . but my first time ever it was, all wet and soapy in the crutch . . . "Tha's had a reet good wash where some men never trouble theirselves to go," she says . . . Come to think on it,' he ended a little sadly, 'she must have been the village tart.'

'Tha's cheered me up,' said Seagrave.

Soames smiled, which was rare for him. 'That's good to hear.'

Chapter Eight

LUIS SAW THEM COMING over the stones and sand by the river, threading their way among the horses and men, long before they seemed to see him. A lot had happened since he and Etienne had separated in the orchard outside Dieppe and it seemed a long time ago. Luis knew it wasn't a long time but at his stage of life a month is long – long enough for change to come between you and the people who you remember as they were when you were younger. A month younger. To Luis now, Etienne walking patiently beside Soames looked like a stranger in his own land, here where Luis himself had come within a few days to feel quite at ease. It was Etienne who seemed like an unhappy outsider, yet something in the way he looked about him and the expression of his eyes and mouth was as if he knew, though he didn't belong to this scene, that the scene in some ways belonged to him. He was like an uneasy man with natural rights here, to Luis who as far as he knew had none anywhere. This made him feel a new distance between Etienne and himself. He ran over to meet them from the water's edge.

'Salut, Etienne,' he said, holding back because he didn't know if it was right to embrace him or not, here where he hadn't seen much embracing going on.

'Salut, Luis.'

'So I see you didn't fall off and land in the shit,' Soames said in his rough but easy French.

'I fell a few times in the water,' said Luis. Even when people were joking it was best to stick near the truth. They suspected you'd lie so you didn't give them reason, unless you had cause to want to.

'At least you're not hurt,' said Etienne.

Why did he think Luis could hurt himself just falling off a horse? Perhaps he was laughing at him. It was better not to answer. Instead he'd tell Etienne what he'd learned from one of the travelling women in France. That would please him, anyway. 'I know Ida's still alive,' he said. 'Someone told me she's alive.'

Etienne took his arm and held it so hard it felt like a punishment. 'Who told you? How did they know? What did they know?'

'It was a woman. They know things we can't know without seeing.'

'Luis, you have a lot of ideas about women out of your imagination. I remember from before. Most women are just people. Women, but people.' You could think Etienne was laughing at him again, but he hadn't let go of the arm and Luis's fingers were beginning to go numb. He pulled away.

'She said she could see Ida where she was. She saw her in a wooden hut, in a town of wooden huts, she said. The woman said we'd find her again one day.' Luis's face felt wet as he spoke, but he didn't think it was from the river. He looked hard at Etienne to see if it was the same for him. It was, but he didn't look happy. What he had must be tears of unhappiness. Perhaps he didn't believe in the *baxt*, or didn't know about it. Luis would explain about that later.

Soames broke in with something in English, sounding impatient, but Etienne only laughed.

'What did Soames say?'

'He said we're like a pair of wailing virgins, standing here.'

Luis was interested in virgins. So far he'd only known the nurses in the camp for Bohemians. 'I've never known one with a hymen,' he said.

'You've got plenty of time in front of you for that,' said Etienne.

'How old are you, Luis?' Soames asked.

'About fourteen.'

'About,' Etienne said.

Soames stooped down from his great height to examine Luis more closely. 'You've got the start of a moustache all the same. Must be the sun. With that I reckon you'll be all right to go in pub. But stand behind me. Come on, I'm half dead with thirst.'

*

Luis drank port in the pub as the nearest thing to the wine he was used to. Beer looked like horse piss and he didn't fancy it. Each time Soames and Etienne bought another drink Luis had another port and he soon began to feel that his feet were off the ground and his head full of something blowing it up like one of the barrage balloons he'd seen near the east coast. From up here nothing seemed to matter much any more, and the smallness of the world down below gave you a feeling of power and freedom. By the time they walked out again into the road Luis's hold on reality was lost, he could tell that himself.

Outside there was a big car and a lot of people standing round it at a respectful distance, watching the people in it. They were standing quietly, the men with their hats off, leaving plenty of space in which two policemen in uniform were at attention.

'What's happening here?' said Etienne as he came out, his voice louder than before as if he too was a bit up in the sky. Soames answered him something in English and they both laughed, but it was an uncomfortable laugh and they kept back behind the people watching.

'What's it about?' Luis asked, hearing his own words as if someone else was speaking far off.

'Rich people. Come to watch ordinary ones enjoying themselves at the fair,' Etienne said. Luis, even far from reality as he was, could hear that Etienne only half meant the sarcastic way he said this.

'Not just rich,' Soames said.

'I know that,' said Etienne.

Another man in a dark uniform was opening the door of the car and helping someone very old get out of it. Luis had never seen anyone who looked so old. Travelling people have short lives. They say they wear themselves out on the road like a tyre. This old man must have been born when the world began. He was tall and thin and bent and white. His head was held down and forward stiffly as if he'd broken it off at the neck and they'd stuck it back as best they could to see him through the little time he had left. Everyone was staring at him as if they were afraid of him, like a Romany king. There was a young girl too, who got out on the other side and came round to hold the old man's arm. She was dressed in a uniform which Luis recognised as a nurse's by the badge on her cap and she looked at the old man softly almost as if he was a baby. Luis disapproved of how this beautiful young nurse gave all her attention to this old wooden statue with bloodless parts between his old wooden legs. Then he realised he must be the girl's ancestor.

'They've seen you,' Soames said in French to Etienne. Luis saw the girl staring at Etienne, and smiling and laughing, and waving her free hand. 'She wants you over there. Better go on, now they've seen you,' Soames said.

Etienne went forward into the empty space between the crowd and the car. Everyone made way for him. He nodded and smiled at the nurse, even bowed a little but didn't touch her, then he held out his hand to the old man who took it at once in both of his, kept it for a moment and returned it like a signed agreement. Like Romanies selling horses or daughters at the fair. For the first time Luis felt afraid of a world which had a place reserved for Etienne but none for him and Ida.

'Who are they?' he asked Soames.

'That old man, he's as good as a little king, up here.'

'Yes. Like a Romany king,' said Luis, confirmed in his guess.

'But a lot richer.'

'Can he order people to be killed?'

162

'He can send them down one of his coal mines under the sea. That kills them pretty quick. It killed my dad all right.'

Luis felt a great anger against the old man and everything to do with him. 'And who's that girl?' he asked.

'His granddaughter. She's the one Etienne was supposed to . . . the one they say he must marry.'

'But he can't.'

'Why can't he?'

'Because of Ida.'

'He's young, Luis. The girl's very young. People change. In the end they go back to their beginning however far they've gone away from it.'

Luis understood these were serious matters but the seriousness didn't stop his head from spinning or stifle the excited, angry laughter that was pushing up in him to burst out.

'What's her name?'

'She's called Glory.'

'Do you think Glory still has a hymen? Soames, do you believe it's still there?'

'That's a ninety-nine per cent certainty, in my book,' said Soames.

If he was right that was an unusual state of affairs for a nurse, as Luis well knew. 'I'm going to see.' He lurched sharply forward and Soames, with only half an arm free and one leg to the ground was too slow to catch him back. He pushed through the people like a ferret and before he or anyone else knew what was happening exactly he was between Etienne and the girl Glory. 'I'm old enough, I want to see.' Probably only Etienne understood his purpose when Luis lunged forward and took the hem of the nurse's skirt in his fist. The next thing Luis knew he was on the ground, there was a lot of noise and loud voices, and Etienne was holding out both his arms standing between where Luis lay with his head spinning faster and faster, and the policemen. Etienne was saying something in a calm voice, very clearly so the noise soon stopped, then he helped Luis up and walked him away, holding him round the shoulders. Soames met them at the fringe of the crowd, and at the same time the old man's driver came up and spoke to Soames. It seemed the old man wanted to speak to Soames too, because of his crutch and uniform. Soames went over and saluted as well as he was able and they exchanged a few words, then the old man stuck his thin shaky old hand out to signal that the meeting was at an end. Luis by now was feeling very, very ill, he turned from the public scene, went behind Etienne, crouched on the ground and vomited everything within him into the gutter. When it was over the sweat was pouring down his face but he felt better.

'Let's get out of here quick, all of us,' said Etienne, and pulled Luis roughly to his feet. 'It's not your fault, it's mine.' Luis agreed about that. Etienne was to blame for obeying the girl's call to him. If a woman wanted you it was for her to come to you, not summon you like a policeman. As soon as Luis had formulated this rule he saw Glory running towards them as they walked slowly in time to Soames's crutch in the direction where all the cars were parked in a field.

'Steve!' he heard her call, and the three of them stopped while she caught up. She spoke quickly for a minute with Etienne, then turned to Luis and spoke to him too, in careful French.

'We're sorry about the misunderstanding,' she said, and smiled at him, a wide smile which caused her eyes, which were very bright and brown but not very big, to nearly close up. Like that she looked like a very pretty sort of monkey. Luis under this smile began to feel a lot better, if rather tired. As she was holding out her hand to him he took it, wiped his mouth on the back of his sleeve, and kissed the hand to show he too was sorry about the misunderstanding. The hand was plump and soft and smelled good. He was quite sure she wouldn't have understood the idea he'd had in his head anyway. Not knowing he'd just been so sick in the gutter she looked pleased at her hand being kissed, and

Luis concluded that the misunderstanding was behind them and that they were now friends. He still wondered a bit about the hymen but obviously it wasn't going to be with her that he would have his first sight of one.

*

Back in the Wordsworth Soames sat with his stump stretched out and supported on a second chair in front of him. Pain dragged his features down and gave him an uncharacteristic tragic mask but Seagrave fetched him a quadruple whisky and the mask gradually lifted.

'What do we do now, to get in the clear?' he asked.

Seagrave was relieved to hear the question. He'd been afraid that Soames, having alerted him but then gauged the difficulties of the situation, would back out. His leg would give him the best of reasons for doing so but he showed no sign of it. Luis was sleeping it off in his house down near the quayside, on a sofa in the front room with the curtains drawn and the door locked from the outside. After parting from Glory they'd fetched Luis's bundles from the French-speaking Romanies who had befriended him, and made a sizeable contribution to their expenses past and future before leaving them with warm evocation of *baxt* on both sides. Luis had slept in the back of the Standard all the way from Brough to Whitehaven like one concussed. Perhaps he was concussed, from falling off too many times into the stony bed of the Eden. That would have to be sized up when he came round.

'We have another drink before anything else,' Seagrave answered, feeling fairly knocked sideways himself. The meeting with Glory, whose existence he had almost forgotten, had been the sort of surprise that forces you off course like a countercurrent in a spring tide.

'If you want my guess, there isn't a lot of time to lose,' said Soames. 'You're not supposed to be here and Luis, he's an illegal under-age immigrant who tried to get his hand up the Lord

Lieutenant's granddaughter's skirt. And me, I'm harbouring him. Locked up, every one of us, we'll be.' He laughed as he did when he approved the way things were going wrong.

'Glory promised to keep quiet.'

'Aye, but what about the old 'un?'

'She says he's only half there, these days.'

'That's the half that'll talk to your brother. Did he ask what you'd done in the War?'

'Oh yes. Of course.'

'And what did tha tell him?'

'I said I'd helped free the French.'

'He won't like that. He'll have thought all this time the War was *against* the French like they used to be in the good old days.'

*

Soames was quite right about one thing, and that was made clear next day when the landlord of the Wordsworth passed the message from William.

'You've to ring your brother at once in his Ministry,' Soames told him, 'and the best of luck with it.'

'I'll have a drink first and do it from here.'

'Fear nowt. It's all one in the end.'

'Not exactly, but thanks just the same.'

William, as foreseen, was extremely worked up. 'I've had old Haweswater on the telephone for half an hour,' he said. 'Gaga he may be but if he gets his teeth into something he never lets go. What the bloody hell have you been up to? You were over at Brough fraternising with the gypsy camp from what I can make out. I suppose it's the *nostalgie de la boue*.' This successful recourse to French seemed to calm him a little, and there was a pause. Then indignation returned in full force. 'So what have you got to say for yourself?' he roared as if he wished all his underlings throughout the Ministry to tremble at the scale of this blowing-up.

But Seagrave had caught a different note concealed in the

ensemble, the tiny piping of doubt. Perhaps Lord Haweswater had actually said something in his favour. To do with Glory maybe. The possibility entered his consciousness for the first time. He tried to rally and align his concerns in their priority. 'What I have to say is, where are you with your enquiries? With all the resources of the Ministry behind you? Where have you got?' Attack was the best approach. There was a silence.

'As a matter of fact that's the other thing I want to talk to you about. There's a certain progress. But not on the telephone, needless to say.' The tone had become strangely reasonable. 'I'm coming up on the night train. To see you. The garrison at Lancaster is supplying a staff car to take me straight over to Ravenglass. I'll be there for breakfast. Arrange to get there by lunchtime. There's probably a bus or something.'

'Can't your staff car bring you on to Whitehaven? We could have a sandwich at the Wordsworth. I'm not keen about going back.'

'Why not? You were born in the place. What's wrong with it?'

'Will you come to Whitehaven?'

'No, I certainly won't. And I can guarantee you one thing, I wouldn't ever set foot inside the Wordsworth if I did. The talk we've got to have is strict security. And by the way, on that subject, Haweswater says you were in the company of a man in uniform. Not an officer. Who is he?'

'A man who was wounded actually soldiering *in the field*, William.'

'Well, inform yourself about transport. Lunch will be at one. If you've got any belongings better bring them with you.'

'Why?'

'The turn of the wheel, my boy, the turn of the wheel.' He sounded in an odd way pleased with himself. Odd, because William's endemic condition was being pleased with himself but not normally in the context of Seagrave's existence. Something must have happened to lighten that burden. He communicated the gist of this conversation to Soames.

'Take the Standard. Go in style,' Soames said.

'You wouldn't come along too?'

Soames thought about this. 'Nay,' he said in the end. 'Words-worth's right for us.'

'Keep an eye on Luis while I'm gone.'

'Don't you worry about Luis. He can pick my brains on his favourite subject. Proper cunt-struck he is, poor lad.'

*

Irrational dismay filled Seagrave as he went through the gates. They used to stand open, signalling there was nothing to fear on either side, but not now. He got out and pushed them back, squeaking on their castors which ran each one along an iron arc embedded in the unweeded gravel. Once you were past them the house was clearly in view. The mass of stone, quarried long ago, lay like a dozing brontosaurus among the trees, dominating the river, the estuary, the sea approaches. It was as he used to see it in his romantic adoles-cence, a sea-beast crawled forth, that on a shelf of rock reposeth, there to sun itself, though as for sun in this locality a sea-beast would generally be out of luck. The Humber staff car was in the forecourt and its driver gave the Standard a contemptuous look as it drew up before the dead centre of the steps where Seagrave got out and left it. He nodded to the driver who grinned back derisively at him, knowing a prole out of line when he saw one.

''Ere cock, if I was you I wouldn't leave yer old crate there bang in the middle of everything unattended.'

'Why not?'

'Well, the Colonel, who is also the squire, a baronet of the Realm, and the next member of Parliament for this dump i'n't going to like it, is 'e?'

'In that case screw the Colonel, the squire and the member,' said Seagrave mildly just as William himself stepped forth from the entrance built like a portcullis to meet him.

'Commie. Where's yer uniform?' he heard the shocked voice of the driver mutter before William boomed up like a cannon on the threshold.

'If you've come in that thing, who's going to take it away from here I'd like to know?'

'Me of course.'

'Better come inside.' William turned to the driver and spoke to him far more genially. 'Er, let's see, Chaplin, that's it yes . . .'

'Parsons, sir.'

'That's right, well, Parsons, if you'd like to go through that arch there and report to the kitchen they'll be glad to give you a jolly good dinner and a pint or two of stout,' he said, and the driver saluted smartly, though to Seagrave's eye he looked as if he understood very well about the cordiality that precedes elections. You could vote for the opposition now and people like William would still be after you with the trappings of old-world courtesy in readiness for next time round.

'Has it ever struck you,' Seagrave asked as they entered the hall, 'how all this linen-fold panelling is very like the lining of the uterus?'

'As a matter of fact I don't recall those surroundings well enough to judge. But if that's why you didn't want to come back here I can understand it,' said William, showing unexpectedly rapid rebound from a joke intended to put him off his stroke. Maybe Seagrave underrated him. William might not be quite the bloody idiot he seemed. He was one, all the same. 'We'll go up to the library. Lead on, if by chance you remember your way out of the womb. There's practically no one here to do anything for one. I've had a small table laid there, no point in being formal.'

The small table was a gate-leg affair big enough to seat half a dozen or so of their more modest ancestors, and on it was laid out a cold meal – salmon, carved grouse, apple pasty with a jug of cream yellow from the cow, Stilton, Carr's biscuits, claret, port, nuts, grapes.

'Even with a skeleton household one can still manage reasonably,' said William. 'Of course none of this is out of anybody's rations.'

'Of course not. And what are they having down below, on their rations?'

'I haven't the remotest idea. And it's no business of ours. All I do know is they're keeping body and soul together pretty well. *And* someone's been coming and going in the cellar. No use making a fuss about it though. They'd leave in a body and go to old Haweswater who's short-staffed. I've brought up a Léoville-Barton '29. Will that do you?'

'I think we want some white Burgundy for the salmon,' said Seagrave, having decided to make no concessions while the going was as good as it seemed to be. William went off grumbling but without real resistance. When he was gone Seagrave got up and walked about inspecting the books. He wanted to check if he'd remembered the line about the sea-beast correctly. He found he had, except that the shelf was of rock *or* sand. For sun-bathing the sea-beast had a choice. Next to *The Poetical Works* in six volumes was a copy of *The Prelude*, decently bound with a tooled spine. The book stood in a dark corner of the room where the faded tones of calf ran indistinctly into the autumn foliage of a tapestry hung on the adjoining wall. He took the volume down. There was a letter stuck in the flyleaf over the poet's signature: 'My dear Sir William,' it began. The dedication was written in a very strong hand, rather large, sign manual of an ego solidly anchored in its own and the general esteem. 'Not seldom, roaming in your fair domains . . . have I seemed to perceive how all things revolve upon each other, as qualities, both in the natural and the moral world, pass insensibly *into their contraries* . . .' There was a good deal more of this before the signature but as Seagrave came to the words in italics he heard William's returning footstep on the last flight of stairs leading up to the library. Quickly and without considering it he put the book into his coat pocket. Things passing insensibly into their contraries, if that was a natural rule, must be taken as covering this switch in ownership of the volume from William to himself. It was the least the family home owed him. He would henceforth have *The Prelude* as fellow-exile.

William was a hearty consumer and in his company you had to look out for yourself if you were to get a fair share of what was going. The meal therefore passed mostly in silence. The claret was excellent and the port seemed to induce timelessness and a sense of distance from the material world, approaching coma. Nevertheless, the impression that William had some special reason to feel pleased with himself came through the well-being as if the pleasure was playing a constant light refrain in his inner ear. Seagrave waited. Where was the hurry? Cracking walnuts in silent thought was an index of patience. William would come to the boil in his own time.

'Have a cigar. Help yourself,' said William waving his hand at a domed silver box in front of him. This was an extraordinary offer, from him. He'd never offered Seagrave so much as a cigarette in his life before. Seagrave took one, breathed the aroma of the leaf carefully and when William went away to pump ship as he called it, he took another for Soames and slotted it in the pocket alongside *The Prelude*.

On his return William put himself importantly into the high armchair that had been their father's usual base. 'Stephen my boy, we've reached – we're about to reach rather – the parting of the ways.'

'What ways, William?'

'Well for God's sake, the ones that have caused our paths to cross in the last stage of a war neither of us might have survived.'

'But we have, and here we are together in what the poet called our fair domains.'

'What poet? What did he mean? You know I loathe poetry. I suppose you're trying to get a rise. You won't. As far as the domains are concerned, you're unlikely to see much more of them after today. If I'd been hit by a bomb it would all have been yours, but now we've come through I'm planning a family.'

'Congratulations.'

'Meanwhile I've found a way for our interests to coincide.'

171

'As the paths diverge?'

William lit his cigar and took a series of puffs, revolving it through a quarter turn before each as if its qualities might vary with rotation like patterns in a kaleidoscope. 'It's really an extraordinary thing that someone as spare as yourself should stir up high-level interest on either side of the Channel, let alone both, but believe it or not that's what seems to have happened. I've been putting in many thankless hours and effort on your behalf. It's reported the refugees living and dead run into millions. I shouldn't tell you this but I will . . .' He drank off his port to give himself the courage of his indiscretion. 'Intelligence speaks of systematic extermination. Would you credit it? Pass the port. Well obviously from a base in Whitehall there's no hope of finding and picking out a single case in all that, even if it's a woman carrying a supposedly British bas . . . baby. Does the girl speak any English?'

'Not a word. French, Spanish and a bit of Romani.'

'As I thought. And all these people are flooding the roads and washing over the fields like . . . like . . . wrack on the tides, back and forth.' William stopped, his eyes round with surprise at himself. An uncharacteristic flash of compassion had forced out of him what even he would have to own to as a poetic image, more or less. 'A number of camps where they and others may have been held for years have been located from the air. But with fighting going on and units breaking and reforming on all sides of all these people, it's a chaos like you can't imagine without seeing it. They're weak and on foot and trying to move west while the military current moves east.'

'Obviously all that's so. It's why I came to you. The only chance for any individual would be if someone was looking for her. That's what you were supposed to set up. In good time for the election.'

At the word election William sat forward in the paternal chair and all his features fell into order, pugnacious and sly, as if a bell had been rung. 'Wait and hear what I've got to tell you. Our services, at my behest, contacted our opposite number in the newly-formed French government in Paris. Nearer the scene of the crime so to speak. And what do I find? That your name . . . our name . . . is not unknown to the Frog intelligence services. My first reaction naturally was that you'd put your foot in it in some sensitive spot as you usually do. Judge my astonishment when I learn that this isn't the case at all. They want you back over there as fast as possible on account of the high value they put on you. They don't want you going astray before they've given you tokens of esteem. Anxiety was even expressed in case your own country might hold you and charge you and make you unavailable for some time to come, frustrating them of their wish to do the honours. Anyway that's the drift. Do you know a man of the name of d'Albaron?'

'Of course I do.'

'A count of some sort, apparently. Not that that means a great deal on the other side of the water as we all know.' William grunted and heaved like a British farmer faced with a livestock pedigree from abroad.

'As a matter of fact he was chief of the Resistance in the whole region. Regarded as a hero.'

'Really.'

'He carried a general's responsibilities, at least.'

'I wonder.'

'A very old family.'

'Ah.'

'His elder brother's a marquis. I know them all quite well.'

'Is he? Do you? Is that so?' William still looked sceptical but as if he would try to recall these mitigating circumstances if ever a thought of Seagrave should re-enter his head in the future. 'So you didn't spend quite all your time hobnobbing with the gypsies then?'

'Don't try and make a virtue out of snobbery, William. They're very fine people by nature. Get back to the point.'

William smiled. It was he who had managed to get the rise.

'Where was I? D'Albaron. Yes. Well he's the source of the messages we've been receiving. No direct contact, naturally. All passed through intermediaries.'

'Oh naturally.'

'The upshot is they think they can help you.'

'Charles d'Albaron thinks that?'

'I don't know his Christian name but that's the burden of it.'

'But it's a most splendid piece of news. He helped before, getting Ida out of the internment camp in the Camargue.'

'Was that when she went to Jean?'

'Yes. He supplied the bribe to the commandant and the truck into the mountains. I owe him more than I can ever repay.'

'I see. Didn't do Jean much of a favour. The long and short of it is they want you back in France and they'll take over where I leave off, thank God, I mean the searches. So first thing tomorrow morning I'm shooting you back over there. You fly from Newcastle in an RAF transport going to some town bang in the middle. I located it on the map.' He pulled a notebook from his pocket and turned the pages tenderly. 'Clermont-Ferrand. They make tyres there, I looked it up. D'Albaron will meet you and after that you're his problem.'

'My passport's only got about a month to go.'

'I've arranged a new one. We have a service for that sort of thing. The photograph may look a bit weird: it was taken when you were about seventeen and I've had it doctored. Valid five years. Plenty of time to settle somewhere in foreign parts and go native. Canada was my first thought but you didn't take to it. See what our neighbours will do for you. Naturalise yourself, after all the red-legged partridge managed to do it on this side.' He handed Seagrave the bright new blue and gilt booklet with the name and qualities of Anthony Eden inside the cover in place of those of Lord Halifax, whose coat-of-arms and coronet had decorated its predecessor. It seemed a bit of a come-down.

'Hang on, William. It's more complicated than you think.'

'It couldn't be. Pass me over the decanter. The port, not the claret. The port, man, the port.'

'There's a young boy here at Whitehaven I'd have to take back to France. He hasn't any papers at all.'

William choked on his mouthful of port and his eyes started from his head. 'A *boy*, did you say? In *Whitehaven*? Good God if it's come to that I can't get both of you out fast enough. I thought you came up here to chase after young Glory Egremont. So did Haweswater. So did she, he says. A *boy* . . . in *Whitehaven* . . .'

It was Seagrave's turn to smile. He'd earned the rise the hard way. 'You've got it all wrong. It's a way you have, William, did you know that? This is Ida's young brother. I've been more or less responsible for him since he was a child.'

'How did you get him to England?'

'He came over with some Romanies in a fishing boat.'

'Smuggled?'

'They do sidestep the formalities, if that's what you mean.'

'Good. No one knows he's here. The RAF can boot the two of you out at Clermont-Ferrand where the tyres come from and no questions asked. It's a great relief.'

'There could be a third man.'

'Who? Not another brother?'

'He's a British soldier who lost a foot and half a leg in the Ardennes. A local man. I mentioned him to you. I think he might like to go back to France too.'

'Well you're not being parachuted. I suppose they can fit him in. And the fewer there are of your friends in this constituency . . . Where are they?'

'Probably in the Wordsworth.'

'Ring them. No, don't ring them. Never take any security risk in a pub. You'll have to go over. Bring them here tonight. The aircraft takes off at five thirty in the morning. My driver can follow you into Whitehaven and bring the whole party back. Meet him somewhere well away from the Wordsworth after dark.'

175

Seagrave thought for a moment about this plan. There was a great rift between here with all it represented and the world in which he knew Soames and Luis and where the balance of disparities held in an equilibrium suiting them all. Here, as Soames had seen at once, it would be too different. 'No,' he said, taking final leave of his origins, 'the driver must pick us up in Whitehaven in the morning. I'll telephone and give the rendezvous. Before dawn in a back street it'll be even more discreet. And you won't be troubled with us here.'

'That's a consideration, I agree. And what your friends on the other side make of this ill-assorted contingent stepping off a warplane is their business. Just as long as they don't send any of you back here.'

'They won't. Charles d'Albaron knows Soames from the Resistance.'

'So he was in that too was he? I presume he's invalided out of the Army?'

'Yes.'

'If not, even a Military Assistant Secretary in the Cabinet Offices couldn't safely fly him off in civilian clothes to the south of France without clearing it.' William rose, threw the end of his cigar into the fireplace and held out a hand to Seagrave as if to pull him to his feet. 'Well, Stephen, I won't detain you. I've taken the line of action you wanted and now it only remains to wish you luck in the future, wherever that takes you.'

'And I'll wish you luck with the election. And the family. Perhaps by the time we meet again you'll be a minister. In the Cabinet not just in the offices.'

'The contingency seems a very remote one,' said William coldly.

'Surely your merits will be recognised for what they are?'

'I referred to the likelihood of another meeting.'

'Well thanks anyway for a lunch such as few people can have seen for a longish time.'

'I didn't want to send you on your way without some ...

acknowledgement of the undeniable fact you were born here.'

After these formal exchanges there didn't seem anything more to be said. Seagrave was glad to leave as William was to see him go. Fraternity had withered on the branch.

'I'd rather like to say goodbye to my old room.' It was a stray anachronistic impulse, a puerile weakness.

'Sorry, you can't. All that part of the house is shut up for the duration. Dry rot.' On the way down the stairs a last thought seemed to strike William. 'By the by, what am I to say to Haweswater about young Glory?'

'About Glory?'

'And yourself.'

'Do you have to say something? She's a nice girl, I like her very much. I'd really . . . but I'm committed. Hard as that may be for you to explain.'

'You're not tied. We all have previous arrangements to get out of when the time's ripe. I have myself.'

'For me, exchanging love ties you up for good. It's a bond. Like giving your word.'

'Always have to make yourself different. Out of it, right out of everything . . . normal,' were William's farewell words as he turned sharply back in under the archway of the door.

*

Soames smoked the cigar that evening in the Wordsworth as provocation, Seagrave thought. No such cigar had been seen in there since the start of the War, possibly never. Cigars of that length and bore were a symbol of the men who owned the coal seams, not those who burrowed them out.

'Where did tha get it, John?' he would be asked by each new arrival in the bar.

'It came with compliments of a grateful cabinet,' he said.

'It's a right big 'un.'

'What's a cabinet?' asked someone else.

'The buggers that govern us.'

Because of the sacrifice of his foot, most people half believed this explanation. It added to the mystique now attaching to him and without which his unusual height and lofty manner would have aroused strong native impulses to cut him down to size. Once he thought he'd got all the mileage there was to be had out of the cigar he withdrew with Seagrave and their drinks into the parlour.

'Folk in the shadow, the better they know you the worse they like it when you're in the sunshine for a bit,' Soames said cryptically.

'Makes you feel a stranger here,' said Seagrave.

'No, nothing'd do that. You'll come back to it one day yourself. Have to, in the end.'

Soames had jumped at the prospect of returning to France so soon and so simply. Seagrave suspected a hankering after the girl who'd followed the Liberation parade round the boulevards at Nîmes. Here in Whitehaven Soames had a connection with a war widow, no longer very young, living a street or two away. He claimed it was a military duty in all circumstances to stand in for a fallen comrade.

'Always keeps her stockings on in memory of poor old Jim who fancied it that way,' he confided to Seagrave. 'Black, they are. Makes a man feel a bit of a ghost, there's the only thing.'

'Will you be going over to say goodbye to her?'

Soames laughed, leaving the question unanswered.

It was raining in Newcastle and an icy wind blew in off the North Sea as they crossed the grass and tarmac to reach the plane. Soames had a lot of pain first thing in the morning and worked it off in blasphemies which seemed to upset the airmen.

'Superstition. Afeard of thunderbolts,' said Soames to explain this unusual effect.

Luis had never been anywhere near an aeroplane before and as he watched the hooded lights of the runway recede through the small round window in the fuselage there seemed an element of disapproval in his wonder. Perhaps hubris was known to have a negative influence on *baxt*. Seagrave could only hope it wasn't so. Copious *baxt* was what was going to be needed now, free from curses and away from this fortress built by Nature for herself. Let her keep it, he thought, as the engines settled into a cruising rhythm, and over the eastern horizon a band of light fine as cheesewire began to cut up into the round throat of the darkness.

Part Three

Chapter Nine

A CAP OF SNOW LIKE A dressing of cream overlay the cone of the highest of the volcanoes and there was white frost on the grass of the airfield. Philippe d'Albaron, dressed in a long overcoat with astrakhan collar, warmer really than the temperature warranted, stood watching the passengers as they crossed from the aircraft to the stepladder which had been wheeled from a shed and over the grass. There was someone on board unable or unwilling to jump the short distance to the ground. In the end this man had to be lowered with the help of ropes because the stepladder had no handrail. Philippe walked in a leisurely way towards the little group finally assembled with their parcels and bundles a few yards from the plane which after a minute or two began to swivel slowly on its axis to put its nose into the wind like a gundog.

'I didn't expect a party but I'm glad to see you all,' said Philippe as his eye ran over each of them in turn and came to rest on Luis. 'Very glad.'

'And I wasn't expecting you,' said Seagrave.

'What were you expecting?'

'Your uncle Charles.'

'Charles?' Philippe laughed with a little contemptuous note. 'You won't be seeing anything of Charles for some time.'

'What's happened to him?'

'He's in prison for refusing to obey the order to return to his post at the Quai d'Orsay. I told you he wouldn't last long after the

Liberation as a generalissimo. Dear old Charles is an innocent under his worldly air. But they won't keep him long under lock and key. Just long enough to separate him from those friends of yours on the far left.'

'So it was you, not him, in touch with my brother's ministry?'

'But of course.'

'What for?'

'To get you back here.'

'I know. But why?'

'Because my master wishes to know you better. Better than through the end of a camera lens.'

'Your master?' Seagrave asked, foreseeing the answer but wanting to hear it spoken.

'*Monsieur le Ministre de l'Information*. Otherwise, Henri Fernand-Félix.'

'You're working for him?'

'His right-hand man. Private secretary, confidant, aide-de-camp if you like. It's the first rung.'

'To where?'

'The future. Fortune and power. The centre of the stage.'

Philippe had come to the airfield in a black official Panhard exactly like those used formerly by the Milice. In a past distant only in weeks. Soames sat beside the driver with his crutches and his stump enveloped against gangrene in an impervious wrapping like a parcel that could weep in transit, Seagrave and Philippe and Luis compressed on the back seat. Luis had manoeuvred Seagrave into the middle place.

'I remember seeing you escorted in a car like this one the day you were due to meet your present master in Montpellier. I assumed he'd turned you in.'

'Ah yes.'

'It didn't look then like the first rung to anywhere except hell.'

'If I had a word of advice for you, my dear Stephen, it would be to mistrust appearances. Cultivate the habit of looking beyond and on the other side. Only the naive like Charles put their faith in unshifting alignments. As a career diplomat he should have known better.'

'Perhaps it's why he didn't want to go back to the Quai d'Orsay.'

The car drove at speed through villages and countryside of this high region on roads almost empty. The surface, compared with those in England, was in a bad state, churned and potholed by the passage of tanks.

'Tell him to drive slower. My friend's wound is only half healed up.'

Philippe shrugged. 'We're late enough. I've got a lot of work to get through today,' he said, and pointed out of the window at a distant château, four-square with corner turrets decapitated at the Revolution, standing on a hillside above the course of a river and a forest of poplars. 'That's where we're going.'

'Is it the seat of the Fernand-Félix family?'

Philippe's laugh this time was wholehearted but held, to Seagrave's ear, a touch of rancour. 'Fernand's childhood was passed over a grocery store in Clermont where we've just come from. The *Epicerie Félix*. The hyphen in the name came along later when he took up the law. He was a gifted child.'

When they reached the château it appeared dilapidated, rough grass and saplings growing up against the defensive walls, shutters missing, roof neglected. A couple of trees blown down some time ago were still half across the track approaching the building, a few branches lopped to leave a passage.

'Fucking shambles round here,' said Soames.

'What does he say?'

'He noticed the lack of maintenance, that's all.'

'Fernand's only just bought it.'

The château was built round three sides of a small courtyard, the fourth closed from the outside by a wall with double doors of grey splitting wood. In the centre of the yard was a stone wellhead. The doorway and windows on one side were late Gothic but round the other two there was an open arcaded gallery on Tuscan columns. The place must have been built when the new style was being imported from Italy, when English houses were still either hovels or keeps.

'Don't waste time looking round. There's nothing at all unusual here except the people. And Fernand hates being kept waiting. This way.'

Philippe led the way along a passage, past a stair rising through a turret from the courtyard, and finally into a vaulted dining room. Seen through the window at the end the distant snow caps hung as if parachuted out of the blue above. The room was crowded with dark furniture including a table on one end of which a lot of papers were laid out. The whole of one wall of this room, between the springing lines of the vault, was occupied by a painting of Silenus and his acolytes surrounded by all the spoils of debauchery, and hung in a gigantic gilded frame carved in the form of fruit, game, utensils of the table and the chase, heads of horse and hound, a swelling breast here and there among the other trophies.

Soames stood beneath the canvas examining the details. 'Old feller's got the smallest tool on him I ever saw on anyone. Pathetic,' he said.

'What does he say now?'

'He says the central figure's not very well endowed.'

'Appearances again. It could be an instance of *multum in parvo*,' said Philippe with something like a return to his old self. 'Translate that.'

'Philippe points out the member's telescopic.'

'Does 'e, well I were pointing out it's microscopic, that's all,' said Soames who had passed on from Silenus to consider a female form near the corner of the picture, fallen and apparently a good deal bruised in the general action. 'She's taken a hammering too, poor cow.' Clearly Soames found the environment inimical and the rough ride in the car had not improved his humour. 'I'm with you, darling, all the way,' he said.

At this moment a door in a low opening in the darkest angle of the room was thrown open so that it crashed back against the stone masonry behind it. Standing there now, the crown of his head several inches below the lintel, was the squat, compressed, energetic form of Fernand-Félix. Like an actor he held his entrance for a lengthy moment, every gramme of psychic force engaged in fixing himself as the focus of unshared attention. Competing with Silenus and the orgy, this was a feat. He was motionless but for the eyelids which beat and fluttered like hovering wings.

'Present us, Philippe,' he said at last, and took a step forward, halting far enough away so that those presented would have to approach for inspection. No illusion of informality was possible, yet his hand, when Seagrave took it, felt dry and warm and even seemed to convey a certain affability by pressure fractionally prolonged.

'I've heard you were with us in the Resistance from the earliest time,' he said. 'I'm grateful to any who served our movement.' He made it sound as if the movement had been peculiarly and emotionally his creature. 'But now we have to face the sequel to all our adventures, isn't that so? Philippe, take these other . . . gentlemen . . . away with you. Install them. I'll send when I need you again.' His tone in issuing orders was more polite than William's, but also more absolute as if – as was certainly the case – the underlying sanctions must be taken a good deal more seriously. He had put a hand through Seagrave's arm and held it firmly so that it touched against his own side as he led him back through the low doorway where he'd come in. Beyond was a small circular room, evidently the ground floor of one of the corner turrets, containing several pieces of valuable-looking furniture. There was a feeling of feminine occupation, the odour of clothes, perhaps, kept in drawers scented with rose petals or lavender, nothing chic. 'Sit down,' said Fernand-Félix, doing so himself in one of a pair of upright chairs. 'In here we're far from the outside world and safe from interruption. The walls are very thick and privacy gives one confidence, don't you agree? And we need to have full confidence in each other.'

'Do we? I put my confidence in what I thought I was being told. That Charles d'Albaron was ready and willing to help me find a girl I'm looking for, a refugee somewhere.' It sounded thin, the sort of story a captive reels off to postpone the start of the questioning.

'Monsieur Charles d'Albaron has plenty of problems of his own at the moment.'

'Philippe mentioned them. I was sorry to hear it. It seems all wrong.' Fernand-Félix said nothing to this but leaning forward slightly he bestowed on Seagrave from large dark, preternaturally brilliant eyes a look of warm appreciation, showing that he too knew what it was to feel for the inconveniences of a dear friend. In every expression, every movement, ran a current of charm, a voltage generated inexhaustibly and without limit. 'But it seems the messages weren't coming from him.'

'They were, naturally, coming from Philippe on my orders.'

'Can you help me then?' Seagrave felt as he put the question just as he had at the moment of taking the photograph in the yard behind the station at Nîmes – objective, curious, concentrated.

'Possibly. Possibly.' A kind of rehearsal of the act of speech seemed to run through the muscles surrounding his mouth, wide and mobile, a tremor like an echo of the fluttering lids. To Seagrave it looked like the outward sign of tactical meditation. 'The more so, perhaps, that your desire is the greater. The more you want it the easier it should be to agree terms. And in France, remember, we respect desire. That's another thing. We foreground desire. The world, after all, turns on it.'

'The grand elementary principle of pleasure,' said Seagrave who in the half light of the aircraft as it crossed the sea and sailed over the broad northern plains had been reading an introductory passage in the purloined edition of *The Prelude*.

Fernand-Félix seemed to listen to this in silence, turning it round in his ear like a phrase of music, with the same sensory keenness. 'There's something familiar there ... a long time before Professor Freud, I think. Will you render what you said into

English please?' Seagrave did so. 'Ah yes, of course, I know it. But your word "grand" in the context has not the same resonance as the French *grand*.'

'Like many English words it has much more resonance. It sounds and resounds.'

'You mean perhaps that it is Romantic,' said Fernand, rolling the 'r' as a mime rolls his eyes, to express susceptibility to the sublime. Then he went on to declaim in English with a strong accent but no want of confidence, ' "The grand elementary principle of pleasure, by which man knows, and feels, and lives, and moves." What magnificent rhetoric, my dear young friend!' He put his hand on Seagrave's knee, almost with affection. 'And all that in apology for pleasure! Which with us needs none. But magnificent, all the same.'

'You read a lot in English?'

'Under the alien heel it came as the breath of all liberty. English then was the impassioned expression, if I may adapt, in the face of all Resistance.'

His own expression was so impassioned that even Seagrave, with solid evidence to the contrary, felt almost won over to the myth of Fernand-Félix as heroic resistant. Nevertheless, they were here together in this little round room because that was not how things had been.

'We must come to the point,' said Fernand, and taking a gold snuff-box from his pocket he opened it behind his hand and carried some of the substance it contained to each nostril in turn. The gesture drew Seagrave's attention to his nose. This noble feature was carved like a monument into the more unassuming surroundings of his face. It gave something ecclesiastic to the whole aspect. 'You have your camera with you?'

'Yes.'

'And your film?'

'I managed to find one or two in London. They're hard to come by.'

'I'm glad to hear that.' The mouth and eyelids continued their local agitation while the nose, superb, advanced a little closer, an engine of siege. 'But I didn't mean new film. Your new film, I will be delighted if you use it to record the present state of this château which I plan to restore to its historical glory. That could be an interesting record. I referred to what one might call your film archive in its small way. Your work of the last months. Since the month of May, to be exact.'

'I left all that in safekeeping with my brother in London.' When he'd said this Seagrave felt it in some obscure way as a blunder. Fernand-Félix obviously believed him because he himself would certainly lodge any potential blackmailing material in a very secure place. It was too late now to withdraw the lie. As soon as uttered he could see new perspectives of danger open out in Fernand's thoughts which seemed to race along them into the contingent darkness. The right tactic would have been to go on showing himself as a unit of no importance, merely provisional holder of certain evidence for possible exchange. Bringing his brother into it put him, Seagrave, in a different light, as someone who might have to be reckoned with on his own account. 'Temporarily and under seal of course,' he added, but the shot had parted.

'Under seal. With your brother. A high officer in your Ministry of Defence, Philippe tells me. How quickly could you recover the film, if necessary?'

'Very quickly I think.' Should he point out that it could be flown over as easily as he'd been flown himself? Better not. It might just be another step in the wrong direction.

'Your brother would send it in another aeroplane?'

'I'm sure he would.'

'Then he must have some idea of the importance of your sealed package.'

'No, he knows nothing about it. He'd just send it at once – fraternally if you see what I mean.' Lying was uncomfortable if the stakes were high, but this particular lie had a picturesque side that made it a pleasure to tell.

'Ah yes, good family feeling. I respect that too. I have brothers. Sister also. Very united.' Seagrave felt surprised to learn it. Fernand-Félix had seemed to him a man too singled-out to be one of a bunch of siblings. The others could only be nonentities in his shadow. 'To return to the problem of your film, placed securely but indiscreetly in a Ministry. I think we understand each other. You're an intelligent young man who can quote the poets on pleasure. That shows a good mind. If one can be philosophical about pleasure one can be philosophical about anything.' He looked for a moment into an imaginary distance as if viewing there his own pleasures in contour. 'I'm interested in possessing the negatives as well as prints of any film in which I appear. I think it a historical duty.'

'I did photograph you during your speech at the Liberation parade in Nîmes. That was certainly a great historical occasion. But all my films are in negative. None of them have been printed.'

'There are no prints in existence?'

'Only negative. As I said.' Fernand would make his own way by degrees to the essential point.

'Good. Good. That at least is something. A print I believe can be very easily doctored. But as you know, I had in mind an earlier occasion . . . than that day of my speech.'

'Yes?'

'One evening . . . at twilight . . . perhaps the light was not sufficient for a clear image? At the railway. Come. We needn't play longer with each other.'

'An entrainment? What I'm interested in is finding someone who was also probably deported. A victim of the process.' From inexperience Seagrave didn't know if he was advancing his counters well or badly. No firm offer of help had yet been made. Time was short. A woman refugee with a small child could die on the road from any of a number of causes – starvation, illness, rape – could you die of that? It seemed like the idea of a death to him. Casual brutality or exhaustion were other ways of ending at any time, out there among the wandering hordes.

'The scene itself and my presence on it were ambiguous. Various accounts could be given. I needn't go into it. But the photograph, assuming the image is a clear one, would only be interpreted in one way. The hostile way.'

'By a hostile viewer.' This was a concession. Almost any viewer of that scene would be hostile. Seagrave saw that he had been eased by charm into letting Fernand-Félix down lightly.

'That's what all viewers are when you overtake them on the road to power. The destination generates the envy. It's the same for poets on the way to immortality. Think of the line "bliss was it in that dawn to be alive" – it seems even Byron was envious. Byron was perhaps a little greedy about other people's revolutions, it's true.' Fernand took another sniff from his gold box. His eyes seemed even blacker than before, a piercing light behind them rendering the black still denser. Quoting the line in English had given him a triumphant look. In a way, he merited it.

'That dawn was a long time ago now. Recently the prospects for some haven't been so good.'

'At your age, the dawn should seem a promise for ever.' Either the verse or the substance in the little gold box had gone to Fernand's head. He was moving out of the corner where his hand could be forced and into the never-never land of eternity's sunrise. He must be brought back.

'What will you do in exchange for those negatives?'

'Have them sent here for examination and we'll discuss those details then. There's a telephone in the château, the line connects through the Ministry. You can telephone your brother at the public expense.'

'Not before I know what you're offering to do for me.' This seemed the right line. Fernand-Félix put out a hand again and patted Seagrave on the knee.

'I'll do things just how you like, my dear boy. You're a charming case of a bucolic lover. You call out my protective feelings. Of course you must first know what I'll do for you, and I'll tell you. I can set the services of my Ministry onto the trail of this missing young person, as soon as we have contact with the first refugees. But my Ministry isn't one of the great agencies of the state – to be frank I hardly expect to remain long in so limited a sphere – but there are also the services of my friend the Minister of the Interior. They can be called on too. The Minister of the Interior is very much in my debt in several respects.' The way he said this made it sound a most unenviable situation for this minister described as a friend to be in.

'Will they start at once?'

'I see you haunted by passion. You'd have the civil servants and their informers running over the Rhine before even the armies have crossed it. The War isn't ended yet, my friend. We're only able to speculate about the fate of all these poor, poor people.' Fernand checked himself here as if even for him there were limits. He smiled, disclosing uneven teeth dominated by exceptionally powerful canines. As if aware of the impression, not wholly favourable, that these could make on the sensitive, the smile was eclipsed as abruptly as it had come. 'But the wheels can be started turning. And the efficacy of our administration is the envy of . . . administrations everywhere. If one holds the key. Even during the Occupation . . .' He left the sentence hanging in the air. 'All the same we must be realistic. It may be months before we find anything definite, one way or the other. We may even never . . .' Fernand pulled himself up short of this terrible faux pas. 'We may even not know till we light on the missing treasure whether we're on the right track.' It was a recovery, if not a brilliant one. Seagrave saw that the most experienced negotiator can slip.

'I'll leave the negatives where they are in London with the Defence Ministry until your own comes up with convincing results.' He'd sat well back in the upright chair and crossed his legs and spoke with a breezy familiarity. It was interesting how easily you got into the way of this sort of thing.

'You realise you're expecting me to mobilise two whole French

Ministries overwhelmed by urgent work, without any proof seen with my own eyes that the image in the photograph is unmistakable . . . enough to make it all necessary?'

'Oh believe me it is. I could get a print run of it over there and sent just to convince you. One of my brother's subordinates could do it. I'd only have to explain on the telephone which one it is.'

Fernand-Félix knew a bluff impossible to call when he saw it. 'You must give Philippe all the description of the girl you possibly can. Have you any photographs of her, you always so ready with your little camera?'

'Just one, not a very good one. It shows her laughing. She didn't laugh often.'

'Well I suppose that may not help us much now.' They were both silent for a moment over the implications of a laughing likeness in the circumstances. 'Don't leave out any physical detail that could identify the subject, alive or not. Even intimate details, if you think of anything useful. Be dispassionate about it. Think of it as filling an anthropometric dossier. That was something done by the late occupiers, on these people. Do it in the interests of the living. You needn't feel uneasy with Philippe, I don't think he's likely to find his interest aroused. That's one of the reasons he's so useful to me. I can trust him with certain missions I would never dream of confiding to a young man like yourself.'

Fernand-Félix smiled again, the canines sliding out of cover and in again like adders at play. Seagrave had a feeling Fernand was quite well-disposed towards him personally; a sort of incongruous affection had entered their relations in the course of negotiation like an animal affinity between combatants.

The floor of the dining room was tiled and, from his position near the door, Seagrave had heard a shuffling advance over it, an approaching presence like ghostly generations returned.

'Henri. Henri.' It was a woman's voice, pitched rather high and in spite of a quavering note having something imperious about it.

194

Fernand-Félix looked put out by this interruption. He got up and went to the door.

'I'm here, Marie-Louise.'

'Of course you are. I know where you are. I know every cubic centimetre of the building please remember. I want something in my secretaire.' She shuffled determinedly towards one of the exquisite pieces of furniture.

'My secretaire, kindly you remember. My secretaire now.'

'Very well, *your* secretaire, if you insist. So vulgarly. Who is this young man?' She wasn't actually at all old but seemed to want to pretend to be as if that was her only defence against unkindness or discourtesy. Seagrave imagined that if she was somehow tied up with Fernand-Félix there could be plenty of unkindness included in the deal. She was very pretty in a faded way, he decided, and not all that faded, with fair hair carried up and arranged with the greatest care to fall about her head in swathes and loops as casual as those of Silenus's fallen playmate in the painting next door. In fact when he thought about it he could see a distinct relation between the painting and this lady's studied appearance, if you subtracted the clothes she had on. She looked a bit beaten too. Maybe like the secretaire the picture used to be hers.

'This is Stephen Seagrave, a friend of Philippe's.' Seagrave missed the lady's name, rattled off by Fernand-Félix as if it was a detail that it didn't concern him to know. She took his hand between both of hers and still holding onto it sat down in the chair he had just vacated.

'An Englishman!' she said in a voice of awe. 'What we owe you! It can never be repaid! Such valour, while so many men here were basely compromised with our enemies!' She looked rapidly at Fernand-Félix and away again, to rest her sharp blue eyes on the face of this uncouth temporary hero standing before her in what had once been her boudoir. Seagrave felt his hand very faintly, very subtly caressed between hers, the lightest minimal friction which put him, as soon as he noticed it, into a state of imminent erection.

He passed his free hand in front of his crutch and bowed forward slightly from the waist.

'I feel very honoured, Madame,' he said, and saw the blue eyes drop down to alight on the sheltering hand like a bird on the worm. 'But I promise you I know a great many heroic French resistants.'

'Do you? Do you know my little brother Charles? Philippe's uncle?'

'Yes of course I do. He was our chief.'

'They've put him in prison now, Henri's friends in the government. Did you know that? A hero of the Resistance already imprisoned by Frenchmen. That's how it always is in France, ever since we let the reins of power fall into the hands of the wretched bourgeoisie.' She looked once more at Fernand-Félix, with an expression both defiant and pleading.

'Nonsense, Marie-Louise. Let me say you talk the most unhistorical absurd nonsense I ever heard. And coming from a family like yours you're lucky to exist at all. The whole brood of your effete forebears could have been wiped out, and better for France if it had.'

'Then you would never have been able to buy my château from me and my farm and my woods down to the Allier, and myself to go with them.' Marie-Louise was in tears now, silent tears which ran down her cheeks like a small quantity of glycerine, while her hold on Seagrave's hand had tightened as if she suspected him of planning to slip out of her clutch leaving her ungratified. In every way, the situation had become most uncomfortable. Someone of Fernand's experience and authority ought to be able to resolve this with less indignity all round, Seagrave felt. 'Or my furniture to give yourself the airs of a nobleman. Or my Rubens orgy to give you ideas you might not have, in your poor bourgeois imagination . . .' Now she directed a barely perceptible smile at Fernand, sly, quick and suggestive, to which he seemed to respond with a lightening of his thundery aspect. It looked as if this sort of sparring was a ritual to be varied and spiced according to circumstances. 'I may not be one of your little girls,' she snivelled, 'but your little girls don't bring you any châteaux with them when they come.'

'Be quiet,' said Fernand-Félix.

'All your little girls bring you probably are the infections they've caught down on the farm.'

Seagrave reclaimed his hand, firmly but not roughly. He found Marie-Louise very appealing in her way, but clearly it was Fernand she was really interested in. He noticed for the first time a sort of narrow day-bed constructed on the round to fit the circular wall of the room, and covered in pink stripy silk upholstery which brought vividly to mind the serried wheals with which Rubens – if indeed it was him – had decorated the figure in the painting. It was high time to make himself scarce and let them get on with it.

Chapter Ten

PHILIPPE NOTED THE details on the ruled pages of an official note-book like a policeman. Seagrave saw *Ministère de l'Information* stamped on the leather cover in black lettering. Philippe was greatly changed from the part-time anarchist he'd been at the university. Now it was not only his functions, which in those days would have roused caustic hilarity, that he took with deadly seriousness. It was power itself, an edifice in which he believed and worshipped.

'I'll take the photograph. This isn't what the Ministry's for, but if it's what the Minister wants I must obey.' Fernand-Félix had been right about Philippe not being inflamed by the details. Even when Seagrave described a beauty spot Ida had on the inside of her left thigh he was unmoved. 'Dark-coloured non-malignant mole fifteen centimetres above the left knee on inner face of limb,' he noted. Seagrave was surprised because he had thought Philippe strongly attracted by Ida; in fact it had been, he thought, a cause of reserve between them. Perhaps the attraction had worn thin in absence.

Soames and Philippe had not hit it off, that was apparent. As soon as Seagrave saw them together he'd realised that Soames's suspension in his own case of general disapproval of the ruling classes was privileged treatment. Soames's criteria were strict and it looked as if Philippe didn't meet them. The reasons for this might never be known. There it was because it was there.

'Any friend of yours can be a friend of mine, but I don't mind mentioning, I'll be keeping my back to the wall,' Soames said, and Seagrave remembered the visiting card passed to Luis at the Liberation parade.

'What about Luis?'

'He'll learn.'

'He told me there were pederasts in the camp where he was.'

'That's what you call them is it? Well if he's met some before he won't be so surprised, will he, when he comes under fire from the rear.' Soames said this without humour, proof that he was ill at ease here. They had been given rooms in an outbuilding at the side of the château walls, crammed with discarded furniture, harness, utensils which had once had a use but now were thrown in here as if the last person to know what it was had long ago disappeared. 'Right graveyard it is,' said Soames, and he looked as if the chill had entered his system through the stump of his leg. By nightfall it was cold, with a cold that seemed at first no more than a touch from the black hand of frost living and waiting under the ground of this high region far from the nearest sea.

'Where is Luis?'

'He went collecting wood; I can't do much and if we don't have a good fire we'll be lumber by morning, same as all this old junk.' Soames banged with his crutch on the side of an upright piano which gave an answering gasp like a sheep not quite dead in the corner of a field.

'How long ago was that?'

'Couple of hours.'

'Which way did he go?'

Soames didn't know which way Luis had gone. It was obvious he considered Luis a free agent and big enough to see to himself while he, Soames, had a bad pain at the end of his stump, disliked his surroundings, and was feeling more and more depressed as the cold grew, and the dark came down.

'For God's sake, Soames, cheer up,' said Seagrave, then he saw that the depression deserved as much respect as the pain. 'OK, I'll go and find a bit of wood myself. We can always chop up some of the furniture, Luis'll turn up in his own time.'

'Good lad.'

*

When Luis eventually did turn up he was silent, as if regressed into a zone of feeling where language had nothing to say. Until he'd thawed by the fire he looked, too, like a frosted plant, withered by it. Slowly the life and colour returned. Soames was watching. 'Now you can lend a hand with these bandages, Luis. If it's not kept clean I'll go rotten from end to end.' Luis jumped up ready to carry out orders as if this grim task came as a great relief. Seagrave went out for more wood, and took his time over it. When he got back the stump was again dressed and the old bandages were burning up in the fire with the blue flame of pharmaceutical alcohol. Soames looked more cheerful though under each eye was a shadow in which a haze of perspiration had gathered like dew in a hollow.

No one mentioned Luis's absence or his return without wood from a wood-gathering mission. Seagrave revolted against his own fears but took the line of silence from Soames's example. Soames was a much more experienced man and had a view from farther off. Nevertheless, the thought of refugees subjected to rape as one of their torments recurred in Seagrave's head and seeped like an oil stain across into his anxiety about Luis. But Luis showed no outward sign of any violence. That was what was most worrying, in a sense. It raised the doubt of complicity. In the past Luis's references to pederasts had always been in a familiar form, part jocular, part defiant like his request for a revolver when left near the Swiss frontier. 'If one comes I'll blow his balls off,' Luis had said laughing, 'then he won't be able to do much with what's left.' Now he was withdrawn and estranged and gave nothing, as if he had nothing left to give.

There was an electric stove in this pavilion, and provisions were brought across from the kitchen of the château by a girl in a black dress and thick black stockings and with a closed face like an apprentice nun.

'Jesus, get an eyeful of this one,' Soames said. 'Grip on herself like an oyster in a shell.'

The girl deposited the prepared dish in the electric oven, turned it on, and laid three places on the rough table standing next to a sink in the passageway. '*Bon appétit, Messieurs,*' she then said, turning her head and tilting it to one side as if trying out a pillow.

'What a pity, that,' said Soames when she'd gone. 'There's a lass from a branch of workers as in bygone days offered many an opening to a young feller.'

'I know that.'

'I expected you to.'

Things had brightened up. Soames went on to recount how before the War there'd been a maid in the kitchen of the Wordsworth worth her weight in gold. 'She was choosy, that was the best. You felt you'd stood up to what you could call informed comparison.'

'What was her name?'

'They called her Lucy.'

'And what became of her?'

'Died young.'

It was a relief to Seagrave not to be expected to dine more formally with Fernand and Marie-Louise and Philippe and Silenus. Soames like a dowser had located a bottle of Armagnac in a cupboard and this they opened without scruple. The dish warming up in the oven was excellent, a deep stew so herby and vinous it was hard to know what else exactly was in it.

'Rabbit,' concluded Soames after debate. 'A thing I never usually eat, seeing it's what my dad called poor poachers' and gypsies' grub. But this animal here's an exception.'

Seagrave waited for the Armagnac and the rabbit and all the ingredients to get through the nervous system before broaching the question of what they should do next.

'The thing I want to know is this,' said Soames: 'what are we doing up here in these blasted hills? And when do we clear out of them and back south?'

'You mean Nîmes.'

'That's what I mean.'

There was that girl there; she was why Soames had come. It was no wonder if he felt a bit restless. Seagrave turned to Luis.

'This Fernand-Félix who is in the government with a lot of power, he's going to help us. That's why we're here.'

'I know,' said Luis.

'How do you know?'

'Philippe said.'

'Philippe?'

'Yes. He said he'd make Monsieur Félix do what we want and help us. If . . .'

'If what, Luis?'

'Nothing. Nothing that matters now.'

'But I want to know.'

'Better leave the lad be,' said Soames in English. 'What's past and done . . .' They sat in a silence in which the process of thought of each of them could be sensed turning like the movement of a clock. 'So it's your mate behind the rescue act and not his uncle. I'm surprised. Makes him out a better friend than I thought,' Soames resumed, though this remark rang false in Seagrave's ears. Soames was making the best of things which if not named might even not take shape. He was trying to keep it moving and he was right. As on the surface of water, movement breaks up reflection.

'I guess he must have a lot of pull with Fernand-Félix for some reason or other,' Seagrave said, taking the same line. 'Actually this place and everything in it seems to have belonged to his aunt Marie-Louise, perhaps that has something to do with it.'

'Including the picture of the picnic?'

'Definitely.'

'So what's happened to her? Bumped off? In prison too?'

'Well yes in a way. As far as I can make out she sold herself to Fernand-Félix as part of the contents.'

'A good arrangement that. You get a scrubber thrown in who knows her way round the premises,' said Soames. Between them they were keeping it light. 'Be illegal in England though. That bloke Wilberforce, a Yorkshireman, he got slavery scrapped years ago. And have you seen her, the auntie?'

'Yes.'

'Nice old lady, is she?'

'I'm not sure it's the right word.'

'Well if the nephew brought you back to meet a powerful minister he's got some of the right ideas.' Soames had an eye on Luis, cautiously, casually. Seagrave had told no one about the photograph in the station yard. No one had ever seen it. He'd had from the first an idea that knowledge of it was too dangerous, it wasn't a thing to pass on to a friend who had no need of it. So Soames must presume the reasons for Fernand's involvement was that Philippe held some dubious kind of influence over him and had brought it to bear in order to favour his own interest in Luis. It would be a dirty scheme but dirty schemes were what Soames would expect from those in power anywhere. It would be easy enough to correct the mistake by revealing the existence of the film. But would it be right? If Soames was really here to catch up with the thin dark girl he'd known in Nîmes, then blackmailing material against a minister in the new government was the last thing he wanted. Besides, Seagrave had a superstitious fear of devaluing the knowledge by dilution.

'It's going to be all right, isn't it? We'll find her now,' said Luis suddenly.

'We've a better chance than before,' said Seagrave. He felt less sure of himself with Luis than he used to, as Luis too seemed less sure of him. Perhaps it just meant he was growing up.

'Of course she'll be found,' said Soames. 'Never you worry, Luis lad, all the forces of the state are on the look-out for your big sister. Think of it. All over France and the Rhineland they'll be, with their eyes skinned.' It was remarkable how Soames negotiated his normal speech into a French vernacular apparently at his finger ends. Perhaps this knack was related to the quickness of his sympathies which had made him respond better than Seagrave to Luis's appeal.

'Then let's go back to Nîmes and the garrigue and wait there. We can't do any more here. I've done . . . And she might make her own way back too,' Luis said.

'That's right,' said Soames, and they both looked to Seagrave for a solution to meet this agreed necessity. Soames spoke again in English. 'The boy needs to be got a long way from here.' There was no need to ask what he meant. Until Ida was found, dead or alive, Philippe could go on trading his influence and his promises and Luis would go on buying them. Or he might. Unless, of course, Luis too was told about the film. But if the knowledge was unsafe for Soames, to Luis it would be deadly. For years to come Fernand-Félix was going to be a power in the land, with special services under his orders. Someone like Luis should know nothing whatever about him.

'I think so too. The only trouble is, we left our old van near Dieppe.'

'And I don't think the friend Philippe will be in a hurry to find us another one.'

'No,' Luis said.

'I'll talk to Fernand-Félix,' said Seagrave.

'He don't look to me a man easy to lean on.'

'I think I know how to though.'

'If that's so, tha's keeping summat to thaself,' said Soames, conveying that he considered himself treated in an unworthy manner. Seagrave laughed.

'Don't you worry, there's nothing in it good for a joke.'

But Soames didn't look satisfied. He was a man who liked to know what was going on around him. 'There's more things interesting in life than just jokes,' he said sternly, and Luis, seeing Seagrave still laughing, asked to have this English humour explained.

*

In the morning Seagrave sought out Philippe, early enough, he hoped, to gain an advantage. But Philippe seemed to have been up and about for hours already.

'You don't sleep if you work for Fernand,' he explained importantly. Seagrave was ill at ease with him, a comrade through several years of fear and danger but whose nature, apparently, he had failed to grasp. He could feel himself recoil.

'I want to see the Minister,' he said, forgetting the devious approach he'd prepared.

'He saw you a long time yesterday. You should have thought of everything then. He's an extraordinarily busy man. He gave me orders to keep an eye on you but he didn't say anything about seeing you again.'

'Then tell him I've got something else I want to say.'

Philippe occupied a room on the ground floor, vaulted like the dining room but much smaller and evidently serving him as both office and bedroom. There was a good fire lit in the chimney and some Italian landscapes on the walls. The bed was a fourposted affair with hangings and Seagrave quickly shifted his gaze to the window from which there was a view up a long agricultural slope to a distant forest. It was a bare-looking scene without hedgerows or trees and with a thin layer of snow over grey grass, stubble and plough. Philippe sat behind a big flat-topped desk which must weigh a ton. He considered Seagrave for a long patronising minute before he answered.

'My dear Stephen, don't mistake your position in the new world we're in. The state is an *immense* machine. The individual is dwarfed unless he's on the inside and has some intrinsic importance, which you'll admit you haven't. What are you? A student still, really, not learning your limitations quite quickly enough. It's only when you've done that that you'll find an appropriate place somewhere.'

'And you? You're finding one?'

'Our cases are not comparable. And then I boarded the moving train. A little later would have been too late. If one means to count for anything one must know how to seize the moment.' He rearranged some papers on the surface before him, clear signal that he had no time to waste. 'And now, *mon vieux*, leave me to work. I'll let you know in good time what's to be done about you and the English soldier.' The telephone rang. 'This will be a confidential call.' He made a movement of the hand towards the door, which, however, opened at that moment to admit his aunt Marie-Louise, dressed in a black velvet robe with a rather moth-eaten fur collar and reaching to the ground. It was wrapped closely round her and showed her off well, and without her make-up she looked quite a bit younger.

'Ah, the little Englishman! But how delightful!' she cried. Philippe had stood up, leaning forward with a half-bow which was also a threat. The telephone continued to ring.

'Tante Marie-Louise, this is my place of work, not a parlour, and allow me to remind you that one knocks. Go and direct the women in the kitchens or anywhere else in the house where you won't be in the way, and leave me in peace in this executive nerve-centre where you are. Very much so.' Seagrave thought this speech to an aunt, even a youngish one, very insolent but Marie-Louise was neither surprised nor offended.

'Dear Philippe. So like your grandfather.' She took Seagrave by the upper arm and began to sweep him away like a puppy caught in the wrong room. 'I'll take this nice young man with me and we'll have some coffee together. *Grands Dieux*, how hard his arm is, like iron,' she said, giving the biceps a good squeeze. 'It even swells to the touch! He must work in the open. In the forests perhaps, wielding axes and things. Not like you, Philippe, going soft behind your big desk, always on your bottom.' As the door closed after them the telephone stopped and Philippe's voice could be heard, soothing and fluent.

The passageway was narrow for walking two abreast and Seagrave enjoyed, as they went slowly along it, the scented presence brushing at his side, a leg occasionally against his own in passing. At the foot of the winding stone stair Marie-Louise withdrew her hand from his arm and said, 'Follow me,' which Seagrave did, a prospect stirring in his mind as the aspect at his eye-level stirred, like beehives active under the black velvet before him.

'Don't make any noise,' she whispered over her shoulder. 'I mustn't annoy Henri while he's working.'

'Are you allowed to annoy him when he isn't?' Seagrave whispered back, thinking rightly that Marie-Louise would enjoy this simple joke.

'Then he doesn't get annoyed, not really,' she said, and gave the sort of giggle you might have expected her to have outgrown many years ago. Was she perhaps an instance of something not uncommon in old decaying families like the d'Albaron, a bit simple but not enough to be locked up? She'd certainly been married, but there was no sign of children about the place. In fact the château felt like a building in which no child had trodden for generations, unrelieved by triviality. Perhaps Marie-Louise tried to make up for it.

At the first floor voices were audible, male and female, and then the closing of a door after which the sound was muffled though you had the impression that at source the volume had probably risen.

'One of those young creatures from the farms,' Marie-Louise explained, walking on tip-toe on the stone. 'Philippe brings them for him.' They continued to the top of the building, the stair turning many times because of the great height of the rooms. 'This way. This is my little apartment.'

There was a warren of rooms up here, to judge by the number of doors in this bare, icy passage. Marie-Louise led the way into one of them. Here too a fire was lit, and it was needed, the raftered ceiling almost lost in the distant gloom above. 'I've got my own little kitchen here where I can do what I like. And prepare lovely sweet things to eat and drink.' She sounded like a little girl, even her voice going upwards and the words coming out in a childlike accent as if she was soliloquising as she played with her dolls. Seagrave had a sudden, disagreeable sensation of having been turned for the moment into one of them. But as she went into her kitchen she looked back at him with the unchildlike smile he'd seen bestowed yesterday on Fernand-Félix. 'Please sit down, I'll bring us some coffee. Some real coffee.' Like her brother in Nîmes she must have special sources of supply.

While Seagrave waited he wondered about what was expected of him. This lady was, as far as he knew, the private property of Fernand-Félix yet there were signs that she didn't think herself bound. That was all right with Seagrave, if that's how things were. Marie-Louise, as aunt of a friend, or former friend, had a certain special appeal; less, in a way, for herself, charming though she was, than as an objective to achieve, a cape to be rounded. He supposed this must be some kind of crypto-Oedipal attraction. If so it seemed a good time to yield to it as it was now becoming subjectively certain that that was what was going to happen anyway. He stood up politely when Marie-Louise returned and as soon as she'd put the coffee cups onto a table he advanced and pressed himself against her, his arms round her waist. If this was rushing things that was because urgency was the mode for heroes.

'Monsieur! Monsieur! What is this?' He pressed a little closer by way of answer. 'But we are in France!' she cried. 'We are in Auvergne, *la France profonde*, not the Seine estuary where your Viking ancestors launched themselves . . . in their long ships behind the great prow of war . . . plundering and raping.' Clearly she was enjoying herself so far. That wasn't the language of dolls, not normal ones. Standing hard up like this they were about the same height, until with a quick movement she kicked off her high-heeled slippers so that now she looked up at him a little, the expression in her eyes one of reproach and encouragement. On her breath was an aroma of oranges in alcohol, mild and mature as if the bottle it came from had slept for decades in the kitchen cupboard. Seagrave suddenly thought of something he should say before going any further, and withdrew an inch or two.

'I was going to ask you to help me.'

'Help you? I don't feel you need help.'

'I mean, later . . . I want your help about something. That's what I meant.'

'Later?' Marie-Louise laughed. He hadn't seen her do this before. Her laughter came from the throat which seemed to throb with it while her good small white teeth opened back as if inviting you to examine the site where the laughter emerged, like a spring at the back of a grotto. 'There's what it means to be *un gentleman*. You declare the ulterior motives in advance.' This remark surprised Seagrave not by its content, but the succinct way it was put. Marie-Louise had other sides to her. 'A Frenchman never does that. He thinks you'll be only too grateful.'

'I didn't like to count on it. You may not be.'

'We'll see about that,' she said. One of her hands which had been resting opened out like a fan on his shirtfront now dropped down and undid the buckle of his belt and the top buttons of his trousers. She then stooped as flexibly as a woman portrayed in a Dutch interior manipulating some domestic item near the ground – a wine-filled ewer or olive jar – and neatly lowered the trousers to the floor, freeing the legs one after the other from his feet. It was a very practised proceeding and the sequel passed off all the more smoothly for it.

*

When they came to the coffee it was stone cold, colder even than the air of the room as if it had slowly taken the temperature of the snow on the hillside visible through the window.

'I won't heat it up,' Marie-Louise said, 'it belongs to a different age.'

'I like cold coffee.'

'Even in winter! It's because you're so hot.' She leaned across from her chair and put a hand on his chest. 'The surface of your skin burns. You should get dressed. Also, Henri may send someone for me.' Seagrave looked towards the door. 'Oh don't worry, the floors here are very thick, he won't have heard anything below. Or if he did he'd have taken it for a barking dog.' She issued her laugh again from far back.

'I've seen no dogs.'

'Henri has very little imagination, except about himself. A barking noise suggests a dog to him, that's all.'

When he had his clothes on again and Marie-Louise had buttoned up her velvet robe – twenty-four buttons from top to bottom, he'd counted – he knew the time had come to broach the favour he wanted. 'Er . . . that other matter . . .' he began. It wasn't a very accomplished overture, he realised.

Marie-Louise looked at him rather sadly. 'The gentleman is about to expose his ulterior motive,' she said.

'What it is, I want to see Monsieur Fernand-Félix again. Philippe's getting in the way. He says he's seen me already and he's too busy.'

'It's true Henri is nearly always working. Everything he does is work. Even the peasant girls from the farm. That's missionary work. He's only a generation or two from a peasant himself, it's too soon for finesse.'

'Would he see me if you asked him to?'

'That would depend on what I told him. One has to use cunning with Henri. I don't know what your business with him is, but it must be important or he would never have had you brought here.'

'It is important. To him as well as me.'

'How badly do you want to see him now?'

'It's rather urgent.'

'If it's urgent it means you want to go away from here.' She looked sad, but it might have been just an accomplished performance, all in the eyes and nothing over the top. Seagrave felt sad too as if having rounded the cape and made a fine landfall he was being forced to sail on, never to return.

'I don't want to go away, but my friends need to.'

'The English soldier? The boy . . . because of Philippe?'

'Both.'

'And you with them?'

Seagrave hesitated. She might find it better value to have him kept here. She was a sort of prisoner herself and he'd read in some novel that prisoners befriend and capture other, lesser creatures to keep them company. This was a moment for guile. 'I had thought so, but now . . .'

'Henri will have to go back to Paris very soon, and Philippe and all the little hangers-on too. Life here can be much more amusing than you know. There are horses in the stables . . . guns in the gun room . . . pheasants . . . stags in the forest . . . I know how the English love blood sports. And the cellar! It was my husband's library.'

'That's what Philippe says about his father's cellar in Nîmes.'

'Of course he says it. It's a commonplace to say about a well-stocked cellar. But behind it lie hundreds of unopened treasures.'

'Yes, I suppose the image of the library's fair enough. It would certainly fit my brother's library.'

Marie-Louise raised her shoulders and eyebrows fractionally. These were quibbles. A book . . . a bottle of wine . . . after all. 'I adore hunting in the forest in winter,' she said, extending her arms behind and above her head so the velvet sleeves slipped back beyond the elbows. 'I mean hunting the stag of course.'

'What would you have to tell him to get him to see me again?'

Marie-Louise sighed. While she reflected on the answer a flicker of expressions crossed her face as rapidly and impenetrably as ideograms rehearsed in Chinese. Secret amusement in the end was all he could read there.

'I'll explain,' she said. 'You don't know anything about Henri, I mean as a man. I think you know something else but I don't expect you to tell me what it is. And I don't want you to.' Seagrave felt that in some way he was being hoodwinked, but knew he would have to make the best he could of that. 'Just as a man he has enough peculiarities. Perhaps the most important to know about is his belief in his own great, unique destiny. I think a lot of men have that. Do you have it?'

'Yes and no,' said Seagrave, and then sensing the inadequacy of the answer added, 'I was taught to believe in the importance of the individual will. Destiny seems passive to me.'

'I assure you Henri believes in the importance of the will. You can be sure of that. I meant he thinks all roads in his life lead to Rome. Do you perhaps see what I mean? The will does its work but whatever happens on his way Henri will get to Rome. And there, naturally and by destiny, he will be pope.' This wasn't said sardonically. The papacy was still the summit of arrivisme. Even in this context, in referring to the Vicar of Christ Marie-Louise gave a slight inclination of the head.

'What does that have to do with getting me another interview?'

'If you want him to do anything he hasn't planned, you have to . . . make him think there's some . . . how shall I put it . . . some fire worth playing with.'

Seagrave thought he got the point of this. 'You mean to prove that whatever happens the road still leads to Rome? Putting destiny to the test?'

'Yes. That's Henri's favourite game.'

'I don't see how it applies to me. I do, in fact, but not over the interview.'

'Don't you? All complications are food and drink to him.' More than this she wouldn't say, treating questions with a cool withdrawal. That was part and parcel of the effect of their difference in age. He was prized for youth one moment and put down for inexperience the next.

While Marie-Louise was in another room dressing herself for the day there was a knocking at the door. Seagrave stood up and went to the window, looking out over the grey snow and cloud and grey air in between. If whoever it was came in now they would find him studying the ground far below for the trail of pheasant or the slotted spoor of stag. Marie-Louise appeared just as the knocking was repeated, more insistently. 'Wait here. I may be some time,' she said, and passed through the barely opened door with the swiftness of a woman half her age and size.

If Fernand-Félix lived on complications, it seemed pretty clear that Marie-Louise would be skilled at providing them. She was now about to promote Seagrave as the latest. Perhaps just interesting enough to catch the great man's attention for half a day. When she returned an hour later she looked pleased but tired. As it was, the elaborate hair arrangement and make-up had aged her by years from her natural state when he'd dealt with the two dozen velvet buttons.

'Poor boy,' she said. 'What a long time, and at your age! But Henri will see you now, at once. Go down to the dining room. Walk straight in. He's waiting for you.'

'Thank you very much. I really don't know how . . . I'm most grateful.'

'Go at once. There'll be plenty of time for all that.'

He wondered what she meant, and what she knew. It didn't sound as if she thought he'd be getting away in any great hurry from this château, the gun room, the cellars, the forest. In the dining room Fernand-Félix was sitting at the end of the long table, dictating to a secretary whom he signalled away as Seagrave made his entrance as instructed. There was an element of unreality and farce in the situation, yet this man was a minister with powers hard to realise at the lower private end of the social scale where you did your best to survive and where, as Philippe had pointed out, small fry like Seagrave were likely to fritter away a lifetime.

'So!' said Fernand-Félix. His mouth worked for a few moments in rehearsal of the sentence to follow. 'It seems we're in some way destined to be folded in one "dark inscrutable workmanship".' He looked immensely pleased with the reference. 'Though I don't believe we're such "discordant elements" after all, you and I.' Once more Seagrave had the feeling of an affinity partly natural, partly projected from overhead like a coloured light on a stage. 'Madame de Tornac tells me ... wait, no pretences between us ... Marie-Louise says you're quite a horseman. He mounts excellently, she says. I know nothing about horses. There are some here in the stable, I suppose they're mine now, let's go and look at them. You can tell me if they're as good mounts as she claims. You who mount so well.' Fernand was teasing him and himself at the same time. He was challenging him into the open, that was part of the game of complications, it was a pastime. Fernand took his arm, keeping him down to his own pace which was slow because of the shortness of his legs, his dignity, and the small unhurried steps he took to reconcile the demands of these factors. Side by side they crossed the courtyard and passed out onto the snow-covered open ground. 'That's the stable,' Fernand said, pointing to a brick building in bad condition on one side of this space. 'These people have been penniless for generations.' The tone was triumphant. The *épicerie Félix* had been a commerce carried on in modest premises but with what result? Fernand had bought up the château de Tornac and could point out with contempt the decay the outbuildings had fallen into thanks to the idle improvidence of a superannuated class. 'Tell me, Etienne,' he said, using Seagrave's Christian name for the first time and squeezing his arm slightly at the same moment, 'your own origins ... Philippe has told me something about them. But in England you have less decadence, at this level. I've seen, I've been *received*, at the château de Cliveden, near the River Thames. The maintenance there is impeccable, despite the War and its privations.'

'It belongs to Americans, that's why.'

'Americans? Certainly not. You're mistaken.' He sounded annoyed, giving no more than a hint of the reservoir of fury hidden within him awaiting employment. 'I was presented to the proprietor. He was a Lord. Entirely of the old school.'

It seemed important not to ruffle him any further. 'I'm probably wrong,' Seagrave admitted.

'Probably? You're certainly wrong. But one can't know everything, and you're very young, and you have mounting on your mind. But your family too has a château, I believe?'

'Not me though. My half-brother.'

'I expect Marie-Louise scented this at once. Women of that sort can place people even before they open their mouths. Of course you have done rather more than that.'

When they got inside the stable they found, as Seagrave had expected they would, Soames and Luis in communion with the two horses living there. Soames examined Seagrave and then addressed him in an undertone in English.

'Been having it off with the lady of the manor, have you?"

'What makes you think so?' Seagrave muttered.

'Never saw anything like it. All over canary feathers.'

'Monsieur Fernand-Félix speaks English. He reads the poets.'

'He does, does he?' said Soames, and turned to Fernand with a respect in which you might not recognise the irony if you didn't know him well. 'I wonder, Monsieur, if you have ever heard of our local poet, of the region of lakes where we come from? The bistro where we drink is called after him. The Wordsworth.'

'*The* Wordsworth? Of course I know him. I read a page of him every day in the original. I read *The Prelude*, in English. Few, very few Frenchmen can boast as much. When I have time I project composing a similar work, if in prose – the growth of a statesman's mind. Most unfortunately I left my copy of *The Prelude* behind in Paris. Philippe is to blame. And here of course there are no books at all, except a shelf or two on heraldry and horses.'

'I've got a copy as it happens, with me . . . in my things,' Seagrave said, regretting it as he spoke.

'You have? Excellent. I knew we had a great deal in common, au fond. You'll lend it to me until I return to Paris. So I can catch up my daily page of the sublime egotist. Since we're all in our way egotists why should not one or two be sublime? Few can aspire to it. Humanity's not a brave thing.'

For some reason, Fernand-Félix was playing for time. It was going to be interesting to hear Soames's view of him later on. Although Soames might not have understood all he said, that gave him the more opportunity to observe. He was observing now, with those eyes set far back inside his head like the lurking but immediate agents of his intuition.

Fernand was observing too. 'I see you're missing a foot, my friend, you've preserved the principal however – I mean your life – and that's good. But you stand there in need of a replacement. In Clermont-Ferrand we have a famous artificial limb specialist. I'll send you to him. It's important to begin the re-education of the limb at the earliest possible moment. In your case the knee could otherwise become vulnerable. I take it on myself. Your government will reimburse my Ministry. But perhaps what you have to do here in France won't allow you to stay long enough to take advantage of my offer?' Soames looked at Seagrave without answering.

'My friends want to go back to Nîmes as soon as possible where we all were at the Liberation. That's what I had to ask you. Travel without authority at the moment is difficult.'

'It can be impossible,' said Fernand simply. 'So you were together at the Liberation?'

'And before. We were . . .'

'And before.'

It had been a mistake to admit that. Fernand-Félix's eyes darted about from side to side as though seeking rats to catch in the corners of the stable building. Seagrave plunged on in an attempt to reach safer ground. 'I was the only one in Nîmes before the

Liberation itself. Mr Soames was with a maquis in the Cévennes and Luis was held in the Camargue. They weren't involved with the Resistance in the town.'

'But as you seem to travel about together now I expect you have exchanged many interesting stories of your various experiences before you joined forces.'

'We've never talked about it.'

'Why not?'

'The present always seemed more urgent.'

'The present exists only as a changing viewpoint, along two perspectives. Before and behind. The one grows from the other, with all that entails. The great difference between men is that some work on the future, others manipulate the past.'

Though Marie-Louise complained of Fernand's lack of finesse it seemed to Seagrave that all that could have been put far more brutally. Many people in positions of power would certainly put it more brutally. Think of William. Here was Fernand reminding him that they were chained together but that it was he, Fernand, who steered their encumbered footsteps. All Seagrave could do was try to make sure that Luis and Soames weren't dragged into the chain-gang after him.

'I don't know about the future, but I know how to keep my mouth shut about the past,' he said.

'I congratulate you on it,' said Fernand dryly. 'There's a slogan used by your Ministry in London, the one corresponding to my own – for the time being. "Careless talk costs lives." I recommend it for your reserve of maxims to keep always in mind.'

That was direct enough. In fact when he thought about it, chillingly direct. 'Do you think . . . do you feel now . . . *Monsieur le Ministre*, that . . .' Seagrave tried to proceed.

'Come, my dear Etienne, come. You may call me Henri.' Fernand's gaze rose to settle on the windows of Marie-Louise's apartment high up on the naked walls of the château. 'Given that we are favourers of some of the same haunts.'

'Thank you, er, Henri. I was asking if you'd be disposed to sanction our return to Nîmes? Now that we're agreed ... about that help you're good enough to give towards finding ...'

'Your missing relation. Help in the search. It's early to talk of finding. In fact orders have already gone out. Philippe sees to that.'

'In that case ...'

'In that case?'

'It would be better for everyone if we were in Nîmes. Here, we'll be in the way.'

'You're not exactly in my way, Etienne. You're on it. But tell me, are you all related in some manner to the missing person?'

'Luis is her brother.'

Fernand examined Luis rapidly, like merchandise in which he didn't deal. 'I see. A beautiful race of people, certainly. And this boy wants to leave also? Do you want to get away from here, young man? Why?'

'To escape,' said Luis sullenly, and then shuddered.

'I understand.' He probably did, Seagrave thought, though what he knew it was impossible to guess. One of the things he understood, to judge by a lightening in the atmosphere around him, was that Luis was no danger. All Luis was interested in was getting back to the Mediterranean, and probably the road. History didn't concern him, Fernand would see that. 'And you, Monsieur,' he continued, turning to Soames, 'you've surely earned a convalescence near the sea before you return to your own country. But you must report your presence to the Préfecture in Nîmes. I will give instructions. You will receive a permit to stay for a certain time. The regulations must be respected.'

'Oh yes. Count on me. I'm sure to respect those,' said Soames.

Fernand gave him a sharp look but Soames was leaning bent sideways on his crutch with his head hanging, like a man only just off the battlefield and with no spare effort for irony. Seagrave looked quickly away.

'Etienne, you will talk to Philippe about the details. A car will be provided for the journey to Nîmes to ensure the party goes there and arrives safely. It will leave this afternoon.'

'In one way I'll be very sorry, after being made so welcome.' Fernand had challenged him into the open and now it was safe there he cautiously was, keeping it light, he hoped.

'You mean sorry to go? But you're not going, Etienne. You and I, we can't separate now. Your friends will go. You will stay with me and either Philippe will put you up in his flat in Paris or Marie-Louise will look after you here. As she wishes. Well, I've seen the horses. Very good. Useless, but picturesque. We must have much less useless picturesque elements in the France of tomorrow. You in England, I know, will preserve them for several generations more.' Saying this, Fernand turned and started back to the château, his footmarks in the snow almost touching each other heel to toe.

'That's awkward,' said Soames when Fernand had entered the courtyard. 'Doesn't want you out of his sight. Or out of hers. I wonder why. Must be due to what you've been keeping to yourself all this time.'

'I can't stay with you, I can't,' Luis broke out.

'No, you certainly can't. Look, Luis, go and put your things and Soames's together so you're ready at once. Don't talk to anyone.'

'Our things are together.'

'Do what I say. I must talk to Soames.'

'And you don't trust a little *gitan* with what you're going to tell him.'

'Don't be stupid, Luis. You know I trust you perfectly. It's for your own safety. You heard what the Minister said – careless talk costs lives. He said it twice. Now go on.'

Luis touched Seagrave's hand lightly as he went off, in a familiar gesture of Ida's when she knew she'd been unjust in some way and didn't know how to put apology into words.

'Walk back slowly in front of me so you can hear but it doesn't look like we're talking. Just in case we're under observation from any of those windows.' Soames set himself going as instructed, hobbling over the grass. It was snowing again lightly, the air blurred with a fine mist. In as few words as possible, Seagrave filled in the gaps in Soames's information concerning Fernand.

'I'd never have thought it of you,' said Soames in a solemn voice.

'Thought what?'

'You'd be such a wily young devil as that. Blackmail and all.'

'Don't you see I'm trying to save a life?'

'Just joking,' said Soames.

'I'm only telling you now in case anything happens to me, before Ida's found. All the Minox negatives are in my bag. Take them with you but don't let Luis see.'

'And only hand them over against delivery?'

'That's it. Now I'll walk the other way and go and talk to Philippe about the car. The less we're seen together the better.'

All the same they had a few more words before the car came. It was snowing more heavily but the misty air was milder so the snow was half-melted as it hit the ground. Seagrave had been thinking about money. Luis hadn't any left, he'd been cleaned out between Dieppe and Brough. What Seagrave still had on him he might need. He hoped he'd live to need it.

'When you get to the other end dig up that cash I buried,' he told Soames. 'No one else knows where it is. You do know where it is, don't you?'

'I do, aye.'

'Then take as much as you need for Luis and yourself, take all you need and bury the rest again somewhere else. No need to say anything to François.'

'I wouldn't dream of it.'

'But to get you a message I'll leave it with him.'

'Well, all the best,' said Soames. 'If things get difficult do what I do, think of the Wordsworth. Watch out with that Minister feller. Writes the story of his life afresh every day, he does. Best read in the world, bar for being born and raised over the grocery store. But he'll edit that bit clean out. Trouble is, he could take it in his head to edit you out too. A stroke of the pencil.'

'But I'm a British subject: the sun can't set on me yet,' Seagrave objected.

'Don't never ever forget that,' said Soames as the car approached through the slush.

Chapter Eleven

Travelling and being with Soames was different from Etienne. Etienne was something between a father and a brother, Luis supposed, and anyway he was the man who in Luis's reckoning was, like himself, a property of Ida's. Soames was a friend only, and you had to be more careful. Luis had never had a friend before. In the camp there had been enemies, victims, and parasites, and when it was time to escape he'd gone on his own. No other *gitan* had befriended him. Of course there'd been the nurses, but there was only one thing you could count them for, one thing to be done with them. With Soames, on the contrary, there seemed no limit to the possibilities because nothing tied him down. If he didn't like a place he moved on, if he disliked a person he looked at the rest of the world over the top of their head.

The civilian driver wore gaiters and a cap like a chauffeur in a film Luis had once seen in Nîmes. The driver was from Paris and he had a cold and distant manner which melted down a bit more each time he stopped for a drink in the villages they passed through. Soames drank in them too and so would Luis have done, if he'd felt better and cleaner. The driver's aim, so he said, was to be drunk before they reached the crest of the mountain pass they had to cross, to reach the valley of the Ardèche and the Mediterranean plain far, far below. He'd driven it once when sober and never again, he said, it was no better than a cart track with a sheer drop to sea level and no wall. Soames said he looked forward to that very much, it would take his mind off his leg. Luis thought Soames should see a doctor about the leg, the last time he'd helped with the dressing the stump had smelled to him like a dead fox in the Camargue, though it looked much the same as before – green and white and streaked with blue like a cheese. Maybe the smell was in his own nostrils and not from outside at all.

The snow as they neared the crest was thick and they stopped to put chains on the wheels. Because the driver was drunk this took a long time, and he shouted at Luis each time his own fingers failed to engage a hook with a link in the frozen void under the chassis of the vehicle. No more snow was falling here now and the mist was thicker as if they were in cloud, it swirled above and about them like water over a flame. A short way over the top you felt you were hanging onto the edge of the world. Then quite abruptly, a hundred or two metres on, the mist vanished, the air above was blue and below you you thought you caught the first wave of warmth. The long valley dropped sharply between grassland and chestnut woods still in leaf, and sometimes, rounding a shoulder of the mountain, you had a glimpse of the plain where olives ripened slowly through the last months of the year. Luis began to feel cleaner, his own smell which had shadowed him these last hours fading.

Soames may have experienced something similar. 'A lot better here. Stump's numb,' he said. By the time they reached the foot of the valley a couple of hours later on the driver was sober again. 'Concentration, that's what does it. Burns the liquor off like nothing else,' Soames explained and Luis stored the knowledge up.

There was a small hotel in Nîmes, dirt cheap, near the station, the place where Luis had been that first time with Ida and Etienne, and that was where they were going to stay while Soames looked round for a new foot. If you couldn't drive or ride a bicycle the cabin in the garrigue was a long way out.

'I know how to drive,' Luis pointed out. 'I learned at Dieppe.'

'Then the day we get our hands on money we'll buy an old crate somewhere and you can get some practice,' said Soames. 'They won't be bothering about things like driving licences. Law and order is for when the War's properly finished. That's when they'll crack down on poor people like you and me.'

'How will we get any money?'

'You leave that to me.'

If Soames said that sort of thing you didn't argue with him as you might have done with Etienne. Obviously if he thought law and order were for later then his system for getting money supplies was not going to be one that Etienne would use, but that wasn't a thing that worried Luis. You had to have money, that was all.

The driver had orders to take them to the Préfecture and report their arrival. The official there already knew all about the foot. 'The Nîmes hospital was bombed by our brave allies from over the ocean,' he said, 'so we're bringing an artificial limb specialist from Montpellier to attend to you tomorrow.'

'Where?'

'Here.'

'That means they've been ordered not to lose us,' said Soames afterwards. 'We'll see about losing us once I've got the free foot.' The last of the pain had left him as they reached the level of the first olive groves, and it hadn't come back. The specialist said the stump was healing unusually well, so that stink of dead fox couldn't have been Soames. Luis was relieved about that. He could keep it to himself, where it had come from.

A provisional wooden foot with a simple one-way hinge was supplied within a couple of days. 'Begin the procedure slowly, as if you were learning to ride a bicycle for the first time,' said the specialist. 'Before you can walk a hundred paces with that we'll have a much more advanced apparatus ready for you. It will be painful, very painful at first.'

Soames was contemptuous of this advice. 'In this country everything's a procedure. We haven't got time for procedures. We must find Mr Paradise and he'll tell us where we can proceed to pick up a very cheap car.'

'We haven't got the money yet.'

'We'll take it on trial and pay next day.'

*

François Paradis had gone back to a job on the railways. He had a little office in the building of the administration near the central station, and even though reduced he looked much too big for it, as if the cubic space could only explode from his presence. He seemed very pleased to see Soames and at once brought a bottle out of a drawer of his desk.

'If you're looking for Etienne, he went to England,' he said.

'Yes, we came back from there with him.'

'Where is he?'

'He'll probably be in Paris by now. He's got a type in the government to search the refugees everywhere for his . . . for the sister of Luis here.'

François looked at Luis and seemed to be considering him as men in authority usually considered him, a likely delinquent whose saving grace was the look he shared with Ida, so that men who knew her, seeing him, were reminded and grew kinder. All the same it troubled them, you could see that, and Luis understood better now why it was so. He'd always known about Ida's beauty but had never been aware how that spilled over onto him.

'Have you been in England too?' François asked.

'Yes, Monsieur.' Luis was afraid of François and counted on subservience to get him safely through.

'I've never been out of France, not even to Spain. But you're a proper travelling people.' François nodded at him approvingly. 'Do you want a drink too, Luis?'

'I only drink wine, Monsieur.'

'You don't need to call me Monsieur. Everyone in the maquis called me François, even those I had to have shot for informing. Well I've got a bit of wine for you. Here.'

Luis decided there was probably no need to be afraid of

François, just very careful of him because he knew so much better than Etienne or Soames could ever know just what sort of creature Luis was, where he came from, how to treat him as the rest of the world down here treated his kind. He drank the wine slowly, kept quiet and listened to Soames and François who were remembering a train journey by moonlight.

'And the operation at the Banque de France, that was good too,' François was saying.

'Very good,' said Soames, 'first class.'

There was a silence which Luis recognised as due to each of them having something to hide, for the present moment, from the other, and he respected that, though he had no ideas about what it could be. Probably something relating to law and order – *gadje* always seemed to be very concerned about them. This word for people of alien race had swum into his head as if he'd inherited it with his skin and eyes, and as soon as he'd used it for François and Soames, even only in thought, he felt more separated from them. They were right, the people like François, to keep him as a stranger. That was what he was. He put down the glass that had had the wine in it.

Soames was saying about buying a car. 'Buy a car? You certainly won't buy a car,' François said. 'You of all people! With what we owe you! I'll find you one at once. And petrol to make it go.' He lifted the telephone, hesitated, and waved his other hand in the direction of Soames's leg and crutch. 'With that . . . you can . . .?'

'Oh yes,' said Soames. 'Nothing to worry about there.'

When François had made the call he wrote something on a piece of paper for Soames. 'I have to stay here . . . the trains and signals, and all that,' he said vaguely. 'But go to this address and ask for Jean-Jacques. He'll provide you with an old car that works. When you need more petrol, go back to him because you won't find it easy to get it anywhere else. You'll pay nothing, that's an order. And you can always find me here when you need me.' He put an arm about Soames's shoulder when they got up to go. 'Your friends here will never forget. And I may need men like you again, quite soon. I hope I will. I think I will. It's a dirty world. Only those who don't fear action can help make it any better.' He turned to Luis and patted his cheek just as he might have patted the dog of a friend. More a thump than a pat, it felt like. 'And the boys too, Luis. I'll need you too, one of these days.'

'Thank you, Monsieur.'

'No no. You must say "François, you can count on me the day you need me".'

'You can count on me,' said Luis, unable to utter the name.

'That's right, and so I will.'

'There's another one doesn't want to lose sight of us,' Soames said as he went painfully along the pavement, leaning on Luis and the single crutch he now used.

'I would be afraid to do anything he didn't like.'

'What I always appreciated about Paradise is he knows his own mind.' Soames thought for a moment. 'He knows the front of it and it's not everyone can say as much.'

'What's he going to do when he hears it's me driving the car?'

'Nothing. Men like Paradise never go back. What they think about is tomorrow. The next operation. And tomorrow again.'

Luis drove with the dash of the self-taught, he could see that for himself by comparing his own system with that of other, older users of the road who scattered at his approach.

'That's right, lad,' said Soames.

When they got to the garrigue Soames said they would settle in there. He gave Luis what cash he had and told him to go down into the town and pay the hotel. 'Bring back some wine and bread and tomorrow's another day,' he said.

When Luis returned it was raining so the water ran in streams off the stony ground; Soames had made a fire in the hearth and was stretched out in front of it in the only chair, thinking. He looked, to Luis's eye, very satisfied about something. 'Change of plan. When the rain stops we'll go down again. There's someone I want to find.'

228

Luis supposed this meant a woman. 'Will I have to get out and go somewhere else when you find her?' he asked.

'Luis, you need to value yourself higher,' Soames answered, and studied him for a moment from his far-back eyes. 'I know what's wrong with you. It's like when my foot was blown off. And I know what'll put you right again. Mind you you're lucky. You don't need a wooden one where your trouble is.'

That evening they went down to a house in the town where Soames seemed to know his way around, and Luis understood what he'd meant. He knew you needed plenty of money if the address was in a good district, and it appeared that money was no longer a problem. When the champagne arrived Soames spoke seriously to Luis, but briefly.

'Have one glass before, and as much as you want after. Do it any other way and even at your age it's not nearly as good.'

Luis took great care not to be drunk, and as Soames had assured him there was no cash shortage he went back upstairs more than once, in order to measure the effect of the single glass of champagne in the intervals. It was all useful experience, and it was still pretty good but what Soames had said was in general correct. The first time was far the best because it put him together again. Soames had disappeared with the thin dark girl and by the time he came back Luis was asleep in a corner of the waiting room. The lady at the desk called it the salon.

'Come on,' Soames said. 'If you can stand you can drive.'

When they were in the car Luis asked why Soames hadn't brought the girl, as there was plenty of money and obviously he liked her so much.

'In the Army, when the time comes for action you keep your different services in their different sectors,' was Soames's explanation. 'Now poor old Etienne, he forgets to do that.'

'What sort of action?'

'You heard what Paradise said. He's counting on us for the day the balloon goes up.'

Luis didn't say so, but he didn't think Soames and François meant quite the same thing. François, formidable as he might be, was only an official on the railways now; but Soames was still fighting a war, he had the habit, and losing his foot probably made him feel he had ground to catch up. Luis didn't believe in any balloon, not here in the Languedoc where all the people wanted was to get back to normal. One of the girls had said so earlier on. 'Just think,' she said, 'in ordinary times there'd be a crowd of gentlemen down in the salon, joking and drinking. Tonight there's just you, you little half-grown devil, and the Englishman with a wooden leg. The Liberation was supposed to do more than that for women in commerce.'

'We pay just the same. Or he pays, anyway.'

'I didn't complain. Only stated a fact,' said the girl, rather sulkily, Luis thought. He decided she wasn't by any means the one he'd most appreciated and wouldn't have been even if she hadn't called him half-grown, and he said this to the lady downstairs while he finished the champagne.

'You listen to me, young man. Come back the day you're head of one of the Banks, or a headmaster or president of the Chamber of Commerce, and then I'll pay some attention to your opinions about my girls. For now, just count yourself lucky having such a generous *patron* bringing you here and letting you loose. As if my house was some sort of zoological garden,' she muttered angrily to herself at the end.

It was after that Luis curled up in a corner and slept until Soames resurfaced.

*

Soames went down every day to François's office in case of a message, he said, but some of these visits seemed to Luis, waiting outside in the car, to last quite a long time. There were no messages but on one day Soames came out and said they were to drive out to the Camargue to look at some land for sale.

'Good territory for horses and going for a song,' he said.

'Do you know the way to it?'

'I've got this plan.'

There was a pontoon bridge over the Little Rhône where the old one had been destroyed from the air, and a short way upstream was the railway bridge, still intact. The last time Luis had crossed the river going this way he'd been standing in the back of the truck that took him and Ida and a lot of others to the camp. Ida had been white and silent with the baby moving about inside, and Luis remembered how frightened he'd been, with fear like a pain, and that the other *gitans* hadn't spoken to them, never did speak to Ida to the day she was taken away. That had been the worst, in a way, because you couldn't understand it. 'There's the road that leads to the camp,' he said.

'That's the way we're going.'

There was old railway track that ran beside the road, the lines rusty and hidden in the grass, and unfenced. Luis knew it was there because it ran straight through the middle of the camp. They said it hadn't been used since long before the War until the day they brought the materials to build the huts along it, but in the old times it took the people on Sundays and feast days from Nîmes or Arles down to the sea and back again in the evening.

'This is it,' Soames said.

'I know. This is where I was. I was here two winters and summers.'

'I mean this is the land for sale. There's the sign up on the post.'

Beyond the post with the For Sale sign were the huts, specially built to look like a Camargue village with thatched roofs but which were really a prison for people of the wrong race.

'This is the camp. The Bohemians' camp they call it,' Luis repeated. He'd stopped the car and Soames was already getting out, pulling himself upright with the help of the crutch. He turned round to speak to Luis.

'Remember what I told you. About keeping different sectors

separate when time for action's coming up. Action and feeling, they have to stay apart. If not you lose both ways.' He walked in through the camp entrance, pushing the gate forcefully open as if it made him angry just to see it. 'Come on, Luis, you're a man now.'

Luis didn't feel like a man, if that meant being able to have the same contempt as Soames for the gate which had shut him in for two years of his childhood, but he followed Soames, partly because he felt even more afraid out on the road by himself.

'OK, Luis, let's get it over. Which was the one you were in?'

'All the children were together in that one there. Not the babies, but the babies didn't last long anyway.' There were only a dozen of the huts in all for three or four hundred prisoners, with hardly enough room to lie down.

'Where did you eat?'

'In the big hut there in the middle. It didn't take long.'

'And if you went sick?'

'The one next to it.' He supposed the nurses must be back on the street in Marseille by now. Everyone had to live.

'And those?'

'The offices. The commandant and the guards. The hut at the end was where they beat the people who tried to escape. They made everyone stand outside and hear, to teach us a lesson they said.'

Soames made a noise without words at the back of his throat. 'It's finished now, Luis, it'll never come back. Those people will have forgotten. I've forgotten what my foot was like. That's how it works. You remember it because you had to listen. But you can walk in and out of here now, and drive away in our own car, and you'll never be taken into that little hut. We'll smash it up before we go.'

They went right round and looked at the fields and inspected the buildings inside and out because nothing was locked up.

'It's a good interesting proposition,' Soames said. 'You'd pull most of it down and make a stud farm maybe. Every worker would have his own cabin and Paradise will get that private railway line he wants.'

'What does he want it for?'

'We don't know anything about that, you and me.'

'Is it to bring building materials? Is that why you said there'd be workers here?'

'Everyone's a worker some of the time. Even a man with a wooden foot, he counts as a worker. If his ideas are right.'

Soames was joking but Luis wasn't going to leave it at that. 'So is Monsieur Paradis going to buy the Bohemians' camp and build a proper house and come and live here?'

'No. Etienne's going to buy it, though he doesn't know that yet. We'll buy it for him and put it in his name. Part of the Seagrave estates.'

'Is it a lot of money?'

'Not to us, it isn't. But it's more money than Paradise can raise without us.'

'Where did we get it, Soames?'

'You like to know something, Luis? That's a question too many. Come on, we're going to burn down the torturers' hut. Go and get the jerry can from the car.'

Jean-Jacques had given them twenty litres of spare petrol and said to make it last, so they only sprinkled a bit round the base of the hut, which was made of wood, to get the fire started and then threw some up onto the thatch to make it quick.

'You light it. That'll do you more good than anything,' Soames said.

'What if the owner comes to make trouble?'

'The type who owns this place made too much out of the occupation to risk any trouble these days. Not for quite a long time too. Go on. Take my lighter.'

The hut went up like a torch under the deep blue winter sky. There was no wind that day so the ash and burnt fragments of thatch floated back eventually onto the ground around them and disappeared in the grass. When the fire was low Luis went in and pushed everything still left into a pile in the middle to burn up so there'd be nothing at all when they went away, but for a blackened patch of ground marking the spot where bad things were done to harmless people.

*

When they came back next it was with François Paradis. He drove the car, even more erratically than Luis himself, and Luis sat in the back and kept quiet. From what he could make out they'd bought the land by that time, or anyway signed a contract for it, but in the presence of François whose huge back was a few centimetres in front of his eyes, Luis didn't dare ask questions in his usual way. François paced up and down the rusty lines, examining the joints and the sleepers and the gravel bed hidden in the grass. 'Did you ever see a train on this line, Luis?' he asked.

'Once. It brought a load of sand and gravel. It's all still there, under those trees.' If François proved to be interested in the sand and gravel that meant he intended to build.

But he wasn't interested in them. All the same, Luis had told him what he wanted to know. 'Good. It must be viable to the main line. I thought it would be. They made the permanent way to be permanent, our fathers did.'

'Some of these sleepers have slept so long they look like they've gone to their last rest,' said Soames. 'Like my father.'

'It doesn't matter. The weight's spread over a long distance.'

'Will you carry the people down to the sea again like they used to on Sundays, Monsieur?' Luis asked, curiosity breaking out.

François laughed. 'No, this isn't going to be a line for recreation. Not exactly. And I've told you, Luis, I told you in my office, don't call me Monsieur any more. I'll be angry if you do. Now you say François. Or comrade. Go on, say it. Say François.' He stood there four-square on the lines facing Luis and waiting to be obeyed.

'François . . .' said Luis in a low voice, comrade seeming to him even more familiar.

'There you are. You see? We can be equals.'

234

Luis knew that was a formality: it wasn't Paradis who'd been made to obey in order to become equal. But he'd learned to understand that older men must be left believing what they wanted to believe at the particular moment, an indulgence much easier than putting up with the difficulties they make for you otherwise.

'What about water? When you were here where did you get your water?'

'There's a well after the trees. It's always full and the water's very good. It was the best thing there was. The only clean thing.'

'A locomotive needs a lot of water,' said François.

'The well always stays full however much you take from it.'

'I told you he'd be very useful,' said Soames. 'He asks so many questions himself he must have a lot of answers by now.' Soames was leaning some of his weight onto Luis when he said this so it didn't feel as if he was talking about him when he wasn't there. Just the same, Soames thought Luis needed justifying to Paradis or he wouldn't have said it. The older he got, Luis supposed, the more he'd need justifying in the eyes of the powerful.

'Well here's a question for you, Luis,' François said. 'Do you know why they took so much trouble to make this look like a real Camargue village?'

'Yes.'

'Go on.'

'So the Americans wouldn't have to believe in prison camps.'

'In the homeland of the Rights of Man,' said François, nodding at Luis with approval.

It wasn't many days after that the message from Etienne came through. Soames was to send him something in the post very urgently. Perhaps it was money he needed. Luis warned Soames that here it wasn't safe to send money through the post. This wasn't England where he'd seen that people were too trusting, because of the sea all round.

'It isn't money,' Soames said, 'but I'm hoping what it is will pay enough for getting your sister back for you.'

Luis's heart – if that was where love stays alive – leaped up when he heard this. Not even knowing that he was *mahrime*, unclean now to the end of his life, could kill off the excitement he felt. 'But I've already paid once for that,' he said.

'I know. She costs dear, this sister of yours,' said Soames.

Chapter Twelve

'The material has been sent to Tornac?'

'Yes.'

'It's here in Paris the Minister requires it.'

'Can't we call him Henri between ourselves? Anyway he told me to call him that. This is a private affair, so far.'

'To me he's the Minister.'

'So he's never invited you to call him Henri?'

There was a silence on the line. Admittedly it was a silly question. 'This is anecdotal. You're trying my patience, Stephen. Ministers have private matters to settle and yours is one of them. That's all. Now, to return to the material the Minister's interested in. It must be sent here.'

'I count on handing it over myself. In photography copyright is involved.'

'The material is photographic?'

'I thought you knew.'

'Surely not just the photograph you tactlessly took at the Liberation parade?'

Evidently Philippe was not au courant. When Seagrave had taken refuge in the Hôtel d'Albaron that night he hadn't mentioned the photograph of Fernand-Félix in the station yard. That had been discreet and he would stay discreet. If Ida had been found thanks to the efforts of the Ministry he wasn't going to do anything to devalue the consideration agreed. Though Philippe must by now know a lot about his Minister, apparently the Minister hadn't chosen that he should know this.

'As you just said, it's anecdotal.' There was another silence. 'I can come up with it as soon as it gets light. By train from Clermont.'

'Just post it to me registered. No, I'll send someone. We don't need you in Paris. Stay where you are and go on keeping Marie-Louise amused.'

'I've got two reasons for refusing that. One, I must see Ida first. It may not be her they've found. Any refugee could pretend to be the woman they were looking for, to get rescued.' He surprised himself by the way he said this, as if his interest was almost impersonal.

'What's the other reason?'

'I've told you, I must put what you call the material into Henri's own hands.'

'You had a gentleman's agreement to do so?'

'I suppose you could call it that.'

Philippe laughed in the old way. 'Then I can tell you the limiting attribute was strictly . . . on one side. Don't count on being repaid in kind.'

'I don't. That's why I'm not handing anything over before I've seen Ida myself. Besides, he's got a book of mine.'

'A book? What book?'

'An inscribed edition of *The Prelude*.'

'Is that some English romantic novel?'

'It's a poem.'

'A poem? Long as a book? Tell me. I wouldn't ask the question if I didn't know for sure that this line isn't tapped. Are you by chance blackmailing a Minister of the Republic?'

'If that's your word for enforcing a gentleman's agreement and as you say the line's untapped, yes.'

Philippe laughed again, but that was the last signal Seagrave ever received from his old self. The new one reappeared instantly and stayed in charge. 'I'll report your conditions and telephone again later tonight. Don't go anywhere.'

'This is where the best night-life in the region is,' said Seagrave. Philippe rang off.

'What did that young sodomite have to say for himself?' asked Marie-Louise.

'Since when have you known he had those tastes?'

'I've assumed it from the day I made a small experiment on my own account. It came to nothing. After all,' she added in her little girl's voice, 'I'm not so very much older and boys have to be started off. He was already fifteen.'

'You seem to me far younger than Philippe. I'm sure you always will be.'

'Come and saddle the horses. There's going to be a full moon.'

Some days they went shooting, others they rode in the forest. The life was healthy and the evenings, as Seagrave had said, far from dull. He disliked killing things but they ate the pheasants afterwards, and Marie-Louise, though quite bloodthirsty, wouldn't handle a gun herself.

'It's a man's thing – too, too horrible,' she said with a pleasurable shudder, and never shrank from wringing the neck of any bird that had to be finished off.

There weren't many pheasants left in the woods now. 'The wretched *people* can all come and take them,' Marie-Louise complained tragically. 'Henri ought to do something about it in the government now that it's all his.'

'Perhaps his egalitarian principles wouldn't let him.'

'Principles! The only principle he knows about is the power principle.'

'Isn't he supposed to be on the left?'

'I don't know where he's supposed to be. Wherever he *is*, it's the centre.'

Seagrave had had plenty of time to feel out the nature of Marie-Louise's relations with Fernand. They were, he thought, by way of being obsessive. In paying off her debts he had bought her and all she owned, and she, succumbing, had slipped into a state of legal privileged captivity. Love-hate for the captor must be a usual feature of the condition. So Fernand's name cropped up even at most unwelcome moments.

'I look forward to the day I get old Henri off my back,' he said once in exasperation.

'I don't want to know any secrets but I don't think you can ever do that, not in France. He never lets go, once he has someone. Perhaps you should return to England.'

'I can't.'

'Why not?'

'I'm a pariah there.'

'Not here?'

'What do you think? Am I a pariah at Tornac?'

'I was a pariah too, until Henri came and paid my debts, and my poor husband's debts he left me, and redeemed the mortgages.'

'My mortgages can't be redeemed. They're part of my life,' said Seagrave rather histrionically.

'You mean the girl?'

'Partly that.'

'A Frenchman would know that nothing in love is ever for ever. Englishmen's senses are all corrupted by romanticism, I think. Chivalry was a long time ago, you know. Look at me. Do I get chivalry? Do I expect it?'

'You expect and get attention and compliments. And a lot more, from me. And all richly deserved.'

'That's gallantry. Quite another thing.'

*

It was late when Philippe rang again. 'We're prepared to let you come to Paris and to meet you. The exchange would be effected at a private address where you'd be taken. But there's a problem.'

'What is it? Go on.'

'On the Minister's orders, I've seen her.'

Seagrave's heart gave an uncomfortable lurch. 'Is it Ida?'

'It seems so.'

'What do you mean, seems?'

'We didn't speak. I observed. She didn't see me. In fact she didn't know I was there.'

'Not the proceeding of *un gentleman* as your aunt would tell you.'

'Those were the orders. I was merely to be the guarantor that you would be getting what you bargained for.'

'Well?'

'There's a change . . . you'd better expect that.'

'I do expect it.'

'It's not for the better, but that's not all.'

'Go on. Go on.'

'She seems not to be alone.'

'Of course she isn't. There's a baby, a small child.'

'I don't mean that. She's accompanied by a man. Crippled. When they found her she refused to leave him.'

'What is he?'

'A French soldier taken prisoner, he says. She says he helped her survive and get out. He can't walk.'

'She must have helped him.'

'If the story's true.'

'Where's he from?'

'He had no papers and he can't remember. All I know is he has the accent of the Midi.'

'Well I'll take them all back to Nîmes and we'll find out who he is and where he comes from. That'll settle the account if there is one. I'll take the first train I can get onto in the morning. Give me a number to ring you when I reach Paris.'

'It's not as simple as you think.'

Surely Philippe's function was to remove difficulties, not whine about them? He sounded as if the whole thing was beyond him.

'What's the matter with you? I didn't say it was simple. All you have to do is what you're told. I'll look after the difficult part later.'

241

'That's right,' hissed Marie-Louise in the background. 'Say he's just a pederast functionary.'

'Your project has been put to her. She doesn't want to meet you here. She wants to . . . be let go. Straight back to the Midi . . . to find her brother.'

'If you haven't spoken to her how do you know that?'

'Through an intermediary. A great deal of trouble has been taken over all this.'

'For Luis's sake?'

Philippe didn't answer that. There was a pause before Seagrave continued. 'I'll have to think. I don't understand what she means.'

'You realise there's no question of the Minister allowing her to go anywhere until the . . . consideration has been settled?'

'Just out of curiosity, what would he do with her if it wasn't?'

'Without the least doubt, send her back over the Polish frontier.'

'Just give me a number where I can reach you.'

Fifteen minutes later the telephone rang again. Marie-Louise, to whom he'd outlined the problem, had gone to bed. 'I told you you'd never get free from Henri,' she said as she went.

'Yes? Well?' said Seagrave into the instrument.

'I wish to speak to Madame la Comtesse.'

'Who is it?'

'The maître d'hôtel of Monsieur le Marquis.'

'Madame has retired for the night.'

'It's urgent,' said the shaky old voice, not much above a whisper down the line from Nîmes which wasn't nearly as good as the one to Paris.

Seagrave went into the bedroom. 'Your brother's butler wants to talk to you.'

'But it's absurd. One doesn't speak to butlers at this hour of the night.' She was capable at any time of taking refuge like this in a world of forms.

'He claims it's urgent. I wish you would. I want to get back to

Philippe and you know how long it takes to get through to anywhere.'

Marie-Louise got out of bed. She was naked. 'Give me my velvet robe,' she said, wrapped herself in it without bothering about the buttons, and went to the telephone.

'Yes, Alphonse?' she shouted.

There was a long silence across which the twittering of the butler's voice sounded, faint and undecoded like the inward transmission on Soames's radio all those ages ago in the Cévennes. Roper came to mind, summoned up by these noises of whose prototype he had been the supposed controller. What would Roper make of this situation? No amount of training could possibly prepare a man to handle it adequately.

Marie-Louise was speaking, kindly and decisively. 'You did quite right, my poor Alphonse. What a blow for us all! For you, for me, for Monsieur Philippe. I'll tell him myself, you need do nothing more. Close all the shutters. I'll come immediately. What? . . . yes, yes, I've a chauffeur here, we'll start before dawn. No, I can't give you Monsieur Philippe's number in Paris. But I can get a message to him quite quickly. Monsieur Charles? He's in prison, we can't telephone him there. Leave everything to me. Rest yourself, Alphonse, and don't touch anything. We will inform the lawyers when I arrive. I'm sure my brother will have provided something for you. And you can count on me, besides.' She put the receiver down and turned to Seagrave.

'We're leaving for Nîmes at once: I was to keep you here under lock and key but this is a crisis. Anyway Henri will have to go to Nîmes too, as he was my brother's lawyer. The selfish old Sybarite has passed, at last. We'll tell Philippe tomorrow morning. I want to get there by first light.'

'What for?'

'The pickings,' replied Marie-Louise, not wasting any words as she swept back into the bedroom to get dressed. 'There's an old Delahaye over at the farm. I never told Henri because I thought one day I might be glad of it. Now I am. They've looked after it for me on the quiet. This should arrange your affair at the same time. You'll be at Nîmes where your hostage wants to go. Go now and pack up your things. I shall have quite a lot of luggage.'

'Are you going to stay away a long time?'

'With luck I won't ever have to come back.' Still half-dressed she turned round to him and put her white, well-covered arms about his neck. 'This has been an interlude passing the time very pleasantly for us both, *mon petit* Stephen. The scene's changing now. You don't know what problems you're going to have to face. I'm not a possessive woman, I leave you free.'

'One could just . . . there's really still lots of time, it's quite early . . .'

'No,' she said firmly. 'You've got to make the Delahaye work. It may have to be wound up. Keep your strength for that.'

'Just . . .'

'No.'

*

It was a bright winter night without frost even near the crest. As the Delahaye ran clear of the forest and came to the head of the pass a full red moon swam into view, swinging over the plain below. On the way down, it would disappear behind a shoulder of hill and then return, huge and foreboding, suspended like a blade above the open valley. By the time they approached Nîmes it was getting lighter in the east and the moon had withdrawn with its menace into the upper sky. The door of the Hôtel d'Albaron opened at the first discreet knock and there was Alphonse, fully dressed as if he'd slept on his feet just the other side of it, like an old horse awaiting the end. When he saw Marie-Louise he began to weep, taking both her hands and kissing them in turn. Marie-Louise was weeping too, with impatience. Slung from her shoulder was a large fur-covered bag matching the coat she wore and more or less disappearing into its volume. She had made no bones about what this was for.

'It's to hold my last chance of freedom,' she'd said.

'In the form of what?'

'A selection of my grandmother's jewellery if I can find it in time. Not everything. I won't be greedy.'

'Didn't you have a share by right?'

'Oh that, *that* was the official share. The legal share, it was swallowed up years ago. This time it's the little supplement an old family owes its last daughter to save her from the clutches of the bourgeoisie.'

'Won't there be an inventory of the jewellery somewhere? If Henri's the family lawyer?'

'There was one. I eliminated it one day at Tornac.'

'Does it all belong to Philippe now?'

'He was my brother's only child. That's the inheritance law.'

Seagrave's sympathies on the question, as far as there was one, were all with Marie-Louise. He didn't think anything was due from him to Philippe, when he thought of Luis.

*

As soon as they were inside with the door closed behind them Marie-Louise got down to business. 'Bring up plenty of coffee to the library, Alphonse. You have some coffee I suppose?'

'Monsieur le Marquis had his special cupboard.'

'Break it open if necessary. And some croissants, I'm sure he had a supply of those too. And Armagnac for Monsieur who has had a very long drive in the dark. After that I don't want to be disturbed *on any account*. I must speak to the lawyers in Paris.'

At the mention of lawyers Alphonse took hold again of one of Marie-Louise's hands. 'I'm so very old now. What will become of me, Madame la Comtesse?' he asked in a voice strangled with despair.

'Would you like to end your days on the Côte d'Azur, Alphonse, looking after my house for me?'

'Has Madame a house there?'

'I expect to buy one shortly. And if you're careful and if you do as I say the place is yours.'

Alphonse shuffled away with a lighter step. 'The coffee and Armagnac and croissants will take fifteen minutes,' he promised.

'I think Alphonse has understood,' Marie-Louise said as they reached the library. 'The telephone's over there. You must ring Philippe, say I'm too upset to speak to anyone.'

'Where will you be?'

'In here of course. Everything was kept in false volumes of the *Mémoires* of Saint-Simon. My brother once showed me. He was a lot older. I was about ten.'

'That was a rash thing to do.'

'He expected something in return.' She was silent a moment. 'Now all I have to do is find them.'

'What if the location was moved since then? You can't pull the whole house to pieces. I don't think I could keep Philippe away long enough.'

'My brother hated change. It put him in mind of the Revolution.'

Philippe sounded angry and harassed when finally Seagrave got through to him. 'What happened to you, in the name of God? I rang for hours last night. No answer. You behave as if you didn't understand what a department of State is. Where were you? The Minister will want to know.'

'I'm sorry not to be announcing better news. Your father . . .'

'What's my father got to do with this?'

'Alphonse telephoned to say he'd had an attack.'

'An attack of what?'

'We don't know that yet.'

'I'll ring Nîmes.'

'I'm in Nîmes.'

'In Nîmes? How did you get to be there?'

'Through Le Puy, then Aubenas, Barjac . . .'

'Don't play the village idiot. I mean how is it you come to be in

Nîmes? Marie-Louise had instructions to keep you busy at Tornac.'

'She's here too. She came at once hoping to see your father before it was too late.'

'Pass her to me.'

'I can't, I'm afraid. She's too distressed to talk on the telephone.'

'You mean it was too late?'

'Yes.'

There was a silence, though not, Seagrave thought, one of grief. 'This is very awkward,' said Philippe. 'It couldn't be a worse moment for me to leave the Minister. He's surrounded by parasites.'

'Won't he have to come too? She says he was your father's lawyer. I was to ask you to notify him.'

'Yes. Perhaps that's the solution. Yes. I'll see him at once. He isn't going to be pleased.'

'Well at least your father's out of reach of all reproach.'

'He may be, but I'm not. Why didn't you ring me last night? You must have been on the road for hours. Where did you find a car?'

'I tried. You know what the telephones are in this country. I couldn't get through.'

'I'd better talk to Alphonse.'

'He's in a state of collapse. Terribly affected. You'd be wasting your time.'

'I'll sack the senile old brute as soon as I get down.'

'You're coming straight away?'

'As soon as possible. Here, we do something called work. And not in bed, either.'

'You'll be coming with Fernand-Félix?'

'No doubt.'

'Bring Ida . . . and her travelling companion if necessary. Then Fernand and I can get free of each other once and for all.'

'You think that, do you?'

'I know it. It was agreed.'

'Knowing too much can be an even worse mistake than thinking one knows everything.' Philippe sounded as if giving this answer was some small consolation for all the annoyances caused by Seagrave and his affairs. 'When I've made the arrangements, whatever they are, I'll inform you by telephone. Tell Marie-Louise the Minister will certainly want to hear her explanations. She must dry her tears and pull herself together.' Philippe rang off.

'You managed that very well. Not everyone's a good liar, it's a gift,' said Marie-Louise. She came across the room to where he sat in the corner by the telephone, leaned over him so her breasts, like trained pigeons, alighted on his shoulder, and kissed him warmly. 'I've found them,' she said. Success had added something heady to her customary aroma, a triumphant secretion held in reserve for the moment of escape through all the long period of captivity and humiliation. She pointed to a pile of ordinary-looking calf-bound quarto volumes on the top step of the library ladder, a grandiose carved affair on wheels with a gilded hand-rail.

'I think I hear Alphonse,' Seagrave warned.

Marie-Louise moved away as the door opened. 'Monsieur Philippe will be here soon, Alphonse. We've explained to him how sorrow has left you a little confused.'

'Certainly, Madame la Comtesse,' mumbled Alphonse with conviction. 'I will certainly always remain very confused about the events of these sad days.'

'That's right, Alphonse.'

When he'd gone, leaving the tray with the coffee standing on a corner of the desk, Marie-Louise went back up the steps and fetched the hollow volumes. 'Don't you touch them. I'm wearing gloves,' she said.

'You've thought of everything.'

'I'd be a fool if I didn't.'

Item by item Marie-Louise laid out the contents of the Saint-Simon. Not for the first time in his life Seagrave was struck by how uninteresting valuable jewellery was when you were at close quarters with it. From a distance presumably it drew the eye to enhance the unattainability of the wearer, close to it just seemed like a lot of little shiny stones. And not even all that shiny, but he kept the reflection to himself.

'Now please imagine for me that you're forty years older than you are and buying presents for your mistresses. What would you choose? I must be sure of selling quickly to a dealer I know at Monte Carlo with a clientèle of old boys who haven't too long to go.'

'It would depend on the pocket money of the old boys.'

'On their last legs that sort of man stops at nothing.'

'The best, in that case?'

'Don't worry about the best. Just apply the male imagination.'

Marie-Louise folded up the selected items in her fur bag. 'I'd have liked to give you something, like a ring, to remember me by. But it might be going too far.'

'I'll remember you perfectly without. Anyway I couldn't have taken it.'

'Why not?'

'The last time I was in this house I was a friend of Philippe's.' As she was reascending the ladder he thought of something else. 'Will he know where to find what's left?'

'Just in case he doesn't I'll tell him.'

'Be vague on detail.'

'Very vague indeed.'

'What will you do now?'

'I'll stay here long enough to see my poor brother under the ground, God forgive his selfish parsimony. Then I'll slip quietly away, never to return.'

'What about Henri?'

'Henri has plenty of other *chats à fouetter*.' She laughed with an unmistakable little note of admiration. 'That expression could have been invented just for him. Whipping cats all the way to the top.'

'Can I borrow the Delahaye to go and find Luis and Soames?'

'But that's it, of course. I make you a gift of the Delahaye. A keepsake. Perhaps it'll even bring you back sometimes, when I'm settled, down on the coast.'

'She's a very fine old machine.'

'I hope if you remember me at all you'll think the same.'

*

Up on the garrigue there was no one, but there were signs of occupation – a spade against a wall, a shirt hanging to dry on a branch of the apricot tree – and inside, the hearth was still warm. Above it on the shelf was a letter for him with an English stamp.

Dear Steve,

I hope this reaches you; I got the address from William who came over to see my grandfather about the election. What a big fat bore he is, you always said so. He calls me the beauteous Glory, I can hardly bear it.

Anyway, the news is Grandpa wants to go and die on the Riviera he says. Now we've pretty well won the War he can relax, the nation can spare him. As some of the time he thought the War was against the French as usual, he's afraid once they realise they've lost they may burn down his villa at Vence. So we're coming out with a male nurse and a female one (me) as soon as William's Ministry (imagine you with a brother in a Ministry) arrange the logistics. That's what William calls them, don't ask me what he means. He says we may have to go by sea, with the Navy!

And why do you think I managed to get leave to be included in the party? I won't tell you, you'll have to work it out for yourself. How far is Nîmes from Vence? Have you got a car there? Is Vence far from the sea? Grandpa says there are lemon trees in the garden of the villa. D'you think there really are, or is it just part of his dream due to being old and mad? Anyway I hope I'll see you. Unless you have too many of what William would call prior commitments.

Lots of love, Glory.

PS I enclose the address. About the commitments – when you were a boy you were always pretty good at wriggling out of things. G.

Seagrave felt strangely disturbed by the letter. It was as if sexuality existed in layers like the soil or the sea, and this appeal came from a long way down. Nearer the surface were the urgent calls for immediate answer; this one was distant but . . . but what? . . . foundational. He went back to the Delahaye and drove into town to ask after François Paradis.

It wasn't easy to view the station and its offices only as harmless, neutral buildings, rather grandiose and theatrical like a music-hall spared by the bombing. The whole ensemble had become a focal point for excitement, hope and fear. A few paces away the Milice headquarters stood shuttered, deserted. Seagrave entered the offices. Paradis hadn't been seen for some days, and there was trouble brewing for him when he condescended to come back. The higher administration thought it was time to remind this hero that he was no longer a guerrilla chieftain and a law to himself. There were plenty of official little men scurrying about here to whom it would be a pleasure if this duty fell to them, Seagrave could see that. Paradis's broad form offered a good target for envy. He made his way on foot back to the Hôtel d'Albaron, leaving the Delahaye under the planes of the avenue. He wanted to exorcise the fears he'd felt the last time he'd walked this way with the Minox under his skirt. Now he had the film safe in an inside pocket.

Alphonse opened the door to him with the manner that no amount of crisis could affect. 'Monsieur Philippe is coming with the Minister in an aeroplane,' he said at once.

'With . . . anyone else?'

'Bringing the person whom Monsieur expects.' It was curious. Alphonse's tone and his words were discretion itself, but from the backwaters of his eye there seemed to come a kind of warmth as if he knew by observation that matters of the heart know no boundaries of caste or race.

'Thank you very much, Alphonse.'

Marie-Louise too, showed signs of a certain empathy. 'I lose you in a romantic cause,' she said. 'But don't forget people change. You may have changed too.' Did she mean because he'd been with her? Had she noticed some change he was unaware of? It was too late to ask. She waited upstairs in the room that had been hers when she was a young girl. 'I'm going to gather the memories and burn them in the fireplace,' she said. Seagrave paced uneasily and unhappily about the hall, the forecourt, and the street beyond, looking out for the convoy of gendarmes that would accompany the Minister from the airfield. The moment, planned, negotiated and bought, was at hand. The afternoon was cold and the winter light beginning to rinse from the sky but he was sweating under his shirt, a cold sweat that seemed to rise from the stomach, like a fever. He yawned from time to time too and though he'd had no sleep he didn't think this was the yawning of mere somnolence.

'Monsieur, they are here.' The hand of Alphonse in its white glove was applying a gentle pressure to his shoulder. He rose from the hall chair like a dreamer lurching forward into a world half realised. The noise of motor-bicycle engines reverberated in the enclosed courtyard, someone shouted an order. It sounded like an operation of the *Hohenstaufen* Panzer Division, moving in hyena packs about the quiet back streets of the town. As Seagrave reached the steps of the house he was aware of Marie-Louise behind him, on the stairs, crossing the hall. He turned for a last exchange of glances. She was dressed in deep black and motioned him forward with a wave of the hand that was a farewell.

The door of the leading car was being held open by a gendarme while a leg ending in a silk sock and highly polished shoe made a descent on the paving stones of the d'Albaron forecourt. It could only be Fernand-Félix, taking command of the terrain. Philippe was on the other side of the car and though now on his own premises he seemed to hurry round to help, and make sure the Minister was successfully transferred to the safety of the interior. Alphonse too was doing his duty, keeping his end up till the moment came when he could skip off to the coast with Madame la Comtesse. Seagrave had a vision of him happy in his white gloves among the lemon trees.

Fernand was out of the car now and he made an impatient gesture in the direction of the motor-bicycles. One by one and as if reluctant to vacate the sound waves the engines slowed and fell silent. 'Where is that little Etienne?' he called out, his voice unexpectedly young. 'Ah, there you are.' Seagrave advanced so he was on the top step of the stair whose two arms encircled a fountain half buried in moss. A second car was turning into the courtyard from the street and immediately one of the gendarmes closed the iron gates behind it. Fernand put out a hand and kept it extended after Seagrave had politely and briefly shaken it. He lifted the envelope containing the film from his pocket and passed it over. 'It will be as well for you if this is what I expect it to be,' said Fernand.

'I assure you it is.'

'And where is Marie-Louise? She has some explaining to do I think.'

'I am here, Henri,' she announced in a voice of mourning, standing at the foot of a pillar just inside the entrance, the black mantilla that covered her fair hair reaching nearly to the ground.

A smile of amusement passed rapidly across Fernand's features. 'My most sincere condolences, dear Madame,' he said, and she inclined her head gracefully and sadly under the mantilla, eyes lowered.

Fernand turned at the top of the steps to face the courtyard and see the transaction completed. The second car had come to a halt just inside the gates. All sound and movement but for the trickling of the fountain through the moss had died out like the closing notes of a dance hung for a moment in the air. It seemed a heavy silence like heavy water, dangerous, deviant. No order had been given to the gendarmes to open the door of the second car and they stood frozen by their machines. Seagrave was frozen too, at the side of the doorway as if the weight of the lintel rested on his head. Suddenly a child's crying came from inside the car, loud and shrill, the cry of a primate but barely a human child's cry, a screaming as inaccessible to relief as that formerly heard from the cellars of the Milice headquarters on the avenue. As he took a step forward the back door of the car was pushed slowly and partially open from inside with a hesitating movement and the crying became more insistent, the sounds pouring out into the courtyard.

At last, with the child looking too big for her arms, a woman came out from the car like an animal out of a shell. Even here in the south she must be terribly cold in those bodiless, colourless rags. Why hadn't they provided her with something better to wear? Her neck and shoulders were uncovered, the frame of bones pushing through the skin. Seagrave removed his coat as he went down the steps two at a time, stumbling over the last which was uneven, and advanced holding out the coat as though to screen an indecent sight. Somehow, unnoticed, Alphonse had got there first. Seagrave wondered for an instant about the state of the sensibilities of the audience behind him. Alphonse was holding the car door, stooping forward and offering something folded over his arm, a woollen shawl, probably what the late marquis draped over his knees when taken out for a drive. Seagrave put the shawl over the child in the hope of silencing it and his coat on the mother's shoulders and looked down into her face, turned away from him towards the closed gates as if to measure the line of escape.

'Look at me,' he said, raising his voice to carry through the child's noise. Philippe had warned him there was change. It seemed indeed radical. Dirt and exhaustion might have a lot to do with it, but the flesh of her face that had given it its serene fullness had burned away, her lower lip whose generosity had been like an invitation was shrunken and stretched, the upper one depressed on one side as though teeth were missing there. 'Please look at me. It's over. You're back.' She turned her eyes to him and he saw that their green had drained from them as it deserts the leaf of a lemon tree after frost.

'Where is Luis?'

'I've got Luis safe.'

'He's mine.' She held the screaming child out as far as her strength allowed, horizontally so its arms and legs punched the air like the feet of a tortoise on its back. 'This is your child.'

Was it? He felt no spring of recognition. The child seemed to look through him at a detested world of its own. He made no attempt to take it from her and after a moment she drew it back against her side. Nothing was going to free her from it. From behind him he heard someone call an order and a gendarme opened one of the gates wide enough for a person on foot to pass through, and then remained standing by it ready to close it again. This was the signal to depart. Seagrave turned in time to see Fernand-Félix enter the house and to catch a glimpse of the black mantilla as the doors closed. Philippe was still at the top of the steps watching him. It was clear he couldn't leave too soon for Philippe. 'We must go,' he said to Ida. 'I've got a car in the avenue.'

'Where to?'

'We'll go and find Luis.'

There was no sign on her face of freedom regained, and he had no sense of speaking to the free person he'd known. Of course with that child in her arms her liberation was notional. 'I haven't come alone,' she said, and motioned with her head towards the car.

'What is it?' He knew the answer but a resistance in him refused to make it easy.

'A companion,' she said, and added something so low he couldn't hear it.

'What did you say?'

'Out of hell.'

'Why doesn't he get out?'

'He can't. His wheelchair was left behind. They wouldn't bring it.'

A rage took hold of Seagrave, not on account of the wheelchair or the disabled man in the back of the car but because of the aberrations of fate, the hostile *baxt* maybe, catching up from whatever was its starting point. He turned fiercely on the group of gendarmes. His fury wouldn't hurt them.

'Open these gates and get the car out of here and onto the avenue. There's a man who can't walk.' No one moved. 'I know you people well. You all joined the Resistance under orders at the eleventh hour to save your skins. This man was wounded in the fighting.'

'What do you know about it?' one of the men muttered. 'You're only a foreigner.'

'I was with François Paradis right from the start.' There was an immediate general movement as when a heavy stone is thrown into a pool. The gates were swung open, instructions given to the driver of the car, two men mounted their motor-bicycles and rode out onto the road as an escort. Another put his face down to the back window as if to exchange a friendly word with the man inside, then straightened himself abruptly.

'It's that swine Eric in there,' he said to his colleague in a voice of astonishment.

The car reversed to turn, then moved slowly forward to pass through the gates. Seagrave, standing beside them, caught sight of the man on the back seat, shrivelled, white-bearded, pulling himself back into the shadow of Ida and the child. Before he went out into the road himself to walk to the avenue Seagrave saw Philippe beckon the gendarme who had spoken, saw the man go over to him at the foot of the steps, answer a question, salute. Seagrave's last view of Philippe was as he hurried back into the house, carrying to his master, presumably, the information just gathered.

Part Four

Chapter Thirteen

THE SPRING HERE ALWAYS seemed previous, not to say premature, coming with sudden force before you were altogether ready, like an ejaculation ahead of schedule. That was Soames's analysis and Seagrave felt the surprise too, even though he'd seen so many more of these springs than Soames had. The onrush was ecstatic but the build-up too brief. Everyone working on the huts at the Bohemians' camp took their shirt off and the late February sun soaked into the skin and soaked the cold out of the bone.

Unlike Luis, Ida had at once accepted the return here to set up some sort of house in one of the surviving huts. The town frightened her and here near the sea she felt safer. Perhaps that was partly on account of the man Eric. You could hide and lose yourself in the vast emptiness of this delta and its sky. Another thing was, as Seagrave soon recognised, that in her mind she was working backwards, as if to find the point at which the *baxt* had turned against her, and the Bohemians' camp lay on that backward road. Let me go back, her eyes seemed constantly to be saying, and not know any more about all that had to happen.

She had put on a little weight and been to the dentist in Arles and her honey-coloured hair grew more thickly now, but about the eyes there was the same shadow, under them and at the edge. 'They emptied the huts on the last night. No one came back. No one they took away ever came back. I hid in a hole some of the women had dug under the floor.'

'Didn't the child scream?'

'It was after that he started. On the road. Not all at once, day by day.'

His name was Stefan – of course, it had to be so – but no one called him that, or anything else. He seemed to exist at a level below nomenclature. The hostility he read, if he could read it, in the eyes of those observing and hearing him he repaid with compound interest. From behind the barrage of his sound he looked on the world with loathing.

'Adolf as a toddler,' said Soames, then quickly added, 'poor little devil's sick.'

'He's very strong though.'

'The problem's up above.'

'Yes.'

But it wasn't a problem Seagrave could face full on. He wished he could, but as Ida was there to take the weight he left it, despising himself, but adamant. A father was for other things, for sound children – God knew what those other things were but they weren't this. A man hadn't the innate skills.

Eric was another unfaced problem. He had to be looked after and helped because Ida wouldn't abandon him. At first Seagrave supposed that, as a soldier wounded fighting for the *patrie*, Eric would make an effort and return to wherever he came from and claim the warrior's due. There was no sign of that.

'We could try and put a photograph in the new local paper and trace your family, or at least your commune.' Seagrave produced the Minox. 'François Paradis could fix it.' Eric said nothing, put an arm across his face and retreated into a permanent silence of icy, hostile fear. Being helpless he had to share sleeping quarters with Luis who watched him suspiciously and without speaking any more than Eric spoke. What had Eric done for Ida to earn this protection at everyone's expense?

'When everyone went away and it was quiet I came out of the hole to look for food. Eric was near the gates of the camp. He was left behind because he couldn't walk.'

'What was he doing there?'

'What was anyone doing there? In Switzerland they knew what they were doing, your sister Jean knew. But you didn't, I didn't. Eric was there, that's all, by the gates. Left there,' she repeated.

'Did he have a wheelchair then?'

'There was a sort of cart they used for taking anyone away who died in the food-line. They had a train for the ones who died . . . where they were supposed to.'

She'd wheeled him halfway across northern Europe on this handcart, him and the child and their bundles.

'What did he do for you to earn it?'

'He had a gun. We wouldn't have lasted long without that.'

'Did he use it?'

'When we had to have food. And if any man came and inter-fered.'

'Has he still got the gun?'

She didn't answer. She sang to the child, that was the only thing capable of soothing it for a time, improvised songs sung in a hoarse voice, a running commentary on her sorrow and the treacherous *baxt*. If the man Eric had been armed, back there in the camp in the north, and was left behind only because of his disability, that implied he hadn't been exactly an inmate, not on the same terms as Ida and the hundreds taken away on the last night. Or Seagrave's father-in-law, come to that, wherever he'd ended. But it was just this aspect of the Eric enigma that Seagrave shied away from, for her sake. So Eric hung on like a secret weight on a conscience, seldom out of his hut, fed and supplied with alcohol for pain but never eating with the rest of them, alien, holed-up as a wounded rat. Seagrave knew that sooner or later someone else would come and take care of the Eric problem and then Ida would have no reproach to bring against herself or him, nothing to make her hate him more than it seemed she already did, through hating Jean.

This hatred of Jean lay between them, not a shadow but a

substantial thing, an iron bolster lengthwise down the bed separating them body and soul. She withdrew when he touched her as if his
touch was the hand of hatred, the denouncer's finger. When he
woke before dawn she would be already gone. Where to? He didn't
ask. Surely not to lie beside a man wrecked from the waist down.
Perhaps to gaze on the free sky and count the stars like coins. It
seemed she couldn't get pleasure without the impetus of love, it
didn't come. She could have commerce, but no pleasure, and even
the first time their relations had not been commercial. The obvious
conclusion he was to draw was that her love had died as though it
was the one part of her that hadn't taken refuge in the hole under
the floor. For Seagrave that was worse than if she'd died herself, on
the road, in the food-line, then he would never have found this out.
He didn't know the right way to mourn the death of a love that had
been as alive as this first light of spring.

The purchase of the land and buildings was completed soon after
his arrival. Any qualms he had about the operation were neutralised
by finding that the hoard of money was unwanted by anyone else.
When Charles d'Albaron was released from prison for his brother's
funeral Seagrave met him by appointment in a café in the town and
asked his advice, in a roundabout way.

'That dossier was closed long ago, when I was still in charge of
this little world down here,' said Charles. 'Try and get a French
bureaucrat to reopen a closed dossier. My dear, you'd be dead
before the dust was even disturbed on the cardboard cover.'

When he approached François with the same scruple he was told
not to be a fool. 'What interests me is that railway line. Once the
land's yours you'll be serving the cause. That should be enough for
you.' François was a fanatic now, with a fanatic's single-minded
logic.

There was still quite a lot of cash left over, accounted for by
Soames including the deductions made for his own and Luis's
therapeutic recreation. He offered to pay that back out of his
pension when he got it but Seagrave pointed out that you can

only redress a balance if you can identify the creditor, and in this case there was no one to stand forward. 'That cash has to be looked on as a common stock,' he said, trying to find a rational status for it.

'OK with me,' said Soames. 'All the same you'd better have it. Someone's got to be party treasurer. And there's still a bit buried up on the garrigue.' Soames very much admired the Delahaye. 'The most thanks I ever got was a square breakfast with porridge and an offer of the same again when the fancy took me.' He now had a more advanced type of foot and was able to practise driving the Delahaye round the deserted Camargue roads. There was pain at every sharp movement but it was worth it. 'The engine inside that car, it's a darling,' he said, kissing the ends of his fingers.

The first time he went as far as Nîmes he came back with some post from the cabin in the garrigue. The most interesting item was a letter from Glory.

Well you see we've got here. Grandpa more dead than alive but he was that before we started. Anyway he's coming round in the sun. And everything. And there *are* lemon trees. I found your note. It wasn't exactly *effusive* let me tell you. You receive a nice letter from a friendly virgin in your own part of the country and all you say is you'll see if you can manage to get away. Some men would be more sprightly than that, believe me (from what I've heard).

A French lady has come offering to buy the little house at the end of the olive grove that Grandpa wants her to have because he liked the look of her as soon as he saw her. In fact he's lost about a hundred years since then. She claims to be a countess. Madame de Tornac. Quite honestly she looks to me like a terrific old tart but after all that's exactly what someone of Grandpa's age probably needs down at the end of the garden don't you think? A professional. She can come up in the evenings and oil his poor old working parts. She certainly looks as if she knows how to set about it.

I'm sure I wouldn't have written the above if it wasn't for the effects of the sun. Plus nurses' training. I don't think I'd better post this letter at all. I'm blossoming in the light here but I'm afraid it's the *fleurs du mal* that are coming out. Perhaps it'll make you think badly of me. Or perhaps you won't think about me at all, with so much else on your mind. So I may as well post it after all and then you'll have to, as a gentleman, so as to answer it. But are you always such a gentleman, Steve? It would be interesting to know Madame de Tornac's verdict on that, she must have known so many who weren't.

Love, Glory.

PS She's got a derelict dear old butler with her and she sent him tottering up with some wine. As you can probably guess, I've been drinking it. I wouldn't be surprised if they move in.

PPS Grandpa says if you like you can come and stay as long as you care to. G

So Marie-Louise and Alphonse had got away safely and were realising their shared dream. It might be amusing to go and see how they were all getting on together. But duty – uncodified but compelling – required him to be here. Even so. And as well as duty there was doggedness. The image of oneself as a beloved being with rights is hard to surrender. If a woman loves you her autonomy is to some extent out of her hands; she can't unilaterally renege. He knew this was an atavistic set of feelings but so, after all, were the feelings tied directly to some part of the body, such as desire and possessive spasm. It only proved the close link between emotions and their biological source, that was what he thought about it. But when Ida was there before him or when he held her unresponding against him these ideas fell away and all he was aware of were the marks of the enemy, the malignant *baxt* on her.

'This 'un's got an English stamp,' Soames said. It was a brown office envelope, typewritten like a bill. Inside was a message scrawled in pencil on lined paper with no heading.

'It's from my brother.'

'Aye, you can see no expense was spared. Must have mortgaged the estate for the stationery alone.'

Dear Stephen,

You will rejoice to know that I have got in at a by-election. When the general election comes it's bound to be a Tory landslide so the future looks settled.

Unfortunately the same cannot be said of yours. Intelligence has been reaching us to the effect that a certain indiscretion in your character and conduct (no news to me may I say) has made you if not *persona non grata* where you are, the object of too close and potentially very embarrassing attention in high places.

This would not be the best moment in the history of the family for any deplorable incident. If you return I think I can arrange something quickly in Australia, but do not lose any time. Go to Marseilles at once and try to get on a British boat. I will send the necessary signals from this office.

Haweswater has gone out to the Riviera but I do not imagine either he or Glory will want to see anything more of you.

Yours, William Seagrave.

'He wants to ship me out to Australia.'

'Don't you ever let him do that. It's never a place for you,' said Soames pithily.

*

There was a troop of horses now, grazing on the land between the camp and the Rhône, unbroken but amiable animals keeping their distance neither too far nor too close in antique cohabitation at this end of the earth. Seagrave and Soames thought about breeding horses and cattle on the land; they thought of opening a hotel in cabins for visitors who liked to rough it and cared to ride, for botanists, zoologists, ornithologists, or escapists of any shade. Or they would flood the land with water from the Rhône and grow rice; or they would plant vines and make wine; or rear game for sale to the murderous shooting syndicates who roamed the delta. These projects, one after the other, came to a halt before the desert realities of this blank space on the map. Nothing flourished here. There was no shade and the soil was impregnated with salt since the enemy had flooded the Camargue from the sea. The horses like cromlechs on the skyline testified to the tragic brevity of life more than to its fertility. The entire landscape, flat and open as the sea itself, was bare, unoccupied, uncultivated. You felt you would be ploughing and harrowing and sowing the bottomless ocean.

It was Paradis who foreclosed these various schemes for good, arriving one day at dawn in a train which advanced slowly, gently over the prairie from the north and halted, puffing and rattling among the cabins. There were half a dozen trucks and an engine from which Paradis stepped down, greasy, grimy and generating a field of vitality and consequence far about him. '*Enfin mes enfants*,' he announced in his voice which would have carried compliance and order to the far end of any camp, 'the Bohemians' camp finds its true vocation!'

Only Seagrave was around to hear him, having woken to find himself alone in the half dark. Whatever your problems the dawn was a good time, the mosquitoes weren't yet in the air and the wildfowl sounded tentative between silences so deep you thought you could hear the distant sea, stirring from sleep. 'And what is that vocation?' he asked in a voice surly even to himself, regretting the broken silence and uninfected so far by the enthusiasm.

'Monsieur is still hardly conscious. He growls like an old farm dog in his kennel.' Paradis banged him on the shoulder to bring him round. 'The Bohemians' camp is our springboard, like the forest in the Cévennes. In good striking distance of the field of action.' He was wearing the campaign clothes he'd worn in the maquis, a mixture of uniform items taken by raid or ambush from either side.

'The action? What action? Where?'

'The bridge between Beaucaire and Tarascon is the target,' Paradis answered, lowering his voice.

'The target?' A first serious misgiving entered Seagrave's mind. This wasn't his country but he'd become so familiar with it he felt a tenderness easily alarmed. 'You're not going to blow it up? With historic towns on either side?'

'We're going to block it. When the time's ripe. Deny passage.'

That was a kind of relief, at least. 'With what end, François?'

'As a sign. It will be the signal for much more general action. Everywhere. I always said the railway's the key to power. This is how great events are brought about. A small spark lights the fuse. Think of the Odessa Steps.'

Seagrave didn't want to think of them. They were a long way off in time and space and he wasn't even sure what had happened on them. All the same François must be serious or he wouldn't have taken this retired train from whatever shunting yard he'd found it in and brought it here with a plentiful supply of coal, as Seagrave saw on looking into the first trucks. So he must be taken seriously, at least as seriously as he took himself. And no doubt he had plenty of followers nostalgic for the times of action. Seagrave felt the nostalgia himself; he could feel a growing impatience for it now as he considered the train there in the heart of this provisional encampment. Action seemed to call from a distance, faintly at first, suggesting a way out of unhappy emotions. François had gone back on the locomotive and was reducing the pressure in the boilers, a jet of snowy steam shooting into a sky still pale, cloudless, without wind. If you didn't do that would the boiler explode? Seagrave looked northward along the lines towards the junction, invisible from here across the wastes of grass, where this overgrown track met the still-functioning line from Saint Gilles to Arles. A brief struggle took place in him between prudent misgivings and the taste for active performance.

'How will we get to Tarascon? There's no rail bridge over the Rhône at Arles.'

Paradis looked at him with the old approval. 'You're right, Etienne, *mon gars*: there's no bridge there; the line turns back like a fishhook on this side of the river. But I shall take my train the other way, by Nîmes, in the night. Full of brave men.'

'That's the main line.'

'Exactly. It's the one to block.'

'But how can you run a private irregular train along the main line?'

'Why do you think I'm a railwayman? For the money? For the promotion? No no. You know that by now. I will be signalled through in the proper way, when the time comes, by men placed in the key positions. That's what the work of my office is,' he ended simply, 'the signalling on the main lines.'

He made it all sound like what Seagrave had heard described in smashed-up smoky London as a piece of cake. That's what a good commander did, simplify the issues for subordinates. Seagrave knew this was only the skeleton: there would be much tactical detail worked out in François's head and it wasn't for him to ask too many questions. Service implied hierarchy and hierarchy meant the experience and exercise of authority, above you and below you respectively. As for service, had he any choice? The Bohemians' camp had been bought in his name with this end in view, that was now obvious. It had been hinted to him and it was too late now to pretend otherwise. Soames had probably been in the know all along. Seagrave didn't resent that. Soames would have had his orders and he was a soldier, a kind of mercenary as well as being a friend. It came back to hierarchy. And then the purchase money had come from François originally even if it wasn't exactly his for investment in revolutionary stock. No one had any exclusive right to the use of this money, it was a floating fund, a free balance, and this was a fait accompli. At the end of the mental summing-up he welcomed the fait accompli. He'd welcomed it, really, at the beginning.

Ida had reappeared from her dawn watch and was standing

beside a tree near the well, looking with fear at the train which like a sea monster had come ashore here in the small bay of her safety. Her hands were folded into each other in front of her as if to shield her belly. The inadequacy of the defence aroused pity, the ambiguous impulse that was always ready, another side of love like the anger he felt also. This love of his was a landscape in which he was the only living thing, but for the changing light he saw it under. Some of the fullness had returned to her face and some of the glow to her skin so that though changed she was recognisable. Paradis was regarding her with unmistakable admiration.

'What has it come for?' she asked.

'Don't be afraid of it,' said François. 'It's only here for a short time. Etienne will look after it, and later we'll take it away.' He spoke as if it was a dangerous animal and she a child.

'I've seen a train in a camp before.'

'This one is to bring a better life. More life. Not death.' He seemed to know what was in her mind though she said so little and remained so guarded.

Ida shrugged her shoulders lightly and raised her hands, separated so they seemed to give a benediction to the train. Or maybe it was a curse they invoked on it, who could tell? Like an escaped animal she was outside the field of interpretation. 'A railway line doesn't lead to freedom. You're not free on a train. The road is the only freedom,' she said.

'The Americans call it a railroad. You must see it like that. Trust me,' said François.

'I don't trust anyone,' Ida answered, but her manner relented and she smiled quickly at him before she turned away again. François seemed struck dumb by this smile as if the current it created, passing through him, had carried away the concrete his self-assurance rested on. That was only for a moment. Real life was not a matter for women's smiles and their effect on you.

'I'll explain how to fire the boiler,' he said to Seagrave, pulling himself together: 'that could save me a lot of valuable time when the day comes; if I get a signal to you in advance you'll know what to do. It takes several hours to build up the pressure.' They climbed up onto the platform of the engine and Seagrave peered into the glowing chamber where the coal fires were now burning low, while François told him the best way to go about relighting it. 'In the end it's common sense,' he said, confirming Seagrave's belief that this lesson was really a manoeuvre against distraction.

'She's still very beautiful, isn't she,' he said.

'The only important thing about what you call beauty is how inefficient and unhappy it can make you,' said François. 'It can make me very inefficient if I let it. Inefficient as a young boy.' The word chosen to designate this fearful effect of his passions if let loose was a kind of ideologically loaded euphemism. The mass of his body seemed to belie it. 'And it's made you unhappy. Beauty and duty and having to go on always being *un gentleman*: that's what they're doing to you, my poor old Etienne.'

'Compassion comes into it.'

'You need to work,' said François. 'For a cause. There's a place for compassion but it doesn't cover the whole sky, not if you're working to an end for a cause. In the Cévennes we didn't think about compassion much of the time – you know that as well as anyone. We never would have known what to do with your Major Roper if we'd lived in a cloud of compassion. Ask Soames.' He spoke with the kind of deliberate contempt that only a readily compassionate man would have needed. William could surely dispatch the quality of mercy with much less strain.

'I must talk to Soames about signals,' François continued. 'The telephone wires are down between Saint Gilles and the Camargue and there's no Baudot, of course. I don't suppose there ever was on this line. It was for bringing the mother-in-law to the seaside on Sundays. Has Soames got radio equipment with him?'

'The only equipment he brought was medical.'

'Yes.' François was used to Soames's leg by now and therefore Soames and everyone else should be too. 'Where is he?'

'Some nights he stays in Nîmes. There's a girl there . . .'

'I know the house. From the outside. Too expensive for a simple railwayman.'

Seagrave laughed. He didn't believe that: it was a Calvinist cover. Not against fornication, against visible extravagance in the pursuit of what Rousseau said should be free to every working man. Or was it Marx who said it? Both of them, probably.

'All right, François, just from the outside. Anyway that's where he sometimes spends the night, or most of it.'

'Why doesn't he keep the girl here and save the petrol?'

'It's like you and your compassion. He doesn't want it covering the whole sky.' Just at that moment the motor of the Delahaye could be heard purring like a great easy cat along the damaged road, among the cries of wildfowl and other animal signals of the Camargue filling the early air. 'That's him.'

They watched as Soames turned into the camp from the road and came to a halt beside the train. 'Just made it in time to jump up slow,' he said through the car window.

'What does he say?'

'Only a country joke, about trains.'

'The time of harmless jokes from the country is over.' Trains were sacred of course, no joking matter when history was in the making, one should know that. The dialectic demanded it. And purpose and the cause were sacred too, and the crusade against useless emotions, redundant humour, costly brothels.

'You must know by now we're serious when it's necessary, François.'

'You're serious when I'm there to remind you. When I'm not, you play about and have private lives. Now, one of you must take me back to Nîmes in that *voiture de gigolo*. It had better be Soames: we can arrange about signals and see what can be done.' He turned to Seagrave with some of the old kindness, from the times before the cause had got the better of it. 'She may come back to you, sometimes they do,' he said in an undertone. 'And if she doesn't, you're young and the women seem to like you.' He waved his hand at the Delahaye. 'There's plenty of fish in the sea. One woman – it's much the same as another. Except Madame Paradis of course.'

'Of course.'

'No one could have done more than you. Being unhappy for long isn't right for a young man.'

How did he know? Had his brief sighting of Ida been enough to tell him all he needed? Or perhaps he and Soames had had a talk some time in Nîmes. 'I'll remember that. And the cause comes first.' Seagrave raised a fist.

François looked hard at him before answering, making sure this wasn't another untimely country joke. 'Better be a common soldier in a cause than a gigolo at large. Even if a soldier sometimes catches a bullet in the wrong place. Where it wouldn't suit a gigolo.' He turned to get in the car, then turned back and spoke again in a low voice. 'Which reminds me.' He looked uncomfortable, a man used to direct speech and uncertain now of the way to frame the coming sentence. 'I think there's a protégé... in the camp... I've heard . . . I think you understood what I said about compassion in times of action. We must be sure of security. In the Cévennes we sometimes had to . . . prune the vine.'

'It's for Ida . . .'

François had got in beside Soames and the Delahaye was already turning. 'When I come back I'll bring some comrades. Here we must be able to work out the plan without risk of any interference. The comrades can camp. The water's good.'

Seagrave watched them go. They both seemed to him older than they used to seem, as if they had been aged by all he'd been through. In François's vital energy there was an element of strain as though too great demands were being made on the underlying structure. They were both still admirable and even lovable, but something had changed. His own life before the recovery of Ida had been still the springtime and that, like the season of harmless jokes, was past. The child had woken and its screams rang across the open ground. The waves of sound engulfed the train, the huts, the trees. It wasn't hunger or bodily needs that were expressed by this unbroken stream of noise, it was a savage existential protest. Life was a lock and the child a key that would never fit in: he turned none of its springs or levers, he could only scream exclusion from beyond a closed door. He was shut off from the world of speech, only song could reach him. It seemed that he couldn't apprentice himself to speech because hatred precluded the necessary mimesis.

'He's a child of the death camp,' Ida had said.

'In England I met a Romany woman who said . . .' For some reason of reserve before others' secrets Seagrave left his sentence unfinished.

'They say anything. Anything they think you want to hear, if it's for money. Did you pay her?'

'No.'

'Then you can believe what she told you.'

Ida said this as if she knew quite well what that must have been. As always he felt a dimension of intelligence and transmission outside his scope, like Soames's radio universe where matters of life and death were quickly settled in codes impenetrable by the ignorant. He found nothing he could usefully say to her. Instead he opened his arms in another attempt to create a fold where they could be wrapped as before. Ida seemed to move towards him, tremble on the brink as the little smile she had for the erotic threshold sketched itself about her mouth and vanished, then she drew away. It was unreasonable, it wasn't just, but it was obedience to a law.

'Why not?' he asked, and she didn't answer. She stood there like a child knowing only too well the force of its feelings. 'Not because of him . . .?' He indicated with his head the direction of the cabin shared by Eric and Luis.

Either the gesture or something in his voice must have roused her. 'He helped me out of the death camp, not into it,' she said.

'Do you know what he was before?'

'It doesn't matter. What was I before? A whore. We have the right to live all the same.'

'You want to live with him?'

'No. He lives with me. He has to. There's nowhere else for him. He's an animal maimed in a trap.'

*

When Soames returned he had a drum of cable, a couple of telephone instruments, and a stamped authority from the railway administration to establish a line between the permanent way near Saint Gilles and the Bohemians' camp. He was in high spirits. 'It's a fine feeling going back to campaign,' he said. 'I'll be honest, I did reckon I were finished.'

'You'll never be that,' Seagrave said rather mechanically as his mind was already on the road. 'How are we for petrol?'

'Paradise had her filled up.'

'Did he say when he thinks of coming back with the comrades?'

'I'd say you've a clear week.'

'All I want is a couple of days. To breathe.'

'Take your time, lad. It'll all still be here.'

'How would you get over to Saint Gilles?'

'Luis has one of those horses half-broken. He can lead me till the foot's used to the stirrup.'

'Keep your eye on that Eric.'

'It's never off him for long.'

A tank full would get the Delahaye as far as Vence where there should surely be no great problem about petrol for the return journey. There were already Americans back on the Riviera, so it was said. Alphonse would tell him where to go, it would be part of Alphonse's function to know about things like petrol. Glory had given him a telephone number and Seagrave stopped two or three times at a bar and tried unsuccessfully to get through and warn of his arrival. Somewhere between here and the Riviera the system had broken down. In a way, that must give protection to the lucky people living there. Marie-Louise, for example, would be harder to run to earth. She would have time to dig in. He wondered if she'd already dug in with Lord Haweswater. The answer might depend on how much she'd got for her grandmother's jewellery. Or on how much more she wanted. Experience with Fernand-Félix would certainly be enough to teach anyone to take heed for the future. The future, as he drove along the almost empty roads in this car made for the highway of the good life seemed like a new land viewed from a mountain pass, possibilities without name or number stretching away in the southern light already touched by the sea. Like the road reeling off at the far end of the Delahaye's long sloping bonnet. As François had said, unhappiness at his age was all wrong, it was an aberration in nature. Had François said that? No, aberration didn't enter into his register of categories for the organisation of life's chances. His register was a homely one. Youth's prospect was a sunlit plain soon crossed, and life was short.

Chapter Fourteen

THE SUN WAS SETTING WHEN he passed through Cannes and had the first sight of the sea, the water and sky both red with no defining line between them. Some warships stood out in the bay immobile but ready like sleeping horses. When he reached Vence it was already almost dark, and he went into a bar to ask his way. No one had heard of Lord Haweswater, war had expunged all memory of the name, unpronounceable into the bargain, but everyone knew about Madame de Tornac even though she'd only just arrived. They called her the lady of the nest egg, so word had evidently got around. When Seagrave at last reached the Haweswater villa it was Alphonse who opened the door to him, and by mute consent neither showed any surprise at seeing the other.

'Mademoiselle Glory is in the garden,' Alphonse said without waiting to be asked about it, and as Seagrave followed him through the house he felt as if he'd known him all his life. 'She has been watching the sunset while Madame la Comtesse is with milord,' Alphonse volunteered. The excitement of a new life was making him more talkative than he used to be in the gloomy d'Albaron precincts. That was all to the good: Alphonse would add his touch of colour to the vital tapestry, Seagrave thought. His pulse had speeded up, he could feel his heart at work like an excavator. Ideas latent but secretly active all through the journey now neared the surface, not in articulate form but as a tidal certainty sweeping him on. 'The young lady often seems sad,' said

Alphonse as he shuffled along, 'and then she drinks more white wine than young ladies usually do, in France.'

'They catch up later,' said Seagrave, thinking of Marie-Louise and her sticky orange liqueurs.

'There she is, among the lemon trees. Excuse me if I don't come down the steps. They're so steep and my knees . . . they've carried me so long.'

'But you get younger every day, my old Alphonse,' Seagrave said and ran down the stair into the garden and towards the grove of lemon trees where a candle burned in a lantern. The air here was warm and seemed to rise gently from the sea far below where lights were strung out along the coast road, and where the late winter sun had worked all day on this bed of air like a blessing on a land of honey. She must have heard his voice because she was standing near the lantern when he reached her, facing the house and the flight of steps.

'I thought you wouldn't come,' she said.

'Why not?' He had to stand close to see her face, even with the candle.

Glory laughed. It was remarkable how easily you could interpret the sound of even so brief a laugh as this one. It was affirmative and victorious, showing that her state of mind exactly corresponded to his. 'Because I've been chasing you. Men aren't supposed to like that.' There was nothing teasing in her way of saying this. It was a plain statement.

'It doesn't count if you've always known each other.'

'You're going to knock over the lantern.'

'That doesn't count either.'

'You'll set fire to Grandpa's lemon grove.'

Seagrave recalled the laws of polite upbringing. 'I suppose I should go in and say good evening to him, before . . .'

'Before you set fire to it?'

'Before Alphonse reports me.'

There was an instant's pause. 'Grandpa is upstairs with Madame de Tornac. He can't very well be disturbed.'

'For how long?'

'Ages. Till supper time.'

'If Marie-Louise . . .'

'Yes? If Marie-Louise . . .?'

There was laughter again in the voice in the half-dark, but this time he wasn't quite so sure what it meant. He had been incautious. About Alphonse too. But there was no way back now. 'I should have mentioned I've met Madame de Tornac. I served under her brother in the Resistance.'

Now the laughter was open: she was laughing at him. 'D'you know when you said that you sounded a bit like William?' She put on a clipped military delivery. ' "I served under her brother in the Resistance." As a matter of fact, I knew. I like your Marie-Louise. We've had quite a few talks, here in the garden at siesta time. I don't think I'd better tell you what she calls you in her lighter moments.'

'Is it all that unflattering?' It was well known that women, when they put their heads together, like to share unamiable confidences about men.

'It may be unflattering for all I know. I've no experience.'

'I'd better hear the worst. At least I'll know if I can do anything about it.'

'I can't.'

'You won't draw another breath till you do.'

'Oh all right.' Her voice had gone up a little. 'I don't know what she means at all actually. She calls you that gifted little Englishman. And by the look on her face I don't think she means your sporting talents, or your intellectual ones either.'

'But as a nurse you must know.'

'Not at all. At first hand. Not at all.'

He could tell that the wine mentioned by Alphonse as mitigator of sadness had been resorted to. That was just as well. He couldn't bear to think of her sad. 'Where can we go?' he asked, looking upward as though it was an air-raid they needed shelter from.

'There's a little pavilion further down,' said Glory, and she took the lantern off the branch of the lemon tree and led the way across dry, stony ground between banks of irises already coming into flower.

*

The metal top of the lantern was pierced with a ring of small lozenge-shaped holes, so that lying back and looking up at the ceiling of this pavilion you saw spots of light moving about up there like dimmed fireflies as the candle flame shifted in the motion of the air.

'That was risky. I didn't think ... I'm sorry. I ought to have thought beforehand, to ...'

'Don't moan. We can't go back on it now. Anyway I think it's all right, by the calendar.' Her voice was jubilant and it wasn't only the wine.

'Let's hope so.' An image of the child in the Camargue crossed his mind.

'If you knew how sick I was of being still a virgin ... and what the other nurses say about it, and talk about risks! With men on leave such a short time. You should hear them.'

'Was that what it meant, then? Catching up?'

'No, it didn't mean that. But it did include it,' she conceded honestly. 'Anyway you know perfectly well how it's always been. Everyone knows. I mean about you, you fool.'

In spite of the testimonials Seagrave didn't feel exactly pleased with himself. If Glory hadn't been slightly drunk he would have been more careful and the conditions more elegantly arranged. Yet lying on the ground with only their pile of clothes under them and looking up at the moving lights on the ceiling, he wondered what more elegant arrangements could have added to the occasion that it didn't have already. He turned his head to look at her. Her eyes were closed and she looked peaceful and very young, the horizontal line of tension on her forehead erased.

'Don't go to sleep.'

'No.'

'There's so little time.'

She opened her eyes. 'You mean before you have to go back? But you're not on leave.'

'No, not on leave. Off-duty. Like a nurse.'

'Duty?'

He wondered what she knew, how much she might have learned from Marie-Louise. It wasn't possible to ask, at the same time it was very uncomfortable being in the dark about it. His life was conditioned by emotional involvements that clashed, not an unusual situation, probably. If he'd been in the Army as William and his world thought he should be, the conditioning would have been simpler. Or would it? Who could tell what went on, for example, behind William's red-tabbed uniform? For all Seagrave knew William was in a state of ceaseless turmoil as he sat dictating minutes at his desk in the Ministry. 'Discipline's what you lack,' they would say. He didn't believe it. They meant the discipline they had to accept themselves. He had his own and that was what they didn't like, the fact that he chose his obediences while theirs were imposed.

'There's a child,' he said.

'I heard.'

'It's sick. Badly sick.'

Glory sat up. Her breasts seemed to follow minutely the fluctuations of the candle-light; they were not large but in the context pre-eminent. 'Have you had a doctor?'

'Yes, from Arles. He says it'll never learn to talk.'

'What will you do?'

'I don't know.' To her, all this was surely accidental, a young man wasn't expected to be continent or even particularly careful – none of her forefathers had ever been, and the only problem lay in extricating yourself with decency. 'But I must go back soon. There are other reasons too.'

'What other reasons?'

'You might call them political, or historical. The come and go of
the dialectic. And the claims of friends.' As he pulled her down
again beside him a voice from the direction of the house could be
heard calling, probably Alphonse sent to find them but afraid of the
steps in the dark.

'Put your trousers on and get off my skirt.'

'You'll have to change.'

'Yes, I can see.'

*

Lord Haweswater seemed quite pleased to have him there, as far as
it was possible to tell. His head was buried in his chest due to too
many drastic falls in the hunting field, and in his iced-over blue eye
there was at least a hint of senile dementia, Seagrave thought,
perhaps from this repeated concussion.

'Remember yer father. Very decent shot. Driven partridge.
Couldn't touch him. Don't recall who was on the throne then, if
anyone . . .' He spoke thoughtfully into his shirtfront, his voice
tailing away at the end.

'You and I last met at Brough in September . . . at the horse
fair . . .' Seagrave shouted, attempting to bring matters up to date.

'I know damn well where we last met. What've you been doing
to me granddaughter Glory?'

'We were admiring your lemon grove. Beautiful. We've just
come in . . .'

'Don't mean that. Don't believe it either. Lot of moonshine.' He
beckoned Seagrave nearer by waving his cigar at him and continued
the movement until their heads were close together. There was a
rich mixture of odours – brandy, cigar, corruption – and Seagrave
had the disagreeable feeling he might at any moment be brushed by
Lord Haweswater's side-whiskers, trained to sprout in a militant
bush across his cheekbones. 'Not much time. Between ourselves,
very fond of the little bitch, doncherknow. Only one of me grand-
children I care about. Make it worth yer while, both of you. Set

yerselves up. Breed. One in the eye for that arse whats'is name too. I'm talking about yer brother.'

He had spoken in a low voice and now he looked finished off, his eyes closed so it was impossible to know if he expected an answer then and there to this abrupt proposal. Perhaps he thought no answer was necessary, but Seagrave anyway couldn't have given one. The proposal entered the field of his conflicts and aggravated them, as it may have been meant to do. The old man could have learned all he needed to know about them from a few words with Marie-Louise. Even senile, he was shrewd, as the very rich must remain in difficult times.

When Marie-Louise appeared the dilemma went into temporary abeyance. As far as Lord Haweswater was concerned it was clear that nothing could compete with her as a focus of interest once she was physically present. He seemed absolutely fascinated and she to flourish in the element. If you thought of her under the harsh rule of Fernand-Félix at Tornac she'd certainly made a good landing. Seagrave kissed the hand held out to him and waited to see what degree of prior acquaintance she was ready to acknowledge. She really did look very well. She'd changed her hairstyle, perhaps been to a hairdresser in Cannes or Nice, the swathes had been cropped and the new arrangement was a studiedly random crown of corn-coloured waves among which, here and there, a pearl appeared as if in witness to the few white strands that had been suppressed. She had dressed for dinner in a long dress and wore a necklace that certainly hadn't been one of the items selected from her grandmother's comparatively modest hoard. This was far too flashy for Seagrave not to have noticed it there, diamonds set in a trefoil pattern and repeated all the way round the neck with stones of equal size. Only the Haweswater coal revenues could possibly, in the circumstances, have run to it. Probably it had come into the hands of the Monte Carlo dealer as part of the fall-out from the Russian Revolution.

'Alphonse,' Marie-Louise cried, 'where is the champagne for

Monsieur Etienne? You know very well it's what he prefers.'
Evidently there was to be no secret. She turned back to Seagrave
and spoke in English. 'Have you come from the Camargue today?'

'Yes, how did you know . . .?'

'I heard from Philippe that you bought some land there. Are you
keeping horse?'

'Whores? Keeping whores?' said the old man, 'what does he
want to keep whores for in the country? You have them in town. In
the country you do better with yer . . .' Once again his discourse
faded away, before he'd announced what, in rural conditions, he
judged was a man's best resource.

'Cecil has a little stroke sometimes, not very serious. A few
minutes of sleep. He awakes refreshed.'

'You never told me you spoke English so well.'

'I speak it as I can. Not well but not bad. You've seen already
there can be mistakes and misunderstandings. But it is proving its
uses now.'

'I hope he lasts a good long time to use it on.'

She shrugged her shoulders in a way which hinted to Seagrave
that settlements had already been made in case he didn't. 'How can
Cecil expect to last long if he exerts himself so?'

'It may be very good for him. Exercise the heart.'

'It *is* very good for him, he says. But . . . what is your expression
in English? . . . if he burns both extremities of his candle it will blow
up.'

'Blow out.'

'Up . . . out . . . I expect each time to be the last.' Lord Haweswater was sleeping peacefully and she drew Seagrave through the
open window onto the terrace overlooking the garden and the
distant coastline. 'I have something important to tell you,' she said,
reverting to French. 'Where is Glory?'

'She went to change her . . . she . . .'

'We must be quick.' She took his arm and held it close to her
side as they moved away from the light. There were weeds growing

up between the paving stones, and against the walls of the house a tangle of neglected plants climbed the limbs of a wisteria. Someone had begun a clearance and there was a smell of extinct bonfire coming over the top of the balustrade. 'You did well to come for her. I've learned about English girls now. They're passionate but their feelings are held in like a stone wall by a mortar of romance and . . . ironies. She believes she can never love anyone else, and that is perhaps right. It's her nature.'

'Aren't you in rather a hurry to . . .'

'Because there is a hurry, a great hurry. You must get away from France. You must. Now is the time. Cecil will endow the girl very generously.'

'He told me so.'

'He approves of you. He doesn't try to buy you. He understands more than you think and he knows about women. Also the world's changing and there's been a war and he's very old. He wants to leave something more than just his coal-mines and his title, something personal . . . a kind of love, to be his immortality. Perhaps you think that vulgar?'

'No. No I don't, but in a way it's not a very alluring prospect for a life. I mean to be old Cecil's little plot of immortality.'

'Oh Etienne, you talk like a *pharisien*, what is that good English word? A prig. You'll be old one day too. Old men and young ones are much the same in essentials. I hope for your sake you find a Marie-Louise then to do for you what I can do for Cecil.'

'Was that all you had to tell me?'

'No. That man, the crippled man, who came with your friend . . .'

'The man Eric.'

'Where is he?'

'In the Camargue.'

'At the place you bought there? Under your roof? You're harbouring him as if it was a sanctuary?'

'He has to be somewhere. He ought to be in a hospital. Like

285

Lord Haweswater he can't do much for himself.'

'Do you know what he was?'

She sounded rather angry. He shouldn't have said that, people get fond of the people they look after. 'I'm sorry, very sorry. No, I don't know what he was but I suspect it.'

'He was an active member of the Milice.'

'How do you know that?'

Marie-Louise spoke very low and quickly, her mouth near his ear. 'Alphonse heard a conversation between Henri and Philippe. Part of a conversation . . . you know in that sort of house there are stairs and passages . . . it seems they'd had some photographs developed. I know nothing of that, I only stayed for the funeral,' she hurried on, 'but in the photographs this Eric was identified. He's a man who knows too much. Probably by accident. For his own good he shouldn't have returned to France. Fernand said to Philippe "get rid of him", Alphonse heard that. But it doesn't matter about that criminal, extermination is right for him. What matters is that I think you're in danger too. That's what I had to tell you. Go away. Go back with Glory from here as soon as you can.' She pointed to the ships out in the bay. 'Cecil came in one of those. It can be arranged.'

'I know. My brother arranged it.'

'Very well then. You see.'

'But I've settled my account with Fernand.'

Marie-Louise laughed without humour, but not unkindly. 'And you think you need fear nothing? If you know something about Henri which he doesn't want known, your account isn't settled while you're living.'

'Then don't you have an account too?'

'Yes, I have an account. But I've taken great care never to know anything dangerous.'

'Suppose he thinks I've talked to you?'

'He knows I wouldn't let you. He thinks I'm fundamentally stupid because I'm part of an effete class but he respects my instincts. Especially for self-preservation.'

'That's the strongest one an effete class has.'

'Just what Henri says.'

'But I think you have others . . . not effete at all.'

'The champagne, Madame la Comtesse,' said Alphonse, looking out nervously into the darkness from the doorway.

*

Every time his eye fell on the ships hanging out there at anchor in the blue they reminded Seagrave of his dilemma by illustrating it metaphorically in their own way. Even without the benefit of tides they swung round indecisively in the water so that prows pointing at nightfall towards the open sea by morning indicated the land once again.

'Why are you always gazing at those boats?' Glory asked one evening when the day's fire from all the clearance they'd done was burning low. 'Do you dream of sailing away for a year and a day, to the land where . . .'

'We could both sail away. William wants to send me to Australia.'

'I don't think I could face that.'

'Not even with me?'

'I doubt if you could make Australia all right single-handed.'

'What about Africa? There's lots of it.'

'I like being where I've a right to be, if you see what I mean.'

He hadn't imagined she would make so many difficulties. Many girls would jump at Africa, he was sure. Her grandfather had spoiled her. Suppose she was going to be like that about everything afterwards? 'And where do you think you have this right to be, Mademoiselle?'

'Where I come from, of course.'

'Not too far from Grandpa's coal-mines.'

'If you come from there you end by going back.'

'Soames thinks the same.'

'Naturally he does.'

What she and Soames had in common as well was this instant capacity for knowing their own minds. Seagrave was aware of lacking the trick of it, so that his actions were impetuous and often more violent than they need be. In a way he was glad of it, as if it meant he was closer to nature.

'You're a canny lot, you Cumbrians,' he said.

'You're Cumbrian yourself. You've forgotten. If you lived there you'd grow cannier too. It's the climate.'

'It's the rock just below the tender turf.'

She had nothing to say to that. It was the first time he'd told her anything that wasn't clearly a tribute to her beauty and how good she felt and tasted in every way. He saw withdrawal in her expression, as if in the flow of their discourse she'd met a foreign body, small but barbed.

'Anyway,' he said, 'I can't sail away anywhere at all now, not just like that. I have dependants.'

'I know. I know.' She never asked about them, put no pressure on him, but this known responsibility was a hurdle for him to cross. She didn't approach it from her side, it was for him to get over it and come to her.

'I don't know what to do about them.'

'I can't help. You've got to make up your mind. You could be a bit canny about it,' she said as a small concession.

The immediate decision was made for him by the arrival of a telegram from Soames.

'Grave murde here return immediately' it read. Did he mean *merde*, a term disallowed by the Post Office and which would have been censored with the mention *texte inadmis*, or did he mean murder? Either way the adjective grave left no choice.

When he said goodbye to Lord Haweswater, the old man, in whose eye Seagrave had learned to read the signs of a much firmer hold on what went on than he used to think, held on to his hand for a long moment.

'Got a place in the Camargue, haven't you? Breed of horse there

I've always wanted to see. Ancient race. Time immemorial. Like you and me.' A sort of wheeze laden with aroma of cigar and brandy issued from him, perhaps some kind of primitive laugh. 'Like Glory to see that too. Don't want her unhappy. Get a ride into the bargain. Might even get up meself, with a lot of help.' He wheezed again and Seagrave from politeness as a departing guest wheezed also, producing an unpractised sound midway between a cough and a death rattle, nothing mirthful.

Chapter Fifteen

PHILIPPE D'ALBARON APPEARED at the Bohemians' camp for the first time soon after Seagrave left for the coast. He arrived in a small black official car from the Préfecture, but there was nothing official about the way he presented himself. He talked first with Ida for a long time, listening, with all the appearances of a feminine assenting empathy with a narrative of woe, to her account of herself, of the child, the extermination camp, the escape and the march to freedom. He must have heard it all before but he listened again. Then he asked for Luis.

'Luis is with the horses,' Ida said.

'I didn't see him when I arrived.'

'He stays out of the way.'

Philippe said he would like to see the horses and would find his own way to wherever they were and then perhaps find Luis too.

'What do you want him for?' Ida asked, her splendid eyes like newly sighted planets looking for the first time fully at him and into his.

'I remember him when he was a child,' Philippe said. 'He was held here in the camp, wasn't he? I'd like to see how he's come on. At the Ministry we feel responsible for people who suffered. Also the Minister wishes to be briefed about this camp in particular, the conditions here, who was held, for how long ... all the other detainees have disappeared *dans la nature*. Luis can give me useful information probably.'

'Luis doesn't say much these days to anyone except the English soldier.'

'Perhaps he'll talk to me.'

'Will you give him money?'

'I can help him, if he asks me.'

Soames was coming back from the horses through the fields when he met Philippe going the other way. Soames had had a fall and damaged some joint or linkage in his artificial foot so he walked with difficulty, using a broken branch fetched by Luis from the river bank and carrying a coil of telephone cable in his free hand. He and Philippe looked at each other with equal distrust on either side.

'Etienne isn't here,' said Soames.

'I know. I'm not here to see him.' Philippe pointed at the cable. 'What are you doing with that?'

'Laying a line to blow up the Houses of Parliament,' Soames said.

'Where's Luis?'

'What do you want with Luis?'

'Listen to me carefully, my friend. Your visitor's permit will expire in a month's time. Renewal is not automatic. You frequent a brothel in Nîmes, which is your own business, but you've been taking Luis there and throwing money about – money of uncertain provenance – and Luis is a minor and even in France that is frowned on. Corruption of morals by an alien. Your permit can be withdrawn tomorrow by the *préfet*.'

'You have plenty of information.'

'I know a lot of people here. Nîmes is where my family has always lived.'

'And of course you also know about corruption of morals in children.'

Philippe laughed but didn't answer this allegation. The phrase was being used in different ways, by him in an administrative and legal perspective, by Soames in a private and puritan one. There was no risk to morals, in Soames's eyes, in a brothel, but plenty in

Hellenic congress of man and boy. Of course Soames had not attended a university. 'Get out of my way,' Philippe said, and strode on, the long coat which he wore unbuttoned swinging about his haunches.

*

Luis saw him coming, with this swaying motion of the greatcoat like the udders of an unmilked cow, Luis thought. What did he want here? Luis felt the familiar uncleanness rise in his throat. He turned back to the horse he was holding by a halter, spoke to it in a low voice in words he kept for communing with the horses when he was alone, a soothing language for himself and them.

'I had a Camargue horse once, when I was a boy,' Philippe said as he came up. 'Very easily broken. Very submissive.' Luis said nothing and didn't look at him but started to lead the horse away. Philippe noticed the saddle on the ground. 'Who's been riding? You?'

'Soames.'

'He's too tall for a horse that size.'

'He's not heavy because he's thin.'

'What was he doing with all that cable?'

'It's for the telephone,' said Luis and at once realised he'd given away something he should have kept to himself.

'The telephone? What telephone? To where? There's no line into the Camargue.'

'It's a home-made telephone from the huts to the fields. If he wants anything. He walks slowly.'

'Yes, I see. What do you know about that train in the middle of the camp?'

'It was brought to get it out of the way. This track isn't used any more.' Philippe said nothing to this but he had taken hold of the halter from the other side of the horse's head and now he stopped so they stood far out in the open ground, alone under the sky, within hearing of the Rhône beyond the line of great trees leaning southward from the mistral.

'Listen, Luis, I haven't come to ask you questions. Your sister – that's what she is, isn't she? – she says you don't talk to anyone. That's a good thing, in proportion. But she says you cut yourself off.'

'I'm *mahrime*. Except in the *maison close*.'

'I don't know what that is, *mahrime*.'

'Unclean. Animals drive out any animal that smells unclean to them.'

'No one drives you out.'

'They don't need to. I go on my own.'

Philippe seemed to think about this for a moment. To Luis, he was only pretending to think, because he'd known about it before he came. Luis had told him, at the time.

'I know a way for you to be rid of all that,' Philippe said.

'There isn't a way.'

'You're wrong. I've talked to someone who knows your laws. To help you. You're young, hardly a man. Life's in front of you. I consulted one of the old travelling people at Montpellier, where they're collecting.'

Luis wondered how true any of that was. Philippe wanted something, he was sure. He must know he could never again have the same thing, not from Luis, that had been a bargain, a sale once and for all. It must be something else. But maybe some of it was the truth. Perhaps there was a way to be not *mahrime* any more. Luis didn't know but he felt a glimmering of some other awareness, like a layer of warmer water in the river as you crossed it with the help of a branch in the current.

'What did they tell you, the old *gitans*?'

'You can purge uncleanness by revenge. Oh I don't mean . . . any private revenges. Revenge against an enemy of your own people.'

'I don't know any enemies. The armies chased them away.' If he hadn't been afraid of Philippe and if he hadn't believed that Philippe by possessing him had acquired a power he would have added, 'No enemies, only you.'

'Your sister came back with a man.'

'He's not a man. He's a cripple.'

'He wasn't always.'

'I wasn't always *mahrime*.'

'Why do you think she brought him? She was coming back to Etienne. That's what Etienne thought. With his child, so he thought. Who is this man? What is he? I can tell you if you want to know.'

Luis took the halter off the horse and spoke to it again for the last time, sending it back over the sere winter ground towards its companions grazing near the river. 'Tell me then.'

'He was a Milice torturer. One of the worst. He's been recognised. Did they torture people here in the camp? Yes? Then you know what it meant. This Eric, that's his name, he's an enemy of your people because he and his kind treated them like shit they wiped off their boots with the end of a whip. That's the truth.'

Luis believed this was the truth. He never spoke to Eric nor Eric to him, but he hated him, he now realised, with a hatred that came the same way as that awareness of the warmer current, in the flow, in the bone, in the dark.

'And that isn't all,' Philippe went on. 'Why did she bring him with her half across Europe in a wheelbarrow? She must know what he was, because he wasn't a prisoner like her. He was in that place because he wanted to be there. He's got a power over her.'

'I don't believe it. It's impossible.'

'And with Etienne, how do you think it is now? How is she with him?'

'Bad. I think they don't even . . .'

'And why? I'll tell you if you can't see it for yourself. It's on account of this Eric. You know a man must sometimes protect his sister . . . Get rid of him, Luis . . .' Philippe turned in the direction of the river roaring monotonously beyond the trees and pointed to it. 'Wash the uncleanness that troubles you away in the water of the Rhône. It'll be lost out at sea. The current's deep and very strong, it pours the stones from the mountains down and out to the bottom of the sea. That's where the uncleanness will go. It'll never come back. You'll be free.'

He had been speaking slowly in a level monotonous voice like the voice of the river, and now he stopped and stood very still, watching Luis as if to see him walk in his sleep. There was a steady wind that day, cold and clean from the Cévennes where the summits were still under snow. But the snow everywhere was melting. It had been a warm month. The Alpine snows were melting before time, pouring into the lakes, and the Rhône was high with them. The sky was a dense blue, bare and rounded as a shield, and over their heads a buzzard circled in the wind in wide, slow circles, with black wings stretched out on the azure shield.

'If I do it will you go away?'

'I'm going now, Luis. But don't forget, there'll be questions afterwards. Even for vermin like Eric there'll be questions. Be careful and I can protect you. The Ministry will protect you. You won't be *mahrime* any more but you'll need to be protected.'

'I won't have to see you?'

'Oh no, you won't have to do anything you don't want, later on, Luis. You'll be quite free,' he said it again.

When Philippe had gone Luis walked slowly back to the camp. Resolution was fully formed in his head, like a detailed action sprung into shape in an instant's dream. Only a doubt about Philippe's last words hung in the background, half-hidden, maybe nothing more than a faded suspicion. He wasn't sure, but now there was work to get on with. He felt elated and somnolent at the same time, knowing just what he had to do.

Soames was at work on his damaged foot, so he was both busy and immobilised. Anyway, Luis knew he could count on Soames afterwards, as much as he needed to. Apart from him there was only Ida, and the child Stefan. Once a week Stefan was taken to the doctor in Arles, and though nothing new ever came out of the consultation Etienne insisted on it. This was his right, even if now he had no others. Paradis had brought them a van and Luis took Ida and the child to Arles and left them at the doctor's house, saying he must fetch something in Nîmes for Soames's broken foot and would come for them later in the afternoon. He then returned to the Bohemians' camp. It was all very simple. Eric was asleep on his bed. He slept a lot of the time because he was drunk most of the day. He was embittered and in pain and his only pleasure was spreading unhappiness over whoever he came in contact with. Life held no promises for Eric, which made it easier to do what must be done. Like with an animal.

Eric's wheelchair, new and paid for by Etienne, was beside the bed.

'Do you want anything? My sister told me to come and ask.'

'I want to go and shit,' said Eric. The smell in the hut was thick and sour even with the door open to the wind. Eric's digestion was crippled like the rest of the lower part of him, and the alcohol made the problem worse. Luis lifted him into the wheelchair with quick, strong movements.

'Give me that bag,' said Eric, pointing to a canvas holdall on the ground next to the bed. Probably he needed some sort of apparatus for shitting but Luis neither knew nor cared to know what it did. There was a small latrine on its own beyond the other huts, a new one since the one used by the hundreds of inmates here during the Occupation had been burned like the torturers' hut, and this one enclosed a hygienic earth pit and wooden seat and was kept clean and disinfected and had a sliding bolt on the inside. Luis lifted Eric onto the wooden seat and waited outside. Could Eric feel anything at all down there? If not, how would he know how he was getting on? These trivial questions passed across Luis's mind like wisps of vapour in a wind. When Eric shouted to be taken away again he put him back in the wheelchair and started in the direction of the open fields.

'You're going the wrong way.'

'The weather's good. I thought you'd like to have a look at the horses. Two of them have foaled. Here . . .' He held out a half-bottle of rough eau-de-vie he'd bought in Arles for the occasion. 'I thought of you when I was in town. You don't get out of that hut enough.'

'Thanks,' said Eric taking it. 'For a little *gitan* you've the beginnings of humanity in you.' He drank copiously from the bottle and put it into his canvas bag in which Luis glimpsed, during the second it was open, what seemed to be a police revolver. It was good to think that Eric lived in fear. It was quite a long way to where the horses grazed, and Eric had several more mouthfuls of eau-de-vie as the wheelchair jolted over the rough ground. Luis took long, fast strides, the wind entering his lungs like the cleansing current of the sea.

'Where are all the fucking horses? It's too far. Take me back.'

'We can't go back now. They're just over there under the trees.'

'If I say we go back we go back, *bordel de merde*!'

Luis continued at a run over the grass, the wheelchair bucking under his hands. You could hear the river now, even louder than when Philippe was here in the morning. The level must have risen, the avalanches from the Alps were reaching the sea, they were rolling the rocks along the bed of the river like marbles.

'Go back! Turn round and take me back, you dirty little black baboon,' Eric screamed into the wind as they sped along. He was trying to reach into the holdall to take the bottle, Luis saw, then it was the revolver he had in his hand and screwing the upper part of his body round in the chair he waved it at Luis behind him. He must be got to the river. He must be disarmed. If he succeeded in wounding Luis they might never get that far. Without stopping Luis leaned forward across Eric's head and grabbed at the hand with the revolver but Eric was excited, drunk, and his arm lashed about like a whip. When the shot was fired they were already under the trees with the river thundering the other side of the retaining bank. Luis felt a blow in his left hand like a heavy stone falling on it from a wall and at the same moment he threw himself on top of Eric so that the wheelchair capsized and Eric sprawled helplessly on the grass. Blood was streaming from the hand and it hurt but the fingers still worked. The revolver lay on the grass out of Eric's reach and Luis kicked it further away before he took off his shirt, tore a sleeve apart and bound his hand as well as he could with the strip of material. Then he set Eric upright again and started to push the wheelchair up the steep bank.

'What are you doing with me?'

There was no need to answer this question. It wasn't compassion that kept Luis quiet but the effort of getting up the bank without overturning again and with a wounded hand.

'I know what you're going to do.'

It was a strange feeling to have this power, the last power you could have over someone – or yourself – to pitch the living thing into the brown flood of the Rhône. Luis wondered what Eric was feeling or thinking, how it was for him, with a minute left. Did he think of the men he'd tortured, according to Philippe, in case he met them again on the other side? Was he afraid, or was he even in a secret way glad because of his crippled state? In a moment it would be over.

'I've got something to tell you. A thing you ought to know,' Eric shouted over his shoulder.

Luis stopped when they reached the top. 'Give yourself a last drink. The water's cold,' he said. It was a weakness. He mustn't have another weakness.

'The woman Ida. You call her your sister. She isn't your sister.' Eric emptied the bottle.

'What do you mean? What do you know about it?'

'I know what she told me, when we were all going to be killed on the road by the English.'

'What did she say?'

'She had you when she wasn't more than a child herself.'

So that was what Eric thought of in his last moments. Perhaps he thought Luis would spare him because Luis wouldn't know who he was, who any of them were any more. Identity and resolution would be undermined by this new information. He was wrong. It made no difference. Sister and mother were only words, the feeling didn't change with them. 'Why would she tell you that? Why you?'

'She had to tell someone. She had you from her brother. That's why the people turned her away. You're unclean, both of you to the end of your lives. Degenerates. Parasites. Fit for the extermination camp. *Gitan* filth . . .' He was calling to the sky and the overhanging branches far above his head as the wheelchair lurched and flew out from the top of the bank and out into the discoloured, swollen, rapid water not far below.

Luis threw the empty bottle after him and saw it speed away on the surface while the wheelchair and the canvas holdall and the body of Eric were immediately engulfed and vanished with the non-floating contents of the river. Then he carefully went over his tracks and those of the wheelchair in the earth of the embankment and erased them and pushed leaves and sticks and loose earth over where they'd been. He recuperated the revolver, counted the remaining cartridges – there were three of them – and walked back to the camp feeling very tired and rather sick, and his hand hurting with a pain hard as the onrush of the river itself. Soames would have to help him.

He explained the whole story to Soames keeping nothing back, except the fact that he now had Eric's revolver in his possession. Philippe might come again.

'Jesus. You've done it now, Luis,' said Soames.

'Yes.'

'First thing's that hand.' Soames had supplies with him for dealing with wounds and pain and together they cleaned the hand and examined it. The bullet had passed through the muscular part between the wrist and little finger and out again without apparently injuring any bone. 'You ought to go to a hospital but you can't. Any doctor who saw that would know it was a bullet wound and the questions would start there. This is going to hurt you.' Soames disinfected the wound and bound it up very skilfully. They didn't discuss how this had been. 'One of us has to drive over and fetch your sister.'

'She isn't my sister.'

'I was forgetting. Which of us is it to be?'

'We'll do it together. You've got two hands and I've got two feet.'

Soames laughed. 'I can see it's cheered you up, pushing that swine in the river,' he said in English.

'Aye, bugger off in river,' Luis agreed using the vernacular he knew.

*

Ida took Eric's disappearance more calmly than Luis had thought she would. Whatever she felt it was deadened like everything else: she was like someone so old as to be only just alive in spite of the beauty which every day seemed to come back a little more. When she was alone with Luis he told her what Eric had said.

'If he was bad enough to push in the Rhône why do you believe anything he told you?' was her only answer. It was a reasonable one but Luis still thought she was hiding something. All the same a look of relief had passed across her face.

'Who was my father then?'

'You haven't got a father.'

'Because we were turned away by the people?'

'Forget about the people. If they turned us away they're no good to you, or me.'

'Since I can remember we were always alone. We must be different.' He turned from her because she'd been lying to him and the child was screaming too loud, and also his hand hurt with a new kind of pain as if it was being twisted off. But he agreed with what she said about the people. She was lying, but she was right about that. Perhaps the people were right too, for them. This must have seemed something very important to them, but to Luis and Ida it didn't. Now they both knew it didn't matter at all. So the people, their people, were strangers.

'I know it was Etienne who told you to push Eric in the river. You don't know his family and I do. They're bad.'

Luis didn't consider this logical. Etienne should be allowed to be as free from his people as they were from theirs. 'It was nothing to do with Etienne,' he said.

'If they ever find the body we'll say it was him, from jealousy,' she called after him as he walked away.

'No we won't,' said Luis, confirmed in his belief that women were creatures of no settled principle. He loved her the same as before, or rather he loved her just as much, but he could see that, ethically, she needed watching.

By the time the gendarmes arrived Luis's hand was much better but still bandaged, and when he saw them coming he put it in his pocket and kept it there. There were three of them and they looked doubtful of their mission, as if they had orders and at the same time felt some much higher authority hanging over them.

'We're looking for the man named Eric.'

'Why do you want him?' Ida asked.

'Suspected member of the former Milice.'

'He's gone. He's gone to Marseilles. His family came and took him away.'

'By road?'

'No. They came in a boat as far as Les Saintes Maries and there they borrowed a cart.'

'Who from?'

'They didn't say.'

'Address in Marseilles?'

'They didn't say.'

The gendarmes looked relieved, as if she was making things easy for them. 'We'll report that, but we'll certainly be back.' The chief of them turned to Luis. 'Are you the one named Luis Karoly?'

'Yes.'

'Orders are you're not to leave the limits of this commune, which is the commune of Arles, without permission from the Commissariat.'

'Can I go to Nîmes?'

'What for?'

'He's got a girl there,' said Soames, silent till now.

'Yes, we know about that, and we know about you. We advise you both to be more discreet in your recreations. There are important men in the town who go where you go. You can go to Nîmes once in two weeks,' he said to Luis, 'and you, Monsieur, will be answerable for him and for his return here. You will both remain under observation and surveillance by order of the Préfet.'

'Once in two weeks isn't very often,' Luis objected.

'Most boys of your age have to amuse themselves. They haven't the money for three-star *maisons closes*. Neither have we. You're very lucky to have it once every two weeks. What's that awful noise?'

'It's a sick child,' said Ida, and turned away to go back to it.

'Where's the father?'

'He went to the Riviera to see an English lord,' Soames said.

'I see why they call it the Bohemians' camp,' said one of the younger men. 'There's no one normal round here.'

'How did that train get there?' asked the chief.

'A railway official brought it. To test the line,' Soames said.

'François Paradis?'

'The same.'

'Another one under observation. All that must go into the report too. It's not regular, a train in the middle of the fields . . . unattended . . . just like that. What's it for? Naturally you don't know.'

When they'd gone Soames sat down on the step of the locomotive, lit one of his small cigars and looked as if he was working out a puzzle.

'How did they know?' Luis said.

'They didn't. They came to find out. That means they only knew the swine Eric might disappear, not that he had. And *that* means they were sent to see if you'd done what you were told to do.'

'Then Philippe sent them.'

'He must have. And not just because he had his reasons for getting rid of Eric. He could have found out in some other way if he'd disappeared or not. The gendarmes were sent as a warning, to show you straight off how you need protection from the law. And that you'll always need it.'

'He thinks he hasn't finished with me, that's what he thinks. But I've got a way to deal with him now if he comes back. If ever I see him again I know what to do.'

Soames didn't seem to be listening very closely. He probably thought Luis was big enough to look after himself from now on, and in a way he was right. Luis didn't know, until he got rid of Eric, what he was capable of. And as he grew stronger in the spring sun he felt himself more capable, capable of anything, his capability expanding with his ribcage, his arms and shoulders.

'Have you killed a lot of men, Soames?' he asked.

'To be honest with you, Luis, I don't think I ever killed anyone. Not for sure. You don't do much killing from a radio post. Why? Are you thinking of going in for it now you've found the way?'

'You're like Etienne. You laugh at everything. Perhaps you do because it's easier.'

Soames stood up from the step of the engine so Luis felt that from his great height Soames must be able to see down into the contents of his head. He therefore expelled the image of the revolver from his thought.

'You could be right about that. What we have to do now is get on with that telephone so we can call Paradise.' The cable was already laid, passing across the open fields, under hedges, from tree to tree over the ditches as far as the railway near Saint Gilles. There it joined the railway telephone network at a point distant from any habitation and all that remained to do was to bring the cable under the surface of the track and connect the instrument in the Bohemians' camp. When that was done Soames called Paradis again and told him in outline what had happened. Hearing Paradis's voice on the line though not making out his words, Luis realised for the first time the implications of what he'd done. No one had been supposed to know about the train and now it would go into an official report to the Préfecture. Still, it wasn't Luis's fault that Philippe had come here and seen it for himself. Soames was speaking again.

'Look at it like this,' he was saying: 'Luis saved everyone else the trouble of eliminating a villain and got himself hurt in doing it. I think he deserves a medal ... agreed, agreed, that's one result of it ... yes, you could say that, it's the tradition, isn't it, a sister ... Well we won't move from here now and we'll expect to hear ... can you get a telegram to Etienne at Vence if I dictate it? Oh yes, I'll word it carefully ...' When he'd done that and his talk with Paradis was finished for the time being, he turned back to Luis.

'Paradise thinks you did right to defend your sister's honour by doing what you did. The trouble is, now they know all about the train the action has to be advanced. No more time for planning. He'll be here with the comrades in a couple of days. He'll warn us when to start getting the steam up. Let's just hope Etienne gets here first. It's his camp that could get blown sky-high, not ours.'

Chapter Sixteen

IT WAS A STRONG SUN AND stripped down on the footplate of the engine you grilled like a chop, but there was no doubt about it, feeding the greedy furnace of this locomotive was amusing, like stoking the maw of a beast behind bars. As long as you shut your mind to the implications. Because the parallel went further. What about when the engine and the train broke out of here to fall on the land, like a beast escaping the bars? Risk laced the enjoyment with a dose of something like foreboding. However, another good thing for the moment was that a young doctor in Arles had come up with an effective sedative for Stefan rather than falling back, as his seniors did, on the assumption that non-stop screaming denoted deficient parenting. It changed nothing fundamentally; the bad *baxt*, more malignant than Cerberus at the gate of hell, was not to be disarmed with drugs. But it did mean that in the comparative silence of the open land you could hear the slow rise in pressure of steam in the boilers, and the call of duck on the Etang de Scamandre, well-named from the river of Troy. What else was this train but a Trojan horse? Seagrave wondered if François had been drawn to the railways by the pleasure of working a locomotive. Probably not so he'd admit it. The class struggle was his pleasure, other amusements a bourgeois pretext to be stamped out. When this was all over he would go into the matter of the class struggle himself and see where he stood. With Glory, for example. When it was over? How could it be over, ever? How could Glory's view of

307

the class struggle affect him unless he abandoned Ida and Luis and everything here? He could give Ida the Bohemians' camp; it was all he had to give, to her and Luis, they would raise livestock, poach and steal and lead a life more natural to them, not wholly indigent but out of the limelight and above all the firing line. Would that do as a solution? No. It wouldn't, but he hung on to the idea of it because he needed sweeping simplicity, faced as he was with a moral dilemma too complex.

The engine had been filled with water pumped from the well and the tender with coal shovelled over from the wagon behind it, and in spite of his hand Luis had done most of this work while Soames and Seagrave lit the fires and watched the pressure gauges and distributed oil according to Paradis's instructions. But you could see that Luis didn't have his heart in it. His heart was with the horses out on the sparse land beyond the iron road. And he was more withdrawn than he used to be, Seagrave noticed, as if he'd formed new judgements on his elders and his relations with them and distanced himself by preference or for survival, even though they'd done him nothing but good. In intention anyway. Looking back to his own adolescence Seagrave could think of no one figuring in it who had done him nothing but good, in fact no one who had done him much good at all, and this gave him a sense of injustice. Probably it came to all parents in the end.

'You hadn't had to push anyone into the Rhône when you were that age,' Soames pointed out. 'Luis had to make himself into a hard man very fast.'

'I think he's hiding something all the same.'

'That's any bugger's right in the world.'

But Seagrave felt that in a sense beyond words Luis blamed him. Perhaps it was the changes in Ida he blamed him for. Was it partly because of them, because Luis was angered by them, that he'd eliminated Eric? How to explain to Luis that his sister had undergone one of those revolutions of feeling, irreversible as any revolution? He would have to work it out for himself, or wait until it didn't matter to him any more, some day. When he was a father himself, maybe, a primal figure to someone else.

François and the comrades appeared in trucks belonging to the railways soon after dawn on Sunday.

'The feast of the blessed insurrection!' François shouted as he arrived. The locomotive snored gently with banked fires in the pale early light and the birds on the Etang de Scamandre, one breed waking after another, started up their own eternal dialectic. François looked excited, his face white, a second day's growth of beard on it, his eyes wide as if straining into a future screened by the mists of doubt and error. There wasn't much about him of the calm that had ordered the lives of fifteen hundred men in the Cévennes. The comrades now numbered about two hundred and not all of them looked to Seagrave very sure of what they were about to do here.

'Just not quite the same good old rabble,' Soames commented. Many of them recognised him however, *flamand rose* back in the right habitat, and as they'd brought enough wine with them to see them through a period of incalculable stress the early uneasiness seemed quite soon to dissolve.

'I don't want to see any of you drunk,' roared Paradis. 'We must keep cool nerves.' His own didn't seem cool and he never would have spoken of nerve as a thing to be nursed in the days of his glory, that was sure. It was a counsel not fit for the field of action. François had been thinking too much, stuck inactive in the office too small for him – he wasn't made for that, his footing had become unsure, the pale cast of theory had got at him, emasculating theory. But maybe he would be his old self again once things got going. 'We won't be stirring from here till tonight,' he continued. 'There's no activity on the main lines between two and five in the morning. We'll go then and be in position on the bridge at Beaucaire at first light. Eat well today: we don't know what tomorrow will be.' While he inspected the locomotive the comrades made their fires. One of them had a sheep from his father's flock and a pit was dug to fill with embers. Seagrave went to find Ida. Every conversation could be the last.

'They won't be here for long. They'll go tonight,' he said.

'Will you go with them?'

'If François wants me.'

'I don't ask for them to go.'

'You don't ask for anything. You never did. You used to give.'

'It was what I wanted then: I didn't have to ask.'

'Don't you want anything now? You must. What do you most want?'

'For Luis to be safe, from what he's done.'

'No more than that?' In his absence at Vence the slow reflux of health had turned into a tide. Her returning beauty seemed like a moral attribute: she was imbued with it, it flooded her.

'You asked what I wanted. That's the answer.'

'I think Luis is safe enough.' He watched her prepare a cigarette from some herb she'd identified among the weeds here. Probably it was something cultivated by the people when they were imprisoned, to while away the months of immobility, off the road. 'But before I used to know what you wanted without asking. It was so easy to know.'

'It was easy to think you knew.'

That wasn't honest. It was recanting. It was as if another woman uninstructed in the past had come back on the roads from Birkenau and stuck a knife in him. 'Is it that that man meant something to you?'

'Eric? No. No. When a man's dead he can't mean anything. You can't say he ever meant anything. You only mean when you're alive.'

'When he was alive, then?'

'No. No.'

Perhaps she wasn't telling the truth now. Perhaps it didn't matter. Even alive, your meaning could die out, like hers.

'And when I die . . .' he asked.

She didn't answer. It wasn't a question deserving answer. Her green eyes were wide, calm, distant. She was dying herself, dying out of the world of meaning and the world of feeling. Perhaps they were the same. The thought that she was failing like a candle in a lantern made this separation easier. In the separation of any death the survivor is passive, and innocent. The candle in the lantern . . . he thought of the garden at Vence. The choice was made for him. The *baxt* dictated it. To call it a choice was only to flatter illusions about free will. And *baxt* cared nothing for pain.

'If I go and leave you all this for yourself will you and Luis stay here?'

'Will you take the child with you?'

'Of course not.'

'Because you don't own it? A sick child can't be yours?'

'I couldn't care for it.'

'Luis says the English girl's a nurse. She ought to know how to care for a sick child.'

Everything was always known, past and future. Things you half hid from yourself were perfectly well known and clear to them. 'She shouldn't have to: it's not hers,' he said.

'No. Perhaps you'll give her a sick child too, one of her own. You won't walk away so easily from that because they're your own people. They know how to hold you. Good enough people for your sister too. People with luck, good luck,' she said, avoiding the Romany word as if people in Seagrave's world didn't deserve it. It had been a long speech, for her, delivered in a voice that slowed as she approached the end as if she feared to break off.

He could hear François calling him, calling someone. It was the release. A coffin of estrangement seemed to be between him and the remains of his love and in the end you must take your courage in your hands and quit the graveside.

'I must go now,' he said.

She brought her eyes back to focus on him with some effort. Their expression was angry but there was something else – a claim,

311

an appeal, it was a compound of expressions put together by feeling or by art, you couldn't tell which. But anger was in the forefront like a high wall. He turned his own eyes away. The light in hers was too strong.

When he reached François, Soames was already there, on the end of the telephone. 'It's my office in Nîmes,' said François. 'On Sunday there's one man there and he's got more to do than take down telegrams in English.'

'For me?' Seagrave asked stupidly.

'Well Soames would have more sense than to get telegrams sent to him here on the feast of the insurrection.'

'This is my address now.'

After a moment François laughed, showing the gold teeth at the back of his mouth which he used to say, in the days of good humour, represented Madame Paradis's dowry. 'This isn't an address, Etienne. This is a field of campaign,' he said.

Soames had written the message down in his rounded handwriting. 'Some of the spelling could be a bit to cock,' he warned as he handed it over. 'Feller at t'other end was too excited for a good signaller. I've done a bit of interpreting.'

Intend coming down to see horses and visit you have found sutable car Monte Carlo Glory will drive it Madame de Tornac will accompany us stop will put up at Julius Caesar's hotel in Arles be with you Sunday afternoon stop Romans extraordinary people Haweswater

'The spelling's impeccable,' Seagrave said. He suspected Glory had dictated the telegram and probably composed it. Inside him a fermentation of laughter and pleasure was rising up like a counterweight but the stern words of François were enough to keep order in his imagination. This was a field of campaign, with its own scale of priorities.

'My English friends will be coming here in a car this afternoon.

They're staying in Arles. I can't stop them but when they get here I may be able to send them away again . . . in time.'

François considered this. 'No, I don't think we'll send them away at all. Isn't one of them, the old man, isn't he someone important? A bourgeois *notable* of some sort?'

'You might call him that. He owns a lot of coal-mines.'

'Excellent. An enemy of the people. Exemplary. This is a stroke of fortune from above.' François raised his eyes, atheist but not emancipated from all belief in the transcendent, to the hard blue dome of sky. Whatever your cosmology may be, the *baxt*, good or ill, has the last word. Seagrave thought he saw the dangers encircling them like the first lappings of a tide.

'Don't do anything bad, François . . . anything inaesthetic.' He remembered the word they'd used about the cleaning up in the streets of Nîmes. 'This enemy of the people is very old. And he's the grandfather . . .'

'I know. Of your new *petite amie*. Ah, when one's young . . . don't worry, I won't hurt a hair on the old man's head. As a hostage he will be a precious symbol. We're an international movement or we're nothing. The name of your old capitalist friend and his granddaughter will be in the world's press tomorrow. We'll send it by telegraph this very afternoon. What is his name?'

'He's called Lord Haweswater. Unpronounceable in French. *Osewatère*.' Seagrave heard Soames laugh in the background.

'A milord. Better and better. The English papers will be full of it. Every coal-miner and all the starving British proletariat will rise with us.'

'I don't think you should count on that.' It seemed that the conflict between fantasy and reality had hit them at last. But arms and weight of numbers were part of reality and on this occasion these vital factors underpinned the fantasy. François was here with his force and he was never a man to trifle with, unhinged or not. He had a short way with troublemakers. And there was loyalty, and affection on both sides to take into account too. The hierarchy of comrades in action, the virile mystique. It was as if the shadow of the distant Cévennes fell across this flat space of the salty delta like a habit of mind. François was already on the telephone to Nîmes, dictating a message to be sent at once to the editorial offices of the new local newspaper that had taken over the press from him after the Liberation, the *Midi Libre* of sympathetic tendency.

'Tell them to get a reporter to the Bohemians' camp in the Camargue. He'll have to ask the way in Saint Gilles. We're holding a party of British plutocrats as hostages of the people. No harm will come to them while our own safebeing is respected. Tell them that, tell them to publish it tomorrow morning. By then there should be a lot more to report. Say that.'

'We're not holding the British party yet,' Seagrave pointed out when he'd finished. 'We can still send them back.'

'I can hear them,' said François who like a cat had specially acute hearing for sounds at a distance. 'And we won't.'

Right enough, after some minutes a vehicle appeared far down the dusty road from Arles, advancing slowly, taking up the full width of the track. It was an old Rolls Royce, a Red Label with horizontal louvres on the radiator, black, huge, tall and shiny as a worn top hat, vastly incongruous sailing through the dry grass. Seagrave ran out into the road to signal it in. Glory was perched in isolation in the chauffeur's open space while in the back behind the glass screen were dimly visible the forms and faces of Marie-Louise and Lord Haweswater, their expressions set as if this car was a revolutionary tumbril. Seagrave remembered that was how people always looked on the way to a picnic.

'You've got here in the middle of an uprising. Or rather the start of one. But we won't tell your grandfather and he may never guess,' Seagrave said to Glory in a low voice as soon as the car came to a halt. 'We can't have him having a stroke out here.'

'An uprising? But I think he'd be delighted,' said Glory. 'Poor old darling, he's been awfully bored ever since you left, in spite of having Marie-Louise. An uprising is what he needs. Don't forget he's an old soldier himself. Are those the insurgents?' She waved at them and several of them waved back. Glory wasn't taking the situation seriously. It was true the comrades didn't make a very fearsome impression, spread about the grass, thinking of girls.

'It's no joke. They're some of my friends and I know them. They're going to hold you hostage. I'd have warned you if I could. We'll try and get you away.' He considered the conspicuous Rolls doubtfully. 'It won't be easy.'

'I don't want to be got away. I wouldn't miss this for anything.' She descended from the chauffeur's cockpit on the side away from the camp and they kissed quickly, fervently, in the lee of the gleaming coachwork. Lord Haweswater banged on the window to be let out, and Seagrave opened the door to give his arm.

'How many acres of this you got here?' were the old man's first words. 'Remember him,' he added as Soames limped up. 'Glad to see you've got yer foot. Damn painful thing. Had a bullet in one once, out in Africa.'

'What were you doing, Grandpa? Was it the Zulu War?'

'Not Methuselah,' said Lord Haweswater irritably. 'Trying to be funny again I dare say. Boer War.'

'How would tha like to go over and look at the horses, Lord Haweswater?' asked Soames tactfully, and the two of them hobbled off arm in arm over the grass and powdery earth on the far side of the track, towards the nearest group of horses grazing by a line of poplars.

'Where is she?' Glory asked.

As if in answer to her question there was a movement, a restlessness among the comrades grouped around their glowing pit where the sheep was being roasted, as Ida passed them on her way to the well. They stirred and turned their heads like a herd disturbed on the African plain. Glory watched her until she went out of sight behind the last cabin in the line. 'Unbelievable,' was all she said.

Marie-Louise was emerging from the Rolls after adjusting her make-up in the privacy left by Lord Haweswater's departure. She was wearing the expression – concentrated and tense – which Seagrave knew as the one that came to her when it was a question of dealing with Fernand-Félix.

'You look preoccupied,' he said, still holding her hand.

'With good reason. Wait till you hear.' She was ornamented with a four-rope necklace of fat pearls held by a diamond clasp and a ring with what looked like a huge yellow diamond in the middle of it. Seagrave hoped the comrades wouldn't think of confiscating them for the people's funds. 'Henri is on his way. He has, of course, his spies on the Côte d'Azur and he heard we were going to the Jules César in Arles. He telephoned me there. I told him nothing but he guessed we would be coming out to see you. Not difficult to guess really.'

'Why isn't he in Paris running his Ministry?'

'He got wind of something down here.'

'What's he coming here for?'

'He says he wants to see me.'

'Do you believe that's the real reason?'

'No. He could have come to Arles. Who are all these men?'

'They're the revolutionaries,' said Glory. 'They're about to bring down the whole fabric of capitalist society.'

'Someone's always trying to do that in France but it stays up,' said Marie-Louise. 'Tyrants like Henri make sure of it by shooting the worst troublemakers. That's what he must be coming for. Could he know about this gathering?'

'If he has spies on the railways too.'

Marie-Louise shrugged her shoulders so the pearls rolled about her neck like foam on the shore. 'But naturally he has.'

'I must warn François Paradis.' François had been watching from the cabin of the locomotive. Perhaps he thought there was less risk of panic among the British if he left it to Seagrave to explain their situation to them. Now he came down from the engine and walked with deliberate steps towards them. 'A new development,' Seagrave said as he approached. 'The Minister of Information is about to arrive.'

'He's Minister of the Interior now,' Marie-Louise corrected, 'much much more important.' She held out her hand to Paradis, rather up in the air in her usual way to save him the trouble of bowing low over it. He took it firmly in his fist and gave it a hard shake.

'Welcome, comrade, to the Bohemians' camp, where history is in the making,' he said, and Seagrave saw his eye fixed on the diamond clasp. 'So the Minister of the Interior is on his way?' His voice now had the jubilant ring to it that Seagrave knew from the days of bravura, and Marie-Louise was smiling at him. 'That will be something for the press to make headlines with.'

'You're not thinking of holding him hostage too?' Seagrave said, catastrophe flashing before his mind's eye. 'Don't forget we have women here.'

'Comradeship at a moment like this knows no gender,' said François sententiously. Or was it a joke at the expense of the crypto-chivalric reflexes of *un gentleman*? That was quite likely. Seagrave himself sometimes felt the real world had pressed on ahead without waiting for him.

'Does Cecil know we're hostages?' Marie-Louise asked.

'Not yet. He was a bit cross when he got out of the car. I expect he was in a hurry to go behind a tree,' Glory said.

'I'll tell him myself. It's hardly what we came expecting but at least I suppose the revolution won't be here in this quiet spot, that's something. We'll be tranquil here while it's going on.' Marie-Louise looked over at the train and the wisps of smoke and steam issuing from the orifices of the locomotive. 'And that thing I dare say is for going up to the front line in.' She gave Paradis another of those smiles with whose effect Seagrave was so familiar.

'I think it is the front line,' he said. François seemed to have swelled still further with importance and approval and the flux of action. Viewing the situation through the eyes of Marie-Louise – at least how he supposed her view of it would be – Seagrave could see the absurdity of its elements, even though she sensed the danger too, he knew that. But Paradis's presence had affected her as it affected everyone, as it had even affected her brother Charles. It was the charisma of natural command, even if here only over a rabble in a field. It was the Bonaparte syndrome, so embedded in the national psyche. Absurdity and the golden calf. Marie-Louise had left to cross the open ground towards Soames and Lord Haweswater and the horseflesh as the sound of a motor-bicycle on the road tore across the calm air of early afternoon like a siren.

'That will be the *Midi Libre* reporter,' François said with relish. 'In just a minute he's going to get the scoop of his young career. Bring him over to see me at the train. He must take away an impression of immediate action.'

'I've never met anyone really important before,' said Glory as she watched him walk away, each assured footstep like the planting of a revolutionary tree.

'He doesn't really think he's personally important. He's an agent of the dialectic and he happens to be the man who knows what to do when the heat's on.'

The reporter was young but not readily impressed. 'I just hope there's something more going on here than a crowd of loafers cooking a sheep in a hole in the ground,' he said almost at once, speaking from the corner of his mouth where he'd stuck a cigarette lit as he got off the motor-bicycle. He'd probably seen a press photograph of André Malraux somewhere.

'Follow me please, and you'll hear all about it. And you stay here and wait for your grandfather,' Seagrave told Glory as he saw the reporter eyeing her as if she at least offered possibilities to justify his expense of time. In François's presence he assumed an even more professional manner. He produced a notebook and a pencil and ran his fingers through his hair preparatory to business.

'I presume this is essentially a workers' symbolic manifestation, Monsieur Paradis? Have you got the backing of your union? Or are you staging an unofficial gesture here?'

'I'm not staging anything. This is the reality. Tell your readers the time of waiting is over.'

The reporter wrote that down. 'And the train? And the British hostages, so-called? Isn't that all rather histrionic? More like staging an event than making history, wouldn't you say?'

'The hostages are to focus attention on the historic events which the train will help us to trigger off.'

'What exactly are you going to do with it?'

'Block the main lines over the Rhône.'

'Don't you fear that the forces of order will come down on you and sweep you away into the river? Aren't you playing with the lives of the men behind you? To say nothing of the hostages?'

'The forces of order will be very careful what they do because we will be holding the Minister of the Interior hostage as well.'

There was a moment's silence as the reporter arrested the flight of his pencil and looked at François hard but uncertainly, assessing his sanity.

'That'll make them think too, those dinosaurs in the Party,' François added in a low voice for himself, his eyes fixed on a point far from the train and the camp and the open air, an imaginary point where in smoky darkness the Party demigods assembled and judged his errors about the historical process. It was easier now to see what had happened. François felt rejected by the cause he'd served all his life, and rejection renders the potent doubly danger-ous. Those demigods had maddened him.

'And how will you be arranging to hold this Minister, Monsieur Paradis?' the reported asked, showing how nothing must be allowed to surprise a seasoned journalist.

'He's arriving here any minute. I shall hold him with the others.' François turned to Seagrave. 'Go and wait for Fernand-Félix out on the road. Don't let him turn back. That magnificent Madame de Tornac must delay him if necessary.'

The Haweswater party, led by Soames, had reassembled around

the Rolls. Lord Haweswater looked in excellent spirits, propped on a shooting-stick and hanging on to Marie-Louise to keep him steady.

'Your man Soames is opening the champagne,' he said as Seagrave came up. 'Lucky in every way having him with us. Hear we've been captured. May have to shoot our way out.' At least he showed no sign so far of throwing a stroke.

'What did you do with that rather pretty little reporter?' Glory asked.

'I must warn you I think there's going to be trouble,' Seagrave said, ignoring her question.

'Then the only thing to do is start our picnic properly straight away. It's what they did when they heard the Revolution was at the gates.' Marie-Louise's appetites and historical myths were always there to fall back on. 'We'll go over under those trees. Invite Monsieur Paradis to join us. I like him.'

None of them seemed to grasp the gravity of the situation at all. The train, the horses, the Rolls, the sun in the immense empyrean, all combined to carry on the comedy they'd brought with them, with the champagne, from the Côte d'Azur. Seagrave went behind the car where Soames was unstrapping a hamper. 'We'll all of us be in real shit up to here in a few minutes,' he said. 'Can't you drive them away quickly, down to Les Saintes Maries till it's all over? The Minister's convoy will come the other way, from the north. I'll cover you here. Paradis's still busy with that reporter. There's no one to stop you and I'll take the responsibility for it on myself.'

Soames looked at him before answering, measuring things as he always did. 'I've already thought on it,' he said.

'Well?'

'I never was for forcing any woman.'

'What do you mean?'

'She won't go, not even at gunpoint. I asked.'

'Who won't?'

'That young Glory won't.'

'Why not?'

Seagrave knew the answer really. Soames was looking carefully at him again. Borrowing from Luis's sixth sense Seagrave read into Soames's mind the thought of how much better ordered these things could be in a disciplined unit like a brothel where everyone, particularly the women, knows what's what. Soames gave no immediate spoken answer but with a movement of the head, drawn-out for emphasis, he indicated the direction of the cabin where Ida lived with the child. 'There's my belief, over that way, if you want to know,' he said.

'The old man then?'

'Won't barely budge these days without granddaughter. Apple of his eye. Bloody touching, it is.' There was no point in urging Soames to try and drive away with just Marie-Louise. She was much too masterful in her devices even for him. 'What's more,' Soames added, 'from what I make out of it this party of folk here is about your best protection with the Minister coming. And you may think me a hard man out of the North but I've come to quite reckon you, in my way, I don't mind admitting it.'

'It's mutual. But what in God's name will come of this?'

'We'll get through. Keep your eyes wide open. Got through other times all right, do the same again, you'll see.' Soames sounded sure of this, but with the certainty more of faith than reason.

One of the trees indicated by Marie-Louise had blown over in the winter and against this Lord Haweswater was leaned up on his shooting-stick while everyone else sat on the ground with the hamper in the middle. From the fires of the comrades the odour of gently roasting sheep and herbs floated over on the heated air. Early leaf already showed on the poplars and gave a broken shade. The sun was strong and the champagne went gently and surely to your head more or less at once. Alphonse had put up a good cold meal, copious, tasty, varied, expensive. The comrades' voices were quite a lot louder than they had been an hour earlier and every now and then an empty bottle struck another in the grass behind them. The train like a patient hunting dog panted quietly in its place on the rusty lines and above the ditches still filled with water the first river swallows weaved and spun. In many ways it was an idyllic scene.

'There's a car,' said Glory.

Seagrave looked towards the comrades where François, having refused Marie-Louise's invitation with a certain regret, was on the ground, relaxed, making a hearty meal of the sheep. Apparently he'd heard nothing, due to the noise going on around him. Seagrave ran across to the road and got there just before the black vehicle from the Préfecture reached the entrance to the camp. He saw that it was unaccompanied by the usual armed escort and he waved both arms to stop it while it was out on the public highway. There might still be time to turn round and go back to the real world and leave them here to unwind the fantasy. He was disregarding orders for the first time and he felt like a collaborator. But luckily or not the driver of the official car paid no attention to him. He blew the horn to order him out of the way and rolled forward to rest on the grass a few metres from the Rolls Royce. Fernand-Félix stepped out of the car on one side and Philippe on the other, like a married couple. Fernand was dressed for the Camargue in a brand new black velvet jacket and brown trousers with a black stripe down the side. Philippe looked uncomfortably from time to time at this ensemble on his chief's stout, short urban physique.

'I'm pleased to see you, Etienne. I knew it couldn't be long,' said Fernand. 'I have your copy of *The Prelude*.' He fished in the inside pocket of the velvet jacket and produced the volume Seagrave had stolen from his brother's library. He saw there was now a plaited silk book-marker in it and for no reason that he could think of the idea flashed across his mind that it was, in spite of its fineness, probably strong enough to be used as a garrotte. 'Inscribed in the poet's hand to your ancestor too. That gave my reading a primal sympathy nothing else in the world could have supplied – "which having been must ever be" – so I don't greatly regret returning it to you. Besides, I think now our prelude is nearly over.'

It wasn't to shelter Fernand or Philippe from whatever was coming to them, it was against eruption of consequences that Seagrave took the risk. 'I'd better warn you . . . while there's still time . . .'

But François's heavy hand was already there on his shoulder, and his voice speaking past his ear. '*Monsieur le Ministre*, I have the honour to place you under arrest. I would say house arrest but here we have cabins and horses and mosquitoes in Etienne's domain but as yet no house.' There was nothing jovial in François's manner as he considered Fernand before him, Fernand with his broad head and superb nose, his short legs of a man who couldn't run far for his life, his wide pelvis, his bottomless guile. 'The arrest is purely formal of course – for the present – I rely on your political understanding. During the Occupation you must have been familiar with the term house arrest and its implications in those days . . .' There was no hint of tremor in the other hand holding the revolver.

Since his first sight of Fernand in the station yard observing the victims for deportation Seagrave had wondered how this star of destiny would appear with the roles reversed, faced with a figure like Paradis. Would he show the sang-froid to be expected of a man of stone? The word – *arrestation* – must have special resonance if what you were used to was the power to deploy the real thing. What courage would he summon up? Seagrave tried to peer beneath the fluttering lids to see what the eyes would give birth to. He saw a simple inglorious fear like his own reflected there, from the other side of the mirror. Fernand was an ordinary man after all. He hadn't moved a muscle apart from the eyelids since François spoke but he was afraid, blue fear emanated from him and spread on the air about him. Nevertheless, calculation was in his life-blood.

'It seems you have a lot of subjects under arrest in Etienne's domain, Monsieur Paradis,' he said, looking round to take in the lie of this land where in the midst of a fête champêtre in full swing his own future hung.

'Those are my men – the others, you're entitled to know – are in the same situation as yourself.'

'You mean you've arrested Madame de Tornac? I warn you she may outwit you.'

François laughed, with a note of embarrassment in his laughter. He too was supposed to be a man of stone, in the field. 'She's a charming woman I wouldn't hurt for anything in the world. Unless I had to.'

Fernand smiled, as if with his canines he'd struck Paradis's weak point and knew now that he was less fearsome than he wanted to look. Platitudes about gender and comradeship would cut no ice with Fernand. All the same, like any hostage-taker, Paradis had gambled his freedom and possibly his head and must be taken seriously. Fernand continued to let his gaze compass the three hundred and sixty degrees of this open scenery. It came to a halt on the reporter's motor-bicycle, then traversed on to finally settle on the train with its vapour curling up into the air where the swallows circled. He had of course known it would be here.

'Your locomotive has the steam up. That means one thing. Your enterprise is in motion.'

'It will be very soon. And you will have a ministerial view. A magisterial view. You will travel with me in the cab of the engine.'

'Where will we be going?'

'To the Rhône bridges.'

Fernand turned his head fractionally in Philippe's direction, no more than a lateral nod. As always there was something hieratic in the deliberation of his movement. It must come from being the hub of his universe.

'To the Rhône bridges? With a regiment of armed men at night? An insurrection?'

'The men will have arms but no ammunition. The ammunition will be left here. This will not be an insurrection. The arms are symbolic.'

'Ah. Ritualistic merely.' A cloud had definitely lifted from Fernand's horizons, it seemed there might after all be no call for physical courage. He looked more sure of himself and his methods and as the reporter approached his motor-bicycle and called out to Paradis, Fernand again delivered a little nod to Philippe.

'I've seen everything there is to see, Monsieur Paradis,' the reporter shouted. 'I've got the material I need. And had a drink on it.'

Fernand turned back to François and placing a hand under the arm that held the revolver he switched into him the floodlight of his charm and attention as if suddenly aware of all François's unique qualities, the one man in the world really worth talking to. 'You're well-known for a brilliant strategist, Monsieur Paradis, a commander of *bravoure* and invention. The world knows it; you proved it in the Resistance. And I credit your motives, in fact I honour them and believe me I share many of the aims. You, Paradis the liberator of Nîmes! We should take you without delay into government. The General himself would profit from your gifts. These great soldiers, you know, they need men of real vision, popular vision by their side. Now let's look closer at this famous locomotive of yours that we're soon going to ride overland to symbolic victory.' As they started off in the direction of the train Philippe turned quickly to catch the reporter just as he threw his leg over the saddle.

'François, wait. Wait a moment . . .' Seagrave called, but Paradis waved him away, no longer alert or ahead of every development as he used to be. He was now Fernand's captive rather than the other way about, moving over the grass with short steps, head down to catch the oxygen of flattery. The dinosaurs had starved him of praise, that was it, and Fernand had guessed it. After a minute the engine of the motor-bicycle started up and the reporter roared away leaving a cloud of dust behind him in the air over the track. Philippe's mission was done. He passed an eye over Seagrave, his oily trousers, his chest streaked with sweat and soot, then without speaking headed off to join the party under the trees. Seagrave followed. Later he would catch François and make him listen to reason. In a way it was lucky this had happened. The fantasy could be halted in time. The steam could be let out again from the boilers. He saw Soames coming towards him as Philippe reached the trees.

'Where are you going? You're needed here.'

'Off to keep an eye on Luis. Pity, there's loads of champagne in yon hamper. But there's no knowing what he could take it into his head to do.'

Soames was right. A guard was needed between Luis and Philippe. Meanwhile Marie-Louise was making the presentations. It was soon evident that Glory, having lost the reporter, was about to pretend she thought Philippe a stunning piece of old France. Why? She seemed in an odd mood now; perhaps she had the curse. After all, Seagrave thought furiously, Glory didn't need any little pip-squeak of a French marquis.

'He's queer as a coot. Thought you should know that,' he whispered in her ear while Philippe and Lord Haweswater stared uncomprehendingly at each other.

'That's not everything, you know. Though I do realise men like you think it is.'

'I think you're being difficult.'

'Well if I'm too difficult for you you know where to go. If she's any easier. Which I rather doubt.'

He saw where the trouble lay. Glory had been unprepared for the visual impact of Ida in the flesh. How could anyone be? He had to admit to himself that on a strictly aesthetic comparison Ida must be seen as in a class of her own. The stock phrase fitted the case precisely. She was like a lone sail on the ocean, bound away from the land to the outer edge. When Fernand arrived to join the group another attempt was made to get Lord Haweswater to acknowledge the newcomers.

'Who is this feller?' he asked irritably. 'Where's Soames?'

'This is someone in the Government, Cecil,' said Marie-Louise.

'Don't know anyone in the Government.'

'No of course you don't. He's in the French government.'

'Not what I meant. I mean, don't know anyone in any government. One doesn't.' He looked tired and full of champagne and ready to fall off his shooting-stick in spite of the supporting tree.

'I read with reverence your poet Wordsworth,' Fernand shouted in English, mistakenly believing that the old man was deaf, yet surely a lover of the regional bard. Was Haweswater after all not the name of a lake? Fernand seemed to be implying.

'Never heard of him,' said Lord Haweswater with as much contempt as if this Wordsworth had been in the Government too. Glory with Seagrave's help led him away to the Rolls where he fell asleep at once, head fallen forward as if shot in the back of the neck.

'I must go and talk to Paradis,' Seagrave said.

'It's your camp, you can go and talk to whoever you want,' Glory said in a surly voice.

He caught her hand as she was turning back. 'You can come too. I want you to.'

'All right,' she said, prompt though still grudging.

'I'm very sorry about all this. You shouldn't be here. I shouldn't let you. If I'd had warning I'd have made you stay in Arles.'

Glory laughed at this pretension. 'Would you? I don't think you could. Marie-Louise said we had to come. She's afraid of something. She thought it would be safer all together.'

'Safer from what? For who?'

'For you I think. She didn't explain. Something to do with the Resistance, or the Liberation. She may not know herself. Didn't a lot of underground things go on? You must know about it.'

'Yes, I think I do.'

François wouldn't listen to Seagrave's warnings about the reporter. 'If the Minister sent a message so much the better. It's just what we want. The maximum attention. The reporter will make the most of it, he's a sharp boy. You're losing your nerve, Etienne. It happens to everyone once. I saw you trying to turn them back. I know why. It's the women here. Some men go soft when there are women around even when the women don't. I must keep you under my eye.'

'If Madame Paradis was here wouldn't you be more cautious yourself?'

'Impossible. Madame Paradis is safe at home in my house in her kitchen. Where she always is.' Perhaps François had misunderstood the question as single-minded egocentrics are apt to do if a question concerns their own affairs. 'My house is very tranquil. It's very secure, I assure you of that.'

The afternoon was so warm that haze rose above the Camargue and the river swallows left the dykes to circle about the open ground where insects, new-born in the heat, hung on the air in squadrons. Low in the eastern sky a full moon like a porthole just clear of the water was discernible through the haze, a pale surprising intruder on the spring day. The comrades lay about the grass recuperating their forces for the night's work and Lord Haweswater slept in the back of the Rolls as soundly as on a bench at Westminster. Fernand seemed to be thoroughly enjoying his captivity. If he hadn't been held here he would have been prisoner of responsibilities it was a great relief to lay aside for as long as this play lasted. He'd continued drinking champagne in sips all afternoon and showed not the least sign of it. Will-power would take care of all that. It was as if he'd fully rehearsed the coming night's production and confidently awaited a successful and amusing show. Meanwhile he entertained Marie-Louise despite herself, and Philippe, who was on duty anyway, with a string of anecdotes about the use of power and its privileges.

When the moon got stronger and the light in the sky began to drain out Paradis roused the comrades from coma and then came across to the group of distinguished hostages under the trees.

'I've decided to advance the hour of action. In other words, we'll start earlier,' he said. 'The moon will be at zenith about midnight. Here in the Camargue if clouds come over it happens soon before dawn; they come in from the sea. We must be in position by then.

The wind's going round to the south. We need the moonlight.'

'There'll be trains running on the main lines,' Seagrave said.

'I've thought of it. Where's Soames?'

'With Luis. There's a mare that's foaling.'

'Go and get him, Etienne. I need him on the telephone. I can't make it work without him.' François looked at his open hands as if they were independently to blame, then folded them to their usual club-like form.

Soames's verdict on the telephone was that the line had been cut somewhere between the camp and Saint Gilles.

'You'd have to know what you were doing and be looking for it to do that,' he said. As a signaller he knew what this meant. Seagrave noticed the thick horizontal creases in Soames's brow. He was ageing and Seagrave felt sorry for him. Soames turned to Luis at his side.

'Run over the fields, Luis lad, and find the place. You know the gear to take.'

'Luis stays here with us,' said Paradis's strong voice. 'There's no time.'

'Who do I obey?' Luis asked with a new insolence in his tone.

'You obey François like the rest of us,' Seagrave said quickly. He said it with misgiving, but in the end he was responsible for Luis's discipline. And safety.

'I'm fed up of obeying,' Luis said. 'One of these times soon . . .' But no one listened.

'We all have to take our chance,' François went on, the volume of his voice still rising. 'On the Odessa Steps they took their chance.' What did he mean? Historical dream was spreading a web over the scene. 'We'll stop at the main line junction and throw the points ourselves. On a Saturday night there's no normal traffic after midnight. It's a small risk, that's all. Nothing to the night we liberated Nîmes.'

'Nothing to the Odessa Steps,' muttered Luis so that only Seagrave heard.

'This will be child's play to that. When the night signalmen see us on the line they'll know who it is and what to do.'

'Let's hope so,' said Seagrave.

François banged the table on which the useless telephone stood with his fist. 'It will be so because I say it's so. Nothing can stop us now.'

'Well at least the British hostages will be safe enough here.'

'Safe here? They're no use to me here. The hostages come with us in the train. All of them.'

'I won't allow . . .' Seagrave began.

'It's not you who allow,' said François more gently now. 'I've spoken to the young woman. She's a nurse and she's intelligent. She's still on service in the War and a nurse could be needed. She's decided for herself. The days of allowing are behind us. Behind you,' he wound up, no doubt thinking of his own régime and Madame Paradis.

As night began to fall Seagrave went to find Ida. He saw her beyond the well, hanging the child's washing to dry on a branch. Her hair was darker than when he first knew her and it hung in a fan shape across her shoulders and down her back, from a ribbon gathering it in at the neck. She turned when he called her and waited impassively for him to come up. In this failing light he remembered his first sight of her under the railway arch in Nîmes and for an instant had the illusion that no time and no disaster had come between them since.

'Have you come to see your child before you go?' she asked.

'I've come to see that you're all right. We'll be back tomorrow or the day after. This can't last long. It's only a gesture.'

'I don't think you should come back. Leave me here as you said. But if anything happens to Luis I'll find you and kill you myself with my own hands.' Ida turned from him towards the cabin where she lodged alone now with the child, away from the train and the men and the rich visitors from the north. At the last moment she turned back quickly as if she'd forgotten something she meant to say. With her index and middle finger she glancingly touched the back of his hand. As she turned away again he saw her eyes dry as desert wells long unvisited, and remembered. But it was late.

The trucks on this train were covered but unlike those of the famous night of Nîmes they had openings along both sides and there was plenty of room because the army this time was so much smaller, a skeleton force. Marie-Louise and Lord Haweswater and Glory were placed in the last truck with a camp bed in case the old man had to lie down, plus the remains of the picnic and the champagne. To the roof of this truck Luis was ordered to lash a short pole with a white shirt tied to it to blow in the slipstream and indicate its non-combatant status, it was hoped.

'If anything goes wrong, if you hear shooting or anything, lie on the floor,' Seagrave told Glory.

'And wait for the counter-revolutionaries to come and rape me.'

'I'll kill them first,' said Luis fiercely. Glory smiled at him and put a hand on his arm for a moment.

'No one takes this business seriously,' said Seagrave again.

'I take it more seriously than you think, Steve. And so does Marie-Louise.'

'Because she knows her countrymen. And she knows the Minister inside out.'

'But he's *amusing*. Amusing people are mostly harmless.'

'I don't think so. And he's not harmless at all.'

'No, I don't really think so either.'

But there was no more time for thinking, or for getting their points of view together on this or any other issue. Paradis was standing mounted on the footplate facing his men. 'Etienne, come here in the first truck behind the engine. Monsieur Fernand-Félix will ride in the cab with me, to see and be seen. Monsieur d'Albaron will go with Etienne who will be answerable for him. The rest of you climb aboard in your own formations. No man will carry any ammunition. Leave it here. Our movement is symbolic at this stage. It's a potent symbol to raise our comrades everywhere. Violence, the recourse of the guilty and the weak, we leave to our opponents – for now. Much good may it do them in the end. We will be fearless but peaceable in our force and when others see it they will join us. *Vive le mouvement! Vive les camarades! Vive le matérialisme dialectique!*' A cheer went up to greet these incantations and the rifles and stens were waved in the air like a stand of phalluses, symbolic in all respects. 'Unload your weapons now and mount!' Luis, who had had an eye on Philippe, went into the second truck and Soames, needing a hand to climb aboard, went with him.

The haze of afternoon had seemed to thicken at dusk so the moon, high up now, was more bronze than silver. Perhaps this presaged the dawn cloud François had spoken of. The Bohemians' train rumbled over the surviving bridge near Saint Gilles, then turned westward, travelling in reverse as far as the main line where it would halt and change course with the engine then leading. Leaning out, Seagrave could see the shirt over the hostages' truck like the standard at the head of a convoy. The line ran beside and above the water of Scamandre, a vast flat motionless sheet among reeds golden in moonlight. The train advanced gently, quietly, and from the water came to the comrades' ears the long patient debate of frogs on this warm spring night of love. Philippe watched the passing scene in silence, the wilderness of reeds, the glassy water and, further on, the hamlet surrounded by vineyards. What was he thinking? Was it he who had given orders for the telephone line to be cut? What message had he sent by the reporter, and to whom? Although they were in a way enemies now Seagrave could only remember that their friendship had been founded on many affinities before divergence in sexual taste undid them. They'd often travelled together by train from the faculty at Montpellier back to Nîmes in the evening or late at night. It seemed a long time ago. When he wasn't expecting it Philippe spoke.

'You see that village there with farms and all those vineyards? The d'Albaron inheritance. The château is in those woods beyond the Scamandre. Everything you can see there – everything – it's mine. And your friends, this rabble they call a movement – all they really want is to get their hands on it and more like it. Change of ownership of all the desirable things in the world, that's what it's about.'

'My brother in England says pretty well the same thing.'

'Any landed proprietor would.'

'So you can work out for yourself easily, what I think of it.'

'You've crossed the frontier, Stephen, the one with no return. Not to mention other indiscretions. Don't expect any amnesty on account of the Resistance. If I were you I'd jump this train the first time it slows down.'

'Like you with the Resistance.'

From the locomotive just behind them François was peering along at the empty track ahead, clearly visible in the moonlight. On the other side of the cab Fernand considered the land, the rich farms on the sloping hillside, the orchards and woods. They stood for the country that the resistants, living and dead, had won for him – the future was his, Vichy forgotten. This earth might be Philippe's, the franchise was Fernand's.

'It must feel strange to a young male brisk as a Camargue bull,' said Philippe in a low voice as if the remark was only an inner reflection, 'quite strange really being turned away at the door by a whore.'

At the junction with the main line the points were ready, the signals were with them. François was right to think his colleagues on duty would make smooth the path. Now the train, with the locomotive at its head, moved eastward and faster along the highway to its objective. Seagrave recalled from the other journey how when the train speeded up the fastening chains on the trucks rattled in a random play over the rhythmic percussion of the wheels. The effect was of the running music of the life process which could only cease when life itself hit the terminus. He stuck his head well out and looked back to the last truck where Glory was. He could see no head protruding there, but after them far back along the line was another locomotive under the moon, following at their pace, without lights, slowing when they slowed, keeping a constant distance. Every signal was green and evidently stayed at green for the train behind, green for Paradis and the Bohemians, green for the moonlit shadow.

'There's an engine on the line behind us,' Seagrave said to Philippe who had placed himself beside the loading door of the truck. Philippe nodded. So he'd known it would be there, as Seagrave had guessed. What was it for? It could only follow them to Beaucaire and the Rhône bridge. In a way it gave protection to the last truck. It stood between the hostages and any following traffic. There were only half a dozen men standing in the coal dust of this first truck with him and Philippe and he didn't know any of them; he didn't remember them from the maquis. The other trucks were fuller. For some reason, conscious or not, there had been no press of men to get in here with them. Probably it was Philippe's presence, a ministerial hanger-on and now a local magnate. Or did some bird of ill omen perch on the roof of this particular truck, or hover in the air over it? The comrades were silent, their fervour, if they had any, subdued. It was very different from the excited tension in the first train, the train of liberation. Politics was a graver matter than mere freedom: it was about power, not love. Maybe power mattered much more in the world but there was no doubt it stirred you less at the surface where the froth shows. Why was Philippe standing in the middle of the truck by the doors? Paradis had said Seagrave was responsible for him. He went and stood near him, facing him so the divide of the doors where they could be opened was between them. Perhaps Philippe meant to follow his own advice and make a break for it. Seagrave put himself firmly before the opening like a bull at a gate. The image was Philippe's.

'Take it from a former good friend, and still a friend,' Philippe said, looking like a student again in the half-darkness with bars of moonlight across his face and form like a heraldic charge, 'jump for it while you can.'

'I'm not going anywhere except in this truck. Neither are you.'

'It was a last . . .' Philippe shrugged his shoulders in the French way that denies defeat. For half a moment he looked almost distressed, no more. 'So be it.'

The train was slowing down. The line ran alongside an avenue of planes at the approach to the town, then among houses and gardens and the quiet roads of the outskirts, a café here and there, a hotel, still a last few lights, a suburb of tranquil people, not like the shunting yards and warehouses they'd passed the other time, the historic time, on the other side of the town. The line rose above street level now, it ran across the arches, on the viaduct that carried it through the main station and out in the direction of Beaucaire. Seagrave knew so intimately the dull orchestral thunder of wheels on this long stone viaduct. You would certainly hear it from the buildings that had been the Milice headquarters, it would have sounded in the ears of the captives in the cellars as they waited their turn, as the ground bass of freedom. Now they were going so slowly it seemed a signal must be against them. How could that be? In the Paradis scheme of ordained things? It was vital to the success of the venture to get through built-up areas without hindrance and onto the Rhône bridge. Paradis's colleagues on duty were supposed to see to it. If the train stopped in the town there was too much risk even at this hour of attracting the notice of some higher official of other political sympathies. Seagrave went forward to see if he could call out to Paradis on the footplate only a few metres away. He might not have seen the locomotive on the line behind them. The detail of the precincts visible on either side was familiar. They were approaching the station, Seagrave knew every window.

'There's an engine on the line after us,' he shouted up to Paradis.

'There's another in front.' They were going at a walking pace now, the brakes sending up a light vibration and judder through the woodwork of the truck. From the opening on one side Seagrave saw a phoenix palm like a giant column in a garden he knew, and the twin spires of the Préfecture, oddly ecclesiastic on a republican palace. Then, through the high arched windows of the station building, the Roman tower on the hill just discernible if you knew where to look in the moonlight. The train was trapped. There had been treason among the comrade-colleagues, or else Philippe's message had done the trick in the proper quarters. On the platform on both sides were gendarmes two deep and armed with rifles. While the train was still just moving Seagrave saw too late that Philippe had managed to undo the chains on the door, and as he leaped out onto the platform he shouted something to the officer of the gendarmes and pointed at the truck behind him.

The sound of three shots fired in quick succession came, it seemed, from the next truck following. The fatal instant became eternity. The train had halted. Terminus was reached. Seagrave had time to feel a huge surprise: there was to have been no ammunition on board this train. Someone had disobeyed. The first two shots smashed some glass in the station windows, the third must have caught Philippe in the arm, the arm that had signalled to the officer. He fell back with his other hand to the place, above the elbow. From the train there was no more firing. The three shots had apparently exhausted the arsenal. Soames and Luis were in that truck. Seagrave had a vision of Ida: he saw her completely, she stood in a brilliant light above and before him, it was impossible to bring Luis's presence to mind without thinking of her. He was already down on the platform going to join the other two, with what purpose he didn't know, a defensive impulse in immediate action. Better than doing nothing. He was facing their truck and leaping towards it with his back to the gendarmes when another volley of shots from several points deafened him, the sound of it so close it seemed to split open like a great ripe fruit inside him, opening a black silence, a sack to slip into, a black bag, red and black, silent as a shell in the end.

Chapter Seventeen

WILLIAM SEAGRAVE WAS BUSY with the coming general election. However, his sister Jean came down for the formalities, driven in a white Packard limousine by a chauffeur, a swarthy, smooth-looking bruiser of the name of Rudi, Soames learned. It was quite soon clear that Jean came with William's authority to act for both of them in finding out whether Etienne had died possessed of anything whatever and if so, claim it.

There'd been a quick funeral in the Protestant cemetery at Nîmes, in an obscure corner of it where the tombstones carried mostly English names. Fernand-Félix insisted on making an address over the open grave and as a Minister no one could very well prevent him. He stepped up onto a flat-topped sarcophagus, as Madame de Tornac called it, so as to get his head above the rest.

'We mourn today a lover of France and of the French, all the French,' he began, his eyes settling at these words on Madame de Tornac, dressed in black against which her pearls and diamonds showed very well, Soames thought. She was a fine woman, wasting herself in some ways. 'He played a part worthy of mention in the Resistance to the enemies of France, and in the Liberation which we all celebrate every minute of every day, even in this sad and solemn place.' The lids stopped their fluttering and for a moment dropped like shutters screening some indecent activity behind a window.

Soames thought of the scene on the platform after the echoes of the shooting had died away. Fernand-Félix had at once climbed down from the locomotive and walked towards the exit. The gendarme officer was leaning over the body on the ground. Fernand, not troubling himself about Philippe and his wound, paused for a moment. 'Dead?' he asked in a clear voice, then nodded his head at the answer and walked on. Only François Paradis and Luis were arrested, the comrades ordered to disperse, the hostages herded into the Hôtel d'Albaron. Alone, Soames had found his way to the cabin on the garrigue and there he'd waited for first light, only a couple of hours away.

'Among his friends of those heroic days there numbered unfortunately some whose political agenda lay outside our young friend's range of understanding. His culture of origin was one not gifted for these ... debates of principle, these ... philosophical confrontations ... so characteristic of our own.' What was he talking about? Was this just part of the French custom Soames was by now familiar with, the serving up again of the national myths in case anyone forgets them? 'Our own historic upheavals, seminal for humanity's growth, have often before inspired the onlooker. My dear friends, I will quote you the words of the English poet Wordsworth, native of the same rustic province as poor Stephen, on the French Revolution as it appeared to enthusiasts. Simple enthusiasts.' He took a volume from his pocket and read in his strongly marked, oddly impressive English. ' "Oh! Pleasant exercise of hope and joy! Mighty were the auxiliars which then stood upon our side, we who were strong in love! Bliss was it in that dawn to be alive ..." ' Fernand-Félix allowed a long pause in which he looked up at the cypresses and monuments and down to the closed faces of his audience, ' "But to be young was very heaven!" I read you these lines from poor Stephen's copy of the work carried in his pocket to the end, stained with his blood, damaged, here at this corner, by one of the insurrectionary bullets that brought his own brief dawn to premature night. Stephen, we will remember you always, with your simple gifts and your rustic interrupted loves . . . all, naturally, within the limits of island culture.'

'What frightful lots of bullshit,' said Madame de Tornac quite loudly in English, rolling the 'r' in frightful around her throat as if she was gargling with it. Soames wondered where she'd learned the other word. She really was a very fine woman. He edged a little nearer. Old Etienne would have understood that, no one better.

'And so, farewell ephemeral sojourner. Out, poor candle.'

No one was listening to Fernand's peroration, he'd lost them by going on too long. He'd never at any moment had any hold on Lord Haweswater who understood no French and claimed to have forgotten the existence of the poet. He was in a wheelchair because of the distance from the road to this corner of the cemetery, and Soames was in charge of the wheelchair.

'Do I have to throw away me cigar?' he'd asked as they passed among the mausoleums.

'I don't think so. It's not like inside.'

'Have to respect local customs. If you can find out what they are.'

Now that the address was over he showed signs of restlessness. 'Better take me the other side of those yews.'

'They're cypresses,' said Soames. 'They plant them for the dead.'

'Only want to have a piss. Any tree will do.'

Soames felt he and Lord Haweswater understood one another pretty well. For one thing, they shared the same view of Etienne.

'Liked him a lot better than anyone in me own family. But for Glory of course. Didn't have enough natural suspicion in him. Perhaps that's one of the things I liked.'

Soames saw there was water running from Lord Haweswater's eye and onto the bushy whiskers; no, from both of them, and he turned away. Maybe that great cigar just made him leak at every opening.

Madame de Tornac came to find them behind the cypresses. She'd lit a cigarette too, now that the earth was being shovelled into the hole in the ground, a flat cigarette taken from a pink packet. Passing Cloud: Soames remembered seeing the advertisements before the War. He'd never tried it, it wasn't a serious smoke. He felt glad she was there as the sounds of soil falling on wood came over to them.

'Now Cecil,' she said, and Soames could tell from the voice that she was going to work off some of her feelings by taking it out on Lord Haweswater. That was fair enough. 'Now Cecil, you must make an effort and be very polite to Stephen's sister Jean. She's asking where you've gone.'

The sister had come leaning on the arm of Philippe, the one not in a sling. She'd reached the graveside after a shaky progress along the gravel paths and her eyes too were watery but not from sorrow, Soames thought. Glory Egremont was on her other side. They made a striking contrast. Glory was slight, white in the face, and dead sober, pathetically sober, whereas the sister looked to Soames the opposite of these things. Perhaps he did her an injustice: it could be the time of life. Philippe hung over both of them with so much politeness you could see he didn't really like standing at such close quarters with women, not at all.

Soames had had a meeting with Philippe, the day after the train. Philippe had come to find him at the Bohemians' camp where he'd returned by rail and foot. Someone had to tell Ida what had happened, and that Luis was in the prison in Nîmes.

'Is he hurt?' she'd asked.

'Not him.'

She had put no questions about Etienne, it was as if she'd never known him. Soames thought a woman owed something more than that, even if she was a whore. He looked down into her face, searching for something in her eyes, for anything, and read there a pain kept in the dark that knocked him backwards, it was so deep.

'You think I did him wrong.'

'I did think that.'

'Shall I tell you why I drove him away from me?'

'I've wondered about it.'

'Because I never could be any good for him. I wasn't made for his life, only for a moment. He had a right to better than me.'

'What will you do now?'

'I can always earn my living.'

She disappeared quickly when she saw Philippe in the distance. Philippe began by asking what had become of Luis's revolver. 'You were standing by him. I saw you both clearly.'

'I took it.'

'Give it to me please.' Philippe held out his uninjured arm, palm of the hand open. 'If you don't I'll have you arrested at once.'

Soames had seen this coming. It wasn't a good time for an Englishman who had fought in the Resistance to be shot dead by the gendarmes on a station platform. It could make trouble for the Ministry of the Interior. This was the moment for an official version. The first shots had been fired from the train, everyone knew that. The Minister's personal assistant had been injured by one of them, another had caught the unfortunate Englishman. It was to be deplored that he was present at all on a scene which was strictly the business of the Ministry and no one else. That only left the weapon in question to be found and put in a safe place.

Under the eye of Philippe's armed escort Soames passed over the revolver. 'I saw what happened and as a soldier I can give reliable evidence of it,' he said.

'But I don't think you will, because I believe you're fond of Luis, in a fatherly way. No one knows Luis's age and he has no papers. If he goes up to the tribunal for minors he'll get an educational sentence and be free in a year or two. Otherwise, it will be prison for the best part of his early life and probably deportation.'

'Who'll make sure of that?'

'The Minister will make sure of it. I came to tell you so.'

When Philippe had gone away Soames told Ida that if there was no trouble made and no talking then Luis would come back to her by the time he'd started a beard. The truth wouldn't do Etienne any good where he was now.

But that wasn't what Glory thought. She came to Soames where he stood behind her grandfather's wheelchair in the cemetery.

'Did you understand what that awful preachy man said, Mr Soames? It was a lie. I saw what happened perfectly well. Steve was shot in the back from the platform, not the train.' There was no sign of any tears, the ashy whiteness of her face was the whiteness of rage.

'I don't know about that, to be honest,' said Soames.

'You must. It was right in front of you.'

Soames looked at Madame de Tornac for help. This was her country.

'Glory darling, Stephen's friends are in prison, remember that. They could be very badly treated and kept there for a long time. We can't get them out but we can take care not to make anything worse for them. The police doctor will say what Philippe tells him to say, with Henri behind him. I mean about which way the bullet came. I'm not a clever woman but I know we have to know as little as possible and leave men to settle their scores.'

'But what had Steve done, to have any score to settle?'

'That's it. He knew something, too much. Mr Soames is wiser. He doesn't know anything at all, and neither do I.'

'I hate this country,' said Glory passionately.

'Impossible,' Madame de Tornac answered. 'It's a logical impossibility: France and love are one and the same thing. What you hate is the bad turn destiny's done . . .'

'The rotten *baxt*,' said Soames, thinking how often he'd heard the word, between Brough-under-Stainmore and the Protestant cemetery here in Nîmes.

'Back? Yes,' said Lord Haweswater. 'To the car. Need a snifter now. So do you, Soames.'

'Only one snifter, Cecil,' warned Madame de Tornac.

'Pay no attention,' muttered Lord Haweswater as they sped over the gravel. 'Interfering woman. Very fine woman mind you, very fine indeed, but apt to interfere.'

On the way they met the sister. She had sunk onto a stone bench near the grave as if buckling under the weight of sorrow, but Soames rather thought he saw in her eye the hungry look of a woman unused to anything like opposition.

'Lord Haweswater!' she cried. 'How kind you are to come for Stephen's burial in this inconvenient spot in your state!' Evidently she didn't beat about the bush. 'The ground looks so hard and stony and dry I wonder they were able to dig the hole deep enough,' she added.

'Don't stop, for God's sake,' said Lord Haweswater, and Soames continued at a good pace towards the Rolls and the brandy while Jean staggered after them.

'I believe you saw something of him these last weeks,' she panted. 'I want to find out if he had a lawyer here.'

'Why?' asked Lord Haweswater.

'Naturally William and I want to know if he left any property.'

'Ask Glory. She's the one he was jumping into bed with. Not me.'

Jean made a gulping sound that could have been laughter, or shock, you couldn't tell which.

'Actually I have asked her. She wasn't very helpful.'

'Get me in the car and shut the door behind me,' Lord Haweswater told Soames. 'And come back when she's gone away.'

Soames turned to the sister when he'd carried out the instruction. 'I was a friend of your brother's in the Resistance, and after,' he said.

'Poor Stephen, he was unfortunate in everything. But a lot of it was his own doing. Of course he was only our half-brother.' She turned away to hurry off into the cemetery again in search of information.

'I can tell you what you want to know,' Soames called after her, and watched her come back. He let her wait.

'Well?'

'Owned quite a bit of land out in the Camargue, did Etienne. If you know where that is.'

'Did he? I see. Good. I don't imagine he made a will, d'you think?'

'He didn't need to. Here the law does it all for you. It all goes to your nearest relations. The lawyer feller's got news for you.'

'What's his name and address?'

The lawyer who had done the sale of the Bohemians' camp had been a resistant too, and Soames and he had had a few drinks together. The lawyer had explained the law about inheritance. The land and everything on it now belonged to the sick child and would be Ida's if the child didn't live to beget another. There was no way round that. It was the code.

*

Up on the garrigue Soames dug the remains of the hoard from the Banque de France out of its resting place among the thyme and the irises. He drove in the Delahaye back to the Bohemains' camp probably for the last time. In the clear light you could see the far blue undulating line of the Cévennes where they'd fought together with the maquis. That was where Etienne had staked his life in a good cause.

'I've brought you this,' he told Ida. 'It was Etienne's.'

'Where did he get it?'

'He won it.'

'I don't want any money. I never took his money.'

'Keep it for Luis. He'll understand. Bury it till he gets out. Don't tell anyone but him where it is.'

'Not even you?'

'Specially not me. I might want to come back and help myself.'

'You can stay if you want.' She only wore a shapeless cotton dress, clean though unmended, but she was easily the most beautiful woman Soames had ever seen.

'Not here. Not now,' he said and turned back to the car. On the road to Saint Gilles he passed the white Packard heading the way he'd come. As far as he could see only the chauffeur was in it, grinning at him with his film-set teeth. He hoped he'd done the right thing by Luis. On an impulse he stopped the car, turned the engine off and got out. He could hear a nightingale tuning up, that must be the first of the year. He had Etienne's Minox in his pocket. Standing on the running-board of the Delahaye he was just tall enough to photograph the Bohemians' camp in its entirety, the huts and trees, the well-head, the horses in the distance, and Ida still standing where he'd left her, a cloth hanging from her hand, looking along the road after him perhaps. He wasn't a practised photographer. Whether or not the picture came out at all was a toss-up, much like everything else.

If you enjoyed this book here is a selection of other bestselling titles from Review

MAN OR MANGO?	Lucy Ellmann	£6.99	☐
WOMAN WITH THREE AEROPLANES	Lilian Faschinger	£6.99	☐
GIVING UP ON ORDINARY	Isla Dewar	£6.99	☐
WAR DOLLS	Dilys Rose	£6.99	☐
ALL GROWN UP	Sophie Parkin	£6.99	☐
WHAT ABOUT ME?	Alan Smith	£6.99	☐
WRACK	James Bradley	£6.99	☐
LATEST ACCESSORY	Tyne O'Connell	£6.99	☐
BETWEEN US	Geraldine Kaye	£6.99	☐
THE CAPTAIN AND THE KINGS	Jennifer Johnston	£6.99	☐
VANITY FIERCE	Graeme Aitken	£6.99	☐
A GRACIOUS PLENTY	Sheri Reynolds	£6.99	☐

Headline books are available at your local bookshop or newsagent. Alternatively, books can be ordered direct from the publisher. Just tick the titles you want and fill in the form below. Prices and availability subject to change without notice.

Buy four books from the selection above and get free postage and packaging and delivery within 48 hours. Just send a cheque or postal order made payable to Bookpoint Ltd to the value of the total cover price of the four books. Alternatively, if you wish to buy fewer than four books the following postage and packaging applies:

UK and BFPO £4.30 for one book; £6.30 for two books; £8.30 for three books.

Overseas and Eire: £4.80 for one book; £7.10 for 2 or 3 books (surface mail).

Please enclose a cheque or postal order made payable to *Bookpoint Limited*, and send to: Headline Publishing Ltd, 39 Milton Park, Abingdon, OXON OX14 4TD, UK.
Email Address: orders@bookpoint.co.uk

If you would prefer to pay by credit card, our call team would be delighted to take your order by telephone. Our direct line is 01235 400 414 (lines open 9.00 am–6.00 pm Monday to Saturday 24 hour message answering service). Alternatively you can send a fax on 01235 400 454.

Name ....

Address ....

....

....

If you would prefer to pay by credit card, please complete:
Please debit my Visa/Access/Diner's Card/American Express (delete as applicable) card number:

Signature .... Expiry Date..............